THE FIFTH COMMANDMENT

THE FIFTH COMMANDMENT

A Red Tail Hawk Production

Stuart I. Haussler

iUniverse, Inc.

New York Lincoln Shanghai

The Fifth Commandment

iUniverse, Inc.

For information address:
iUniverse, Inc.
2021 Pine Lake Road, Suite 100
Lincoln, NE 68512
www.iuniverse.com

ISBN: 0-595-33071-1

Printed in the United States of America

CHAPTER 1

▼

"Doctor! Right now I'm a frustrated jurist in my own court! Just what in the hell…ahem…excuse me…what is it you want from me?"

"The opportunity to tell the truth, Your Honor. To know what the County Attorney is doing here and what he wants from *me*."

"Doctor, this is a court of law. In my court, any court, we have rules, the simple fundamentals of law. You must answer the questions put to you, Doctor. We'll get to what you want to know. I suppose your attorney wants to know also." Stopping abruptly, the Judge looked at the County Attorney scornfully and snapped, "and so do I."

The Doctor seized the opportunity and countered, "Yes I do, and yes he does, and I'm glad you do, Your Honor, but I feel the law is not serving me. The questions are structured so only a restrictive and governed absolute answer of yes or no can be given, and no qualifying an answer is permitted, and to that I strenuously object!"

"Easy, Doctor. I disagree, Doctor."

It was evident to the Doctor that his interruptions were irritating the Judge, but he was going to continue lecturing him. He had done it before when the Judge had been a patient. "I expect you to, Your Honor, we live in different worlds, you and I. You in the world of being an adversary. I in the world of being a willing partner to improve the quality of everyday life. I am a Doctor. I live as a Doctor, me, just me, in my world where there are no absolutes. There, for me, most of the time there are no singular, restrictive, absolute answers to questions…like yes or no."

"I hear you, Doctor, and you know I do. We are worlds apart, but this all sounds like course 101 in something. You're working me…lecturing me and, by God, in my world it may be cause for me to hold you in contempt for lecturing this Court!" The Judge paused, frustration written all over his face. He really didn't want to be scolding this man in an open forum, but his Court was his Court no matter how deep the feelings he had for this Doctor. His mouth curled as if to signal he was about to smile. The curl disappeared as he took a deep breath and he continued, "Or…I just might recuse myself from this case, but no, for now, I'll resist doing that for I care in this instance about what has happened and…" the Judge, now totally exasperated, paused.

$$* \qquad * \qquad * \qquad *$$

Judge Nicholas Hickman had come from absolutely nothing and—entirely on his own—made it to the top, and he never forgot it for one minute. He never had a family, not one relative. He was summarily shuffled from one orphanage to another and, when old enough, from one foster home to another. He fought alone, all of his life through the ugly and the unthinkable that was his existence. He never married, for he had convinced himself he didn't understand or feel the kind of love necessary for marriage. His work was his mate. As a sitting District Judge he had to rotate through the various courts. Despising Domestic Relations Court, he reveled in Criminal Court, for there he could throw the book at the likes of which he had had to contend with and tolerate as he fought his way through the circumstances of his life as an orphan. He saw too many get away with too much, so when he handed down prison sentences he always felt he was somehow evening the score.

This Doctor, J. R. Rollins, that now stood before him, he knew only too well, for one Christmas Eve this Doctor had restored his facial bones to their proper positions and closed a large laceration, still evident to the keener eye even after these many years. It extended from his left ear, down across his face, under his jaw and onto the right side of his neck. The scar gave an added dimension to his large size. The parotid gland had been laid open but the external carotid artery had only been nicked. As he put it to his secretary, Marsha Manning, the next day through his wired jaws, "The car struck the bridge abutment and my facial bones were reshuffled by the dashboard."

Knowing he was out of serious trouble she looked down at him, half worried and half angry, and questioned him as a mother would, "How did it happen?"

"Harvey, ah Harvey, the White Rabbit had the audacity to jump out in front of my car, Manning."

Bending down she placed her mouth to his ear and hissed, "Drunk? Drunk, weren't you? Yes or no?"

"Yes."

Hearing the answer she kissed his forehead, stood, turned and left the room, never to discuss the why's and wherefore's.

Drumming his fingers on the bench as he remembered what this Doctor had done for him, he turned his attention back to the present and thought, *"Get after the Doctor's attorney and if that doesn't work, head for my chambers,"* and he snapped, "Mr. Ortman, can I prevail upon you to instruct your client that he must answer the questions as asked and not expand and or express his opinions. Just give the answer to the question, and if it means a yes or no answer, so be it. Do you understand my meaning of what I want you to convey...Mr. Ortman?"

"I understand, Your Honor, however, the Doctor, my client, does not feel his best interests are being served when his replies are restricted to a leading question by having to answer only with a yes or no."

"Mr. Ortman…counselor…as you know you can object to a question, on behalf of your client, and ask for clarification and ask the Court to have the question restated. Then, Mr. Ortman, I can rule on your objection, that is all this court is asking you to do. Again, Mr. Ortman, do you understand me? Now, before you answer, remember: If you and your client refuse to cooperate I'll throw you both in jail until you are willing to tell me you will cooperate with this court. In fact, I want you to join me in my chambers." The Judge stood and as he did, "Ah what the hell", slid from between his teeth, and he forcefully added, "Mr. Ortman, while walking to my chambers, think! For your client's sake, your sake, the court's sake, damn it man…THINK!" There was a long deliberate pause and then Hick continued, "Mr. Ortman, once again…THINK, and one thing for you to think about is that this is a preliminary hearing, so what is the County Attorney doing here? Do you know? I'm adjudicating the law for you, Mr. Ortman, and Mr. County Attorney, you help him think and you might help me understand what you're doing here also. More about that when we reconvene, and when we do I want the objections flowing from the right direction so we can resolve what in the hell is going on here. Do you get my meaning, Mr. Ortman?" The Judge saw the befuddled look on Paul Ortman's face, so before he could respond the Judge interjected, "Don't answer that, Mr. Ortman, just do your research during the recess. Show and tell comes later."

A female voice boomed out from the back of the courtroom, "Just one minute, Judge Nicholas Hickman, Your Honor!"

Knowing the voice and the face that belonged to it before he saw it, he knew what lay ahead. Without hesitation or anger in his voice he called out into the shadows of the courtroom, "All right, Manning, I won't even bother to object to your outburst, go on, and if I might ask, where are you?"

The voice boomed out even louder. "I'm right here, put your glasses on and your thinking cap, Nicholas Hickman, for I come as a friend of this Court, and you, and I think Mr. Ortman, and for certain his client the Doctor."

Judge Hickman sat back down and as he did instructed Henry Justin, his bailiff, "Henry, except for you know who, clear the court, and see to it the rest make it to my chambers, and Henry, see to it they have coffee. I have a feeling this court will be in recess for a bit. Gladis, we don't need to record what Manning has to say. Come back…you'll know when."

Gladis Pitman was the consummate court reporter. She was prompt, objective, honest, with a fast mind and was extremely accurate and attentive. She lived alone and her work was her life. She was always present for Judge Hickman when needed and her transcripts were always ready in twenty-four hours, always. She was known around the courthouse as the shadow because you never knew she was present in the courtroom. She always used hand and eye signals to communicate with the Judge or would tiptoe to the bench when something went awry. Judge Hickman liked her because she was always there. Manning told her that one day and she merely replied, "It's easy to work with and for him, Manning. I have a crush on him, just like you do."

In response to the Judge's order Henry Justin, at six-foot-three, two-axe-handles-wide, very black man stepped forward to face the Judge and responded in a very deep and resonant voice, "It will be done, Your Honor."

Hick smiled to himself and thought *"Henry means it, he always means it."*

*   *   *   *

Henry Justin, twenty-two years ago, stood before Judge Hickman and was about to be sentenced by him to three-to-five years in the penitentiary for assaulting one Dicey Brown. Dicey Brown's rap sheet was long and left no doubt in the casual observer's mind that he was a gambler. A crooked gambler at best. He had been shooting craps with

Henry Justin and some other men one Saturday evening. Henry caught him switching dice, loaded ones, at a crucial moment in the game. Henry never hesitated and beat Dicey to within less than an inch of his life. Dicey remained in a coma for about four months, which in itself was a blessing for Dicey for he did not have to endure the pain associated with the healing process of the many fractured bones in his face.

The District Attorney waited patiently to see if the charges against Henry would be for assault or for murder. Dicey lived and the charges were for felonious assault. Henry' young and inexperienced attorney, one Paul Ortman, had done a good job, with some assistance from Judge Hickman, laying out the infamous record of Dicey Brown and it was with some reluctance that the jury foreman read the jury's finding, "Your Honor, we the jury find Henry Justin guilty of simple assault, but please, Your Honor, without the intent to kill. We ask the court to consider probation and, Your Honor, we think Dicey…"

Judge Hickman hurriedly cut off the foreman, for he realized the foreman was about to stray from the jury's charge. "Thank you, Mr. Foreman, thank you, members of the jury, for your deliberations and your finding. I would like to meet with the jury immediately in my chambers. This Court is now adjourned."

Not only Henry's eyes, on the fateful day of sentencing, looked up at the Judge but behind him a multitude of his neighbors and friends eyes stared straight ahead at the Judge. Judge Hickman's eyes moved from one black face to one white face back to another until he had counted fifty-two faces. He had read the probation officer's report but at this moment all he could remember was that Henry Justin was the choirmaster at the African Methodist Episcopal Church. He thought to himself, "*My God, is this the Choir?*" He was right. The Judge shook his head as if to shrug off the absurdity of his question and redirected his eyes to Henry's. They were dark and the face was black and the softness of Henry's demeanor struck him and he asked, "Henry Justin, are you a God-fearing man?"

Without hesitation the resonant bass voice boomed out, "I am, Your Honor!"

"Do you fear this Court, Henry Justin?"

"I fear this Court, Your Honor, but not you as a man."

Judge Hickman's eyelids narrowed and through the slits Henry Justin saw what he needed and quickly asked, "With your permission, Your Honor?"

"Proceed, Mr. Justin, but with caution, for neither I nor this court fear you as a man."

"No offense intended, Your Honor. I'm saying I do not fear God but I do fear what he has allowed to be created by his right hand...the hand of justice."

The eyes of the two men locked and Judge Hickman's demeanor became even more judicial as he quickly addressed Henry. "Mr. Justin, the jury has found you guilty of simple assault. I hereby sentence you to two years of probation under the condition you swear to this Court you will not gamble."

Henry only heard the word probation as Pat Krel, Court Probation Officer, had instructed him to hope for. This word would be the key to his future. On hearing the word, Henry readily responded without emotion, "I so swear, Your Honor."

"Not so fast, Mr. Justin. Bailiff, the Bible."

The Bailiff handed the Judge a large Bible and Judge Hickman instructed, "Step to the bench, Mr. Justin, and place your right hand on the Bible and so swear."

The large black man stepped forward; his reverence for the book was obvious as he attentively placed his huge hand on it and meekly said, "I swear to my almighty God that I will never gamble again. I will travel only on the path of righteousness."

Judge Hickman smiled his inward smile, as he often did when defendants, by their words, confirmed the jury's findings and he responded with, "That, Mr. Henry Justin, was more than I could have asked for or expected. This Court specifically appoints Mr. Pat Krel as your permanent probation officer. The Bailiff will take you to his office. This Court stands adjourned."

There was silence as the Judge left the bench and made his way to the door of his Chambers. He entered and, leaving the door ajar, saw the many black and white hands wrap around Henry Justin and then heard a quiet restrained voice say, "Thank God, thank God almighty."

The Judge closed the door and as he turned he thought, "*There's more to all of this.*"

Judge Hickman picked Pat Krel as Henry Justin's probation officer because he respected Pat's integrity and the sincere, judicious, and complete manner in which his pre-probation evaluations had always been handled. He had limited conversations with the young man but appreciated the concern he expressed from time to time about each case under consideration. His investigation and evaluation of Henry Justin had led Pat to one conclusion, as per his letter to the Court.

Your Honor:

These personal remarks on my part are in addition to the preceding pre-evaluation for probation material normally gathered for your consideration. I believe my following remarks will best summarize my impressions of Henry Justin. Henry Justin is a pillar of his neighborhood. A God-fearing and a God-serving man. He never drinks and only gambles when in need of money for his role as choirmaster. He is educated by his own hand and his passion is singing. I have taken the opportunity to observe him with his choir. They practice for four hours, three nights a week. He is an orphan, no family, not married, and works as a handyman for the Schumacher Chevrolet Agency and has since he was thirteen. Kyle Schumacher, president of the agency, states his title of handyman belies his importance to the agency. He stated, "For Henry, I prefer the title...substitute for anything or anybody." Mr. Schumacher had no reservations about putting up the bail money, but bail was denied. Your Honor, you must one day hear Henry Justin's singing voice. The quality of his voice represents the inner quality of the man. As an orphan I believe he harbors a resentment, a hatred of those who prey on others who by circumstance find the street their home. He had no reservation about striking out against the likes of Dicey Brown. I believe he would do it again but his contact with the Dicey Brown's of this world only occurs when he is in need of money for his church. Henry's street reputation is one that he can only be beaten at dice by someone who can cheat with perfection. I would welcome the opportunity to work with Henry Justin.

Sincerely,

Pat Krel

Judge Hickman understood what Pat was saying and followed his recommendation. It would be for Marsha Manning, the Judge's secretary, friend, confidant, and would-be lover to bring the two men's lives together.

✳   ✳   ✳   ✳

When Henry had closed the door to the Judge's chambers a figure that had been standing aside in the shadows slowly emerged while saying, "Are we alone?"

"Yes, Manning, we're alone…in my court."

"Phooey, Hick! Who cares if it's your court. I object to your even sitting on this case. You should have disqualified yourself. This man, this Doctor, put your face back together and nurtured you not only through the healing process but became your close confidant and ally. He needs *you* working with him, not against him…now!"

"I know all that, Manning, for heavens sake, this is only a preliminary hearing. A hearing to see if there is cause to even suspect J. R. of wrongdoing."

"Excuse my departure from the discreet terms of normal verbal communication, but where are *you*, Hick? Lost? Up your own backside? The powers that be in this town, the two-faced social bastards of this town want his ass…and, by the way…they'll have yours if you let them destroy J. R. anymore than their wagging lying tongues have already done."

Seeing how the veins in her face were bulging from anger, Hick acknowledged, "Calm down before you blow a fuse, Manning. You're usually more right than wrong and have been for the years I have known *you*. In fact, I'll say in matters of great concern, concerning us, you have more often than not been right, but..."

"But what? This time I'm wrong, Hick? Don't bet the farm or anything else on that. I'm right again, Hick. There's people who want J. R. to die...that way he'll go away and their sick agenda can go on forever. They'll have put away a Doctor. Don't *you* have your ear to the ground anymore? They want him to be put on trial for murder and they want him convicted and executed. This would be their masterstroke on the picture of power and control they imagine."

"Murder? You're kidding, Manning, what in the hell are you talking about?"

"I'm right, Hick, about two things; where your head is and that certain persons want the execution, one way or another, of J. R. Rollins, M.D. Oh, lest we forget, there's a third thing; he has been a friend of yours and mine for many years. I know you'll at least agree with me on that."

Her words bore into him; Nicholas Hickman looked confused and hurt as he usually did when Marsha Manning went on the attack. He met and hired her thirty years ago as his secretary two days after he opened his small office at 514 the Truitt Building, in Omaha, Nebraska.

*   *   *   *

Omaha was a long way from the streets of Newark, New Jersey, but he wanted to stay in Nebraska, for it was the only Law College that even considered his application for admission. Hick was turned down the first time but a letter from the chairman of the admissions committee, who noted the strong letters of recommendation, suggested he find a way to come to Lincoln and be interviewed, which he did, and the next year he was accepted. His first year was a financial struggle. He waited on tables at the Country Club and swept and cleaned the Trailway Bus depot nightly. His academic prowess was quickly recognized, and rewarded his second year. The Dean called him in and told him he had been awarded the Henry J. Finelly scholarship for the next three years.

Nicholas Hickman distinguished himself and graduated with honors. He was sought after by many firms in and outside of Nebraska. He decided his progress to date was what it was because he had always set his own course and he would continue to do so in the future. Money for the small waiting room and office was acquired first by writing briefs and doing research for a large firm. There was a small neighborhood Rexall drugstore around the corner from the modest apartment he had rented. It was there he met and one day hired Marsha Manning. The drugstore, with its soda fountain and six small tables, was the general meeting place of the neighborhood for breakfast and lunch. Carl, the manager, was gruff and sometimes just plain rude but everyone knew this was a coverup for his soft under belly. Carl always knew when someone needed a helping hand with the check and understood when they would double up on their bill…it meant they were over the hump and he would reward them with his infrequent but fleeting and elegant smile.

Carl's sharp eye and habit was to invite those in need to have supper with him at five. Since they didn't serve a supper meal he would always suggest, "Well, I have no one and I like to cook and I like company."

Ed Bender, pharmacist and owner, was as carefree as a bird in flight and never interfered with Carl but shared his concern for others in need. When Carl put someone on the "cuff" by waving them off about the check he he would inform Ed, who would then insist their other needs from the store be met and he would add, "We'll just be putting this on your bill with Carl for now."

Their reputation for generosity and caring spread, and they were never disappointed this Pharmacist and Lunch Counter manager, for sometimes years would go by but their kindness was never forgotten, for letters flowed in almost every day from those befriended, not only with words of thanks but with the money owed. It took one young adventurer ten years but the letter came along with the money owed. Ed mentioned the ten-year lapse to Carl and he grumbled, "He was a good kid. I expected him to pay and by God, he did…they all have and do."

One day, while sitting at a table after observing the routine of helping others, the Judge to be, Hickman, saw a pretty young woman be treated by Ed and Carl as all who were in need were. The next day, as fate allowed it to be, the counter and tables were full. All but his. The girl had a cup of coffee in her hand as she approached the table. "Room for another?"

Hick stood immediately. "Please…be seated."

"I'm Marsha Manning, well…thank you."

Somewhat surprised by the thank you, Hick asked, "For what?"

"Standing! Not all men are so considerate. Your name?"

"Why, ah, Hickman, Nicholas T."

"Nicholas T. Hickman, I am pleased to meet you."

"Yes, well, ah, would you have me call you Marsha or Miss Manning?"

"You're right, it's Miss but call me Manning. What would you have me call you?"

"Ah, if you don't mind, Hick."

"Hick?"

"Yup, Hick."

Marsha Manning's hand trembled ever so slightly as she sipped from her cup. Slowly placing the cup back in its saucer and seeing Hick watching her every move she asked, "What do you do, Hick?"

"I'm a lawyer, just starting out around the corner."

"Around the corner?"

"Sure, second floor, Room 514, Truitt Building."

"That's a good building for a lawyer."

"How do you know that?"

"Sorry…it was just a little pun. Forget it."

"Well…all right. What do you do, Manning…need sugar or cream?"

"I drink it black and I do nothing and you know it."

"I'm sorry, you're right. I saw Carl reaching out to help you as he and Ed have helped others, me included. I'll rephrase the question, what would you like to be doing?"

"Well, Hick, get used to it, our paths have crossed and I always tell the truth. First, I would like to be working at anything that makes me enough so I don't have to be on the dole and constantly worrying."

"You could be a whore."

Taken aback by the remark, Manning's eyes flashed and her jaw set and then she shot back, "A what?"

"A whore!"

Quickly understanding what he was doing, Manning changed her expression from one of resentment to acceptance and blurted out, "You're right, by cracky. I could be! But! But! There's something more than money that keeps us all going," she added defiantly.

Carl was listening watchfully, pleased that these two were engaged in conversation. Hick responded, "Really? What?"

"Dreams."

"Dreams? Of what?"

"I refuse to answer. You're a lawyer, right?"

"Right! But…what are your dreams?"

"Like anybody's dreams, Hick, like yours. To change the subject, you need help?"

Manning's changing the subject for some reason momentarily flummoxed Hick, but he quickly recovered and perfunctorily snapped, "Yup! Someone to work with me. I need an anything and everything person. Want the job?"

"I'm it."

"Don't you want to know what I'll pay?"

"Nope. The job is a dream come true and something is better than nothing and that's what I have now…thanks to you."

"Then, you're hired!"

Manning lowered her head and Hick saw the first tear hit the flat distorted reflection of her face in the coffee cup. Ripples formed from the continuing tears and without hesitation Hick's hand shot across the table to grasp hers and then he quietly assured her, "Manning, not to worry. Listen to me. How much I can pay I don't know. We'll be in it together, I know it. I guess what I'm really saying is you're hired, but not really…will you work *with* me?"

Manning slowly lifted her tear-stained face and as she did Hick noted she wore no makeup and thought, "*Not only pretty, but it's natural.*" As Manning raised her free hand to wipe away her tears, Hick's hand grasped it, held it tightly and after a moment he whispered, "Let them be. I'll always remember how they sparkle. They are the beginning of our relationship."

As their hands dropped slowly to the table they tightened even more, Manning felt what she would always feel for this man who had reached out to her. LOVE.

Carl smiled to himself and then rushed to tell Ed what he had heard and seen, for they both liked these two young people and early on had figured them as a pair for some reason. Together they watched from behind a display of stacked mouthwash and took pleasure in what they were observing. Nodding their approval they quietly returned to their stations to await what they agreed was an inevitable outcome from this newfound relationship.

For Hick and Manning, through the years, an abiding friendship developed. Once they tried sleeping together but Hick did not understand the secret intimacy love necessitates between a man and a woman. He didn't understand it, how he was feeling about this woman. For some deep inner reason he refrained from consummating the physical act. It was an awkward moment and difficult for them both. Somehow Manning understood and held him in her arms until they both fell asleep. She didn't feel rejected. She wisely knew from their many conversations his life on the streets left him with this void of understanding about intimacy with that special person. She knew he didn't want to just use her so she hoped in time he would find the emotions he lacked. There never was any physical relationship after that night but something else took its place…in both of them. Manning argued with herself many times as to whether it was friendship she felt, a budding romance, companionship, or just convenience based on necessity. She would dismiss any doubts she had about him by muttering to herself, "Ah, what the hell, I love him and that's all that really matters."

*   *   *   *

Now, as Manning stood before him, she felt frustrated and with anger in her voice demanded, "Nicholas Hickman, are you listening to me? Tell me, are you paying any attention to what I am saying?"

"I am, Manning, but you're all over the place and I don't know what you're talking about."

"Then, as I have said, your head is up your rear, Your Honor!"

"Please, Manning, don't talk like that in this court. You know it diminishes the stature of the court and I don't like it and besides, someone might hear."

"Is that all that worries you?"

"No! I am a man who came from the streets; I know its language; that type of language represents a failure to have acquired a vocabulary and erupts from frustration. I have never used it to express myself to you and you have only done it on those occasions you seem to feel that I am lost, hopelessly lost. You think these shocking words will turn me around but, Manning, just tell me what I need to know."

*   *   *   *

Henry Justin had moved back into the courtroom quietly. He always sensed when Marsha Manning was on the attack. He cared for her very much because of the way she treated him, respecting him and influencing the Judge to take him on as Bailiff after the incident during which the previous Bailiff, Peter Caslin, had had his throat slit by one Mike Johnston.

Johnston was a street thug and a murderer. Where the knife came from no one ever learned but as he was being sentenced by Hick he suddenly threw his cuffed hands out and spun around and the knife cut through Peter's skin and severed his external carotids and his larynx, causing him to drown in his own blood. Hick tore his robe off as he rounded the corner of the bench confronting Mike Johnston as he completed the circle he began. Hick grabbed both hands still holding the outstretched knife and bent his arms back and pushed, causing the knife to bury itself into Mike Johnston's throat. There was a gurgling sound as he screamed and fell to the floor next to Peter Caslin. Hick called out, "No one move until he is dead. It won't be long."

Gladis Pitman, court reporter, quietly fainted.

"It didn't take long," is how Hick responded when the County Attorney inquired as to why he hadn't sought help for Mike Johnston. "I'm from the streets, Mr. County Attorney. What I did, I saw played out many times before. Mike Johnston's modus operandi was exactly what street knifers do, to not only kill but to intimidate. My reaction was to turn the final results of his actions back on him. More questions?"

There were none from the County Attorney but Manning had quite a few. She harped at him about it for several days. "Hick, you're a Judge, not a street fighter. You may be six-foot-six and weigh two-hundred-seventy pounds but you've been off the streets too long."

"Here you are wrong, Manning. One never forgets such things."

The words caused her to immediately acquiesce and she replied, "That may be but I have enough problems around here and losing you is not going to be another one. Now…once and for all…do you remember Henry Justin?"

"Certainly. The black choirmaster."

"Right. Well, he has an appointment to see you this afternoon. Today, Hick, today. About replacing Peter. Today after the funeral, Hick, today, and I won't take no for an answer."

"I know you won't take no for answer but do you mean you want him as my Bailiff?"

"Right!"

"Why, Manning, he's a convicted felon!"

"That was three years ago. Pat Krel tells me he's clean, and will stay clean for you."

"What's that mean?"

"Haven't you seen him in your court over these last few years?"

"Certainly, I've noticed him, how could I have not. Pat makes his probationers come to court from time to time and so he informs me when they are coming. His intention is to refresh their memories as to what could happen…if they stray from the righteous path he's outlined for them."

"No, Hick. Justin comes to see and hear you. He admires you. He is grateful to you. He was in court the other day and saw what happened. He came and talked to me to say he didn't have time to help because you leaped to the occasion before he really understood what was happening. He knew you could handle it. That's more than I can say. Well?"

"Well, what?"

"Will you see him?"

"Do I have a choice, Manning?"

"No!"

The no was thunderous and Hick flinched, but quickly replied, "I didn't think so."

"I'll go get him."

"Go get him? You said after the funeral."

Manning knew she had to continue to overwhelm Hick if she was going to get things her way, so she took a deep breath and rattled off, "When I called Henry yesterday and told him I wanted him for your bailiff he was flabbergasted. I set it up for him to come in about four o'clock, Hick., as I said, after the funeral…but he was waiting when I came in at seven this morning. Now that's a good sign, he was anxious and all slicked up, Hick. I have him waiting in courtroom three. He wouldn't even go to lunch, but I took some to him."

Manning stopped to take a deep breath before she went on, after which she saw the beginning of a smile forming on Hick's face and just as quickly it faded as he said, "Manning, if I didn't love you, I'd bop you one. You assume and presume too much sometimes. You rattle my judicial bearing. I know you do it because you love me and think you know what's best for me but I'm telling you don't know in all instances. Now listen to me, woman, this is *my* Court and I make the decisions concerning this Court. Do you understand?"

"Right. But…"

"Right what? But what?"

"Right about whatever you say, Hick. But you said you love *me* and you know I love *you*."

"Right, Manning! Oh, what the hell, now you have me doing it."

"What?"

"Enough, Manning, enough. We'll talk about it over cocktails and dinner at my place tonight. Get Justin. Do we have time?"

"Plenty, the funeral's at three, it's only two o'clock. I figured you'd finish that one o'clock sentencing earlier than you did. You were windy."

"Manning!"

Manning knew by the tone of his voice she had pushed too long and too far, so she capitulated with, "Sorry, Judge, Your Honor, Sir!"

"Manning, I'm no fool. Your mind is made up and if I go against you, once that happens, based on past experience, I'm done for in more ways than one. Go after Mr. Justin. Bring him here to my chambers and then you disappear. Give me a half hour to visit with him, then come and get me so we won't be late for the funeral."

Manning was reaching for the door handle as she listened, her back was to him and she had a large self-satisfied grin on her face as she sweetly muttered, "Yes, Sir!"

A few minutes went by, giving Hick time to think about Manning and what she meant to him. Suddenly he was brought back to actuality by a soft but firm knock on the door. He called out, "Come in, Mr. Henry Justin. Please come in."

As Henry opened and walked through the massive door into Hick's chambers he saw Hick stand; walk around his desk, and extend his hand in greeting and say, "Welcome, Mr. Justin. Please be seated with me here at this table."

The table was small and positioned in front of a large arched window that offered a commanding view of the Courthouse gardens. Hick's office was the most admired office in the complex because of the historic content of period furniture and the spectacular view of the gardens and fountains. Hick only used his desk when dealing with matters before his court. All other matters and personal visitations were conducted at the small table.

Hick took particular note of the apparently new black suit Henry Justin was wearing on his six-foot-two frame. His shirt was starched stiff and dead white. His black tie was narrow, and struck Hick's fancy. His black high-top boots bore a spit shine and his demeanor was one of self confidence but apprehension glistened in his eyes as they met Hick's. Henry spoke, "Thank you, Your Honor, for requesting to see me."

"No thanks needed, Mr. Justin. You have your own private booster, and her name is Manning. What would you have me call you, Mr. Justin?"

"Henry, sir!"

Hick smiled as Henry's rich bass voice filled the room and then replied warmly, "Henry it will be, and Henry, your thanks and mine for your acquiring this position go to one Marsha Manning, affectionately known around here as Manning. She's already told you that, hasn't she?"

"Yes, Your Honor."

"Call me Judge, Henry."

"Yes, Judge. Yes, sir."

"No sirs, Henry, just Judge."

"Yes, Judge."

"We don't have long before we have to attend Pete's funeral. That's Peter Caslin, Henry, my former bailiff."

"I know, Judge, I was in the courtroom when it happened."

"Right, Henry, right, Manning mentioned it to me. Let's get to the point. Oh, but before we do, I would ask about the good looking suit you have on. Tailored? Manning?"

"Manning, Judge; she insisted. She called me a month ago and took me to Mc Tier's Clothing to be outfitted."

"A month ago, Henry? A month ago? I'm surprised."

"Yes, Judge, all she only told me was that she had plans for me."

"That would fit. Uh-oh, that means more than one suit."

"Three, Judge. Three of everything and all black but the shirts. Did I do wrong?"

"No, Henry, *you* had no choice, for you have been embraced by one Marsha Manning. You are now under her protective custody. Even if I didn't want *you* for my bailiff, and I do," the words *I do* did not go unnoticed by Henry even though he was uneasy in the presence of the Judge. As the Judge continued Henry's eyes filled with tears. Noting this, Hick pulled his handkerchief quickly from his pocket and extended it to Henry as he continued, "Henry, she gets what she wants, as you will see, and you and I will have nothing to say about it. You're hired, appointed, selected, or whatever. You start now…ah, can you?"

As Henry wiped his cheeks he replied, "Yes, Judge, I can, and thank *you*."

"It's a hard job, Henry. A few months from now you may not thank me. The hours are long and what we will share together goes from an emotional landslide some days to an emotional standstill on others. Be prepared for the worst, for it will happen as you saw the other day. We will talk more as time goes on. My door is always open to you, without knocking. I will have another bailiff familiarize you with the formal duties of a bailiff when we return from the funeral. You start tomorrow morning at six-thirty. Oh, yes, you will be paid $27,000 a year. Plus the 'hoo, hoo'. Manning will explain it all. Can you accept?"

Henry was overwhelmed. The most he had ever made was $6,000 a year. His face brightened as he bolted to his feet, taking Hick by surprise, and belted out, "I accept, Judge, I accept and praise be to God!"

"Exactly, Henry, praise be to God, and let's not forget Manning. We'll find her waiting in the car."

The doorway to the Judge's Chambers was large enough so the two men walked through it side by side. The image projected as they strode down the main hallway of the Court House would be repeated many times and noticed by many as the years passed. One, a Judge of the Court, the other the Bailiff of the Court, and when encountered they left no doubt in anyone's mind that they shared two common purposes they acquired early on in their relationship. And they were what, you may ask? Well, it was to see that justice was swift, for justice delayed is justice denied, and to let all others know that they support each other one-hundred percent in every way.

$$* \qquad * \qquad * \qquad *$$

Manning wasn't bothered one bit by Hick's protestation. She merely countered, "I'll say what I want, when I want if justice can be better served, and more importantly, if I feel better saying it."

"All right, Manning! Calm down. Tell me, what it is?"

Manning heard his plea and the way he said "all right" she knew he was ready to capitulate. She seized the moment, "I need Henry."

"What for?" Manning glared at him and he retorted, "All right, all right, Manning." Hick swung around in his chair, and to the eyes peering at him from the shadow by the door to his chambers he instructed good-naturedly, "Come on, Henry, come on, and oh, tell those waiting it will be a bit longer."

Henry opened the door, delivered the message and then, turning back into the Courtroom, closed the door.

Hick looked at Manning and inquired, "Okay, what next?"

Never hesitating, Manning turned to Henry. "Henry, the secure room, is it available?"

On hearing the question, Hick's eyes moved from Henry to Manning and he demanded, "What secure room? What the hell's going on! How do you know about the secure room? What a dumb question...I should know better. There are no secrets around here as far as you're concerned...forget it. Ah, let me rephrase it. Why do we need the secure room?"

Henry smiled as he picked up the phone hanging behind the Judge's bench and dialed security. When the phone was answered, Henry asked, "Clear for Judge Hickman?"

"Clear," came the reply.

Manning was listening and watching Henry and asked impatiently, "Well, Henry?"

"Clear."

Hearing "clear" she looked at Hick and smiled an all-knowing smile.

Hick was watching her intently and snapped, "Looks like collusion to me, Manning. Answer my question. Why the secure room?"

The lines at the corners of Manning's eyes deepened. Her lips tightened as she acknowledged, "There is no collusion now, and there has never been any between Henry and I against you. Others, heavens yes, but never you, and I might add, when we are in 'cahoots', and I like that word better, Hick. Not as heavy as your word, but when we are in cahoots it is to help you and even sometimes to save you from yourself."

"Manning, consarn it, you're lecturing me. Cut it out. Get to the point."

"You're right, absolutely right. We need to talk to you. Henry and I have knowledge, very sensitive knowledge, about J. R. We want to share it with you and it is for your ears only. Talking in this room is like standing in the middle of Main Street."

Hick shook his head at the remark and realizing his dilemma, Henry spoke up, "Judge, if you please. Take Miss Manning's arm and follow me to the elevator."

The tone of Henry's voice suddenly validated the seriousness of what Manning was implying. Hick quickly stood, and moving to Manning, took her arm and marshaled, "Lead on, Henry."

As the elevator door shut, Manning watched as Henry pushed three and then quickly double pushed four. The elevator rose and stopped between the third and fourth floors. Henry turned to the side of the elevator and ran his hand down the edge of the mahogany panel and the panel opened. There was a door behind the panel with a push button security lock. Henry pushed 55215, the door opened into a single file corridor that ran between the elevator shaft and a large cold air return. Walking twenty-five feet they encountered another door. Henry pushed 51255 and Manning thought, *"Same numbers, only backwards."*

What Manning didn't realize, because she was watching Henry, was Hick watching her. "Now you know, Manning."

"What? Ah…what?" She stammered.

"The numbers. Remember, double three, double four. First door, numbers 55215. Second door, same numbers, backwards."

"Right." Manning answered and Hick explained, "This room is not only a place to not be overheard but could be a great place to hide."

"Who dreamt this up?"

"Merritt Lawler, the county architect, put all this in the building's original plans but never divulged its existence to anyone until that crazy Mike Johnston killed Peter."

"You mean no one saw it in the plans?"

"Manning, there's a million ways for him to have hidden this arrangement. He came to me about it after the incident and said he had originally figured one day we would need something like this. He sensed the breakdown in civility and the increase of violent crime necessitated this room for the very purpose you and Henry seem to think is necessary today. Right?"

"Well, Hick, he was right. It amazes me this room went undetected and unused for all these years. What we have to say needs to be said where no one other than yourself can hear it. There are just too many ways to eavesdrop."

Henry opened the door and flicked on a light switch revealing a small room with a large table and eight chairs. There were paper and pencils set out on the table and the only other item in the room was a refrigerator. Manning took it all in and asked, "No phone?"

"Impossible to do, Manning, without giving away the room's existence. There is a cellular phone in the end of the table. The refrigerator has some fluids if anyone would need some," Hick replied as he sat down at the head of the table. Henry and Manning sat down on either side of the table and Henry asked, "Your Honor, would you like some juice or pop?"

"No thanks, Henry."

"Manning?"

"No, Henry, I think we should get on with what we have to say to Hick. He has people waiting. I suggest we stick to the specifics so we can save time and if we can convince His Honor about these specifics, we can go into details later."

"You're right, Manning, people are waiting, convince me."

Manning, closing her eyes and lifting her eyebrows at his sarcasm, exhaled out of the corner of her mouth. Taking a deep breath, she opened her eyes and looking at Henry said, "You start, Henry."

"Well, Your Honor, my street ear tells me there are a number of prominent citizens involved in drugs and sex with youngsters, minors."

"Go on, Henry. Who?"

"Judge Batemen, Police Chief Wentzel, Publisher Conway, businessmen Tyler, Givens, Remco, and Beasley."

After the names sank in Hick, obviously taken aback, quietly remarked, "I'll accept what you say, Henry. I'm not shocked, I can believe anything, and coming from you I know it's the truth, but what does this have to do with J. R. Rollins?"

"Givens wants his wife, but in reality he has his wife."

"So?"

"They've bought a contract on Watland."

"J. R.'s partner?"

"Yes, Your Honor, one and the same."

"Doctor Rollins and Watland have had a serious falling-out about fees and procedures that Doctor Watland has been charging and performing. They have argued publicly in Doctor's lounges. Doctor Rollins cuffed Doctor Watland outside of their office several weeks ago."

"Cuffed him?"

"Yes. Police were called and it took three officers to separate them and seventeen stitches to close Doctor Watland's lip."

A serious look came over Hick's face. "Phew! Manning, I have the feeling this is just the surface, isn't it?"

"Yes, Hick. Susan Rollins wants the social position Givens and his money can give her. I don't think J. R. realizes what's going on, I know he doesn't. Oh, about their divorce he does, but not the seriousness of having him accused of murder to discredit him or...tell him, Henry."

"They might murder him, Your Honor. You can hear them deliberating on the tapes as to whether that would be a good idea or not."

"The tapes! What tapes?"

"The ones in my pocket, Your Honor."

"Where did *you* get them?"

"Dicey Brown."

"Dicey Brown? He's the one that had something to do with your problem way back…with gambling and you promised…"

"Yes, but he's converted to the ways of the Lord, Judge."

"Henry started working on him, Hick, right after you sentenced him."

"Okay, but I'm lost. Where'd the info come from in the first place about all these people, sex, and drugs?"

"One of the girls in my choir, Barbara Jones, she works at the Givens house. She was close to Mrs. Givens before she died. Walter Givens kept Barbara on for his children's sake and because he needed someone to run his house. Barbara was a patient of Doctor Rollins. She overheard a telephone conversation and came to me about it. I went to Dicey, he put the word out on the street and the word came back there was a tap on the phone. Seems the publisher of the Omaha Sentinel, Robert Conway, is nervous and doesn't trust anybody. He had their phones and meetings tapped. The tapper, Matt Hughes, owed Dicey."

"What did he owe Dicey?"

"A favor, Your Honor."

"Henry…straighten it out for me."

"Big money from before Dicey found and accepted the Lord."

"You're sure of this, Henry?"

Manning interrupted, "Hick, you're pursuing the wrong path and besides, Matt Hughes is dead."

"Dead?"

"Yes, as of yesterday."

"Back up, Manning. Someone was after Matt Hughes because of the tapes he gave to Dicey?"

"No. He was in debt…way over his head…and behind in his payments, like six months. Kansas City took him out."

"Kansas City, Manning, what does that mean and how in the hell do you know these things?"

"Well, Kansas City, Hick, is where the big betting money for Omaha is laid off. What Matt Hughes couldn't get through his head was they were serious about wanting their money. Eighty-thousand-dollars worth. How do I know things? I work for you."

"What's that have to do with it?"

"Why, Your Honor, all those lawyers that sit in my office waiting to talk to you, talk to me. I've kept my ears open."

"You never cease to amaze me, Manning. Okay, I'll listen to all that later. This is confusing for me and it's obvious you two aren't confused. What are they, your conspirators, trying to do today?"

"They want *you* to find cause to bind J. R. over for trial and the charges are to be for murder, slander, and libel."

"I never heard anything like that implied, Manning."

"No, you didn't, as least not yet with all the wrangling that has been going on. The Doctor isn't going to slaughter as easily as they thought he would, but I'll bet you'll get an ear full about it in your chambers. They'll cut to the quick and try to take you off-guard with their accusations."

"Based on what?"

"A letter from the Doctor to his sons about their mother and the tapes."

"I know about the letter; it's his right to communicate with his sons; I don't know about the tapes."

"It may be his right but not as far as the plaintiff is concerned, and the sons are lined up against their father. Use discovery to expose the tapes…Your Honor."

"Discovery, Manning? That's Ortman's job. As far as the tapes, and a few other matters are concerned I'll go after Villella," Hick stopped, looked as his watch, and exclaimed, "Good Lord! It's been forty-five minutes. I have to get back. Henry, Manning, now summarize for me, details later this evening, my place for dinner."

Henry looked at the Judge intently as he said, "Your Honor, it is very serious for the Doctor in many ways and for us. But there is no cause for this action against the Doctor."

"Manning, what say you?"

"Ditto, Hick, ditto. We're now in it up to our necks. We'll be taking on the big boys in this town…but Dr. J. R. Rollins has committed no crime; he is the one who has been done to. The root of the whole matter is the Tenth Commandment has been broken and we must see to it the Ninth isn't and also deal with the Seventh."

Hearing Manning's words Henry intoned, "A-men, A-men."

Hick stood smiling. He was proud of them both and Henry's insight into the law pleased him, for it showed Henry had been paying attention through all those long hours spent in his court room. He cheerfully exclaimed, "You two never cease to amaze me, or have I already said that? I don't know all the Commandments by their number. Just that there are ten. Which one should I be concerned about as I go to meet those people in my chambers?"

As if rehearsed Manning and Henry spoke as one, "The Ninth: Thou shalt not bear false witness against thy neighbor."

"I'll see to it. I'll go first, Henry. follow in about ten minutes. I'll be ready to go on with the hearing in about twenty minutes. No one is to be in the court unless they are a part of the hearing."

Hick turned, left the room, and made his way to the elevator to return to his chambers, all the while trying to remember which Commandment was which. He couldn't. Opening the door to his chambers the serious look on his face caused those waiting to wonder, and well they should. He went to his desk and, dropping down into his chair, began by bringing himself to his full height while looking scornfully at the County Attorney, Joseph Villella. He spoke, contrary to his facial appearance, soulfully, "All right, Joe, just between us all here informally gathered, clear it up, what are you aiming for in this preliminary hearing. I'm confused or not well informed. I thought this was a matter to determine if a letter from a father to his sons could be used to bring a slander action against the father. An equity case where someone has doubts, a supposed tort, about circumstances not covered or discovered by law. Right? I was flattered and made to believe my judicial capacity and temperament was desired by all parties as a part of this action."

"They were and are, Your Honor, but the Grand Jury handed down the indictment late yesterday afternoon. This action was scheduled; the plaintiff's attorney deferred; I took the opportunity."

"To what, Joe?"

"As I said, present you with the indictment, identify the accused, have him plead, arraigned, and then booked."

"Joe, you want to…no, let me ask, are you supplanting the plaintiff's attorney, as I have said, in this or what I was led to believe was an equity case?"

"Yes, Your Honor, this is to be an action at law, for I have reason to believe and can produce prima facie evidence that a felony has been committed…to be exact, murder, and that the Doctor acted as a co-conspirator…an accessory to murder. I expect you to so find and to bind him over for trial with no bail. I have the indictment from the grand jury, I repeat, the accused has been identified. I expect him to plead not guilty but I also expect you, on hearing the evidence, to have him arraigned…with no bail. The True Bill takes precedent over any action for libel or slander."

Hick was watching a seething Paul Ortman moving forward in his chair. He was about to jump up and object when Hick stopped him by asking, "Calm down, Paul. Tell me, when you saw Joe this morning didn't you wonder what he was doing here?"

"I asked!" Paul yelled as he jumped to his feet.

"And?"

"He said I'd find out as matters proceeded."

"You weren't suspicious?"

"No, Your Honor, this was a civil matter and he has now turned it into a criminal case with an indictment and all. I didn't even know there was a grand jury impaneled."

"Neither did I, Paul, so I can't reprimand you for not knowing what was going on around the courthouse." Quickly turning to Joe, Hick, on the attack, snapped, "Okay, Joe, now you tell us why we feel like mushrooms."

"I petitioned Judge Batemen to impanel two days ago so I could get a True Bill to prevent flight."

Hick closed one eye, raised his opposite eyebrow, shook his head slightly and muttered, "Judge Batemen, Joe? Why not me? Don't answer that one, Joe, but answer me this, why would a man flee when he hasn't the foggiest notion he is going to be charged with anything other than slander, libel, or both for writing to his sons?"

"Because he's guilty of murder, even as if he pulled the trigger."

J. R. Rollins moved forward in his chair and shouted, "Murder! Are you crazy?"

"Like a fox, Doctor. I knew what would come out in this action and I didn't want you fleeing…God knows where."

Recovering from the surprise, Paul Ortman rose to his feet thundering, "Your Honor, this is highly unusual; high handed to say the least. I…"

"Hold it, Paul, not so loud. I run this court." Once again, Hick's scowling face turned to Joe and demanded, "Joe, he's right you know. You've brought an action before this court, or are trying to, without first informing *this* court. You pulled a bait and switch. You could have amended the civil action, or dropped it so as to inform the court. Why didn't you?"

"No time, Your Honor."

"Phooey, Joe, phooey! This office opens every morning at six-thirty."

"I couldn't get here this morning. The press of my case load."

"Weak excuse, Joe. The worst. You better give me cause as to why I shouldn't throw this whole thing out. Who do you have to test, the Ninth Commandment? Before you answer remember this, make it precise as to your evidence and it's legitimacy or…I'll rule on both matters in the defendant's favor and blow *you* out of the water. Don't try and tell me I can't, for what I see this morning borders on fraud, deceit, and contempt for this court, MY COURT, Mr. District Attorney. If necessary, through precedent, I'll cite chapter and verse, as to what gives me the right to throw the book at you. I repeat, this is MY COURT. Think now before *YOU* answer. It seems I just can't get anybody to think this morning. I'll wait."

Knowing Hick as he did, the tone of his voice and his direct implication Joe had besmirched the integrity of the court caused Joe to know he was in trouble, big trouble. He felt he had the necessary evidence but wouldn't reveal the telephone call he had received. For now he'd backpedal, stall, and to that end, in a very patronizing way said, "I was wrong, Your Honor, I apologize to the court, and especially to you, Your Honor."

Hick knew he had Joe on the ropes and that he was groping for a way back. He sensed he wanted to stall until open court. He thought, "*Sometimes these guys are like children, anxious to fess up, but try to be clever about it.*" Hick asked, "When did you have a grand jury impaneled?"

"Three days ago, Your Honor, I went to Judge Batemen when certain facts were brought to my attention. The True Bill was handed down yesterday."

"You sure moved that along in a hurry and, in fact, you did have more than ample time to inform this court, didn't you, Mr. County Attorney?"

"I did and there's no excuse. I apologize again to the Court, Your Honor. It doesn't seem to be my morning."

"Not as far as telling it like it is and it isn't going to be your day, Joe, unless you now get to cause."

"I have tapes, Your Honor, and will present witnesses willing to testify the Doctor contracted for the murder of one Matthew Hughes."

"Paul, how do you respond? Want a postponement so this can be done proper and legal like?"

J. R. Rollins reacted immediately by shaking his head negatively, and to get Paul Ortman's attention reached over and pulled violently on his coat sleeve. "One moment, Your Honor...please."

Paul bent down and conferred with his client and suddenly J. R.'s whispering became a shout as he said, "Under no circumstance delay! I wave my rights to a trial before a jury. I want a hearing, a trial, whatever it takes...NOW!"

"No need to answer, Paul, we all heard the Doctor...that is, unless *you* want to go against his wishes."

"Not on a bet, Your Honor. We'll proceed to court and see what the District Attorney has."

"You are all excused, gentlemen. I'll see *you* in my court in fifteen minutes. Be ready."

The room quickly cleared and Hick was left with his thoughts. He pondered and shortly picked up the phone and dialed Judge Harold Bateman.

A low voice answered, "Judge Batemen here, what is it?"

"Harold, it's Hick. I have a strange situation going on in my court this morning and I..."

Harold interrupted, "I know all about it."

Remembering what Henry had accused Judge Bateman of being a part of, Hick, contrary to his usual decorum and good nature growled, "You know all about what, Harold?"

"Joe came to me to impanel the Grand Jury, and I know about the True Bill handed down."

"And you knew about the action scheduled in my Court today?"

"I did."

"And you don't think it improper or at least peculiar I was not informed?"

"Why, Hick, you sound piqued."

"As the Presiding Judge, Harold, you have a responsibility to keep the rest of us informed. In case you've forgotten, I'm not sitting here on anybody's side. I'm here to see justice is done and I don't like being sandbagged or blind sided by anybody. Especially by the Presiding Judge. Do you have an explanation?"

"I don't have to explain anything."

Hick wasn't surprised at what he had just heard; he rather expected it, but the veins bulging on the side of his neck gave visible testimony to his extreme anger. He never really liked or trusted Harold…so…he waited purposefully for the silence on the phone to speak for itself, for his anger, and then he interjected forcefully, "No you don't…but…you can be held accountable for wrongdoing and you will be."

"That a threat?"

"Take it to the bank, Harold."

"I think you ought to disqualify yourself. You're prejudiced in favor of the Doctor. If I remember correctly, he's the very doctor who put your face back together."

Hick smelled it. The man was mentally rehearsed and his voice was defiant. The immediate urgency and convenience of the suggestion to have Hick disqualify himself showed something was building or had been put in place which had him as part of the outcome. Hick rebelled, "When do you plan to show cause?"

"Most likely when you render your decision; it will be thrown out on appeal."

"What decision?"

"I don't know…yet, but I suppose I will this morning. Also, Hick, I'm a witness for the prosecution."

Hick's mind cried out for more information based on what Manning and Henry had given him earlier. He replied, "I'll look forward to that, Harold. You'll find I am not asleep at the switch. This is going to be interesting, for in my court I eagerly wait for the opportunity to exercise the judgement of contempt. Also, I am learned when it comes to tit-for-tat. I want you to know there are more than one set of tapes."

Harold never had a chance to respond, for Hick dropped the phone in its cradle and cried out, "Ha, ha, let's see how you like that, Harold ole' boy!"

Harold's hand shook as he placed the dead phone back in its cradle. He waited, fleetingly thought, and then picked up the phone and dialed Hick's office. Ten rings, but there was no answer.

CHAPTER 2

▼

The Sapphire Diner on the North Kansas City river road was the gathering place for most of the second level two-bit gamblers, trigger men, and would be's. Charlie Umbigolata, the owner, paid no attention to them unless they tried to stiff him. Everyone in the place, any time of the day, knew Charlie had nothing to fear from any of them. His roots went back to the all-out gang days by way of his father, Antony. Antony was better known in his day as "The Silencer." The modern uptown gamblers, trigger men, drug dealers and movers of women all over the world still were tied to the North Side Diner by telephone. Every booth had its own phone and a twenty-four-hour occupant. The "dinner tabs" were sent out each month, as Charlie would say, "To the uptown hoy-pa-loy. Even though they moved up they still liked and never forgot Charlie's food, and besides the tab for sitting rights, they ran up healthy food tabs." Then he would laugh.

Louie Donata sat in his booth in the north corner of the diner. The booth was just past the turn of the aisle as it led to the mens room. He could see everyone who came in but they would have to strain to see him. The booth also gave ready access to the door in the men's room leading outside if he needed to make a quick exit. Louie had inherited the booth when he went from being a runner for Sam Hirsch to contact man and bookmaker. Sam was the only Jew entrenched in the

Kansas City scene and that was because he had the contacts and people in Omaha. Sam's specialty was finding the best and quickest way to lay off some of the fast big money shoved on the table by the star players in Chicago, Omaha, and Kansas City.

He also had the best stable of gunsels readily available, but this he denied. They were cheap if needed to maintain order and discipline in the ranks. Otherwise, for a hit they were expensive, very expensive.

Louie smoked cigars incessantly and Charlie had to install an exhaust fan right over the booth to cut down the odor. There was an extra monthly tab but Louie didn't mind, for the fan made it more difficult to hear what he was saying. This morning his phone was busy as always and he was having a hard time satisfying himself with coffee and his usual apple fritter. He had laid off better than two-hundred thousand from Omaha on the Sunday Dallas-Green Bay game and was slightly agitated because he was just plain hungry. He hadn't even taken a puff of his cigar and had to keep relighting it. He saw Charlie's large hand with the familiar diamond pinky ring reach across the table with a fresh cup of coffee and heard him say, "Getting rich this morning, wop?"

"Charlie, why do you call us that?"

"I don't like being Italian. I'm not like all *you* dumb dago northerners. My people had papers."

"Charlie, I'm offended."

"Louie, you ain't smart enough to be offended, that's why you're a wop...without papers."

Louie was clearly offended and his hands went up and to each side as if he was a balancing act and as his head cocked to one side he seemingly pleaded, "Explain, hey...for me...Charlie...explain my not bein' smart."

"Louie, look what you do for a livin' and the Jew gets all the dough. That's smart?"

"Charlie, I gotta eat."

"You should be an apple fritter. That's about all you eat…and I see you haven't touched yours. Hand it to me, you dumb wop, and I'll warm it up for you."

Louie handed Charlie the fritter and as he did his smile revealed the gaping holes of his missing teeth. Charlie, looking down at him, disdainfully asked, "Louie, do you even go out with broads? Will broads go out with the likes of you?"

"I'm too busy."

The answer brought a smile to Charlie's face as he stood looking at him. He shook his head as he turned and walked away muttering to himself, "Dumb dagoes never get it. Can't add two and two."

$$* \qquad * \qquad * \qquad *$$

Sam Hirsch sat in his sumptuous office on the twentieth floor of the Kinner Towers Building. His gambling and prostitution empire had no equal. Sam didn't do drugs. Not that he hadn't done them but when he first ran into Kate Shields, twenty years ago, she was a heroin addict but that did not stop him. He fell in love with her. Kate had come from a wealthy Dallas family and had tried to break into the entertainment business as a singer but couldn't make it fast enough to the top; got in with the wrong bunch and took to recreational drugs, as she put it, to ease the pain of failure. Eventually prostitution was the waybill of her habit.

Sam had started out in Chicago with the mob, for his father sent him from Omaha to "get smart." Sam didn't take to the heavy-handed tactics he saw used time and time again. On occasion, for relief, that became more frequent as time went on, he sought out a small restaurant and bar on the west side called Donny's. Donny Vestuva and Sam hit it off. Donny had left the rackets and as their friendship grew he sensed Sam didn't like them either. Donny's "Pa", as he called him, ran a fierce, tight-lipped, Sicilian-only family of south side hoods with no equal for violence. Donny subscribed to their right to be what they wanted to be and understood the value of the family but wanted no part of the violence. Pa set him up in his "club" and promised he would be left alone, with protection, to find his way.

Sam only drank on Friday nights at Donny's. He would sit alone in a dark corner Donny reserved for him. His routine was two bourbons straight up and a side of soda on ice. Six of the largest shrimp Donny could buy and his special horseradish sauce were routine.

One night as Sam walked in Donny greeted him with excitement rather than his normally business-like voice. "Sam, Sam, Sam! Tonight, wait till you hear what I have. I'm moving up. Gonna give this joint some class."

"What's cookin', Donny?"

"This broad I got…wait till you hear her."

"Do what?"

"Sing, you clown, sing. Wait till you hear her."

"Where'd you find her?"

"Pa! He felt sorry for her and sent her down."

"Pa sent her? Why? Break it to me easy."

"She's hooked on the big H, but what a voice. Wait till you hear her."

"Oh, brother. An addict?"

"Yeah, like I said, temporary like, but wait till you hear."

"That's all you have said, 'wait till,' since I walked in. I'm ready already."

"To your table, Sam, to your table. The shrimp and bourbon await. I'll get the six o'clock show on the road just for you."

Sam walked to his table and as Donny had said his booze and shrimp were waiting. He didn't have to wait too long, for as soon as he sat down the lights dimmed and a spotlight fixed on Donny, who began with, "Ladies and gentlemen, patrons of my club, I take great pleasure in presenting to you, for your enjoyment, the most beautiful voice of love. Ladies and gentlemen, Miss Kate Shields."

The spotlight faded and quickly reappeared. Standing demurely with hands clasped and head down was Kate Shields wearing the black tailored knee-length dress, with a strand of white pearls around her neck, that Donny had bought for her at Lord and Taylors. Her black hair glistened and her blue eyes accented her beauty, for she wore no makeup. Her lips had a natural pink glow and her prominent cheeks slightly shadowed the side of her face and, coupled with the diminished light from the spotlight, formed a soft halo around her head as she began to sing.

Donny found his way to Sam's table and without a word sat down, drink in hand.

After several songs Kate paused and just looked out over the darkened room. The small orchestra could hardly be heard but the notes from the piano attempted to fill in where her voice had left off, but to no avail. There was no applause, rather a stunned silence, a silence that often accompanies the recognition that a rare talent was being discovered.

The room remained dark and, starting up again, Kate sang for forty-five more minutes. It had now been an hour and forty-five minutes since she started. On completing the song "Near You" the spotlight faded and Donny jumped to his feet, leaving Sam in total darkness. Quickly the spotlight reappeared with Donny walking into it saying, "Ladies and Gentlemen, there will be a short intermission before Miss Shields returns. I know she would appreciate your applause."

As the lights in the restaurant went up there was a thundering, cascading wave after wave of applause. Much to Sam's surprise the room was packed. People were standing, drinks in hand, dumbfounded by the voice and beauty of what Donny had introduced.

Sam turned in his chair and saw Donny shaking hands as he returned to the table. He sat down and excitedly spewed out, "See, Sam, see! I told you! I told you she's the very best, nothing like her. Is there?"

"No, there isn't. How is she?"

"Nervous, but in a strange calm way."

"She need a fix? When under pressure that's when they usually do."

"No, Sam, they had her in the tank for over six weeks. Pa says, and I believe, she's dried out and if we keep the show going she'll find herself in singing," Donny answered, clearly agitated by the question.

"She is the show all right," Sam said, trying to smooth things over, "I didn't realize that much time had gone by and that the place had filled up."

"Let me tell you. Larry, my Captain, opened the doors to let the heat out when the place filled up and he said they're standing outside. He's serving drinks on the street, and listen to this, the beat cop said he couldn't do that but when he heard Kate, he O.K.'d it and stayed with everyone else. He's still here. Said he never heard anyone like her. She's wowin' 'em!"

"I could just sit and look at her, Donny, she's a looker."

"No, Sam, no, it's not her looks for me. It's the voice. They can't see her outside but they can't leave. Can you stay?"

"Donny, I haven't been motivated to stay any place this long since I came to Chicago. I'm going nowhere. I think you have a winner, a star. Can you keep her off the stuff?"

Donny was taken aback again by Sam's persistence about the drug problem, for he was lost in the artistic ability of this young woman as well as her physical beauty and stage presence.

Sam saw the hurt flash again in Donny's eyes. "Sorry I said that, ole' chum. You're right, she is absolutely the best. I'll help you and your Miss Kate Shields any way I can. How old is she?"

"Twenty, Sam, just twenty. How old are you?"

"Thirty-eight, Donny, just turned thirty-eight and ugly."

After that night Sam became a regular but drank booze only on Fridays. Months went by and Kate's strength grew with her popularity. Revues occurred weekly and offers poured into the club but she never wavered, and one night startled Donny with, "I'm going to call it quits, Donny. I've learned my lesson."

"What are you talking about? This place is just a beginning. You have a great future."

"Not in singing."

"Not in singing, Kate, what are you talking about?"

"I'm in love."

"With whom?"

"You're not surprised?"

"Shucks, Kate, if you're in love I'm thrilled for you. You've come a long way and you've dragged me and my club right along behind you. Pa was right about you."

"I was off on the wrong track; he saved me from myself."

"Yeah, he did. Pa surprises me every once in awhile. You know dealing in that stuff is his shtick, along with a few other choice ones. But he, well, he sees somebody in a predicament and he makes them a special somebody. It's like he makes them family and won't let anything or anybody hurt them…just like family."

"You really think so?"

"I know so. The word went out on the street about you, direct from him. If anyone had sold to you or done, or does, anything to you, they're meat for the grinder. You're family."

Kate was taken aback by Donny's words and offered, "Donny, I'm flattered Pa feels that way about me."

"He does. He sneaks in here about twice a week to hear you sing. Says you're his protege. Did you ever sing for him?"

"No. I've never met him."

"What? Then how did he get you to me?"

"When I left the hospital they said a very prominent man, a very powerful Chicago man, wanted me to stop by and audition for you at your nightclub and I did."

"Pa is something else. In fact, you know, I think he was glad when I wanted out of the rackets. He can't, but I wish he would get the hell out before..." Donny stopped and looked pensive as he sat by Kate's side. She said nothing. Then, shaking his head somewhat sadly, Donny continued with, "The conversation started out you're in love, you're quitting. Who is it?"

"Sam."

"Our Sam?"

"I'm glad you feel that way. I sit and talk with him every night. He loves me but doesn't know it. He's unhappy, Donny."

"Yeah, I know he's unhappy. He's no gunsel but he has one in and to his head."

"Who?"

"His ole' man. He'll never let him change like mine did."

"Do you think he'd change for me?"

"Want an honest answer?"

"Wouldn't have asked if I didn't."

"The answer is no, he won't change for you, me, or anybody else. I see it in his eyes. He's not a gunsel but he's a gambler. He doesn't lust to gamble but lusts to take it away from the suckers who do. I guess it's in his blood...but listen, you could bring the beauty, the class, the balance to his life. You, Kate, could keep him from the really bad stuff that happens to a guy in the rackets."

"I'm going to try."

"Good. Has he told you, have you told him about loving one another? Did what I just say come out right?"

"I understand. He doesn't know. He's never told me but I know and he will...tonight."

So it was. That night Kate proposed to Sam as she held his hand. Donny sat listening at what had become their table. Sam didn't seemed surprised by her words, rather he listened intently and when she was through said, "I should have said it to you, Kate. I didn't think I was on your mind or even a list that way or that you could ever think of me that way. I say yes, I'd be crazy not to, I will marry you, and the sooner the better."

Kate's other hand reached across the table to grasp Sam's free hand as she asked, "Why wouldn't you think I could love you, Sam?"

"Hell, for starters, I'm ugly, Kate."

That didn't make any difference and in a matter of days they were married. Kate retired from the Club but not until she found a replacement for Donny. Kate went back to school, traveling extensively in their first years together. She became prominent in charitable organizations yet kept a low social profile. She and Sam spent as much time as they could alone. She bore two children, a boy and a girl.

When Sam's father died, Sam moved the operation to Kansas City. Their home on Wilson Parkway was elegant and always referred to by the uppity's at the country club as the Kate Shields Hirsch residence. Never was Sam's name brought into a conversation. It was if he didn't exist but his money and power did, and when spoken his name brought fear in many circles.

The ringing phone broke Sam's concentration on the past, he reached over and picked up the receiver and said, "Sam Hirsch, here."

"Caveat emptor."

So as to honor the caller, Sam sat up straight in his chair and announced, "What buyer and beware of what, Your Honor?"

"Hick to you, Sam."

"Never, Your Honor, not after what you did for my father."

Hick's mind raced back in time. Sam's father, in his later years, became careless and was indicted for fraud as a result of a real estate dispute. He made a big mistake out of anger and was caught. The matter dragged on but by the time he was tried, convicted, and about to be sentenced, he had developed stomach cancer. Sam's physician told Pat Krel, the probation officer, he had maybe three months to live. Pat passed the information on to Hick and on the day of sentencing an almost comatose Isadore Hirsch was helped to his feet and held tightly by Henry Justin as he heard Hick pronounce sentence. "Isadore Hirsch, you have been found guilty of one count of fraud. However, I have taken into consideration the good as well as the bad you have done in and for this community. You stand before me and on the threshold of meeting your maker. Therefore, I sentence you to three years of probation, restitution in the dollar amount as contained in the fraud indictment and a fine of $3 million. The $3million will be paid by you personally this day to the Omaha Home for Orphans. You have contributed before. I have made arrangements with the Sheriff, your son Samuel, and your bank to have this matter concluded today, before you return to your sick bed. I remand you to the Sheriff and, Mr. Hirsch…may God be with you and have mercy on your soul."

Sam never forgot what the Judge had done and returned that afternoon to his office to thank him and to relate to him what had happened at the Omaha Home for Orphans.

"Your Honor, the whole school turned out in the gymnasium. It was the Headmaster's doing. He said Father had given a lot of money over the years and had refused recognition but under these circumstances he felt it was time to say thank you in a big way. You let him know ahead of time. Didn't you?"

"A Judge has many responsibilities. We hate no one, we only administer the law. Go on, Sam."

"Father, Your Honor, on his own insisted on riding with the Sheriff and before he knew about the ceremony he contacted the bank. The check to the school was for five million dollars, not three."

"Phew! Five-million…and your father?"

"We took him back to the hospital, he was weak. The Rabbi is with him. The Doctor says he won't make it through the night."

Hick stood, extended his hand across the small table where they sat, saying, "Thank you for telling me. Remember, I am your friend."

"I know, Your Honor. I thank you again and if I can ever help, never hesitate to call on me."

*   *   *   *

Hick had called Sam numerous times over the years and they had worked together on many projects and Hick never hesitated to call him. Hick's mind raced back to the present in a matter of moments as he related, "There has been a hit on one Matt Hughes, gambler. He was reportedly into you or someone for about eighty grand. Rumor of possible contracts on J. R. Rollins and William Watland, M. D.s. So whoever bought the one contract and is contemplating the others best beware, for I'm on the case."

"Hughes owed us but we would never touch him. He can't pay it back if he is dead. The others I don't know anything about, Your Honor. Can I call *you* right back?"

"I'm due in court but I'll wait."

"Two minutes and I'll be back. Shalom Aleichem."

Sam hung up the phone and immediately dialed the Diner.

"Sapphire Diner, Charlie."

"Wop, it's the Jew. No time for bullshit. Know anything about a hit on Matt Hughes or a bid for a hit on a J. R. Rollins or William Watland? They're doctors in Omaha."

"Hughes owed *you*. That *you* know. No hits or bids for six weeks. Okay, Sam?"

Sam and Charlie respected and liked one another but most of all, understood one another. Sam could tell Charlie was holding back. Most likely for money. They liked one another but nothing was for nothing. Sam sighed, "Okay, Charlie. For my friend, His Honor, I was hoping *you* knew or heard something. Cut in on Louie."

Charlie punched hold and rang Louie, who was about to take his first bite of an apple fritter.

Charlie had mandatory control over all of the phones. He could listen in, cut in, or cut them off.

He liked to tell those who wanted a booth in his place, "I'm control central. What goes down around here I know about and I can thumbs up anything or thumbs down anything. If you don't like the rules of the Sapphire Diner, hit the street any time. I know what we're all about but I'll only let things go so far. We've been here a long time and will be here longer, much longer."

Louie, seeing the light blinking on his phone, quickly slammed down the fritter, picked up the receiver and growled, "Yeah, Charlie, yeah."

"Don't yeah me, you dumb wop. Pick up one, the Jew wants you."

Louie was doing a slow burn as he snapped, "Charlie, does Sam know you call him the Jew?"

"Why in the hell don't you ask him, right now!? Wop!"

Louie punched the button with vengeance but knew he would never ask Sam that, for he was afraid, he didn't have the guts to…and meekly answered, "Sam. Louie."

"Louie, who hit Hughes?"

"We didn't, Sam, you know that."

"Find out who did."

"How?"

"Louie, what in the hell do I pay you for? Don't answer that. Look, for starters, work on Charlie. I have a feeling he knows something or at least can find out. Second, find out if there's a bid for or contract out on a J. R. Rollins or William Watland of Omaha. Get back to me, pronto."

"Okay, Sam, Okay. How Pronto?"

"Five minutes at the most." Sam hung up and dialed Hick, "Judge Hickman?"

"Is it you, Sam?"

"Yes, Your Honor. Nothing here. Hughes owed us but we didn't hit him. It's against my policy. About the others, I've put the word out for info and will get back to you as soon as I hear."

"Could someone else, other than a Kansas City man, have hit Hughes?"

"Sure, but I wouldn't know why or who, yet I'll guarantee we were the only ones he was into. The word was out on him."

"Sam, I have to get back to my court. I need information as soon as possible. Call Henry on the bench phone if you have something for me. Just tell him it's you and I'll get right back to you."

"Goodbye, Your Honor. Shalom Aleichem."

Sam hung up the phone, picked it up again and dialed Louie. Louie's mouth was full of fritter and he had just picked up a cup of coffee to wash it down when the light on the phone blinked. He swallowed hard, muttered a profanity, and picked up the phone to hear, "Well?"

"Nothing yet, Sam, but I'm working on it."

"Louie, I've had to remind you twice I pay you big time. Not for nothing, Louie, but for action. I want results fast and you now have ten thousand to spread around for quick action. Get it?"

"Ten minutes, Sam, I promise."

"I'll be waiting."

Louie was standing as he dropped the receiver in the cradle and the fritter on the table. He turned and hurriedly walked down the aisle to where Charlie stood watching him and as he approached Charlie he bellowed, "What now, wop?"

"There's ten thousand if you've got something for me in two minutes."

"I figured the Jew would come across. I can tell by his voice when he's hot on something and money is no object."

"How can you tell?"

"That's for me to know, you dumb wop."

The perceived insult by Charlie was wearing on Louie and he snipped, "Thirty seconds has gone by."

"I'll supply what you want to know, my little Italian jerk, in thirty seconds. Sit down and listen."

Louie did as he was told. In fifteen seconds his mouth opened and his jaw dropped in disbelief at what he had heard. Fifteen seconds more and Charlie was through and asking for his money, "Now *you* have it, jerk. Hand over the ten thousand of the Jew's money and don't try to argue with me."

"But, ah, but are *you* sure?"

"Louie, my patience is wearing thin with you in general and I'll only tell you one more time. Hand over the dough or hit the street."

As Louie stood, he reached in his pocket and pulled out a large roll of thousand dollar bills, counted out ten and hurriedly handed them to Charlie saying, "I believe you, Charlie...I...believe you, but will Sam?"

"He'll believe, cause that's the way it is, and tell him more will follow. What you have is just for starters."

Louie, still not believing what he had heard, walked back to his booth and dialed Sam.

"Louie?"

"It's me. I got what you wanted."

Louie repeated what Charlie had told him and it took thirty seconds. He still didn't believe it but knew it had to be true because it came from Charlie's mouth.

When he was finished Sam said, "Money talks."

Sam hung up the phone dejectedly but immediately and unhesitatingly picked it back up and dialed Hick's Courtroom.

CHAPTER 3

▼

Hick hung up the phone, stood, drew himself to his full height and, realizing he hadn't removed his judicial robe, moved toward the courtroom door and paused before it. He took a deep breath and thought *"T his is going to be interesting."* He took another deep breath as he forcefully opened the door and immediately looked around the courtroom. His mind accelerated and informed him, all of the participants in the action were present and in their proper places, but someone was missing. Suddenly, Hick whispered to himself, "Harold, dear Harold is missing."

Henry's voice intoned, "Please rise for Judge Nicholas Hickman, for this court is now in session."

Hick strode to his chair and, looking down on those who waited, asked, "Mr. Villella, do *you* intend to call Judge Harold Batemen as a witness? I was previously so informed."

Joe Villella was taken aback by the question, for he had intended Judge Batemen's appearance to be a surprise. "Why yes, Your Honor, he is a witness and should be here any moment."

"Good, Mr. Villella, we will wait for the presiding Judge."

"Well, ah, Your Honor, I had intended to call him at a specific point in our deliberations and that will be not be for awhile."

"Well, Mr. Villella, not the way this court functions. I don't want surprises, I want everything up front. In fact, you should have disclosed this witness to Mr. Ortman. I believe that is the right of the defense to have disclosure. Want me to cite the legal precedent?"

"No, Your Honor, not necessary, I have erred."

"Mr. Villella, you have two minutes, he is in his office, accompany my bailiff and procure the Judge. Now! Mr. Justin, if you please."

On hearing, Mr. Justin, Henry stood and moved toward Joe Villella as he thought, *The Judge is upset, very upset.*

Joe nodded at Henry and they walked together out the main door of the Courtroom without a word. They knew what they had to do.

In the Courtroom there was no sound of interest, confusion, or wonderment as to what was happening but there was a wave of anticipation that swept the room.

In what seemed like an eternity for those waiting, but in reality was but a few minutes, Joe, Henry, and a very obviously irritated Presiding Judge Harold Batemen returned. As Joe and the Judge moved to the Prosecutor's table, Henry assumed his position next to the door of the Judge's chambers and to the right of the bench. Joe started to speak but Harold Batemen's hand found his arm and he called out, "Hick."

"It's 'Your Honor,' Judge Batemen. We're in court, *my* court."

Harold was taken aback and he flushed inordinately. He started to spew out an epithet, but judicially restrained himself; twisted his body to the right, dropping Joe's arm and as he turned back to face Hick, went on in an apologetic tone, "Of course. Your Honor, I find this rather unprecedented for you to have the District Attorney and your bailiff come to my office, interrupt me, and forcibly remove me from my chambers and bring me to your courtroom."

"Why?"

Harold flushed again but this time the veins in his neck swelled and began to protrude over his collar and up the side of his neck, quickly followed by beads of perspiration forming on his forehead. He was now clearly irate and dropped any pretense of judicial restraint as he thundered, "You lowly piece of shit out of the sewer, how dare you play cat and mouse with me! How dare you insult the dignity of my office! You don't belong in a courtroom!"

Hick was enjoying this outburst more than he ever realized or imagined he could, would, or should. He knew Gladis was taking down every word so he let Harold's words float through the room and reverberate from the walls and then fade into total silence. There was a look of wonderment on the face of each person present in the room. Hick took particular note of the County Attorney's look of anguish. The anguish, the look, so often seen when an attorney knows, *"It's hit the fan and we're down the drain."*

Hick ruffled his robe then stared at Harold, thereby giving him time to realize what he had just done, as well as said. Harold Batemen, seething, pulled a chair from under the table, and as he did, the legs squealed as they slid across the floor, breaking the silence. Hick looked at Paul Ortman and Joe Villella and in a restrained judicial voice commanded, "Please come to the bench."

The two Attorneys proceeded together to the bench with a look on their face that anticipated the worst. They leaned forward and heard Hick say, "Gentlemen, do you know what is coming next?"

Both men looked at one another, then back at Hick, all the while shaking their heads in the affirmative as he whispered, "Good! Now take your seats and Joe...I expect you to control your surprise, and your surprise witness, or I'll deal with you just as contemptuously. Am I understood?"

"Yes, Your Honor."

"Good."

Hick waited for the two men to return to their seats and gave ample time for Joe to inform Harold that something was about to happen. Hick prolonged the waiting period, for he saw the veins once again distend in Harold's neck as Joe leaned over to confer with him.

When Joe was finished, Harold sat back in his chair waiting. Harold was straining on the leash of contempt for Hick, but held his tongue.

Hick let him suffer the early humiliation of waiting. When Hick sensed the intensity of anticipation in the courtroom had reached its peak he spoke, "Will Judge Batemen please rise and face the Court."

Even though this was another humiliation, Harold immediately rose to his feet, turned his face toward Hick and glowered. Hick endured the insult and then proclaimed, "Judge Batemen, this Court takes note of your remarks concerning this court. I hereby hold you in contempt of this court and its traditions. Therefore, I sentence you to five days in the county jail, commencing at the conclusion of your testimony."

"I won't go!"

"Seven days. Don't try me or I'll make it two weeks!"

Harold was totally befuddled. With frustration, he looked down at Joe and cried out, "Don't just sit there! Damn it, do something!"

"Your Honor," Joe pleaded to Hick.

"Yes, Mr. County Attorney?"

"Your Honor, you are sentencing the Presiding Judge of this District to jail for five, I mean, seven days."

"Yes, Mr. County Attorney, I am."

"But, Your Honor, you can't, you simply can't. Consider the consequences."

"I can and I have. What are the consequences you refer to?"

Joe was at a loss on how to answer. He looked around as if searching for help but found nothing but the faces in the courtroom staring at him, waiting for his answer, which was, "*You* know, Your Honor, why, this is a Judge. He didn't mean what he said, he was angry, he…"

"Just one minute, Mr. Villella, would you like me to have the court reporter read back what this man said?"

"Why, ah, no, Your Honor, that's not necessary, I remember."

"Let me ask *you* then, if *you* sat where I sit and these remarks were made in your court, what would you do?"

"Why, ah, before I sentenced another Judge to jail I would…ah…ah…" Joe didn't know what to say, then suddenly words spewed from his mouth, "Why I'd make him apologize to the court!"

"No, it's obvious you don't have a Judicial temperament, Mr. County Attorney." Then turning back to face Harold, Hick continued his remarks to Joe, "You should have suggested that to your witness and then he should have offered it to the court. An *apology*, that is."

Harold jumped to his feet and Manning's voice cried out, "Henry, Hick, watch out!"

As Harold moved forward Henry was upon him in a matter of seconds and had his arm tightly wrapped around his neck and was choking him when he heard Hick command, "Stop, Henry, and to you Harold, I say, contain yourself, NOW!"

There was total disbelief at what was playing out by everyone in the room. All Joe Villella could say was, "Oh, my God."

Hick moved around the bench and towering over Harold insisted, "Before you do anything more, think, man, think! This is a court of law and, by God, I will uphold its dignity at any cost. You make one more move and I'll put *you* in jail for a year. You are about to commit a felony. You have other avenues of redress against this court, and me. Save your energies and maintain the thought of other avenues to control your anger for now."

Hearing Hick's words, Harold now realized what he had done. He turned from Henry's arms, walked back to where Joe stood and said, "I don't believe what I have done, what I have said."

Joe took his arm and quietly pleaded, "Be seated, Judge. Please be seated."

Hick returned to his chair but Henry did not move. Hick sat down and signaled for Henry to step aside.

"Your Honor", Joe called out, "I would ask the Court for a fifteen minute recess, but before you move on this request may I address the Court?"

Hick knew he was now in control and stipulated, "Both requests are granted. Go on."

"Your Honor, I must ask the court to forgive what has transpired this morning. I feel that I am to blame, for in my haste to incarcerate

Dr. Rollins I held you suspect and had no right to do so. I did not use good judgement. I had no reason to believe your court would treat the indictment in any other manner than a judicially proper one. By creating this climate of suspicion I have brought discredit to a sitting and Presiding Judge. I apologize, Your Honor, and I beg the court to reconsider its contempt citation of Judge Batemen and bring upon me whatever the court feels is prudent and necessary."

"Mr. County Attorney, I have heard your words and you are correct about your suspicions. They were and are without substance or merit. Judge Batemen, please rise."

Harold Batemen had returned to reality and was stripped of his haughtiness by the prospect of being incarcerated. He rose not defiantly but meekly, for all to see he now stood in fear of the very court so many others stand in awe of each day. He started to speak but Hick continued, "Judge Harold Batemen, this court recognizes the plea of the County Attorney. This court has reconsidered the contempt citation and hereby rescinds it. However, for the record, I resent you felt it necessary to attack me personally in my court. My chambers are not hallowed. However, this room is and my chambers are available to *you* at any time to cite any grievance you have against me, real or imagined. I believe we both have something to say to each other. I will look forward to such a meeting, and the sooner the better. We will now recess for fifteen minutes."

The back of the bench phone rang and Henry moved to pick it up while keeping his eye on Judge Batemen. As he put the phone to his ear, he intoned, "Judge Nicholas Hickman's court, A-men."

"A-men, Henry? It's Sam, I have what the Judge needs. What's going on?"

"Yes, Sir. Nothing is going on, sir. We are finally in recess. One minute, please sir, the Judge, he is walking into his chambers."

Hick had heard the phone and knew who it was. Going to the small table overlooking the gardens he picked it up and said, "I have it, Henry," then, "Is it you, Sam?"

"Yes, Your Honor, I have what *you* need, or at least a start. The word is this whole matter is big. A part of something bigger."

"That doesn't make sense, Sam."

"I know, but for starters the contract on Hughes was a part of the doings of my son, Donny, in Chicago."

"What?"

"I know, I felt the same way when I talked to Charlie at the Sapphire Diner."

"The Sapphire Diner?"

"North Kansas City control center for mob action. Charlie Umbigolata, the owner, keeps tabs on everything in Chicago, Omaha and Kansas City. It only took him thirty seconds to name Donny, Batemen, Conway, and Givens."

"My sources tell me Hughes owed you eighty thousand."

"He did and that's why I wouldn't have him taken out even if I operated that way. Which I don't. As I have said, they can't pay if they're dead."

"Just what did Charlie, what's his name, tell you in two seconds?"

"Donny had the contract on Hughes, Conway had real tapes and altered tapes, and Batemen was running the plays in the courthouse and the big money comes from Givens and more information would follow."

"When?"

"I don't know, Your Honor."

"What about your son?"

"I sent him to Chicago, like my father sent me, to get street smart. I'm just a gambler. I like to take other people's money because it's easy. The percentages are on my side. I don't do drugs, prostitution, or murder, and I don't do business with people to have it done or procured. Donny is not me. He's twenty-seven and what he's done means he's putting the move on me. He wants my seat and I can only suppose he intends to expand. He's down and dirty."

Hick heard the anguish in Sam's voice and responded to it, "I'm sorry, Sam. Any danger?"

"I will be eventually if what I suspect goes down."

"What can I do?"

"I think whatever you're involved in will eventually lead to Donny. He's probably a bigger player than I even think or know about. He wouldn't dare challenge the Chicago mob but he needs Omaha to get to me."

"To get to you, Sam, you're his father."

"That makes no difference to him but he needs money, power brokers, crooked judges, police, punks attached to guns, all loyal to him to take me down and that's a lot."

"Take you down? My God, man, I say it again: He's your son!"

"Your Honor, with all due respect, this is not your concern in any way, whatsoever. My life and my son's life are not comprehendible to most. The inner workings and relationships are at best fragile. Worry not for me, for I know how to handle such transgressions. I will be back with more for you as soon as Charlie gets back to me. I would have you know, I do have emotions, for my son is my son, and my heart aches. But it is my place to forgive him and his transgressions when the time comes and it will. Keep alert. Shalom Aleichem."

Hick dejectedly put the phone down and muttered, "Shalom Aleichem, Sam, and may God be with you."

When Hick answered the phone, Henry placed the extension back in its cradle, still carefully watching Judge Batemen and the others as they emptied the court. He followed them out at a discreet distance into the main corridor and walked down the hall toward Manning's office. The hall from Hick's chambers was the only other way to her office, and knowing the Judge was on the phone with Sam, Henry did not want to disturb him. Suddenly, Judge Batemen turned, stopped, then defiantly walked back to Henry with Joe Villella on his heels. The Judge walked up to Henry and, with head back, looked up at him and snarled, "I'll remember, bailiff, you putting your arm around my neck. I'll not forget! You will pay!"

Joe reached out to take the Judge's arm and pulling on it demanded, "Stop now, Your Honor, don't make it any worse for yourself...than it already is."

Judge Harold Batemen spun around screaming, "What the hell do you mean by that, Mr. County Attorney?"

Joe was aware Henry was watching and listening intently and quietly said, "Mr. Justin...Henry, I believe you were on your way to Manning's office. Please continue."

"Yes, sir."

Joe watched as Henry stepped to one side of the Judge, halted, made eye contact with him, then took three more steps. He put his hand on Manning's door; it was ajar, pushed it open and walked in. Once Henry was in Manning's office and the door was shut, Joe, still holding the Judge's arm, turned to face him. The lines in his face had deepened and they left no doubt in Harold's mind Joe was not to be trifled with. Harold was about to apologize once more but Joe stopped him with, "I would remind you, Judge Hickman damn near threw *you* in the slammer and I wouldn't have blamed him. If he finds out you threatened his Bailiff, I believe you'll be on your way. I would remind you...you are the presiding judge of this courthouse. Where in God's name is your judicial decorum?"

Harold Batemen was a wily man and had been all of his life. Born to wealth, he basically bought or cheated his way to the top. He recognized his own deficiencies early on and skillfully used seclusion to hide his dishonesty and inadequacy. No woman could stand by his side for long, for his evil ways soon became apparent with intimacy. Even his sainted mother shunned and finally cast him aside. Before she made her final decision about him, her parting words to him were, "I'll give you credit for one thing, you are a clever rogue, Harold, but then, poor darling, you eventually will give yourself away and be your own undoing."

Harold struggled with that rejection, but not much, for he had convinced himself he never really liked his mother much…either. He was a BIO'er (born in Omaha) and his family's wealth opened doors in spite of himself. His monthly card game at the club was his only social contract with his peers and once a month suited him fine. He preferred his pornography, but at this moment he was seething with anger about what he considered insubordination by Joe Villella, the "mere" County Attorney, and a street person nothing, Nicholas Hickman. He wiped the spittle from the corner of his mouth with his sleeve and half whispered, "You'll all pay…and you'll pay dearly before we're through with you."

Joe now understood why he and other lawyers never really liked the man. He had never revealed himself as a person, in court or otherwise. His rulings and judicial decisions were classic copied textbook and cold. Devoid of any sensitivity or awareness, that the law, like mankind in general, was evolving and not static. He was also haughty. About what, no one could conceive but it was something to joke about over a drink.

The lines in Joe's face disappeared for he realized he, for the first time, had gained insight into this man, this enigma. He casually and carefully remarked, "Your Honor. Daniel Webster once said, 'There is nothing so powerful as truth, and often nothing so strange'. I will see Your Honor in court…presently."

Judge Harold Batemen, not to be bested, snapped, "Maybe you will and maybe you won't."

"I will!"

"How can you be so sure!"

"He's called the Sheriff, Your Honor."

CHAPTER 4

▼

Henry shut the door to Manning's office, looked and saw D. T. Osbon sitting across from Manning. They had a startled look on their faces and Manning asked, "What was that all about, Henry?"

"A continuation of unbridled anger from the courtroom by his Honor, Judge Batemen."

"So I gathered from what we heard of his voice, but what precipitated it?"

"My putting a choke hold on him."

Henry looked at D. T. Osbon and realized he had not said hello and offered, "Hi, Mr. Osbon. Always good to see you."

"Hi yourself, Henry, always good to see you and your shining face but it's not shining this morning."

"I know, sir, there's days like that around here."

D. T. Osbon was an eighty-two-year-old multi-millionaire that most people in Omaha did not know about. He once told Manning and Henry, when asked why he was not known, "It's simple. Store not your treasures on earth where moths, rust, and thieves break through and steal. Rather store thy treasures up in heaven, or something like that."

D. T. had in reality done much for the city and its people in his own way and continued it on a daily basis. He lived, when asked, "With

Josh and Emily Stratheim, butler and housekeeper respectively, but they're really my best friends," and then always added, "They understand the dark side of me."

Several years back, at Josh's behest, D. T. had taken to coming each day to the courthouse to sit in the various courts to find areas where he could put his wealth to use. This soon led him to the library next to Manning's office. He saw her one day retrieving material for Hick and as he willingly confessed to her, "I was taken not just by your good looks but by your demeanor."

To which Manning replied, "I'm just a girl, so tell me, for a man, what's the secret meaning of the word demeanor?"

His sincere reply came unhesitatingly, "Why, it's your body," and from that day on they had been great friends.

Manning approached him one day about a new adventure in the Hall of Records. "D. T., this place is a virtual trove of the past. It could be of great interest to you."

"I'm suspicious, Manning, but go ahead, tell me why?"

"Why, yourself. How long have you lived here in Omaha?"

"Fifty years or thereabouts."

"Well then, it could bring back memories, clear up some mysteries of the past and...ah...help uncover secrets and let you see what it looked like compared to now."

"Manning, it doesn't fit. You want me to do something. Right?"

"Why, D. T., how perceptive of you. Will you?"

"Well, as I have said, why? And now what?"

Manning spelled out Hick's history as an orphan, foster child, and the like and asked D. T. to see if he could find a way to trace back and find out who Hick's parents were. He appeared to be fascinated with the story as she told it but when she was through he asked, "What good will it do him?"

"Wouldn't you want to know who your mother and father are or were?"

"I do know."

"Stop it, D. T., will you help me or not? It will be a great thing for him if we can find something out."

D. T. couldn't resist Manning and quickly agreed under one condition.

"What's that, D. T.?"

"I have a conference every Wednesday with you over lunch."

"Done! You pay?"

"Manning, there's always a price for research."

Thus Manning's W. L. & S. day came to pass and from eleven-thirty to three she was out of the office.

Knowing this, Henry continued by asking, "D. T. find anything yet?"

"A great deal, Henry."

This perked Henry up and he asked with renewed enthusiasm, "What, D. T., what?"

"I've found the first foster home he was in."

"Where?"

"Lodi, New Jersey."

"Where's that?"

"New Jersey?"

"You know what I mean, D. T."

"I know, Henry, just kidding you. I don't really know where Lodi is, but by this time next week I will. I'm going to the Record Hall in Lodi."

Manning interrupted, "D. T., you're like a dog with a bone. It's time for us to be on our way. Wednesday lunch and shopping awaits."

Looking concerned, Henry asked, "Manning, after this morning's session, do you think you should leave?"

"Why?"

"We may need you. "

"Henry, I have a feeling the fore-nooner session you're in for will be short and lead to a postponement. Want to bet?"

"Not against you, I don't.

"Good!"

Manning and D. T. stood, turned, and walked to the door. Stopping, they turned back to Henry and in unison chimed, "See you later, alligator," and left.

A moment later the door opened and Manning stuck her head back in and chided, "Now, when I return, don't let me find that either of you have messed with the docket. Understand?"

"Understood,...yes 'um, it's understood," and the door closed again.

Henry always used "yes 'um" as a counter to any of Manning's unbridled dictates, for he knew it irritated her no end. She even confronted him the first time he did with, "You're doing that to irritate me, Henry Justin! You're implying that I consider you stupid. Aren't you?"

Henry kept her waiting for an answer for suspense and to give himself time to come up with a reply. He looked at her sheepishly and half defiantly said, "Yes 'um."

Manning stomped her foot, but said nothing. Henry could tell she was really irritated when she turned and walked out of the room jabbering, "You're like a child. A smart aleck, a teaser, and so forth but you don't bother me, cause nothing could be farther the truth. I know how I feel about you and the Judge." Henry was smiling at his tact when suddenly she barged back into the room shouting at him, "Because…you're both family to me!"

"Yes 'um" became his unchallenged counterattack and it amused the Judge enormously. Henry one day told him the story of how it came to pass and the Judge pleaded, "Please, Henry, think of something I can use to counterattack."

They both admired and loved Manning for her free spirit and unbridled honesty. Henry thought he understood her feelings and relationship with Hick but he really didn't. They both had become family for him and he knew they felt the same way about him. Henry had spoken about it once to his now friend Dicey, and Dicey complained, "They can't feel that away about *you*, man, you're black."

Incensed by what he heard, Henry retorted, "What the hell does that really have to do with anything? We're all God's children and you are hung up about the color of the skin? It's what's underneath the skin that counts...man! They're my friends and we care about each another."

"Think they love *you?*"

"Sure they do. We'd do anything one, for the other."

"I can't believe but if it makes you feel better, so be it."

"Well, Dicey, that's the *way* it is with us, so to hell with you!"

When Manning and D. T. left, Henry walked down the hall from Manning's office to the Judge's Chambers. The hall was short, wide, and with a high ceiling. Manning, over the years, hung Hick's degrees, honors, certificates of membership, and honorary citations all over the walls. The ones she didn't particularly care for she had Henry hang high up, so no one else could read them, "And, I don't have to look at them at all," she would snicker. The hall saddened Henry, for like himself, there were no pictures of family. The walk from Manning's office often caused him to shudder in remembrance of his childhood as an orphan. He would, when not on the run, stop at the end of the hall, look back and say, "Well, that was the past. I have a family now."

When he knocked on the Chamber door, Hick's reassuring voice would always ring out, "Come on in, Henry, come on in."

This day it was the same and as he walked in he remarked, "Judge, how do you always know when it's me?"

Hick was sitting at his desk and turning to the right to face Henry he replied, "Manning never knocks."

They both laughed and Hick asked, "Henry, do we have some coffee?"

"Yes, Judge."

"Good, pour two cups, then come over to the small table and visit with me."

Habits tag along with familiarity. So the need for coffee and conversation became a habit between these two men as they learned to care for one another. It was a way for Hick to lighten the weight of judicial responsibility and caring. Once, early on, he told Henry, "When, seemingly, the pressures of this office become taxing and I must find someone who understands, from my perspective, the stewardship of life. That someone to listen, to advise, is going to be you, Henry. You're with me each day and you'll know and understand."

Henry's answer finalized their relationship, "I am flattered, Your Honor, but more important for you I do understand, completely, what you are saying. I've been there, like yourself, alone."

They exchanged opinions about Judge Batemen's conduct and Hick reassured Henry that if the Judge would attempt to retaliate against him because of the choke hold, Hick would retaliate in kind. The discussion had a soothing effect on them both and then Hick reminded, "We're out of time of time, Henry. I would suppose we are over time."

"By two minutes, Judge."

"Well, then, let's go. We can't put it off forever, not that I wouldn't like to."

Henry pulled himself to his full height, brushed his coat and walked to open the courtroom door, and leaving it open for Hick, he then walk into the courtroom to announce, "The court of the Honorable Nicholas Hickman is now in session, please rise."

Hick was right behind Henry and as Henry's words faded he strode through the doorway to the bench, looked about and noticed Harold Batemen was not present but saw some new faces. Looking at Joe Villella, he asked, "Mr. County Attorney, are you ready to proceed?"

"The State is, Your Honor."

Hick smiled to himself at the "The State is" remark but let it go and turned to face Paul Ortman and J. R. Collins and asked pointedly, "Mr. Ortman, are you and your client ready to proceed?"

"We are, Your Honor."

"Good. We left off in a furor. The court has taken note of those who were present and I would ask the State's Attorney, Mr. Villella, what happened to your witness, Judge Batemen?"

"May I approach the bench with counsel for the defense, Your Honor?"

"You may."

When the two men stood before the bench Joe whispered, "As to the matter of the Presiding Judge, Your Honor, he is being difficult."

Hick couldn't resist and replied sarcastically, "Difficult, Joe, really?"

"Yes, Your Honor, he says he has matters before his Court this afternoon and they take precedence over anything else."

"Really, Joe, you really believe that?"

"Yes, Your Honor, and I suppose, here I go again, it's my fault."

"Why would you believe that, Joe?"

"Because I told him earlier he would be on and off the stand early and his schedule for this afternoon would not be in jeopardy."

"How presumptuous of you, Joe. Shall I recess again and have the Sheriff serve him with a subpoena?"

"Good Lord, no! Your Honor. He'd become a hostile witness. In fact, he already is. I let him know how I felt about his actions."

"Joe, now that's interesting. Would you like to enlighten the court as to your thinking?"

He looked at Paul and said earnestly, "Paul, if I answer that for the Judge will you hold what I say inviolate?"

"No."

"Why not?"

"You're trying to slap a murder indictment on my client and you want me to restrict what I'll use to defend him?"

"You're right, Paul. Your Honor, can I then just confide in the court?"

"You're excused for a moment, Paul, while Joe confides in the Court."

"I object to the court's intended action, Your Honor."

Hick bristled and it was obvious as he replied, "I'm fed up with both of you and the way this whole affair is proceeding. There never has been any protocol from the beginning. The whole affair is nothing more than a pseudo legal skirmish, Paul, but I'll do what I think I have to do to get to the bottom of this mess. If it goes to appeal I don't care what anyone else thinks because I'm dealing with it today. I want to remind you both once again, it's basic, I represent the interests of the people of this state. You know what you represent. I'll ask you both one more question. Paul, do you believe I am against your client?"

"No, Your Honor."

"Good! Joe, do you believe I'm for his client?"

"No, Your Honor."

"That's progress! Now I ask you, do you both believe I represent the people of the state of Nebraska? And I want that answered in unison, men, say it in unison."

"We do, Your Honor."

"Good…finally…basic…101 law prevails. We know what we're all about now…. sit down, Paul."

Paul said nothing, turned and returned to the waiting defendant, J. R. Rollins.

"We're alone, Joe, go ahead."

"I don't trust Judge Batemen, Your Honor."

"Why?"

"Rumors…his attitude…and…and…a hunch."

"I'll have to discount everything but the hunch, Joe, you have a pretty good track record as far as I am concerned. Do I make myself clear?"

"Yes, Your Honor."

"Well then, get to the point, man. The point."

"I can present what I feel is sufficient evidence to warrant going ahead with the indictment and incarceration of the Doctor on charges of being an accessory to murder."

"Well, I think we might be getting someplace. You seem to be zeroing in on at least a point. This morning you kept saying he was a murderer. Now he's an accessory. Oh, well. Who are your witnesses?"

"Tape and voice experts."

"Okay, Joe, we can't go any further with this tete-a-tete without Paul, not that it hasn't been interesting. Let's go back to open court. Sit down and proceed when you are ready."

Hick smiled and turned to Gladis saying, "We're starting up again, Miss Pitman."

"Yes, Your Honor."

"The court recognizes Mr. Villella when he is ready."

"Your Honor, the prosecution would like to play an excerpt from a tape recording for the purpose of identifying for the court to whom the voice belongs."

"I object, Your Honor."

"To what, Mr. Ortman?"

"The tape. There's a lack of foundation. Where did it come from? Who recorded it? Why, and how did the prosecutor get it and whose voice is it purported to be?"

"I haven't had any time, Your Honor, to lay a foundation."

"I know, Mr. Villella, but we're on our way. Overruled, Mr. Ortman. Proceed, Mr. Villella."

"Thank you, Your Honor. The state will now present the recording."

A small boom box had been placed on the prosecutor's table and he pushed the play button. A voice began, "I have put the final bulbs in the basket as you instructed. When will you plant?"

A second voice was heard, "This afternoon I will prepare them for planting."

"Then what?"

"We'll wait for the second planting."

Joe Villella reached over and flicked off the switch, turned to address the court with, "Your Honor, I would now like to call Mr. Victor Donner to the stand."

Hick moved to the edge of his chair and instructed, "Bailiff, swear in Mr. Victor Donner."

Hick went back to his thoughts about what he had just heard, *"God, how juvenile, can this be for real?"*

Henry nodded at the Judge when he was through swearing in the witness and Hick instructed, "Proceed, Mr. Villella."

"Mr. Donner, please tell the court your name, address, and occupation."

"'Victor T. Donner, 2236 North Coulter Street, Scottsdale, Arizona. I am a voice analyzer."

"What's that? I've never heard of it before. Please explain to the court."

"I listen to tapes, or any recording, to determine from various electronic impulses what is being heard and many times attempt to match voices."

"Match voices?"

"Yes, everyone's voice has impulse characteristics, wavelengths, like fingerprints, they are repetitive for the same word or similar words. Peculiar and specific for each voice."

"Did you listen to the tape just played?"

"I did."

"Were you asked to make a comparison to any other voice?"

"I was."

"Whose voice?"

"A Doctor J. R. Rollins."

Paul Ortman was back on his feet in an instant and crying out, "I object! Where'd you get his voice? Who said it was his voice? How much are you paid…"

Hick interrupted, "Hold it, Mr. Ortman. You get your chance on cross examination. Let the man testify."

"Yes, Your Honor, but for the record, this is absurd."

"From a legal standpoint, Mr. Ortman, so is your objection at this time. Proceed, Mr. Villella."

"I have no further questions at this time. Your witness, Paul."

"Your witness, Paul," was dripping with sarcasm, bringing a quick rebuke from Hick.

"Gentlemen, it's obvious we're finally going somewhere with this case. The court also recognizes we all are from time to time on a first name basis, but outside of this courtroom. I would remind you that while in this courtroom I will not have that familiarity interfere with our formal proceedings by using it to elicit contempt or sarcasm for one another and you know exactly what I mean. One more comment from the bench. This has been some morning. However, from now on I will no longer conduct seminars or offer suggestions. I am going to start leveling fines and contempt citations. Both of you know the rules…play by them…or else. Mr. Ortman, your witness."

"Mr. Donner, you're from Arizona, is that correct?"

"Yes, sir."

"Yes or no will be adequate. Tell me, **Mr.** Donner, what percentage of your time is devoted to pursuing your occupation in your field and what percentage of your time is spent as an expert witness?"

"I'd say about fifty-fifty."

"Fine. How do you charge, as a witness, by the hour, the case, or what?"

"By the case, plus expenses."

"Can you estimate for the court what you will derive from this case?"

Immediately Joe was on his feet, growling, "I object, Your Honor. What he charges is no more important than what I make or what Mr. Ortman makes."

"Objection overruled."

"But, Your Honor…"

"Mr. Villella, you know what Mr. Ortman is after and further, you know it's a legitimate question. Please answer the question, Mr. Donner."

"I was guaranteed fifty-thousand dollars and expenses."

The words *fifty-thousand dollars* brought Hick back to the edge his chair.

"By whom?" Paul hurriedly asked.

"A Mr. Robert Conway."

"You mean the newspaper publisher?"

"Yes."

"Did he tell you why he wanted you in this matter?"

"Yes."

"Don't leave us in suspense, tell the court why he wanted you."

"He felt it was his civic duty as a citizen."

"How did you get to the County Attorney?"

"Mr. Conway sent me to Judge Batemen and he had me meet with the County Attorney."

"That seems very convenient."

Joe Villella jumped to his feet and started to bray, "Please, Your…"

Hick quickly interrupted him, "Stop, Mr. Villella, it's my pleasure. As if I didn't hear you, Mr. Ortman. What did you say?

"Sorry, Your Honor."

"Fifty dollars, Mr. Ortman, I warned you both. This is my court and I want the decorum I want and believe me the next time you step over my line it will be one-hundred and double after that. Go on."

Paul Ortman turned, and seemingly dejected by his rebuke, walked to the defense table, bent down, and whispered in J. R. Rollins's ear, "We scored big on that one. I think we are beginning to pop the rats out of the woodwork."

"How?" J. R. asked hopefully.

"Later," came the quick reply.

Hick insisted, "Mis–ter Ort–man!"

"Yes, Your Honor, I will go on. Mr. Donner, how does one become an expert in…"

Joe was back on his feet with, "I object, Your Honor."

"Why? I don't know where Mr. Ortman is going but the court isn't convinced you established Mr. Donner as an expert witness. Where're his credentials? You know, Mr. Villella; schools, colleges, degrees, teaching, et cetera."

Joe sat back down. Paul continued but would now be on the attack. Paul smelled something, and for all intents and purposes Hick had overruled Joe's objection. To irritate Joe he started out, "I'll rephrase the question."

As he paused to think, Hick immediately interrupted, "Don't rephrase the question. Continue the question. Miss Pitman, if you please."

Gladis never hesitated or skipped a beat. She was always attentive and in step with Hick and his rulings and she read, "Mr. Donner, how does one become an expert in…"

Paul smiled, shook his head slightly, and added, "Your occupation?"

"I have four years of college and graduated as an electrical engineer. I served four years in the United States Navy as a lieutenant on the USS Patrick Henry in charge of missile launching and tracking. I also worked for Magnetic Tape Imaging Corporation for ten years as chief of research and development. I formed my own company five years ago, Donner Digital." Paul knew he had lost that one. Credentials like this man's you normally didn't hear from expert witnesses. Most were hustled up from some legal magazine classified section and were then easily discredited by their own words or with a little help would hang themselves. Yet something didn't ring true. He continued, "Impressive, Mr. Donner, impressive. That's all for…oh…one more thing, a personal query on my part. How is your company doing?"

"Not well."

Joe started to his feet. Hick scowled at him and Paul jumped in with, "Sorry to hear that. I'm through with the witness, Your Honor."

Joe was furious that Paul got that in. Hick smiled inwardly, thinking, *"Paul's learning,"* then said, "Gentlemen, it's almost noon. We will recess for lunch and return at one-thirty. Oh, and gentlemen, I have been musing and want you to know that during the recess I will decide if I should step-down from this case. Two reasons with two factors; First reason: am I prejudiced in favor of the Doctor or prejudiced against the way the State brought this case to my court. Second reason: today is Friday, my last day sitting as a domestic relations judge. I move next Thursday, after a three day hiatus, to Criminal Court. This case is going to be scheduled as a criminal case after today if the County Attorney has anything to say about it."

The disappointed look on Paul Ortman's face didn't escape Hick's attention and he continued with, "Mr. Ortman, I can see anxiety written all over your face, just hold on. I haven't ruled yet if there is sufficient evidence to bind this matter over." Paul smiled and Hick continued, "as I was saying before I interrupted myself, Judge Jason January, my colleague, sits with me next week in Criminal Court. I believe, if this case is bound over, his proclivity for objectivity could better serve this entire matter. Enough said. We stand in recess until one-thirty."

Joe and Paul stood and without any hesitation or reservation moved toward one another. Joe spoke first, "I pray for both our sakes, Jason January doesn't sit on this case and that's what I mean, he'll sit on it and us."

"Maybe he won't. Maybe Hick will throw this whole thing out. However, if he doesn't, I know January won't give us any room to squeak. He never does. Just pray Hick sees the light that you have nothing."

"Paul, I have plenty, but in case he doesn't throw me out, we best go talk to him."

"Think he'll tolerate our trying to influence his decision?"

"He might, but what the hell, he's pissed at both of us and by the way, Paul, that business of getting in about Donner's company's profitability was a nice stroke but I doubt it will make any difference."

"Thanks a lot, Joe, but you're wrong. Let's go before he makes up his mind."

"God forbid he hasn't already."

CHAPTER 5

▼

As Manning sat across the table from D. T. studying the menu, D. T. remarked, "Do you know something?"

Putting her menu down, she looked over her cheaters to study him. Raising her left eyebrow while closing her right eye she snapped, "Okay, D. T., what?"

"You know something?"

"Here I go again, D. T., what should I know?"

"When you were a little girl did anyone ever spank you for being naughty?"

Manning looked confused by the question, and to stall so she could think removed her cheaters, thought and then with the determination of a shrew answered, "No one would have dared. Besides, I was never naughty. I was always a nice girl and still am…but…D. T., that's not really what you're after, is it?"

"Nope."

"Then stop the horsing around and get to the point."

"I want to know if you know something, I don't think you know, or at best suspect."

"D. T., I've been in Hick's court all morning and your question only makes me believe one thing."

"What?"

"You would have made a great lawyer, D. T. You missed your true calling. Your question is a something, a real study, only a lawyer could dream up. However, for the sake of our conversation, Counselor, please rephrase the question so that, one, I can understand it, and, two, I can answer it."

D. T. was smiling, as Manning described it, "his cute, Irish, I believe in Leprechauns smile with its spell I can never resist". She was right, he did have her under his spell, but he broke it by saying, "I'll put it another way. Does His Honor know about this flight of fancy you have me pursuing?"

"I'll tell you right now, D. T., you've changed the whole meaning of your question. I'd go so far as to even suggest you've changed the subject. Right?"

"Wrong."

"You are prevaricating, D. T., and that's just another word lawyers use to say you're lying."

"Darlin', my darlin', please answer my question soon, it seems they want us to order."

"To hell with them," Manning said indignantly as she spun in her chair and then disapprovingly looked back at D. T. and continued her tirade, "and besides...oh, you little devil of a Leprechaun, I don't see anybody wanting anything and besides, I refuse to be rushed. I come here every week with you to take my damn time so as to enjoy my food." Taking a deep breath, she smiled, wiggled in her chair and went on, "and the answer you already know. His Honor doesn't know and you know it...I'm doing it, and I've never divulged what I am now going to say to you because something tells me somehow, sometime it will be important to his life if we can find out about his family. Also, my little, big rich, wonderful friend, he asks about you for he sees you in my office...oh, from his door of course, for he would never deign to be seen in my office, other than when the bloody courthouse is closed for the day and I don't jump quick enough with the scotch to suit him...so he can tittle on his booze. Whew! Now, D. T., that's a windbag lawyer's sentence and it takes a good set of lungs…so…I've let it all hang out. What say you?"

Manning flushed and waved her napkin as she waited for D. T. to reply. D. T. was studying her as she did, then picking up his menu and waving it so he created a small breeze for her, answered, "I think I'll have the spinach salad. I like bacon."

On hearing his words, Manning closed her eyes, shook her head from side to side while muttering, "Brother! You guys are all the same."

✳   ✳   ✳   ✳

The phone rang and startled Sam, for his mind was preoccupied. He reached for the phone and as he placed the receiver to his ear he heard, "Jew, this is the wop."

"You're an angry wop, that I can tell. What's up?"

"I wish the hell I really knew. It's my business to know what's coming down around here but today I don't."

"Calm down, Charlie, you're confusing me."

"Yea, I know, I keep hoping you'll interrupt me and tell me what I want to know."

"About what?"

"Sam, I can't say. I heard something and I'm mad about it but you know what goes on around here I can't repeat, cause' if I do I'm as good as dead and your business would be over."

"I understand. Is it about me? Don't worry about this business, it's covered no matter what happens to me."

"Thanks for understanding but I can't say if it's about you but…"

"But what, Charlie?"

"The dumb dago, your Donato, he knows."

"Then I'll find out."

"Can you do it without him knowing or suspecting?"

"I can't say, Charlie. I've got to hang up and think this out."

"Sam, whatever you do, keep it under your hat or I'm history."

"I'll say nothing, Charlie, but I didn't think you were vulnerable to anybody or anything."

"You kidding? If they even suspect I've broken the oath of silence they'll come after me in numbers, relentlessly, until I'm a goner."

"I never heard anything, Charlie. So long."

"Jew, don't hang up yet. Don't worry about me, just worry about yourself and, Jew, this wop has always respected you."

Sam choked, "I feel the same way about you, Charlie, the same way." Lowering the receiver slowly back in its cradle, Sam thought about Charlie's last words to him. Then he spun around in his chair angry, but at what he didn't know. He stood and began pacing while he thought out loud to himself, "Louie? What the hell is Louie up to? Is he up to something alone or is he in with somebody? I've always trusted him, treated him right, what could be his beef? Not enough money? He wants to move up…or out maybe? Nah! He doesn't have the guts to go it alone, plus he doesn't have enough smarts or contacts. Or does he? Think, man, think!"

Sam sat back down in his chair, and when in doubt, as he always did, he called home. The phone rang twice and a voice formally stated, "Good morning, oh, I mean good early afternoon, the Hirsch residence, Mary Beth speaking, how can I help you?"

"It's Sam, Mary Beth, and it's how may I help you, not can."

Sam couldn't resist, because Mary Beth said the same thing every time she answered the phone. She just couldn't get it through her head what Sam wanted her to say. Sam loved to correct her, for it was his way of teasing. Kate had found Mary Beth years ago at a home for unwed mothers as she was about to have her baby. She was alone in the big city, penniless and scared to death. The administrator called Kate because she new Mary Beth and Kate both needed help. Mary Beth needed help for her life in general and Kate needed help around the house plus some companionship.

As it turned out their need for one another heightened when Mary Beth lost her baby during delivery. They bonded and Sam often observed when they seemingly ganged up on him, which they often did without any reservations, 'You two are more like mother and daughter than anything else.' He was right.

"Oh, Sam, I'm sorry. How may I help you?"

"Mary Beth, guess."

"You need Kate, Sam. I can tell by the sound of your voice. Just one minute, please."

"Sam waited for what seemed too long and then Kate spoke, "Sam? Mary Beth says you're in trouble. What's the matter?"

"Oh, brother. Kate, that Mary Beth is something else but she's right and I love her."

"Get to it, Sam." Sam related his conversation with Charlie and asked, "Well, what do you think?"

"One minute or maybe two, Sam. I have to think."

This was Kate's way and Sam was used to it. He waited.

"I've thought, Sam."

"And?"

"One of two things. Louie or Donny."

On hearing his son's name Sam remained composed and asked, "Why not Louie?"

"Simple. No class, no guts."

"Why Donny?"

"You've been telling me he's going to put a move on you one day. He's not like you, Sam. He's once removed."

"Once removed?"

"Sam, my dear Sam. You and I, most people, see the past and the future. Donny only sees the future and what it means to him."

"He's your son, Kate."

"He's our son, Sam. Maybe the genes didn't line up right or the blood didn't mix the way it should have."

"What else? Anything else?"

"It just occurred to me it could be them both."

"Donny and Louie? That's a joke!"

"Think about it, Sam. Louie knows your operation inside and out."

"No, he doesn't, he just thinks he does."

"What do you mean?"

"Kate, my love, I'm a gambler, a damned good gambler, and a good gambler always keeps an ace up his sleeve...just in case."

"I figured as much, Sam. That's why I love you. Be careful."

"Thanks, Kate, for the talk and help. I knew I could count on you, and Kate, the feeling's mutual."

"Say it, Sam, say it, then get on with what you have to do."

"You're the best thing that ever happened to me, Kate. I love you."

"Why, thank you, Sam. Thank you. See you at dinner."

The phone clicked and Sam began to ponder as he set the receiver back in its cradle once again. Suddenly he remembered what he had to remember and he picked up the phone, once more dialed and waited as it rang.

"Judge Hickman's chambers, Henry Justin, Bailiff, speaking."

Sam smiled as he said, "Sam here, Henry, doing double duty?"

"Mr. Sam, no sir. It's Wednesday, you know, Manning's day to lunch and shop."

"I forgot, Henry. The Judge there?"

"Yes, sir! He's contemplating, that's why I answered his phone."

When Hick heard Henry say Sam he reached his decision and called over to Henry, "I'll take the call, Henry."

Hick moved from the small table to his desk and took the receiver from Henry as he sat down. "Hello, Sam."

"Hello, Your Honor. Contemplating?"

"Yes, Sam, I was, it's the case I mentioned."

"To that there may be a link."

"With what?"

"I can't go into it right now but I need your help. I think...in fact my being tells me my son is getting ready to move in on me."

"As I said, Sam, that distresses me. How do you know?"

"Indirectly, Your Honor. I really can't tell you but I have a hunch we can help one another."

"How?"

"About this Matt Hughes, your Doctors, my son, they're connected somehow."

"You said you really didn't know anything, Sam. For me, it's really about one Doctor somebody's out to do in or have put away. I have other information about corruption but it is more hearsay and rumor than fact to date."

"I know, Your Honor, but tell me, where are you?"

"Where am I?"

"Yes, with your contemplating. I surmise it's about the case you're involved in today. The Doctors."

"You surmise correctly and it's one Doctor I'm concerned about. He put my face back together when I needed him. I like him, respect him, and he needs me now as a friend, for he is being attacked for what reasons I really don't understand. As I have said, I only have conjecture, rumors, my own hunches and hearsay to go on. However, I resent the obvious, his sons have turned on him and this distresses me as I am appalled at your suggestion your son is capable of the same thing. What's going on? Did God reconsider, call Moses back to the Mount and strike the Fifth Commandment from the tablets?"

Hick struck a nerve, for Sam could not answer. He gulped in an attempt to clear his throat for his tears were now streaming down his throat as well as his face. Hick heard the gulp and used the time he knew Sam would need to recover to wipe his own face. He then asked, "You all right, Sam?"

"Sure, Your Honor, but, but I can't answer your question, Moses and I aren't on speaking terms, for I have sinned."

"What you've done, or haven't done, Sam, isn't the point."

"That could be a good discussion some day. I have an idea for today. What have you decided?"

"I'm going to step-down from the case and expend my energies in defense of my friend, J. R. Rollins. To deny I am prejudiced would be to deny my friendship for the man. Some things are more important to me than the judicial chair I find myself sitting in. Jason January can adjudicate this better than I ever could. He's no nonsense, objective, and could tie a knot in the devil's tail before he knew what happened to him. I have the rest of the week off, I'll start working on J. R.'s situation immediately."

"A suggestion, Your Honor."

"What, Sam?"

"Call Judge Samuel Wenter Waterford; he's ninety three, has all his faculties, but is crippled with arthritis. Stubborn as a mule. Lives here in Kansas City at the Stoddard Arms on Wornal Road with a retired Marine colonel who calls himself Charles Wentworth. His name is really Col. Felix Brannigan, but that's another story in itself. Tell either one, or most likely both, when you meet them one on one, Hirsch, brother of Joe, said *urgent*. I can't get near them or call them on the phone but I can call on them for help. Explain to them what is happening and when you are through tell them I said, "what about CMD for Louie". That's all you'll need to say. They'll take it from there with a yes or no. Oh, and, CMD stands for controlled mind device."

Hick thought to himself, *"This all sounds crazy but what the hell, Sam's a straight shooter."* He responded, "I'll do it. Anything else, Sam?"

"Yes, a phone number for the Judge is 517-334-6940. When they answer say, "Is Thurmond in?" and then listen intently to what he says. He'll tell you when he will see you. Good luck and keep in touch but, Your Honor, from now on we must use special communications. Judge Waterford will tell you what you need to know when you meet with him. So long."

Hick was saying goodbye when he heard the receiver click. Without hesitation and looking at his pad he dialed 517-334-6940. There were three rings and he heard a stern voice say, "Hello."

Hick replied, "Is Thurmond in?"

"Hold on please, a window's open and I can't hear you. Can you hold on while I close it?"

"Yes."

Hick pushed the receiver to his ear and heard another voice ask in the background, "Who is it?"

"I couldn't hear it all, Judge. The noise from the window. Something about a Thurmond. I'll shut it…the window."

"Oh. Well, ten-thirty in the morning is when you have to take me to the clinic if I'm up to it."

"Let me find out whose on the line first, Judge. Then I'll talk to you about that."

"Fine, I'll wait."

Hick heard a window slam, then the clicking of someone walking back to the phone. The original voice asked, "Still there?"

"Yes."

"Good. Sorry for the delay but the window, you know. It's closed. What can I do for you?"

"I wanted to know if Thurmond is in."

"Thurmond? No Thurmond here. You must have the wrong number."

"I'm sorry."

"Not at all. Sorry to have kept you,"

The phone went dead. As Hick knowingly jotted 'ten-thirty tomorrow' on his pad, Henry's voice prodded him back to the matter at hand, "They're ready, Your Honor."

"Good! I am too, but give me a few minutes, Henry, I want to talk to Judge January first."

"Yes, Sir, he's on the phone."

"How did you know, Henry?"

As Henry handed him the phone he added, "Deduction, Your Honor, deduction 'cause I've been around you long enough."

Hick smiled as he took the phone and asked, "You there, Jason?"

"You bet. Henry called and said he thought you might want me so I've been hanging on. What's up, as if I didn't know."

"What's that mean?"

"It means, Manning came up here this morning and let me know what was going on and Henry has filled me in with more details. Hick, your people know you. You're lucky and they're lucky to have one another."

"Thanks, Jason, but will you?"

"I already have it scheduled for tomorrow morning at nine o'clock. I called bonehead Harold and told him to clean my docket because I wanted to sit in criminal court tomorrow morning. He took over what I have left for the week. He seemed relieved to hear I was taking the Rollins case, but he won't be too happy for too long."

"I don't understand."

"Simple. The three of us; Manning, Henry, and myself, knew you were going to wash your hands of the case. We just anticipated you."

"What if I had changed my mind?"

"You didn't and won't, so what's your beef?"

"None."

"Good. Get back in court and drop the bomb. I'll be down later."

Hick cradled the phone and signaled for Henry to go ahead. Henry had been listening and, taking the cue, walked into the courtroom and called out, "This court is now in session, please rise for Judge Nicholas Hickman, presiding."

Hick stopped next to Henry and with a large smile said, "Henry, I don't know how you do it but every time we open the court you do it differently."

"I know, Your Honor, it doesn't get stale that way."

Hick laughed to himself and made his way to the bench. He sat and looking out across the room was surprised to see Harold sitting right behind Joe Villella. He thought, *"Joe must have put the prod to the bloke but are they in for a surprise."* Hick sat back in his chair and began, "Mr. Ortman, Mr Villella, I have taken into consideration my personal feelings regarding the matter before the court and have decided to step-down. I have asked Judge January to schedule the case and he informs me he will take the case and be ready to hear it at nine in the morning."

Paul and Joe looked at one another in dismay. They knew what lay ahead for them. Looking at Hick and in unison meekly said, "Yes, Your Honor, thank you, Your Honor."

Hick snapped his head to one side and exclaimed, "Good! Court dismissed! No wait, wait just one minute, gentlemen, there is something else," Hick stood and cast his eyes on Harold, who was smiling, having heard what he wanted to hear. Hick continued, "I am stepping down from the bench. I am not retiring, I will be a partner in the firm of Harding, Kimball, Roberts, and Hickman, starting in the morning."

The smile on Harold Batemen's face gave way to a scowl as he jumped to his feet calling out, "You can't do that, you have to give the court notice!"

"Sit down, Harold! I can still find you in contempt but I won't and I'll do as I damn please. Court dismissed."

There was total silence and disbelief on the faces of those in the courtroom watching Hick start for the door to his chambers. Henry was a step ahead of him and flung the door open, stepped back, and as Hick passed him cried out, "Hallelujah, the Lord be praised!" turned and slammed the door shut.

Hick turned back to him and instructed, "Have a seat, Henry, and listen to what I say." Henry sat wide-eyed and grinning, eager to hear.

"I've been thinking about this for quite some time. Quitting, that is. After this morning, Harold and all, I figured enough is enough. The indignity I suffered at Harold's hands," Hick stopped to wink, "gives me just cause to quit rather than give notice and resign. I've carried this letter in my pocket," Hick stopped and reaching in his coat pocket pulled out an envelope and handed it to Henry, "for two years. It's from Lance Harding. Go ahead, Henry, open it and read it out loud."

Henry fumbled in his pocket for his glasses, then with the envelope Hick had handed him, he pulled out the letter and read aloud,

Dear Judge Hickman,

With your permission, as per our several conversations and my persistent telephone calls to you. We will reduce to writing how we feel about you. Whenever, and if ever, you decide to resign from the bench and will consider joining our firm, the following joint stipulations as set out will be eagerly and willingly met. One: Your compensation will be double your present compensation as a judge. Two: Your secretary, Marsha Manning, will remain your secretary. Three: Your bailiff, Henry Justin, will be retained as a clerk in our office. Four: Miss Manning and Mr. Justin will be compensated at an amount equal to one and one-half times their present compensation. Five: Mr. Justin will be enrolled, if he so desires, in an accelerated pre-law course at Omaha University. Six: we have offices prepared for you all. What remains is for you to turn on the lights.

Hick, we anxiously await your call. Please make it soon.

With sincere and deep personal regards, for the firm of Harding, Kimball, and Roberts, we remain,

Lance, Mark, and Bert

Henry's voice was quavering as he finished. He quietly folded the letter, placed it back in the envelope and handed it to Hick with eyes cast downward. Hick reached for the envelope and as he took it he patted the back of Henry's hand saying, "Well, what do you think of that?"

Henry removed his glasses, carefully folded them and placed them back in his pocket; rubbed his eyes and as he cast then upward, remarked, "Manning know?"

"No. I…ah…don't think so."

"I know why. If she doesn't."

Hick chuckled as he replied, "Why?"

"They dealt with you at home. She must have never been there when they called."

"You are talented, Henry, in many ways, and most likely your observation is correct. But!"

"But?"

"We'll see what she says when we tell her. Not much escapes her and her networking. What do you think about your situation?"

"Your Honor, wherever you go, if I can go, I will. You gave me my opportunity and I give you my loyalty."

Both men stood and as they embraced one another the phone rang. Hick picked it up and answered, "Judge Hickman."

"Hick, it's January. Batemen just left. Poor bastard doesn't know what he's in for, yet. He recited how you up and quit and how he challenged your right but that he will be thrilled to see your backside as it leaves the building. I'm all for you, wish I had the balls to do it myself. You'll be taking on Rollins?"

"I haven't gotten that far, Jason, but it's a great idea if he'll have me."

"Well, I'll bet you, Ortman—and I know you like him but he's slow, Hick—he'll be glad to turn it over. Go for it. I'll see you in court maybe?"

"Not tomorrow, Jason, but maybe next week. We'll see."

"Whatever, Hick, it will be my pleasure to finally tangle ass with a lawyer who knows what the hell he's doing."

No sooner was the phone dead than it rang again, startling Hick. "Hello, Jason? Did you hang up?"

"It's Lance, Hick,"

"Hold on, Lance, I want Henry, my bailiff, my friend, to listen." Hick punched the speaker phone button and pointed to a chair and then his ear for Henry to sit and listen. Henry nodded his understanding and Hick remarked, "Go on, Lance."

"Hi, Henry and Hick, the firestorm of your announcement has spread across the street to our building and I'm calling to see if we can turn on your office lights?"

"You can. We'll have to clear out of here tonight when Manning gets back. I want to make it quick and clean. Surgical. I'll need help and a meeting tonight with the partners. Possible?"

"Done. There's twelve of us here. When the doors shut at five we'll head over with boxes. Get you settled in and have our first meeting. Okay? Something up?"

"We'll look for you at five, and yes, there is something up. I don't know how big it is but it's big. I'll spell it out at the meeting and remember, Lance, if it's not your cup of tea I can go elsewhere."

"That I know, Hick. I know you and my partners. Wait and see, we'll get behind you whatever it is. Wait and see."

"Thanks, Lance, it's always nice to have friends, especially when you need them."

Hick hung up the phone, turned to Henry and asked, "Can you find Manning?"

"No problem. She told me this morning that shoes were her thing today. Each Wednesday she picks one thing and hits the trail. Today it's shoes. Only one kind for her, and only one place to get them she told me. Prevata shoes at Dorothy's. I'll call her."

"No, no, no, Henry. Don't call her to come back. Call her to have her wait for you to come and get her. Then on the way back, break it to her. What's happened, that and then I'll fill in the details."

"Yes sir, that would work best. I'm on my way."

CHAPTER 6

▼

Harold Batemen left Hick's courtroom elated. He felt certain the master plan he and his associate had agreed upon would now proceed with ease. He recognized that Jason January was a formidable tactician in the courtroom but his primary desire was to put people in jail. Or so he thought.

Gertrude Boltinghouse had been his secretary for twelve years. He hardly ever talked to her, much less confided in her. Yet, he liked having her around, for she, "well you never know she's around but she does her job", he would often say about her to others. Harold did not have his own bailiff. He preferred to use anyone available on a day-to-day basis. Harold Batemen built no loyalties and had none.

Gertrude looked up as he walked in her office and inquired, "Everything all right, Your Honor?"

"Fine, just fine and dandy, as the saying goes. I'll be in my chambers. Busy. No calls for an hour."

"Yes, Your Honor."

Harold went straight to his desk, picked up the phone and dialed.

"Givens Manufacturing."

"Mr. Walter Givens, please. Judge Harold Batemen calling."

"One moment, Your Honor." The young woman rang Walter Givens' phone.

"Yes."

"Judge Batemen is on line one, Mr. Givens."

"Tell him…forget it. No. I'll take it."

✻   ✻   ✻   ✻

Walter Givens was a no-nonsense businessman who knew what he wanted and with his money usually got it. He had a weakness; lust. A lust for women. Other men's wives or girlfriends. He searched the world over for prostitutes, high-class prostitutes, but they never satisfied the desire he had for other men's women. He had decided years ago that it was the conquest. To be able to turn a woman away from a man she had and was committed to. Once the conquest was complete he would quickly throw them over and set out on his next seduction.

He had surrounded himself with all of the proper trappings of society. A beautiful wife, children, servants, and home but that was never enough. He had left a trail of broken marriages and relationships across the continents, yet to this day had gone undetected as what he really was. There were several scrapes with jilted husbands and lovers but all were conveniently and easily settled with various amounts of money. Some had to be ended violently. Contracts came with varying price tags but he had always picked the most expensive, which led him to an international consortium of dedicated assassins, not low-class hit men. His trail was on file with Interpol but to date they had not laid a finger on anyone who could connect him directly with any of the deaths. All had been classified as, "Coincidental association with the woman in question."

He despised Harold Batemen, but Harold came along with the group that had evolved over the years out of their individual needs for cover and commonality of purpose or, best said, individual deviant behavior. So he tolerated him but thought his lust for pornography was about as sick as the two others who were pedophiles. He picked up the phone and asked, "What, Harold?"

"Judge Hickman dumped the Rollins case and has left the judiciary as of today."

"Harold, as I said earlier, our agreement is we don't contact one another in any way unless it's a real emergency."

"This is."

"Why?"

"He's poking around looking for information and asking questions."

"How do you know that?"

"I have his phone tapped and he has been calling Kansas City. A call to Sam Hirsch, gambler, who seems to have confirmed his suspicions and is leading him to someone named Judge Samuel Wenter Waterford."

"Do you realize what you just said? Did it ever occur to you someone may have your phone tapped?"

"Why would they?"

"You're kidding me, you must be, but let me ask you. Why in hell did you have Hickman's phone tapped?"

"I don't like him and I was trying to get something on him."

"Why, Harold?"

"So I could discredit him."

"Silly and stupid, Harold, just damn foolishness, from what I know about the man he is as straight as an arrow. You're the one someone should be listening in on and just may be listening right now."

"I don't care if they are. I want Hickman taken out."

"I don't know what you're talking about, Harold. I didn't hear you. Tell me what you said at the meeting tonight. Goodbye."

Walter Givens hung up in disgust and muttered to himself, "Damn fool. I'll bet that little twirp of a judge plays with himself when he looks at his dirty pictures."

Harold was furious and muttered to himself, "All that prick understands is how to stick it in some other guy's wife and make money."

*　　*　　*　　*

As Louie started out the door Charlie called after him, "Wop! Leaving that phone of yours naked?"

"Naw, I know you'll cover it, Charlie. If anything comes in, take the message. I'm gonna check my car battery."

"Sure, Louie, sure you are."

Louie walked out the door and strode to his car, opened the door, climbed in and jammed the key into the ignition, twisted it. The engine turned over immediately. Louie slid in behind the wheel, and making a point of taking the plug to his cellular phone jammed it in the cigarette lighter and waited. He picked up the phone and dialed.

A voice asked, "Louie?"

"Yeah. Quick. He's watching."

"Take him and Sam. I'm ready to move."

"You're sure about Sam?"

"Couldn't be more certain."

"It's done."

Louie jerked the plug out of the lighter and threw it on the seat and slammed the car door. He leaned against the car as he took out a cigarette and lit it. He took a deep drag and rolled the smoke around in his mouth, inhaled and as he spewed it out his nose heard Charlie yell, "Hey, Wop! Better get your ass in here, it's Sam."

Louie threw his cigarette on the ground in disgust, stomped his heel on it, and growled under his breath, "I'll wop you. You'll see who's the wop."

Charlie was holding the door open for him and when Louie strode in he laughingly added, "At least you're one wop who knows how and by whom his bread is buttered."

Louie begrudgingly picked up the phone and calmly said, "Sam, it's Louie, sorry, I was checking my car battery."

"So Charlie says, Louie. So Charlie says. But I'm not so sure."

"What do ya' mean by that, Sam?"

"One thing, Louie, I have a lot of ways I keep tabs on you. I know about you and my son, Donny."

"Donny?" Louie felt the sweat break out on his forehead and his hand tremble as he waited for an answer.

"Yeah, Louie. Donny! Remember my son, Donny Hirsch, of Chicago."

"Sam, what are you saying?"

"It's an old saying, Louie. You'd double-cross your old man and have a million reasons why it would be okay, just like Donny. Right?"

"You're wrong, Sam, you're wrong."

"When you're through I'll be waiting for you, Louie. Here at the office. Uptown, Louie. We'll have a drink and talk about it."

"Sure, Sam, sure. I'll be there."

"Oh, Louie, take it from me, you are the dumb wop Charlie always says you are."

The phone went dead and Louie stood there, soaking wet from perspiration and shaking with fear, then anger set in as the phone slipped from his fingers and crashed to the table. He didn't sense Charlie standing behind him and he spat out, "You'll get yours, you damn Jew. Just wait and the wop of all wops will too."

"I know the Jew, Louie, but who's the wop? Watch out, it might be you."

Charlie turned, walked down the aisle and called out to the counter man, "Give Louie a drink. Bourbon straight up and send along the bottle. The one marked courage. The wop needs it bad."

Louie no sooner sat down and the counter man was sliding a glass of bourbon and a bottle over to him. Under his breath Louie snarled, "Get the hell away from here."

Ben Talmadge, a sixty-seven-year-old retired hit man was night man for the phones. There was never much activity unless someone suddenly had an overload of betting and needed to lay it off. Ben's job was to find Sam so he could broker it. Ben slept most of the time but wore earphones turned up so he would wake up if the phone rang. This night when he walked in, for some reason he slid in next to Louie and proclaimed, "Man, you smell like a distillery," taking note of the bottle he asked, "you gonna' drink the whole damn bottle?"

"I'm sober. What's it to you if I do?"

"Not a damn thing to me, but Sam wouldn't like it."

"How in the hell will he know? You gonna tell 'im?"

"Nope, but Sam knows everything. Haven't you found that out yet?"

"Wop? Is that what you wanted to say?"

"What do *you* mean, wop? What's that got to do with anything?"

"That's what Charlie calls me, a dumb wop."

"I don't know about that, Louie, but if *you* think Sam doesn't know what's going down, you better think again and get it straight; if I wanted to call you a wop...I would and not worry a damned second about it!"

Louie knew he had pushed Ben too far and realized he was still dangerous, so he tempered his voice and said, "I know, I know, but things can change."

"Yeah, the graveyard's full of changes."

"Changes?"

"Yeah, from life to death."

Sam hung up his phone. Opening a desk drawer he pulled out his "safe" phone and dialed. There was one ring, two rings, three rings. He hung up and repeated the same procedure twice. The third time a gruff voice snarled, "What's up. Sam?"

"Yeah, it's me. I'm not sure but Donata is on his way down. Call *you know who* and back me up as planned."

"Louie?"

"And Donny."

"What *you* predicted is coming down?"

"I suspect it is."

"Sorry, Sam, your own kid and all. Still want me to handle it like we agreed upon?"

"Absolutely."

"You really sure, Sam?"

"Like I said. Do it."

"What about Donny? You never said."

"Don't touch him. Leave him alone. He's my son."

"God save us, Sam. Your kid is out to do *you* in and *you're* saving him?"

"That's the way it is. If it happens, watch over Kate. I've tripled your stash."

"I'll see to it she's covered for life, Sam, if."

"Thanks. Cover me. Now!"

Sam hung up the phone to wait for Louie.

*   *   *   *

Louie slid out of the booth, not saying a word. Wobbling slightly, he made his way to the door. Charlie watched him but said nothing. Louie walked to his car, opened the door, and slid in behind the steering wheel. Reaching over he opened the glove compartment and rummaged around until he found what he was looking for in a small paper bag. He opened the bag; turned it upside down and let the metal object fall on the seat between his legs. Sliding his hand in his coat he pulled his gun from its holster and let it drop to the seat. He slipped the silencer onto the barrel of the gun and as he moved to get out of the car he slowly put the gun back in its holster and hissed, "Shit, I hope Charlie didn't see. I know he's watching. I just know it."

Charlie was watching but didn't see the gun. Louie made his way back to the door and moving to open it Charlie called out, "Forget something?"

Louie thought, *"you forgot to say wop,"* but answered, "No, Charlie, just need to talk to you. Private like."

"Follow me, Louie, we'll use my office."

Charlie never let his back be exposed. He always had others go first. Even when he sat in a restaurant his back was always to the wall but this time, for some reason, he went into his office first. Louie saw his opportunity. Reaching into his coat he jerked the pistol free from its holster, aimed it at Charlie's back and pulled the trigger. Charlie heard the all too familiar sound of the silencer but it was too late. The bullet smashed into his back to the left of his spinal column, breaking a rib whose parts then became projectiles tearing his lung apart. Falling forward from the impact of the bullet, Charlie threw his arms out so when he hit the floor he rolled over on his back. His head was leaning against the wall and he could see Louie's face, for Louie had bent down and was now eyeball to eyeball. Charlie coughed and blood spewed from his mouth. He took a deep breath and the blood he inhaled caused him to cough again. As he looked up at Louie his eyes were ablaze with fury and he blew out blood with the words, "Just a minute before you finish me off," and he gasped for more air.

Louie wiped Charlie's blood from his face with his sleeve and as he did Charlie spat out with what was his last breath, "You damn wop!"

The words caused Louie's face to contort with anger. He pulled the trigger again, and the bullet smashed between Charlie's eyes as the words, "you damn..." were forming in his mouth. Charlie's head bounced to the floor from the impact of the second bullet and fell to the right.

Louie stood over him seething with anger and whispered, "We're even, you damn wop," and then laughed.

Louie jammed his pistol back into its holster. Walking into Charlie's bathroom, he washed his hands and face and wiped Charlie's blood from his coat. As he walked out of Charlie's office he quipped to the dead body, "See you later, Charlie, and thanks, it was *my* pleasure."

It would take Louie the better part of thirty minutes to make it to Sam's office.

When Louie left, the counter man, as instructed by Charlie, went to check on Charlie for as Charlie said, "Just in case."

Seeing the carnage he immediately went to the phone and dialed a number given to him by Charlie. A stern voice answered, "Joe Umbigolata here."

"This is Cappie, Charlie's counter man."

"Yeah, I know, Cappie, I know. What's up. Is it what I think?"

"Yes. I'm doing what Charlie instructed me to do. Call you. He's dead. Louie Donata did it."

"What else did Charlie tell you to do? In case."

"Shut down the counter and take over."

"Do you know how to do it?"

"Yes. He showed me."

"Then do it. I'll be there in the morning. Where'd Donato go?"

"Charlie told me he was on his way to the Jew's."

"Cappie, I repeat, do like Charlie said, do like I said," and the phone went dead.

Cappie opened Charlie's top desk drawer and reaching in found the key taped in a small recess. He walked to the coat closet, opened the door and pushed the hanging coats and pants aside, revealing a small locked metal door. Opening the lock with the key he saw a switch and flipped it on. He re-locked the metal door, rearranged the clothes and closed the door. He left the office, went to his kitchen area and shut down the stoves and ovens. He dimmed the lights and placed a sign on the counter, 'closed' and sat down to wait as Charlie had instructed him to do, in case.

Joe Umbigolata was in Detroit and as he always put it, "Watching my store."

As Joe slammed the phone in its cradle he cried out, "Damn, Charlie, I'm sorry! I'll even it up!"

*   *   *   *

Joe walked to his office door and opening it yelled, "Mark Umbigo-lata, I want *you.* "

A very large, younger man turned to look at Joe, rose from his desk and as he walked into Joe's office asked, "What's up?"

"Charlie's dead. Donato did it. He's on his way to the Jew's, most likely to take him out. Get on the phone to K. C., we've got maybe fif-teen minutes to ace him before he hits the Jew. Get to it."

The young man's face showed no emotion as he stood to leave and Joe added, "This place is yours. I'm on my way to K. C. to take over. Run this place well. I don't want to come back and be disappointed. Understand?"

"Don't worry, Joe, I'll take good care of both things you want."

*   *   *   *

Sam had two parking spaces in the building garage. His Continental was in its usual space. Louie pulled up beside it and got out of his car. He took off his outer coat just in case he had missed some blood and walked to the elevator. Turning his key in the elevator switch, he heard the familiar click, then the hum of the elevator. The door opened and he stepped in. The door shut and the elevator started to rise before he pushed a button, and it took him by surprise. He pulled his gun from its holster and stood to one side of the door. The elevator stopped on the fifth floor, Sam's floor, and the door opened. Nothing happened. Louie slowly moved around the door to be confronted by Donny who said nothing. They walked directly to Sam's private office door. With gun in hand Louie knocked.

"Come in, Louie, the door's open."

Louie turned the doorknob enough to slightly open the door. Step-ping back, Louie kicked it open with his foot as Donny stood and watched. They saw Sam's back, for he had turned to the left to rise from his chair so he could greet Louie. Louie fired two shots rapidly, catching Sam in the back, which threw him forward, face down into a corner. Louie walked into the room, and Donny hung back. Louie heard the bullet pass his head and slam into the wall. Louie fell to the floor, rolled over and saw Donny was gone. He crept back into the corridor but saw nothing. He had no idea where Donny had gone. Scrambling to his feet he heard the elevator humming as it ascended. He muttered to himself, "You son-of-a-bitch, I shoulda' known. What the hell, I gotta' get outta' here!"

Louie waited, and when the humming of the elevator stopped, he put his key in the switch; heard the click; then the humming as the elevator began to descend. Louie flattened himself next to the elevator door and waited. As the elevator door opened he spun out in front of the door with gun extended but the elevator was empty. He entered, pushed the button marked "Parking" and muttered, "I kill the Jew, and then the kid was going to kill me. What the hell's next?"

The elevator stopped and the door opened. Nothing happened. Louie pushed himself up against the wall of the elevator, then swept through the door with gun extended. Again, no one.

Running to his car and looking in, Louie saw it was empty. Opening the door he slid behind the wheel, jamming the key into the ignition. Twisting that key was his last act. The explosion obliterated his car, Sam's car and two hundred feet of garage in every direction.

Across the street two men stood watching and waiting with hands cupped over their ears.

Hearing and feeling the explosion they dropped their hands and one man quietly said, "Woulda' had it Louie woulda' knew what was going to happen before it did but this is what Donny wanted. Just in case."

The second man asked, "Just in case what?"

"Just in case he missed Louie."

"You mean, you mean, we could have stopped him from taking Sam out? Why didn't we?"

"I don't know. That's the way Donny wanted it and that's the way we did it. Cum'on, there'll be cops all over the place before long."

A solitary figure watched as they ran down the street, walked to a phone booth, deposited money, dialed, and waited.

"Mark Umbigolata here."

"It's the man."

"Right! What happened?"

"Someone got here ahead of me. They vaporized him. I'd say it was twenty feet of cordite."

"Cordite?"

"Yeah! The smell, I know it. Military like, maybe. I'm a TNT man but cordite, it's good stuff, cheap to buy and easy to get off the street. A big boom but not all over the place. If you know how."

"Yeah. If you know how. Your money has been stashed."

"What for? I didn't do nothin'. I just watched."

"A deal is a deal. I'll need you soon."

"Okay, kid, okay. Tell Joe."

Nitro knew he should leave but his hands were clean and he liked the excitement that came before, with, and after an explosion. As the fire engines, police cars, and spectators appeared from everywhere, Nitro stood thinking to himself, *"Man, what a way to get attention. Nothin' like it."*

Nitro's MO was a familiar one in Kansas City and when it happened he was always hassled. He was first and foremost the best hit man money could buy. He was quick and left no traces because he usually blew away the evidence. He even liked the hassle because he knew it would take weeks, months, even years for the police to find out who he wasted. After about an hour of watching he heard one policeman tell another, "It was Sam Hirsch somebody wanted; somebody else blew up the shooter."

Nitro smiled at the remark and moved away from the onlookers. He wanted to get home, for he knew his MO would have the police knocking on his door. Having lived on the shady side of the law most of his life, Nitro had no problem eluding anyone when he wanted to. He deftly slipped into alleys, down side streets, and through buildings with the ease of a cat that defied suspicion or detection. He would always pop out right in front of his very upscale apartment. Which he did this day.

Letting himself into his apartment he went straight to the refrigerator, for beer was the companion of his weakness and passion, nitroglycerin.

Nitro poured his beer and while savoring its taste pushed down on the button activating his answering machine and heard, "Nitro. I have some business. Call. John Q."

Nitro shook his head negatively, smacked his lips, drank from his glass and quipped as he refilled his glass, "John Q., I'll have nothing to do with you...you damn gunsel. Well, what the hell, a buck's a buck. One never knows. I'll call."

*   *   *   *

Hick sat in his chambers overlooking the courtyard. He was pleased with himself and what he had done. He was trying to convince himself by thinking, *"It's time for a change, I'm way overdue for a change."* Hearing a soft knock on the door, he looked over his shoulder and called out, "Please come in. The door is open."

J. R. Rollins walked in while asking, "Am I interrupting you, Your Honor?"

"Why of course not, J. R., and it's Hick to you."

"No, Your Honor, I can't call you that. You're my senior. I wouldn't be comfortable doing it."

"I understand. Would you have me call you Doctor?"

"No, sir, I'd prefer J. R."

"Very well, J. R. it is. What can I do for you?"

"You resigned today because of me. Did you not?"

"I'd have to say a partial yes to that. Your situation seemed to ignite an anger or maybe a desire. A hidden desire to move on. I was just telling myself, before you knocked, it was the right time."

"Will you help me?"

"Well, J. R., I already am, but for the sake of correctness in such matters I must respectfully request that you allow me to complete my duties here. When I am an official member of the firm of Harding, Kimball and Roberts, then I will be able to explain. That relationship will start in about two hours. So until the first of the week, for I will be out of town, we must use discretion. I want to help you because you helped me, but more importantly, I believe what we never got to today, the actions of your sons, is deplorable. I do not consider it manly. I will expand on my feelings at another time and place. Have you discussed this with Paul Ortman?"

"I have and he is willing to step aside."

"I would prefer he didn't. Ask him to call me and you be on your way so we don't cause ourselves any trouble."

"Yes, sir, and thank you."

J. R. turned and started for the door. Hick had turned his head back to the window and as he looked out over the forming shadows of nightfall he called out, "J. R., one moment, listen to me. If I had a son I would want him to be just like you."

The silence told Hick he had been heard and the soft click of the door's latch told him his words had been carried out of his chambers.

*   *   *   *

Stepping into the courtroom J. R. wiped his eyes as he heard Paul Ortman ask, "What did he say? Will he take you on?"

"He will but he couldn't say much. He wants you to call him. He won't be available until the first of the week."

"I can't wait, we go to court in the morning."

Paul Ortman walked to the door of the Chambers and opened it. As he walked in he started to speak but stopped and looked about the room. There was a light on the Judge's desk The green-shaded lamp cast a soft glow about the room, competing with the long slender shadows of twilight flowing from the courtyard through the large window. The outline of Hick's head and shoulders caught Paul's attention. Instantly sensing he was witnessing a moment of transition in another man's life he became acutely aware of the magnitude of his intrusion on this moment. Embarrassed he began to back away when Hick, without turning, spoke, breaking the importance of the moment.

"I know it's you, Paul. I knew you were with J. R., and I expected you. Will you join with me at Harding, Kimball, and Roberts?"

Taken aback, Paul sheepishly asked, "Will they have me?"

"Let's find out."

Hick stood, walked to his desk and picking up the phone instructed Paul, "Turn on some lights."

The phone rang, a voice answered, "Law offices."

"Lance, Hick."

"Yes, Your Honor."

"Lance, do we have room for Paul Ortman in the firm?"

"Everybody is here. We're waiting to come over and start moving you. Let me get you on the speaker phone. Okay, now, ask again."

"Do we have room for Paul Ortman in the firm?"

"Hick, that didn't take long, all heads are affirmative."

"Thank you, gentlemen, fellow lawyers, see you shortly," Hick hung up and turning to Paul asked, "You heard. What say you?"

"Yes, yes, yes!"

"Good. Go into Judge January's court in the morning; get a continuance. He'll give it to you. He's not ready and he always likes one leg up. I'll call you tomorrow from Kansas City. Now get out of here before someone accuses me of collusion or something worse. I'm not officially in private practice until five o'clock."

Paul turned without a word and left. J. R. was waiting for him and with both thumbs held high and with a large grin he gleefully told J. R., "I'm a partner! Can you believe it? Just like that with the one and only Judge Hickman in Harding, Kimball, and Roberts. Wow! Let's get going, there's a lot to do tomorrow morning. Follow me."

Ten minutes later Manning and Henry walked from Manning's office down the hall and into Hick's chambers without knocking, for the door was wide open and a local easy listening station was blaring away. Hick was intent on scooping up material from his bottom desk drawer, so he didn't hear them when they walked in. As he lifted his arms and stood from the squatting position to deposit the contents of the drawer in a box, he saw Manning's hands moving up the side of her dress to her hips. When their eyes met he greeted her somewhat sheepishly, "Oh, I've been waiting for you two. Glad you're back."

"Yes, Your Honor, we are. What, might I ask, are you doing?"

"Packing."

"Oh yes, packing. Henry told me you've quit."

"Not quit, Manning. I resigned as of…"

"Henry mentioned that."

"You're not upset?"

"Why should we be? Henry and I know where our bread is buttered."

"You're upset, Manning, but time and the tide, you know, dictate action. Today it was change. I don't have much time, so listen, you two. The Harding, Kimball, Roberts office will all be here after five to move us over. We are all hired and so is Paul Ortman. You'll like the arrangements, offices, salaries, et cetera. Lance Harding will explain it and you explain what you can to him. Manning, I need a ticket for this evening to Kansas City with an open return. Find me a room close to the Plaza for two days. Paul will be taking Doctor Rollins back to Jason's court first thing in the morning. Have Lance go with him. I want a continuance. Henry, you start to glean everything you can from the street about what you told me in the quiet room. Dig into these men's past and present activities, and Henry, get a tail on Judge Bateman. If there's a weak link, he's it. One more thing, so I don't leave you hanging, there's evil afoot, more than meets the eye. I like J. R. Rollins and detest what is happening to him. I am first and foremost an officer of the court and I'll be damned if I'll sit and let anything happen to him. He's innocent and someone, maybe me, should take a stick to his son's hind end. I have to go home and pack."

Manning spoke up, "One minute, hold it. If you think all that explains anything, forget it. You're upset, aren't you?"

"Yes, damned upset."

"Be specific."

"I can't. I just sense this is bigger than I think. I haven't been a Judge all these years for nothing. I can smell a rat, a big one."

"What's in Kansas City?"

"Manning, I don't know. Sam Hirsch, on the QT, has steered me to a specific man. Sam's under attack, just like J. R."

Manning, looking at Henry for a sign that he understood what Hick had just said, saw him shrug his shoulders. She turned her attention back to Hick and fussed, "I'm confused but I'll work on it. Be on your way. I'll do what *you* want and call *you*. Henry, take him home, help him pack, then get him to the airport."

Hick started to the door, stopped, turned and returning to Manning folded his arms around her and exclaimed, "I don't understand it all yet, but in the meantime, until we do, thanks for caring for me...for loving me."

Manning squeezed him tightly and whispered, "Now that's more like it."

One hour later as Manning sat observing her new office, the phone rang and she picked it up saying, "Law Offices, this is Marsha Manning, secretary to His Honor Nicholas Hickman. May I help you?"

A strident voice, consistent with most impersonal police officers replied, "Yes. This is Detective Gary Peluso, Kansas City Homicide. Am I to understand Judge Hickman is now at this number?"

"You are, Detective."

"Good, is he in?"

"No, His Honor is gone for several days. Can I take a message?"

"Can you get the message to him?"

"Detective, you'd be surprised what I can do, in other words, yes, I can."

"Good. Tell His Honor a Sam Hirsch was shot to death this afternoon in his office. On Mr. Hirsch's desk was a note instructing whoever found his body to call His Honor, and to inform him, quote, 'I have met my fate,' unquote."

Manning thought, *"I wonder what that means?"* Then she quickly asked, "Anything else?"

"Well, the only other thing he asked was to notify his wife."

"Well?"

"Well what?"

"Did you...Detective?"

"No, not yet, I notified your office first. Now I'll notify his wife."

"Detective, I'll get the message to the Judge; you go on and notify his wife...for God's sake."

Manning hung the phone up in disgust and muttered out loud, "My Lord, those guys act like murder is just another everyday happening."

A voice just outside her office asked, "What guys?"

Before Manning gave a second thought to who asked the question she answered, "The police."

Lance Harding stepped around the jam of the office door and standing before Manning replied, "To them...it is...just another happening."

Manning, embarrassed, rose to her feet to reply, "I'm sorry, I didn't see you, Mr. Harding."

"Lance to you, Manning, and you know when it has to be Mr. Harding. I wanted to welcome you three together, but it seems the Judge is starting off like the rabbit."

"The rabbit?"

"Come on, Manning, Bugs Bunny, not Harvey."

"Oh, you know about Harvey?"

"Manning, I venture to guess everybody knows about the Judge and his meeting up with Harvey. Those were his less behooving years and are known especially to the lawyers. Did he tell you to tell me anything?"

"Behooving years? That's a new way to put it. Oh well. Yes, he wants you to know everything we know and right now…but that's not much. First, the police officer that just called said Sam Hirsch is dead."

"The Kansas City Hirsch?"

"Right, and that is where the Judge is off to for two days. He said Sam led him to someone but he didn't say why or what for."

"What else?"

"He's taking on the J. R. Rollins case with Paul Ortman. There's a hearing before Judge January in the morning and he asks that you go along with Paul; he wants a continuance. He'll tell you the rest when he calls."

"Done. Where's Paul?"

"In his office but…Lance?"

"What's the matter, Manning?"

"Are we proceeding too fast? Are we taking over your office?"

"Manning, not to worry. We could not be more pleased or excited to have you, Henry, and the Judge. We've wanted him to join with us for years. Never thought it would happen but it has and we know he'll inject a new direction into this place that has been sadly lacking. We need the new direction, a new enthusiasm for the law. We were getting stale. Practicing law should be fun and exciting."

"Lance, my friend, stand back and get ready. I have a feeling, knowing Hick, we're all in for the ride of our lives."

*   *   *   *

Police Detective Peluso hung up the phone and dialed Sam Hirsch's home number.

"Hirsch residence, Mary Beth speaking. How may I help you?"

"This is Detective Gary Peluso, Kansas City Police Department. Is Mrs. Hirsch in?"

"Yes."

"Well, if she's in, may I speak to her?"

"Just one minute, Detective Peluso."

"Brother!"

"What was that, Detective Peluso?"

"I was exclaiming…forget it, Mary Beth. Mrs. Peluso, I mean, Mrs. Hirsch, please."

Detective Peluso heard Mary Beth put the phone down and again exclaimed, "Hell! I'm not even married. Brother! Oh, what the hell."

Kate Hirsch picked up the phone and asked, "How may I help you, Detective?"

"Mrs. Hirsch, this is Detective Gary Peluso, Homicide, Kansas City Police Department. If I sent a car for you, would you be willing to come to the police department?"

"What is it, Detective? Sam?"

"Yes, ma 'am."

"He's dead, isn't he, Detective?"

It was against police rules of procedure to inform a relative over the phone that their loved ones were deceased. This is so someone can be present when the news is broken in case there may be an untoward response. Detective Peluso took note of the calmness in Kate's voice and thought, *"Go ahead, tell her, she's a cold calculating cookie just like all these gangster broads are,"* so he responded, "Yes, ma'am. He's dead."

"When? Where? How?"

Gary paused as he thought, *"Yup, she's one cool number,"* and then continued, "About thirty minutes ago. His office. Shot twice in the back."

"Did he suffer?"

"We believe he died instantly, ma'am."

"Where is he?"

"In an ambulance on his way to the morgue."

"When can I have him?"

"It would be best if you would come to the station. There are a few questions and after the medical examiner is finished you are free to make arrangements."

"I'll start to make them now...and then, Detective, I'll be on my way."

"Yes, ma'am, I'm at 2302 Lovett, third floor, room 305. There's an elevator."

"That's not the police station."

"No, ma'am, it's not. It's our southwest Homicide station."

"I'll be there. Goodbye, Detective."

The phone went dead before Gary could reply. He slammed the phone down and yelled, "Brother! This isn't my day, all these dippy broads, ah what the hell, I'll have ham and cheese on rye, hold the mayo!"

Kate re-dialed the phone and a slightly Jewish accented voice said, "Shalom, Rabbi Krupinsky."

"Kate Hirsch, Rabbi. He's dead."

"Well, we knew that would happen sooner or later. What would you have me do?"

"He's on his way to the city morgue. I am on my way to 2302 Lovett, third floor, room 305 to see a Detective Gary Peluso and answer questions. It's the southwest homicide station."

"How convenient. I'm just around the corner. I'll meet you there and then we'll go to the morgue. I'll have a hearse on the way. Bring Sam's Tallith. The one without pockets. We'll bury him tonight and then you will start Shivah That's how he and society want Jews to be buried, quick. What about Donny?"

"I'll call him. If he wants to come, he'll come. He can stand over the fresh grave and shed his tears if he has any to shed."

"You're his mother, Kate. How could you say that?"

"It's easy. I know my son better than anyone. I'll see you at the station…and, Rabbi."

"Yes?"

"Shalom."

The phone went dead. Kate dialed again, waited for four rings, hung up, and re-dialed. She waited for three rings and hung up. After the third time and two rings there was an answer.

"Yes, Mother. It is you, isn't it?"

"You have someone else using my code?"

"I wouldn't dare, Mother. You're the only one I allow to call me without any restraints whatsoever."

"How sweet of you, Donny. I have news for you."

"Go ahead, Mother."

"Your father, Sam, has been shot in the back twice and is dead."

"That doesn't surprise me, Mother, it goes with the business, and…it's bound to happen to us all, sooner or later. I noticed you stressed the word back and that, Mother, is the way it is done in this business."

"I can't answer you, Donny. You're impossible. I am burying your father tonight as soon as the police will turn him over to me."

"I can't make it but I will be there in the morning to take over the business."

"Very well. I know nothing about it."

"I do. I'll let you know when I'll arrive and, Mother, tell Mary Beth hello for me."

"I will not! Donny, why don't you leave Mary Beth alone and find a nice Jewish bitch?"

"Why, Mother, if I didn't know you married a Jew, I would suspect you're anti-Semitic."

"And my erstwhile, half–Christian son, I believe you are the personification of chutzpah. Walking, stalking, breathing chutzpah."

"Mother, are you inferring something?"

"I infer nothing, I tell you, you are my son. That means nothing to you but it gives to me a discretion God only gives to mothers and fathers. I, who bore you, now tell you from this moment on you are in danger…from me. I, your mother, find you offensive for you have fallen far from the tree and I must assume the responsibility for your fall from grace. Hear my words and remember them, for I mean what they say."

Donny Hirsch didn't know what to say. He was at a loss for words and for the first time in his life he felt fearful. The silence bespoke his fear and apprehension to Kate and she seized the opportunity by saying vengefully, "I will finish this call, Donny, by saying two things; keep your hands off Mary Beth; your father and I will be waiting."

*   *   *   *

Kate slipped the phone into its cradle and sat down crying. Crying not so much for Sam, but for her son. Sam warned her of what was going to happen eventually to him, so the shock was not as great as it might have been had he not. Kate lived inwardly with what Sam did but her outward life was divorced from the reality and entanglements Sam faced from day to day.

Kate had seen her son evolve into the despicable person he was since his junior year in high school. She often complained, "Sam, it's as if someone injected Donny with the devil's evil intent. In one day he changed."

"That's not possible, Kate."

"It is. Are you trying to tell me you haven't seen the change in him?"

"I've seen it. There's a difference. You're right…as usual…about such matters. He seems cold and detached. Let's work on him. I'll bet all kids go through this."

Donny never changed and Kate was glad the day he left for Chicago, and she never looked forward to his returning home.

*   *   *   *

As she sat thinking about Donny, Mary Beth walked over and, placing her hand on Kate's shoulder, felt her shudder.

"Kate, are you all right?"

Kate reached up, took Mary Beth's hand in hers and squeezed it. "I'll be all right, Mary Beth. I'm upset. This thing about Sam. It's so convoluted. Donny…Mary Beth, he'll be coming to Kansas City. Please stay away from him, he is nothing but trouble."

"Why, I never did *anything* with Donny!"

"I know that, but he won't stop until he compromises you. Do you understand what I am saying?"

"Yes, I do. The way he looks at me. The things he says, no…the way he says things. He frightens me."

"And me. Stay close to me at all times. We will be in our seven days of seclusion starting tomorrow. Have there been any calls?"

"No, but Mr. Hirsch left this envelope with me the other day to give to you in the event anything happened to him. He seemed to know…somehow he…oh Kate, I'm so sorry."

Mary Beth handed the envelope to Kate and hanging her head began to cry. Kate immediately responded, "Mary Beth, don't. Not yet, buck up, the hardest days are ahead. Save your tears. Here, let me read the letter out loud."

"Dear Kate,

I have given this letter to Mary Beth for safekeeping. All of my affairs, as you know, are arranged to meet any contingency. We are both prepared for what is going to happen. Be strong and fear not. I have been from time to time in contact with Judge Nicholas Hickman of Omaha. I have spoken of him to you on several occasions. I have recently been in contact with him. In the event anything happens to me, please advise the Judge immediately. This is imperative. Do not delay."

Lovingly, my Dearest Kate, until we meet again,

Sam"

Kate kissed the letter and placed it on the table. She moved with a sense of urgency and picking up the phone dialed long distance.

"AT&T Long distance. How can I help you?"

"I need the telephone number for the courthouse in Omaha, Nebraska."

"One moment, please."

"Omaha directory assistance."

"The courthouse, please."

"One moment, please."

There was a pause and then a recording. "The number is area code 402-551-5005. I repeat area code…" Kate pushed down on the button, disconnecting the operator and dialed the number.

"County courthouse. What extension, please?"

"Judge Nicholas Hickman's office, please."

"The Judge has resigned and is now with the firm of Harding, Kimball, and Roberts. The number is area code 402-551-5290. Did you get that?"

"Yes, thank you."

Kate dialed and as the phone rang, Manning dropped a box of books on the floor and reaching over, retrieved it from between two boxes. Somewhat out of breath she said, "Judge, I mean, Nicholas Hickman's office. Marsha Manning speaking."

"Ms. Manning, this is Mrs. Kate Shields Hirsch in Kansas City. My husband, Sam Hirsch, was an acquaintance of Judge Hickman. My husband was murdered this afternoon and…he…" Kate's voice cracked.

"I am so sorry, Mrs. Hirsch. Please take all the time you need."

"Yes, why yes, thank you. Sam left instructions for me to notify Judge Hickman immediately in the event anything untoward happened to him and…"

Kate's voice cracked again and Manning interjected, "The Judge is on a plane to Kansas City this very moment. I will notify him immediately, Mrs. Hirsch. He will be staying at the Ritz Carlton, room 514, and I will have him contact you."

"Thank you, uh, Ms. Manning. My number is 417-334-6940. Thank you again. Goodbye."

Hurriedly pushing the boxes and papers stacked on her desk to one side, Manning dialed the phone. "John Kincaid's office, Helen Hartwell speaking."

"Helen, it's Manning, again. The Judge is on flight 202 to K. C., seat five, first class. He just took off ten minutes ago. Can you patch me in, it's an emergency?"

"You bet, Manning. Let me go to the board. Hang on."

There was a pause as Helen walked to the screen that gave her the information on every flight arriving or departing Omaha. Picking up the phone she told Manning, "They'll be delayed in a holding pattern for about fifteen minutes before final approach. There's a phone on board if the Judge needs it. Any credit card works but if he doesn't have one, I'll tell the pilot to throw the switch for him. Here we go."

Helen picked up a microphone and pushed a button on the large desk at which she now sat marked Control Tower and heard, "Tower."

"John, it's Helen."

"Roger, Helen, long time no hear, what's up and what can I do for you?"

"Emergency, John. Contact pilot, flight 202 to K.C., patch me in."

"Roger. Continental flight 202, this is Omaha Tower. Come back. This is an emergency."

"Omaha Tower, flight 202, Captain Webster."

"Go ahead, Helen."

"Captain, this is Helen at John Kincaid's office. You have Judge Nicholas Hickman on board, seat five, first class. Convey message, Sam Hirsch murdered this afternoon. Contact wife at home. Give the Captain the number, Manning."

"417-334-6940 and, Captain, the Judge never has any money or credit cards and can't find them if he does."

"Helen here, did you read all of that?"

"No problem. Over, out."

"That should do it, Manning. Like I told you, he's covered the whole time he's there. Just like you wanted."

"Thanks, Helen. Lunch one day. Lots to tell, we've moved."

"I know."

"How the hell could you know? Why, we're just doing it."

"It's a small world, Manning, a very small world...specially when you are as big as Judge Hickman. Plus, knowing stuff is my business. See ya'."

Manning shook her head and began to laugh as she hung up.

Captain Webster looked at his copilot and as he removed his headset remarked, "Murder. That's a good reason to call. Take over."

The copilot gave a thumbs up and the captain walked to Hick's seat and looking down at him asked, "Are you Judge Hickman?"

"I am."

"Your Honor, could you give me some identification?"

Hick fumbled around in his pockets, then remembered he had put his wallet in the throat of his left boot. He pulled it out and handed the pilot his driver's licence.

"Thank you, Your Honor. Omaha Tower just contacted us and there is a message for you. I have written it on this paper. Please feel free to use the phone by the cockpit door. It's ready to go...no charge."

"Thank you, Captain. I never carry money and always have trouble finding the right credit card."

"So they say, Your Honor."

"Yes, of course, Manning would say that, she's my secretary."

"Manning. Yup, that was the name," grinning the Captain shook Hick's hand, turned, and walked away.

Hick put on his glasses and read., "Sam Hirsch, murdered this afternoon, contact wife at 417-334-6940."

Hick undid his seatbelt and walked to the phone. He dialed and waited for the myriad air to ground connections to be completed, then heard a voice say, "Kate Hirsch."

"Mrs. Hirsch, this is Judge Nicholas Hickman, I am on a plane to Kansas City. I have been informed about Sam, please accept my sincere regrets. Can I help in any way?"

"Yes, Your Honor, I know about your meeting in the morning. Sam told me. I must talk to you. I intended to bury Sam at sundown but the coroner delayed us. He will not release the body until after midnight. I, therefore, plan to bury Sam at sunrise. I will then meet you at eight o'clock in the morning at a restaurant called Plaza De Copia on the Plaza. It is ours. There will be a closed notice on the door but walk in, the door will be open, and I will be waiting. Thank you."

The phone disconnected, taking Hick by surprise. He returned to his seat thinking, *"That was different! There seemed to be mixed emotions."*

The hostess interrupted his thoughts by saying, "Plenty of time, Your Honor, before we land, they're stacking us because of a thunderstorm. Drink?"

"No, thank you."

The plane landed thirty minutes late. Hick's thoughts were preoccupied with Kate Hirsch. He couldn't put his finger on what was bothering him. The plane landed and the stewardess touched his shoulder, breaking his concentration long enough that he went through the motions of leaving the plane and walked to the baggage area where he had to wait, lapsing back into his wondering. He thought, *"What really bothers me about the conversation with her was she just hung up. No thank you for calling or goodbyes. Or did we get disconnected? No, Your Honor, that's not it. She just didn't seem distressed enough for a woman who had just lost her husband. She wasn't sick he was murdered. She was too busi-nesslike about burying him and just as perfunctory about the burial in the morning, and meeting me. Maybe they didn't have a relationship? Maybe she is just plain tough."*

Suddenly Hick realized he was standing alone by the conveyor but his bag was at his feet. He looked about and saw a sky cap beckoning to him from the exit. Picking up his bag and walking to the sky cap, he handed him his claim check remarking, "Guess I was lost in my own thoughts."

"I noticed that, sir. This is your bag, isn't it?"

"I haven't really checked."

"It was the only one left on the conveyor, so I figured it was yours and put it by your side. Let's check the numbers and be certain."

"I must have been in outer space."

"They check, sir. Think nothing of it, people do it all the time. Become preoccupied, that is. It can set you up, even as big as you are, so be alert from here on out."

Hick reached in his pocket and took out the dollar bills Manning had given him, handing three to the sky cap.

"Not necessary, sir. Not really necessary, but thanks. Oh, were you to meet someone?"

"No! Why?" Hick's words stung the atmosphere as if he were in his courtroom. He saw the effect they had on the young sky cap and embarrassedly said, "I apologize for the sharpness of my reply."

"Think nothing of it. I asked because some guy has been circling around. Watching you. He's gone now but I can tell he had his eye on you, and I would suspect even now."

Hick looked around and asked, "What's he look like?"

"Black hair, blue eyes, six foot, medium build, grey overcoat, black brief case, suntanned. Looks like any businessman."

"That's a pretty good description."

"I'm airport police, Judge."

Hick was taken back by the word 'Judge' but instantaneously put two and two together and asked, "It was Manning, wasn't it?"

"I don't know Manning, Your Honor, but Omaha Airport Authority police alerted us to cover you. Somebody else will pick you up when you leave here. I thought the guy I mentioned might be him but he just doesn't fit. He might be new or doesn't know what he's doing but that's not been my experience with the FBI"

"FBI?"

"FBI, Judge, you're important to your people."

"Sounds like my people have gone overboard."

"Now, Your Honor, it's nice to be worried about. Maybe they figured you don't get out of town enough and could use a little backup in the big city."

Hick smiled. "Omaha's no cow-town but I get the point, officer, I get the point."

"Good, I have a cab waiting. Follow me."

Hick picked up his bag and followed the officer through the large automatic glass doors.

They walked to a waiting cab and the officer opened the back door and instructed, "Just throw your bag in and follow it."

Hick did as he was told and the officer slammed the door; stuck his head in the open driver's window and looking at Hick said, "Meet Eddie, the cab driver. Also known as officer Mike Groton, Kansas City Police. He's for specials like yourself. He's yours until you leave Kansas City. Right, Eddie?"

"Anything you say, Sky cap."

"Your Honor, you can see we're all comedians, too. Eddie here will take you to the hotel and as I said, any place you want to go in the morning and during your stay and then bring you back to our safe-keeping. Good luck."

"Thanks, officer," Hick called out as the window rolled up. Turning his attention to the driver he added, "Ritz Carlton on the Plaza...officer."

"Yes, sir, Judge."

"You're well informed, too."

"Yes, sir. I won't try to kid you, you're under protective custody while you're here. I'm flexible and will accommodate you in any way. I will divulge nothing about your activities to anyone. This is a courtesy our city likes to extend to certain folks and especially the judiciary. There's a lot of kooks out there, Your Honor…heck, you know what I'm talking about."

"I'm afraid I do. Thanks, Officer Groton."

"Best call me Eddie, sir."

"I understand. Pick me up at eight-fifteen in the morning."

"Yes, sir."

Nothing more was said until Eddie pulled in under the marquee at the Ritz Carlton. He stopped, turned to Hick and with a smile and a quiet voice instructed, "Move forward and appear to fumble for money. We have been followed. I'll pick you up in the morning. Sit a minute until the doorman gets into position. He's a police officer. Your only exposure is to the front door and he'll cover you and I'll be right behind you with your bag. Leave it and when inside pretend that you forgot it."

The door to the cab opened and the doorman said, "Welcome to the Ritz Carlton, sir."

Hick did as he had been told and within moments he was in the lobby. He turned, and looking at the doorman said, "Sorry, I left my bag in the cab."

Just as the doorman turned Eddie walked in and handed the bag to Hick whispering, "We've got his license number and two of our unmarked cars are following him. He left. We'll nail him. I'll let you know who in the morning, or sooner if necessary."

Hick smiled and, handing Eddie the roll of bills he had in his hand, replied, "Thanks for the help. Dinner's on me."

"No time to argue, Your Honor." Eddie spun around, money in hand, and hurried out the door.

The doorman said, "Follow me, sir. We'll get you checked in."

As they passed the Bell Captain's desk the doorman instructed to a lone bellhop, "William. Take the gentleman's bag and follow us."

Walking up to the desk the doorman rang the bell and a young woman sprang through an office door calling out, "Welcome to the Ritz Carlton."

The doorman seemed irritated by the fact that she was not present at the desk and snapped, "This gentleman is pre-registered. Room 514. Keys, please."

Hick watched the reaction to the doorman's words. The young woman was visibly nervous and haltingly said, "The keys, yes the keys, they're right here. The room is ready."

At the word "ready" Hick was alerted. His mind cleared and he reached for the keys at the same moment the doorman reached out. Using his other hand Hick grabbed the doorman's wrist, and with a firm voice insisted, "Back off. I'll take the keys."

The doorman's hand and wrist went limp as he meekly replied, "Yes, sir."

Hick turned his attention to the young girl and countered, "Five-fourteen."

"Yes, sir. Have a good evening."

The doorman backed away and returned to the main entrance. William, the Bellhop, had moved to the bank of elevators and was holding one. Hick walked in and said, "Fifth floor."

The bellman pushed a button and as the elevator started to rise, Hick sprang forward and slammed his right fist against the stop button and circled the bellman's neck with his left arm. He then kicked the back of the bellman's knees, causing him to crumple to the floor and as he did, Hick grabbed his right arm and began to twist. The bellman cried out, "Hold it, Your Honor, I'm one of the good guys, I'm a police officer!"

"I've had a lot of people telling me that ever since I got off the plane, but there's one problem," and Hick twisted his arm even more.

Now in real pain William cried out again, "What?!"

"No one has shown me their badge or I. D."

"Give me a chance and I will."

"I've been there before. Use your left hand."

William, now visibly in pain, reached into his bellhop tunic and pulled out his wallet, handing it to Hick.

Flicking it open Hick found a police badge pinned to the flap and a card identifying the bellhop as William Holly, Kansas City Police Department, Badge number 715. Hick dropped his arm and reached down to help. The officer was smiling as he said, "You're tougher than hell, Your Honor, I could feel it in your grip. Sorry no one bothered to show you I. D., it would have saved my arm."

"Hurt bad?"

"No, sir, but I'll never forget you."

Hick's eyes were penetrating as he looked into the young officer's and he summarized his feelings with, "Good!"

Hick reached over, pushed five and the elevator started its climb. When the door opened, Hick stepped out with his bag and looking at the officer said, "Thanks. I'll take it from here."

The young man shrugged his shoulders, nodded his head and as the doors shut said, "Good night, Your Honor, and I don't think I'll be worrying about you."

Hick smiled, turned and walked down the hall to room 514. There was light streaming out from under the door. He put his ear to the door and heard nothing, placed the key in the lock and slowly turned it. When he heard the tumbler click he kicked the door open with his foot and slid sideways into the room. Looking around he saw nothing out of order. The room was large with a bed and sitting area. He looked in the bathroom and found it well appointed.

Closing the door he remarked, "My entrance was missing the most important ingredient...a gun," and while laughing at himself heard the phone ring and picking it up snapped, "514."

"Mr. Hickman, this is Tori calling from the Cloud Room Restaurant. We have a table ready for you at your convenience. A delightful bottle of our finest Chablis is on its way to your room. A gesture, sir, from Marsha Manning."

"Thank you, Tori, but I am going to shower, enjoy the wine, and wait about forty-five minutes for you to send down the dinner Miss Manning ordered for me. I have to rise early in the morning but tomorrow night might be another matter."

"Certainly, Mr. Hickman. How did you know about the meal?"

"I know Manning, Tori, I know her very well."

There was a snicker and then, "I understand and I hope to meet you tomorrow night. Please call and let me know what time you would like dinner if you decide in our favor."

"Thank you."

Hick hung up the phone, removed his coat, and rummaged through its pockets, finding a carefully folded piece of paper on which was written, "Open Me." Hick opened the paper, knowing full well who it was from, and read,

"Dear Hick, Would expect when you find this you have arrived safe and sound in Kansas City. Hope my arrangements didn't upset you. Henry and I felt we should use the courtesies offered to the Judiciary when traveling from city to city.

Just in case you would want to call, our new office number is in the little black book in your right inside pocket. I would imagine we'll be here late this evening.

Rest well and have a safe return.

Love, Manning"

Hick reached for the little black book and found the new number and dialed, aware that if he didn't he'd hear about it.

"Law Offices, Marsha Manning speaking."

"Is that the way you're going to answer the phone?"

"What do you want, like, offices of some other guys and the most Honorable ex-judge Nicholas Hickman?"

"It needs to be improved around the edges, but for starters that will work."

"Sure. How'd the trip go? Did you get my message?"

"Just like you planned it. I see Mrs. Hirsch early in the morning and my backside has been watched every moment since stepping off the plane. I assume it will continue until I get back on the plane?"

"Good, and it will."

"Why did you do it, Manning?"

"Your Honor, we are beginning to mess with some pretty big fish."

"What's that mean?"

"That means methinks the fish already know what you're up to and they have the big bucks to shut you up."

"You think they would resort to that?"

"Hell, yes! Don't you?"

"Yup."

"Good, for once you understand…he understands, Henry. Henry's here with me. We're the last bastion, finishing up, and we are covering for one another."

"Bastion?"

"Wait a minute," Manning opened her dictionary and read, "Bastion: there's a lot of stuff, here…I like this best, 'Any well-fortified or defended position'. And we better be."

"Manning, you sound worried about all of this."

"Not really, Hick, we've been through worse and will again. But, I always feel we should go into these matters with our eyes wide open and backs against the wall."

"Who worries you the most?"

"Walter Givens."

"Why?"

"Money. Four-hundred million if you believe the last report, and I do. Plus…he takes what he wants, that's how he wound up with J. R.'s wife."

"You and Henry been researching?"

"No, not yet, no time. We just haven't told you everything. But we will...and Hick, you picked the right law firm. They are so excited about having you associated with them. Our offices are beautiful. They were all charming to Henry and I, couldn't do enough. The place looks like we've been here forever. Say hi to Henry."

"Hi, Henry."

"Hi, Judge. I agree with everything Manning has said."

"You better, Henry, she has her ways."

"Yes, sir, but I'm serious, these are nice folks; and wait until you see my office. Can you believe I have an office?"

"Yes, Henry, I believe it but there's one thing missing."

"What, Judge?"

"The L. L. D. on your door. Get to it, starting tomorrow."

Henry swallowed hard, "Yes, Judge, I will," he handed the phone back to Manning, turned and left the room.

Manning watched him leave and asked, "What did you say to him?"

"Why?"

"He left the room."

"I didn't say anything to hurt him, Manning. You tell him, the Judge is always right and you do what he says."

"Always right? Sure! Can I say something personal?"

"Certainly."

"I love you, Nicholas Hickman, and always will. Take good care of yourself and come home to us safe and sound."

"I love you, Manning. My life wouldn't be much without you at my side. Goodnight."

Hick hung up the phone for he knew emotions were swimming excitedly to the surface. The formality of their relationship, for this moment in time, had been put aside allowing their love to surface.

CHAPTER 7

▼

The seven men, Harold Batemen, Judge, Robert Wentzel, Police chief, Robert Conway, Newspaper Publisher, Clyde Taylor, children's store owner, Walter Givens, International Construction Co., Donald Remco, Physician, Tad Beasley, Automobile Dealer, gathered every three months or when they felt threatened. Originally they were all members of an investment club that met monthly. They never made money but their meeting was an excuse to get together to eat, drink, and—at first—allude to what really interested them most. Six years ago, after a golf outing, the other members of the club had left and the seven remaining were totally uninhibited from the alcohol they had started to consume at one o'clock on the first tee.

It was eleven o'clock and Walter Givens, wobbling to his feet, asked, "Anybody see anybody?"

Lifting his head off the table and slurring his words Robert Conway asked, "What in the hell does that mean, or have to do with? You'd think we're drunk or something?"

"No, you dumb shit, I want to know if anybody's around so I can say what I want to. Get it?"

"Sort of."

Pouring a drink he didn't need, Donald Remco yelled out, "Hell! I think anybody's that sober has gone home and that includes the help."

Still standing but weaving in a small circle, Givens slurred, "I feel good. Can everyone left hear me?"

There was a chorus of drunken, "hell yes's"; Givens belched and went on. "Good! Listen up. I'm sick and tired of this crap of working my ass off and not getting any. Now before you say anything, if you can, I'm goin' around the table. Tell me what you like best."

"Hold it! Walter, you get more ass than all of us put together. No, that's not right, I've been drinkin', let me see...you get more ass in one week than we all get put together in a year and that counts the nothing Harold gets. Right, Harold?"

Harold Batemen opened his eyes and retorted, "Overruled. What I get isn't related to the original whatever Givens did, Beasley. Continue, Givens."

"Fine, Harold, what's number one on your list...you do have one, Harold?"

"Sure, I like a new porn movie every night. Or at least pictures I haven't seen. You know, new stuff, every night. How about you, Walter?"

"Like I said, more ass at least twice a day. Fresh, eager stuff. A machine that doesn't want to turn off."

Robert Conway smiled as he suggested, "You ought to come with Clyde and me once in awhile. Those eleven, twelve-year-old girls have more moxie and movement than you'd think and they like it any *way*."

"Hell, I hear you two go for any age, any sex, Bob," Donald Remco said sarcastically.

"Hell, I hear you go for those sixteen and fifteen year olds."

"Beats the hell out of screwing the cradle."

There was silence at these words and Walter knew a sobering effect was setting in. He sat down and pleaded, "Now, now, gentlemen, we all have our idiosyncrasies or whatever; let's not be stickin' it to one another or judgin', it's all in fun. I think we can help each other in a lot of different ways. Let's meet in three weeks. Screw this investment club. We need to see to it we get what we need to get. All in favor say 'aye'!"

There were seven ayes and it was that night the evil began.

Walter Givens called each of the other six the next day and when sober they were even more eager to get together and explore what they could do to support their lust…as a group.

Walter owned a modest Inn north of the city on the river. He held nefarious personal and business meetings there to avoid detection. Customers at the Inn's restaurant were few and far between so the tenant welcomed the opportunity to accommodate the group every three weeks.

For six years, with each others cooperation, they had increased their perversions to a point of total satisfaction and had developed a false sense of protection from exposure in the community.

Regardless of their perversion they liked to share their stories of conquest. Except Harold. On several occasions he attempted to express the sexual gratification he felt by reading and watching pornography. The others were dismayed but not surprised that was all he wanted. Realizing they were put off by his stories, Harold stopped sharing his feelings after Tad Beasley asked, "You don't even play with yourself, Harold?"

Nothing was ever said again. They knew they needed the Judge just in case and they were right. The Police Chief, Publisher and Judge were invaluable when it came to impeding inquiries from reporters eager for a story, young policemen sensitive to what they were hearing on the streets, and from the Count Attorney's office.

Then something went wrong. Out of smugness and a false sense of superiority, they overreached the system. Walter Givens met J. R. Rollin's wife at a social function and the attraction was mutual. He for the unrelenting sex and she for the position and money he enjoyed and a hidden illness she didn't realize she had or was willing to face. Their affair was daily.

Even a week together on "vacation" for a business meeting and a National Womans meeting was not uncommon. The affair was flagrant, but their spouses had no reason to doubt and as they would later recount, "We were naive."

Walter's wife passed away and, trying to protect his name in the community, he had schemed to have J. R. Rollins murdered but the group prevailed upon him to frame J. R. Rollins for murder. J. R.'s wife filed against him for divorce, not coordinating her actions with Givens, and J. R. 's attorney insisted he respond by cross-filing, which he did. The matter had been in the lawyer's hands for months, during which time J. R. had lost the affection and love of his two sons since they were living with their mother and subject to her constant maligning of their father in her attempt to preserve her own persona and not disclose the true nature of her relationship with Walter Givens.

Harold Batemen was upset and uneasy about what had happened in Judge Hickman's office and the failed attempt to have J. R. indicted for murder. Now, at the end of the day, as he recapped and sat worrying he saw Jason January, who he despised more than Hick, in charge of the case and Hick resigning his Judgeship and instantaneously joining the firm of Harding, Kimball, and Roberts. He was informed about Hick's moving after five and the fact that he was on his way to Kansas City to see Mrs. Hirsch in the morning.

He was the last to arrive at the Inn because time slipped away from him as he sat reflecting on the results of the day. Harold walked to the table and all were seated and their eyes followed him for Walter had pre-warned them with, "Harold's in a twit".

Harold's teeth were set, his jaw muscles twitching, and his eyes were ablaze with anger as he hissed through his teeth, "We have to do something. Hickman is moving at a pace we will not be able to counter unless we move now. He must be wasted before he leaves Kansas City."

Walter Givens was taken aback by what he saw and heard. Harold had dropped his meek, self-effacing appearance and emanated the raw fear and willingness to fight that any cornered animal demonstrates. He asked, "Harold, what evidence do you have to warrant this concern?"

"I don't need evidence. I have experience. I have a gut feeling. I understand men like Hickman and January. They don't like me and they don't like you and we are giving them cause to come after us, which they will. I have seen and felt this determination in their kind all of my life. They are the modern day moral equivalent of crusaders and because of our lusts, different from theirs, they consider us individually an anti-Christ and collectively depraved."

No one said a word. Some looks of concern came over several faces and Robert Conway, publisher, covered his mouth and whispered to Paul Wentzel, police chief, "Is he nuts?"

"No, he's right, in a convoluted way."

Harold heard their whispering and exploded, "You consider yourselves normal?"

Now Walter Givens exploded, "Harold, you may be a judge, but you're no psychiatrist!"

"Just answer my question. If not out loud, then to yourself and then if you want to protect your ass and our asses collectively, you'll see to it Hickman as well as Rollins are eliminated."

"Rollins? I thought the idea was to get him for attempted murder. To put him away," Walter asked condescendingly.

The veins on the side of Harold's neck and face were distended and his eyes ablaze as he lurched forward over the table and yelled, "Dead men don't tell tales. Damn it! Can't you understand that? They're coming after us. I know it, and you'll be sorry if you don't take my advice."

Walter regained his composure, stood and advised Harold, "Sit down, Harold, before you blow a blood vessel. You've all heard Harold's opinion, do I hear a motion?"

Harold jumped to his feet demanding, "I move we arrange a hit on Hickman and Rollins tonight."

Robert Conway called out, "I amend the motion to strike out Rollins."

"Question," Paul Wentzel called out. "Why not Rollins?"

"Because he is going to be indicted in the morning. If he would suddenly die this could raise questions in the District Attorney's office and elsewhere."

"Any further discussion?" Walter asked.

There was none. Harold said nothing, for what he really wanted was to see Nicholas Hickman disposed of, for he didn't care two hoots about Rollins.

"The original motion as amended would be to hit Nicholas Hickman. Those in favor signify by raising your hand."

All hands rose and a large smile broke out on Harold's face. Paul Wentzel looked at his watch, it was five past six. He reached for the phone sitting on the table next to him and dialed as the others watched and listened while he said, "Willy, top brass. A. Nicholas Hickman, Judge. B. As soon as possible. C. Tonight and tomorrow, your town. Ritz Carlton," Paul Wentzel hung up the phone and looked about the table continuing, "It will be done. I move we adjourn until it happens and then meet again to plan our next move."

"We haven't eaten yet," Harold complained.

Tad Beasley stood and as he walked past Harold, on his way out of the room, leaned over, and suggested, "Why don't you go home and eat while you look at your dirty pictures? Your Honor."

Harold jumped to his feet and as he spun around his fist smashed into Tad Beasley's face, knocking him into the wall and Tad's limp, unconscious body slid down the wall onto the floor.

The other men stood motionless and Paul Wentzel thought to himself, *"We're done for. Conspiracies die by the hand from within."*

$$* \qquad * \qquad * \qquad *$$

Hick slept well. However, getting to sleep took awhile because he went over and over in his mind how much Manning meant to him. He argued as to why he couldn't feel what he knew he had to feel for a woman. Something was missing in his life.

Plenty was missing but *one* thing, just *one,* was blocking his under-standing. He promised himself he'd work to find what was missing.

When the wake-up call came he had been up for an hour. He felt rested and enjoyed the warmth and leisure of a long shower. Hick dressed and walked down the corridor to the hospitality room where he found coffee, rolls, and juice. He picked up a paper and returned to his room to watch the news and weather. At seven-thirty the phone rang. Hick answered, "Good morning."

"Good morning, Your Honor. Your driver, Eddie, is waiting."

"He's early. I'll be right down."

Hick put on his coat and was in the lobby in a matter of minutes. Seeing the doorman he walked up to greet him with "Sorry about last night…at the desk."

"No problem, sir, William explained our failure to establish who we are."

"Have a good day, officer."

The doorman smiling, winked, looked around and in a low voice replied, "Eddie, your driver, is in the coffee shop. He's early."

"So it seems. He's my driver?"

"Things change, Your Honor, usually for the best."

Hick shrugged his shoulders and followed the pointed finger the doorman had extended in the direction of the coffee shop. He walked to the door and saw Eddie sitting at a corner table with another man who had his back to Hick. The room was almost empty and as Hick started toward the table a young woman approached and he waved her off. Standing at the table Hick looked down at Eddie and then moved his eyes to the stranger. He had black hair, blue eyes and it was the sun-tan that caused Hick to realize he was the man at the airport. Hick spoke, "Morning, Eddie. You're early?"

Eddie had started to his feet saying, "Good morning, sir. I'm early for a reason. Coffee?"

"Fine."

Eddie turned a cup over and filling it slid it to Hick, then sat down saying, "I'd like to introduce you to this person but I can't. There's a schedule to keep and he has something to tell you first."

Eddie looked at the handsome young man and instructed, "Go ahead."

"What I have to say won't take long, Your Honor."

"You know who I am?"

"I'm paid to know."

The obvious tension between Eddie and the stranger alerted Hick and he replied, "Paid to what?"

"Know who you are."

Looking at the young man with disdain, Eddie interrupted, "All right, all right, cut to the chase, don't dance around the point. You know the agreement." Eddie abruptly turned to Hick and dropping his eyes continued, "Your Honor, this nameless scum," at the word "scum" the young man started to his feet and Eddie's hand slapped the table, rattling the coffee cups and saucers, startling the young man and Hick. Eddie lowered his voice and continued, "Sit down, scum, and if you don't think you want to, better check where my right hand is."

When Eddie sat down at the table, upon greeting Hick, he had slid his hand across the holster on his belt pulling the .38 out and was now pointing it at the young man.

A waitress walked up to the table and asked, "Would you gentlemen like to order?"

"Not now," Eddie snapped, "maybe later."

The girl felt the tension in Eddie's voice and immediately turned and walked away.

Eddie continued, "Spit it out, scum, now!"

The young man had dropped back in the chair and he countered, "Okay, okay, take it easy. Put the piece away."

"You watch too many movies, it's a .38; get on with it."

"Okay, Your Honor, I'm hired to separate people from this world for a price."

"He means a hit man. He has to say it that way or he knows I'd run him in so's to clean up the streets."

"You want me to go on?"

"You better have at it."

Hick spoke up, "Who and why does someone want to separate me?"

"You're perceptive. I'm here, for we were contacted to assist you into the next world by some prominent community leaders in Omaha. However, there's one problem with them. Their money's good, but they're deviants. The worst kind, we won't do business with them. Not all of them exploit children...sexually...but some of them do and those scum have tainted the rest. Am I understood?"

"Perfectly," Hick answered shaking his head in disbelief, "but tell me, I just don't understand."

"Well, Your Honor, I understand. I'm an educated man. I'm an attorney but I do what I like best and I'm good at it. My firm knows scum," the young man stopped and looked at Eddie as he repeated, "real scum. There's plenty to do in this world but hurting children in any way is against our code of honor."

Eddie spoke up, "That's it, Your Honor, *you* heard it. Code of honor, my foot, what a joke. He won't tell you who hired him and he was hired but he was called off by his boss when they found out about the lust for children some of these bozos share."

There was a wonderment in what Hick had heard and he said, "Just one minute, Eddie," then turning to the young man, enjoined, "Young man, I feel sorry for you."

"Don't! I like what I do and as I said, I'm damn good at it."

The young man stood, smiled, threw five dollars on the table and said, "It's for the coffee, Eddie. See ya' around."

Hick and Eddie sat and watched him as he walked away and then slip the waitress another bill and walk out of the restaurant.

"Sorry about that—him—Your Honor. My captain figured you'd probably believe it more if you heard it from the horse's mouth and in the scheme of things, that guy's a horse for the mob."

"Is he really a lawyer?"

"Beats me. If I knew much about him he wouldn't be walking around. I think they rotate these guys from one place to another. It makes it harder for us to put a finger on them. He was contacted last night around six. He might have been on his way out of town and you can bet he is now. Let's go, Your Honor, or you'll be late."

The two men walked out a side door and Eddie walked toward a black Lincoln and as he opened the rear door, Hick asked, "Moving up in the world, Eddie. A Lincoln?"

"The Captain figured we'd best change our MO from cabbies to limo drivers. Personally, I think it's all a bunch of baloney but that's the way they want to run it. We have both and I'll admit I like the Lincoln better. You should sit in the back, sir, it makes it all look more real."

"You know where we're going?"

"Yes, sir. Plaza De Copia."

"Did I tell you that last night?"

"I don't remember, but I know."

"Let's go."

The Lincoln pulled up in front of the restaurant and Eddie parked in a no parking zone. Both men exited the car and Eddie slipped a card in the front window that read, "Police".

Hick took note and said, "That sort of gives away something. Doesn't it?"

"Maybe, but we won't get a ticket or be towed away."

They walked to the massive hand-carved doors of the restaurant. Each had a large black wreath attached. A small note taped by the door handle read, "Closed until further notice."

One door was open, as Mrs. Hirsch said it would be. Hick opened the door and Eddie followed. The restaurant was well lit and appeared ready for the evening dinner crowd.

Background music was softly playing and a delicious aroma caught both men's attention. Hick looked around the room but saw no one and then heard, "Right this way, Judge Hickman."

Hick proceeded toward the voice and as he walked by the piano saw a beautiful woman sitting behind it. Signaling for Eddie to stay where he was he proceeded toward the woman saying, "I didn't see you…Mrs. Hirsch?"

"Yes, Judge Hickman. I am Katherine Shields Hirsch, please call me Kate. And you?"

"Why, ah, Kate, I'm Nicholas Hickman. I prefer Hick."

"Rather informal for a man of your stature."

"I'm not a judge any longer. As of yesterday."

"So I understand."

"News travels fast. The young man with me is a police officer. He's watching over me."

"I know," Kate said matter-of-factly, as a furtive smile quickly developed and she added, "and a good morning to you, Officer Groton."

Hick's face showed the surprise he felt at Kate knowing Groton's name. Kate took note of Hick's surprise by continuing, "So that it doesn't cause you any wonderment, Hick, it's our business to know such things about each other. Sam taught us well."

"I can see that; and about Sam, Kate, I'm sorry, very sorry."

"I know. Sam always spoke very highly of you and the way you treated his father. He always told me when he had talked to you. He enjoyed the candor of your conversations. That is why I wanted to talk to you before your meeting. Before I start about that there is a wake, a Jewish wake, if there is such a thing, for Sam starting at six this evening, here at the restaurant. I would be pleased if you would attend. I would have you meet our son, Donny, " Kate paused, for she saw the harsh look that had come over Hick's face, "not to worry, Hick, I know he saw to Sam's death. Sam was expecting it. These things have a way and a life of their own."

Sam was taken aback by her casual explanation devoid of any emotion, and a harsh, "What's that mean?" slipped out of his mouth.

"It means be persistent, walk softly, and carry a big stick."

As Hick looked at Kate Hirsch he saw a demurely beautiful woman in complete control of herself. He took note that her hands were folded calmly in her lap and never moved. Her body movement was minimal, her facial expression an incomplete smile, feline-like; but her eyes, the pupil of her eyes were strikingly black and as he studied her eyes he saw the telling sign of the mystery of this woman. The irises of her eyes were also black. There was a demarcation between the pupil and the iris so that the size of the pupil appeared normal, yet on closer examination the black iris explained the reason why she captured attention. The cold blackness of her eyes was the curtain, an impenetrable curtain to who she really was or what she may be thinking. Outwardly she was warm, but was this really her?

Kate was watching Hick, and her smile lengthened as she asked, "What do *you* find?"

"About what?"

"Me. You're studying me. What do you find?"

"I don't."

"Ah, you've discovered my eyes."

"How did you know?"

"Sam always told me that if people wondered about me and then studied me, my eyes, my black eyes, would confuse them. He said they were a wall in front of the real me. What do *you* think?"

Before Hick could think he answered, "Does it really matter?"

Kate was taken aback. Moving her hands and shifting slightly in her chair she regained her composure and answered, "Your point is well taken. Some other time, some other place."

"What?"

"We'll talk again."

Hick looked at her eyes again and once more there was no meaningful sense of the moment in them. They were just black.

Kate, sensing his dilemma, interjected, "About your meeting. I know little about the two men or what they represent but Sam asked me to be certain that after you see them you meet with me and I'll divulge information to you that will have more meaning after the meeting than it would now. We can talk at the wake. Now how about a nice breakfast?"

"For three?"

"Your officer friend is certainly included."

"Good. Even though I ate earlier, suddenly I'm famished."

There was small talk while they ate and for a few minutes after they finished. Kate seemingly dismissed them with an abrupt, "I would imagine you must be on your way," and without another word they left.

Hick climbed in the back of the car and as they pulled away from the restaurant he asked, "You know where I'm going?"

"No, sir."

"Stoddard Arms on Wornal Road."

"Now I know where you're going…Waterford and Wentworth who is also known as Brannigan."

"How do you know about them? Judge Waterford and Col. Brannigan."

"Big, long story, Judge. I don't think it has anything to do with what you are seeing them about, and then, again, I may be dead wrong. Most likely I am. Those two are special."

"Officer Groton, what's your rank?"

"Detective, Homicide."

"They assigned a detective to me, a homicide detective?"

"You're important Judge, very important. We don't want you to get hurt while you're in our city, or anyplace for that matter. I was assigned to you because I'm familiar with the scum like that hit man we talked to earlier."

"What about Kate Hirsch. Do you know anything about her?"

"'Does anybody?' is an immediate answer, Judge, but to answer your question I never have known anything about her and still don't," and thought to himself, *"But what I know about her husband I'll keep to myself…for now."*

Hick was thinking to himself, *"I'll bet he knows plenty about Sam,"* and then replied, "I agree. I'm going to call you Detective."

"Yes, sir."

"Detective, what did *you* make of her?"

"Not much. She didn't want us to know anything. She reminds me of a character in a comic strip, Steve Canyon. The character was an oriental woman. Long silk gown, black hair, beautiful but mysterious. She had complete control."

"Of what?"

"Whatever she was a part of. Everybody."

"Was she honest?"

"Which one?"

"Both."

"Straight as an arrow. Both have breeding, are educated, and prepared to face anything, anytime."

"I get the feeling, Detective, Mrs. Hirsch is hiding something."

"Judge, I'd bet she is. She's hiding one hell of a lot of things and I have the impression she lets things out as she wants to and when she wants to. Like tonight."

The car came to a stop at the entrance of the Stoddard Arms. Detective Groton opened his door, stepped out and opening the door for Hick remarked, "We're early by twenty minutes. They're on the 5th floor."

"What number?"

"Judge, they are the fifth floor. The whole floor."

Hick smiled and as he stepped out noted the doorman was watching him intently. He whispered, "I'll walk slowly and kill a little time."

"Whatever you say, Judge."

The doorman stepped in front of Hick as he started to stand up and blocking the way asked, "Your name, sir?"

"Thurmond, to see Waterford and Wentworth."

"Yes. If you'll wait here I'll see if the Judge and the Colonel are expecting you."

As he brought himself to his full height Hick purposely brushed up against the doorman to check for a weapon and snapped, "Hold it! What's your name, Mr. Doorman?"

Not anticipating Hick's height and bulk the doorman stepped back with his head held back and holding onto the brim of his hat while looking up meekly replied, "Baldwin, sir!"

"Well, Baldwin, I'm early and you know they don't like that anymore than they like a person to be late."

"You know them, sir. If you're early you wait; if you're late you leave early. They're a pair to draw to, sir, but as you know they are nice men."

"A dichotomy, Baldwin, they're a dichotomy."

"Whatever, sir. What time is your appointment?"

Hick looked at his watch and replied, "Five minutes to go."

"We'll wait four. Step right in and have a seat."

Baldwin held the door open and, knowing he wasn't armed, Hick walked inside while asking, "I'm a street person. I noticed the scar across your face, tell me about it."

*   *   *   *

Detective Groton was all ears and as the two walked in the building he held back to pull out his cellular phone and dialed while muttering, "This Judge is something else. A street person? Yeah, right, okay. it's Detective Groton, give me the Captain."

"Captain Thurmond."

"Captain, it's Groton. The Judge has been delivered to Wornal Road. He's going to a wake later for Sam at the request of Kate Hirsch. She's quite a broad."

"What's that mean?"

"She doesn't seem too upset about Sam."

"Maybe, just maybe, it's a front."

"Could be."

"What about the Judge?"

"He hasn't said anything to me about his meeting with the daring duo."

"Watch it, Detective. The Judge and the Colonel are men of distinction. Men of history. Men who gave their all."

"Tell me, Captain, if you feel this way, why are we always leery about what these two are up to?"

"Like I said, Detective, history. Stay with the Judge and keep your eyes and ears open. Report back again after the meeting or whenever you can."

"Yes, sir."

*   *   *   *

Hick didn't take a seat. He stood in front of the elevator door waiting and again asked Baldwin, "What about the scar? Get it from the street?"

"Nope, Korea, many years ago. I was attached to a Turkish commando unit. The Turks were dedicated to putting the fear of God in the slant eyes. They could lop off a head with a garrotte with one snap of the wrists. They really put the fear of tomorrow in the gooks when they would cut off their genitals and cram 'em in their mouths. That was some kind of an oriental no-no."

"What about the scar?"

"Oh, yeah, I forgot. One of them was showing me how to spin around with a pig sticker and slash off a head. My mug was too close as he spun around. Took about a hundred stitches to close it. Bled like hell but I got a Purple Heart even though I didn't get it in combat. Not much fun but stature in the unit came with it, the scar, that is." Baldwin looked at his watch, laughed, and opened the elevator door with his key while beckoning for Hick to enter. "We'd best start up. Only one minute to go."

Nothing more was said. The elevator stopped and, opening the elevator door, Baldwin stepped into a magnificent alcove and reached for a large brass door knocker. Pulling it out he let it drop and a loud bang erupted. He turned to Hick and instructed, "Step out, Your Honor, and wait. It will take them about thirty seconds to answer the door. I'll leave you for now."

Hick looked at him with surprise as he replied, "How'd you know who I am?"

"Not me, Your Honor, them. They know everything that happens around here or is about to happen anywhere."

Hick stepped out into the alcove and as he turned to ask another question Baldwin shut the door and was gone.

As Claude Baldwin, Sergeant, USMC, retired, started down in the elevator he thought, *"Judge Nicholas T. Hickman, District Judge, Omaha. Wonder what he's up to?"*

The elevator went to the basement and Baldwin exited. He walked to a door marked "Building Maintenance", took a key from his pocket and opened the door. He quickly shut it and a voice called out, "Has he arrived, Sarge?"

"Yup, he's up there waiting for the door to open, go ahead and plug them in."

A young man sitting in front of a large console began throwing switches and, when he did, a bank of twelve cameras flickered on and began to monitor the fifth floor residence of Judge Samuel Wenter Waterford and Col. Felix Brannigan, also USMC retired. Reaching over he flicked a switch marked audio and they heard, "Who was it?"

"It's our guest, Judge Thurmond."

Judge Waterford swept through the doorway of the study into the foyer. Hick's size took him by surprise and he asked, "What's your real name?"

Hick, smiling as he extended his hand, answered, "I think you already know my name, Your Honor, and everything else there is to know about me."

"Maybe! What do you know about us?"

"Nothing."

Judge Waterford shook Hick's hand and asked, "Met Wentworth, haven't you?"

"Yes, when he answered the door."

"That's not his name, it's Brannigan, Felix, Colonel, USMC retired. We're both retired. I was a federal judge. He has a nom de plume for a bunch of reasons. Call him Felix, me Sam, and what do you go by?"

"Hick."

"Okay, Hick it is. Come on in the study, there's always a fire. Right, Felix?"

"Right, Sam. It's going even in the summer, we just turn up the air conditioner."

The three men walked in the study and Hick began to walk around the room and take note of the many displays on the walls. Military medals, citations, battle flags, insignia pictures, signed autographs of U. S. presidents and other dignitaries from around the world. Sam and Felix sat in front of the fire and Sam called out, "Come on, Hick, sit down. Don't be so nosey. We need to find out about you and what you want. We only have so much time."

Hick did as he was told and asked, "How much time do I have?"

Felix smiled and Sam snapped, "Contrary to what Sarge told you, he's the doorman; you have all the time you want. Need a drink, a beer, anything?"

"Scotch, straight up."

"I had you sit down too soon. Help yourself, right over there, on the table. Chivas, it's the best; in fact, make it three. Felix and I never turn down scotch, that's why we keep it around. You're one up, Hick. Any man who likes his scotch this early can't be all bad."

Hick poured three scotches and, after handing them to the two men, sat down. Judge Waterford spoke, "A toast to the United States Marine Corps."

The men drank and Sam Waterford spoke again, "What do you want with us, Hick?"

"Sam Hirsch said you have the means to help me."

"Sam's dead," Felix interrupted.

"I know. He knew it was coming at the hands of his son or by his son's will. I have had another case of two sons turning against their father and I have a host of prominent men in my city, deviant men, driven by their lust for sex. They're violating any and all codes of moral behavior. I have had my fill of it and I am going to defend an innocent man, a Doctor. Doctor J. R. Rollins from his sons and I want to impeach the others I mentioned, for they have broken the laws of moral conduct. Moralistically and legally they are felons."

Sam was studying Hick intently and let his words fade for effect and then said, "That's a mouth full. Garbled, but that's why you quit as a judge?"

"Exactly."

"Well, you are on to something, and others in your community share your feelings of guilt and failure."

"Guilt? Failure?"

"Hick, you've been a good judge, an upright citizen, but you and others have had your heads in the sand like an ostrich. Depravity of this magnitude takes time. Sodom and Gomorrah weren't built in a day. I'm just glad some of you have finally awoken and want to spit out the bad taste you have in your mouths. I'll tell you it's been going on for a long time."

"How do you know this? About my city?"

"It isn't only your city. It's all around us. But others have sought us out from Omaha. We are already involved."

"How?"

"Well, as in all matters, certain ingredients are necessary for the pot to boil. The first contact was from the clergy of your city. They are aware and cite as Christians and Jews that Jesus said on the day of judgement God would be more severe with cities rejecting the gospel than he had been with Sodom and Gomorrah. We had no contact, but they came to the federal court, here in Kansas City, seeking relief. It seems your police and judiciary are tainted. The court asked Felix and I to use our resources to validate what has been suggested. We're in the process now. I forgot, the second ingredient was Sam Hirsch, the Jewish mobster. Sam was a likeable person, one on one, but he dealt in crime daily. His ire was roused when he found out his son, his own flesh and blood, was willing to take him down or to have him taken down to promote the son's own well being. It stuck in his craw. I told him it was retribution. The third ingredient was Joe Hirsch, Sam's brother. Inventor, dreamer, a brilliant man who sees into the future. He can help you. Felix and I are what's left of a cadre of military and judicial crusaders, if you will."

Felix interrupted, "We are really knights of the scotch table. It's what keeps us going."

"That was supposed to be levity, Hick. Don't let him fool you. He's the one who will brief you when the time comes. Have you considered that you might be more effective in the judiciary?"

Hick was taken back by the question but retorted, "Not at this time."

"Then you haven't closed out that possibility, have you?"

"Can you help me? Will you help me?"

"He's losing patience with me, Felix. Still has the fire in his belly. How can we get him to Joe and bypass the watch dog downstairs?"

Felix walked to a desk, opened a drawer, pulled out a phone, dialed three numbers, and, before pushing the intercom button, asked, "Okay if Hick hears?"

"Why not."

"I thought you would agree. Yeah, Moffet, you've heard?"

"Yes, sir."

"What about Groton? Have you tagged him yet?"

"Before he got here. He's on line. We're recording."

"What's he up to?"

"Not much. They don't have much. He's talked to his Captain, that's about it."

"Good. Can you have the Captain call him and send him on a wild goose chase until the wake?"

"No problem."

"Do it. Tell Sarge to go out and tell him the Judge will be tied up for lunch and won't be free until about four. Wait about a half hour before the Captain calls...what's his name?"

"Detective Groton."

"Yeah, that's it. I forgot."

Hick listened intently but the look on his face told Sam that Hick wasn't putting it together, so he interjected, "What we are capable of doing is listening to anyone now or anytime in the past. We can also simulate someone else's voice and have what we simulate say anything we want. We are being monitored and recorded as the Detective has been recorded. We are going to simulate his Captain's voice and lead him astray. Questions?"

"Plenty. I don't understand."

"It's complex and based on a theory originated in the 1960s called Chaos Theory, which runs hand in hand with quantum physical theory. Are you familiar with either of these?"

"I've heard the word quantum, but have no knowledge of what it is really all about."

"We will clarify it eventually, but simply put, we can listen to anyone, anywhere, and hear what they have said or are saying. Scientists postulate that once there was chaos in the universe and then the universe and its systems became ordered by God's will. But systems, such as the weather, are not predictable over long or short periods because, somehow, systems can revert to a seeming state of chaos. It's a disordered state of otherwise uniform matter. That help?"

"Not really, but I'll work on it. Are you saying you can pull up Hitler's voice from the past?"

"Ah, ha, see, you're getting the idea. We can. Once a voice is identified, because it has specific characteristics, just like a fingerprint; there are no two alike, the voice can be recalled most of the time, but sometimes chaos rears its confused head."

"Who and what are behind all of this?"

"We will introduce you to him as soon as we send Detective Groton on his way. How about another scotch?"

"I don't think so. I'd better keep my mind clear for what's to come."

"Good thinking, but I don't have to, so pour me one. Felix, what about you?"

"No thanks, Sam. Remember: I have to drive."

Hick was taken by what he had heard yet confused by what Sam Hirsch had led him into. He blurted out, "The specific characteristics of a voice, like a fingerprint. What are they?"

Walking to Sam with a drink in his hand, Felix raised his eyebrows at the remark and handing the drink over exclaimed, "He's catching on!"

"Right, Felix, he is." Lifting his drink to Hick, Sam continued, "You have the right kind of mind for what you will hear, you're not a doubter; you start to look for answers and they will be supplied. I drink to you," Sam took a drink from the glass and swallowed after which he made a sound of satisfaction with the scotch, "good stuff. Felix, be on your way, I will see you later at Sam's wake."

"You think you should chance it, Sam?" Felix asked with a worried look on his face. "If I'm not up to it, I'll let you know."

Felix gestured for Hick to follow him and informed him, "We will not be going down by the usual means but by a special elevator to the parking garage; it's separate from the regular garage. Further underground. You're a big man. The elevator will be tight for us both, but most importantly, watch your head."

Hick walked to Sam, shook the outstretched hand that awaited his, and said, "Glad I had the pleasure of meeting you and I'll look forward to seeing you later."

"The feeling is mutual, Hick. I don't think you've learned a great deal from Felix and I but as the day goes on you'll learn a great deal. I know you're wondering, but Sam Hirsch didn't lead you wrong, we have what you need to clean up your town and set things straight. Goodbye for now."

Hick followed Felix through a door at the back of the study and down a small hallway. The wall at the end of the hall was blank but Felix reached out and rubbed a small worn area of paint and a door slid open, revealing a very small elevator.

"Step in, Hick, and I'll follow, but as I said: From here on out, watch your head."

The two men barely fit into the elevator but were soon standing in a small open area. Hick remarked, "Seems like we're down pretty deep. More than five floors."

"You're right, we're down about ten floors. This garage has a passage we take under the streets and Brush Creek on the Plaza. North about eight blocks, we'll come out in the lower level of one of the Plaza parking lots. It's a great way to get out of the apartment and not be detected."

"How is it that you have it at your disposal?"

"Hick, you have an inquisitive mind. Guess that's why you made such a good judge. The answer to why it's at our disposal and other questions I'm sure you have will all be self-evident before too much longer. Bits and pieces won't help, I'll just let it all fall into place on its own as we go along. Our apartment, garage, and this passageway were part of a mobster's layout in the thirties. He was part of the Tom Pender era. He liked to live in style and when Brush Creek was lined with fourteen feet of Pender Cement, they put this tunnel in. It confused the police for quite some time how the mobster could seemingly move in and out of his apartment without their being able to detect his movements."

Hick smiled as he replied, "Do the police know now?"

"I know they do."

"Strange, very strange, but it's your show."

"Now, now, Your Honor, don't be testy. I know this all seems peculiar, to say the least, but be patient and soon you'll know what it's all about."

The two men got in a small Fiat sitting next to a Cadillac limousine and Hick remarked, "Does that Cadillac fit down that small passage?"

"When it has to and that's not too often. It was the Judge's and sometimes he likes to go in style when he goes. He has a very bad heart, shouldn't drink, but I learned long ago not to argue with him as long as he takes his pills. His greatest line was when he retired permanently from the bench. He retired many times but was constantly called back for one reason or another…no other man like him, he stood at the dinner, after the accolades, looked around at the many, many dignitaries and said, 'Thank you. Now that I know everything no one wants to listen,' and he sat down to a stunned group. He was right that night and he still believes what he said and so do I. Let's go."

Felix started the car and soon they were moving down the long dark tunnel and eventually came to a cement wall. Felix pushed a button on the dashboard and the wall opened behind stacks of bailed cardboard boxes. Driving around the boxes they came out in the basement of a parking garage and made their way to the street level and exited. Nothing was said. The car moved rapidly down an expressway and within fifteen minutes they pulled up in back of a large brick building. Felix remarked, "This was once a Jewish Temple. They sold out and were going to use it for apartments for the retired but the deal fell through. A Rabbi, Sam's Rabbi, Rabbi Krupinsky bought it for one buck."

"To do what?"

"He lives here."

"Alone?"

"I'll let him tell *you* the rest of the story. You'll find it interesting."

Felix and Hick walked to a large metal door and Felix pounded on it with his fist.

"Doesn't he have a doorbell?"

"No, he doesn't like company."

Suddenly the metal door slid open and a large man in a black suit with a white shawl around his neck said, "Felix, I knew it had to be you and the Judge. Come on in."

Hick was taken aback by the fact that he was known and expected by this man. As he was ushered in by Felix, Hick smiled and shook his head slightly. The door was slammed shut with a bang and he found himself standing in a well lighted, large, empty room. The smile faded from his face and was replaced by a frown.

The Rabbi was watching him and asked, "Like my house? Don't answer that, I was just joshing you. Welcome to my operation. I'll cut to the quick for I know time is short for you. I go by the name Rabbi Meinhart Krupinsky. I am really Joe Hirsch, Sam's brother, and I'm not really a Rabbi. In fact, I'm a Christian, but it's a good cover. Our parents were half and half and I became the one half and Sam became the other as it relates to religion and good vs evil.

I didn't and don't know much about him and what he did for I am and have been too busy and consumed with my own projects to worry about his nefarious affairs over the years. There was a distinct difference between us, as if we really weren't brothers. You would ask then, how did he come to send you to the Judge and Felix? Simple. I told him if he ever saw straight or needed straight go for Thurmond, 5th floor, Stoddard Arms. Your presence is the first time Sam used this knowledge."

"May I interrupt as you go along?"

"Sure. I'll call you Hick, too. Okay?"

"Hick it is, but what does 'if he ever saw straight' mean?"

"Not crooked, right from wrong. I want you to realize Judge, I mean Hick, we have been listening to you since you got off the airplane last night."

"Why?"

"So you'll become a believer. You need help and we are in place to help you."

"In place?"

"Yes. In Omaha. One of our people is in place and laying the ground work."

"Ground work?"

"Gaining evidence against some of the very people you want to see behind bars and/or at least punished. We are working with the federal district attorney, for we are going to use federal law to indict these people."

"I'm not interested in federal indictments."

"You will be. You will be swept along the path you are presently on and right into the Y of convergence."

Felix saw the look of dismay associated with frustration sweep over Hick's face and he interrupted, "Hick, I mean, Your Honor, Joe has a habit of confusing people because he lives in a world we are not familiar with. The Y of convergence is his way of saying your case or cases will lead you to the case he is involved with in Omaha. There are connections of the parties involved in both instances that are not yet clear to you, but they are to us. When Joe is confusing I'll try to straighten it out. Like I said, he's in his *own* world. Further, Your Honor, I am not comfortable calling you Hick. I like, 'Your Honor', better. It gives you the respect you deserve and adds to the position you will have to assume."

The look of dismay prevailed on Hick's face and it caused Joe to snicker and then say, "He's doing it to you, Your Honor, and he's right about the Your Honor business, what I have a tendency to do. Confuse people. What he's saying in a half-ass way is they have plans for *you* in this whole matter. The matter being a sum of the parts."

"What plans?" Hick wanted to know.

Felix was glaring at Joe and then smiled saying, "Ah, what the hell. Joe is Joe. The Judge wanted to wait until *you* were fully informed by Joe as to his capabilities to assist *you* and then offer *you* a federal assignment as judge in the case we are building in Omaha."

"I've given up the judiciary, gone into private practice," Hick said with evident surprise and a hesitant determination.

"You'll want to rise to the occasion, Your Honor. Reserve your decision for now. Un-tether your mind and follow me," Joe said as he pointed to a door marked "No Trespassing," and walking through the door remarked, "That sign kills me. If anyone tried to walk through the door without me, they're dead. I have one of my gamma-D-detectors set up and the beam melts atoms."

"You'd kill someone for breaking and entering?" Hick asked.

"No one would ever know if it did happen, and that includes me, because there wouldn't be anything left to detect."

Felix intervened by saying, "It's the perfect death ray, quick and doesn't leave any residual traces, and no notice, no warnings."

Joe's eyes flashed as he added, "This is a very sensitive area, Your Honor, as you will see. I don't have time for second guessing anybody. We've been hurt in the past by trusting. Our adversaries are like the devil himself and you know it, Felix."

"Only kidding, Joe, only kidding and you know it," Felix snapped back.

"Right, Felix, but remember we're trying to win the Judge over. Don't make us out as heartless."

"Aren't you?"

"Felix, Felix...but come to think of it, you may be right, however, we are damn good at what we do. Follow me."

Joe opened a large door and they proceeded down a corridor to an elevator. Stepping inside, the elevator automatically started down. Joe spoke, "The elevator started down and will take us to the fifth lower level because it read my mind as to where I wanted to go, after it identified my person and understood that I still have clearance to be in the building. The fifth level," Joe stopped talking as the door of the elevator opened and the men stepped out into a large room with about ten people monitoring screens and evidently listening, for they all had earphones on, and then Joe continued, "is our listening post. These people are intercepting, recording, or surfing for specific voice patterns on demand from specific governmental agencies such as the CIA, Military Intelligence, and limited FBI pursuits. We limit FBI involvement, for they are not set up for clandestine operations to the extent they need to be so as to protect their source of information. Too many knowing lips can sink a ship. Our location is now known to all of sixteen people and now you, Your Honor, are one of seventeen."

"I'm honored, but why am I included?"

"We have stated our purpose when we informed you that Judge Waterford has recommended you for the federal judiciary position in Omaha. You're that important, so you must understand the nature of our abilities and their accuracy to allow such material to be placed in evidence."

"Now I see. Could this be construed to be tampering with a judge, make him partial?"

"Sounds like a Felix to me, Your Honor, a joke that is. All I can say is, this is our attempt to inform you as to our collection methods and if that could be construed to be tampering then take it up with Judge Waterford, for I am just a sleuth."

"And a damn good one," Felix called out.

"Follow me to my office, gentlemen."

The three men walked into a large, beautifully paneled room and Joe shut the door. There was a large desk and several tables with what was clearly monitoring equipment. One table had six phones sitting on it in different colors. A large projection screen had been dropped from the ceiling in front of a long oval conference table. Joe spoke, "Please be seated at the conference table, it will be more comfortable and we can see the screen better. If you press the button on top of the table in front of each chair, Your Honor, a server will rise and it contains any type of liquid refreshment you might desire, please feel free at anytime to avail yourself of it."

"There's even scotch, Your Honor," Felix said as he sat down.

"Even scotch," Joe quipped and added, "Oh, please excuse me while I tend to a few messages I see on my desk."

Hick watched as Joe walked to his desk and sat down. He was a large man in height and his girth was massive. His beard was long but meticulously trimmed. There were deep crow's feet on the side of his eyes and they extended back almost to his ears. A large scar starting at his left ear extended across his cheek to the mid point on his chin, not too dissimilar to Hick's. When he smiled the scar seemed to be an extension from the corner of his mouth. His hands were large and the liver spots were extensive across the back of each hand. He slipped the shawl from around his shoulders, letting it slide to the floor. He removed his yarmulke and dropped it on the top of the desk and threw his feet up over edge of the desk, revealing his black cowboy boots with white stitching. Picking up a stack of papers he quickly browsed through them and then dropped them back on the desk and walked to the bank of phones. He had sensed Hick's eyes watching him and, turning to Hick at the table, commented, "The different phone colors are for a specific agency throughout the facility. Blue FBI, green CIA, red Naval Intelligence—they're our biggest customer—and so on."

"I see you wear cowboy boots."

"Bad back."

"They help?"

"That's what Captain See thought."

The words, Captain See, brought Felix to his feet with his voice pleading, yet demanding, "For God's sake, Joe, forget it."

"Sorry, Colonel, very insensitive of me."

Hick felt and saw the hurt both men were experiencing, and asked, "Who was Captain See?"

Felix turned to face Hick and replied with a military resolve, "Captain See and his wife, Laura, were killed the day they were married. Both were a part of Naval Intelligence and singled out to be killed as a part of a tit-for-tat international vendetta. I can't go into detail but their death threw our lives into a turmoil. We became captives of the winds of chance. We lost our direction, our purpose; we resorted…"

Sensing Felix was losing his composure, Joe hurriedly interrupted with, "Their deaths cut deep. We can't forget. Most of the people involved with the Captain and Laura went their separate ways. Some of us, for one reason or another, have continued on. I'm sorry, Your Honor, it is hard to talk about, to think about. I'll give you the file before you leave."

"I didn't mean to be prying. I just want to get to know you and what you're all about."

"I understand, in fact, you're doing *very* well considering you've been thrown into a situation about which you know nothing." Joe paused, looked at Felix and asked, "you all right, Colonel?"

"I apologize. I'm fine."

"Good. I'll continue, Your Honor. I want to capture your attention and have you understand we can capture any spoken voice from any time and are in the process of identifying other sounds. Cannons from various wars have specific sounds depending on the size of the projectile explosive load. We must have a norm or a standard for comparison so we can isolate the specific characteristic of the sound wave which is transformed into a specific subatomic particle. I am ahead of myself…back to the basics. All physical phenomena should be explainable by some underlying unity. The big bang theory is one basis of our thinking relative to the creation of what we know. However, in some minds, such a theory would have the Universe expanding too rapidly to allow uniformity. Therefore, the chaos theory has been postulated which states that the Universe was at one time uncontrolled, not ordered, maybe being created, then through the intervention or design of a supreme being, which in itself could be an unknown physical occurrence, but like some scientists, I accept God as the creator. The Universe, under His direction, became a series of controlled systems, some predictable but not all. The weather, being a prime example, for over long periods is not a predictable ordered system of the Universe. Therefore the chaos theory evolved. This theory attempts to find order in the unordered systems.

The control interactions in matter are gravitation, electromagnetism, and the nuclear forces, one a strong force with a short range holding atomic nuclei together and then a weak force that is responsible for slow nuclear processes like beta decay.

I became interested in subatomic antimatter even though ordinary matter is overwhelming and there is little antimatter known to us. We know that when nuclear particles and antiparticles meet they annihilate each other with a release of great energy. I will return to this area but I have not gone on to embrace the grand unification theories that want to give a sense of order and completeness like the concept of symmetry, for it is merely an attempt to interject desire to explain, not as a discovery process. For in physics these symmetries of demonstration are known to be only approximate. I do not believe in a grand unification theory, too many holes. I believe the Universe is expanding with controlled matter and with chaos, and things occurring at random and those things yet undetermined. The word *things* being an all encompassing grand title or definer.

To capture the voices and/or sounds that we do and identify them necessitates a superficial understanding of the phenomena of sound. Sound wave carrier frequencies have side bands with complex variations of subatomic particles; quarks, strange quarks, and others heretofore undetected. These nuclear particles, particularly the ions which can be electrically charged or neutral are the fingerprints of a particular voice or sound in conjunction with quarks.

Electromagnetic waves created at low frequencies have a resonance factor and we can control the mass of the resonance once recaptured. We have resonant circuits to select or reject currents with specific voice frequencies. From the particles of the side bands we restructure the original electromagnetic waves they were a part of and convert them to the electrical oscillations necessary to produce a voice. Let me summarize. The original sound waves are never lost and their identity is secured by the subatomic particles of the side bands. We must have a sound master to identify resurrected utterances of the past. We can generalize previous cannon sounds but the specific cannon type can only be identified if we have a sound record of a specific cannon. Why is the sound not lost? Because of the specific subatomic particles created in the side band and because space is curved. The exact degree of curvature in the neighborhood of heavy bodies is known; however, curvature in empty space is not, for there are no points of reference. The subatomic particles I refer to have a unified spin to the left or counter rotation. Supposing this in empty space the same recovery of sound appears feasible. That's it, in a nutshell."

"And he's the nut," Felix quipped, but he had been watching Hick as Joe was explaining his theories and discoveries. The look on Hick's face was a study of total and complete involvement. The movement of his eyebrows, when in doubt about what he heard. The shifting in his chair with uneasiness when he didn't fully comprehend and the closing of his eyes when contemplating were the outward signs of his involvement in what he was hearing. Hick moved to the edge of his chair and asked, "How do you find a specific instance of a captured voice pattern? The year it was said, the day, the time?"

Joe Hirsch slapped the table and exclaimed, "Wonderful! You understood, but more important, you believe. You didn't dismiss what I said or offered. Wonderful!"

"I not only understood but I believe in your belief, not…a…but 'The Supreme Being' brought order out of creative chaos to leave some disorder for man's determination. Maybe the chaos is a path to greater understanding and discovery. An expanding Universe. Never static, always evolving to satisfy humanity's spirit of discovery *yet* leaving our willingness to accept truisms of the physical and spiritual worlds. Like the Ten Commandments."

Joe, excited beyond belief, was on his feet crying out, "The Ten Commandments, how beautiful an analogy! How appropriate, how fitting; how Kosher." Joe sat down and then pleaded, "Give one minute for me to answer your question." Joe wiped his brow with his sleeve and continued eagerly, "a unique computer program on a series of CD-Rom discs holding all of the spoken words or particular sounds we care to identify. Then through a quark color deterioration detection method we have developed, we match the unknown to the unutilized quark of specially dated crystals. We have a schedule of dates back to 4000 B.C. that can be matched through the computer to the year and dates of the Lunisolar, Roman, Julian, Gregorian, or Christian calendars for accuracy. Taking that into consideration we now postulate Christ was born on December 25th, 4 B.C., not 1 B.C."

"Do you work alone?" Hick asked.

"Couldn't do it. I have five of the most brilliant minds, none of which is over forty-two, working with me day and night."

"How old are you?"

"Seventy-six."

"Have you published any of your findings?"

"Not a word. Our reason for being is for the defense of the Republic for which we stand and hopefully through you can assist layman variety justice."

"Why?"

"I don't make the decisions as to why and I don't care. I have at my disposal what any scientist would die for. We are able to achieve what we do because of what is so readily available to us without any questions or delays. Delays because of money slow down the scientific quest for more knowledge. We have developed ordnance that is mind boggling and continue to do so. Ordnance was my factum of credibility for those who understand the importance of that which is hidden but lies ahead of progress and must be discovered for there to be progress."

"And," Felix interrupted, "he is their willing slave."

"Not a slave, Felix, it's my life."

"That it is and every time I hear you explain what you're up to, I creep a little closer to understanding."

"A, hah, but what is more important you believe and through your believing or your faith will come revelation."

Hick was on his feet and stretching. Turning to Joe he asked, "Do you have a practical example for me of a voice I would know that you have intercepted and recorded?"

"Your Honor, we are well prepared for such an inquiry. I am pleased you brought it up, for this is further evidence of acceptance and understanding. We have a chronology of a voice *you* know very well. The voice of one Judge Harold Batemen." Hick showed his surprise by raising his eyebrow and tucking his chin. Joe went on, "However, we have picked yesterday in your court as the time and place for a remark Judge Bateman made to and about you. We actually have about everything this man has ever said. We do not want to prejudice you about him in any way. So we will not disclose anything further than what you are about to hear. Listen."

Joe went to a small console, pressed several buttons and the voice began. The voice of Harold Bateman. "You lowly piece of shit out of the sewer, how dare you play cat and mouse with me! How dare *you* insult the dignity of my office. You don't belong in a courtroom!"

Hick smiled as he saw Joe slam down a toggle switch and the recording ceased. Turning to Hick with obvious contempt for what he had heard, Joe fumed, "Oh, how I'd like to say something, Your Honor, based on what I know, but that's out of the question for now. What do *you* think?"

"You actually did it like *you* said?"

"Absolutely. Right out of the 'ether.' We were listening."

Joe laughed heartily and was soon joined by Hick and Felix. Slapping his hand on the table Joe asked, "Scotch anybody? It's time for one, you know, and this Rabbi loves his scotch."

CHAPTER 8

▼

The pounding on the back door of the Temple went unheeded. Detective Mike Groton in his frustration cursed between pounding blows, "Damn it, I know you're there, answer the damn door!"

Flipping out his cellular phone he dialed Judge Waterford at the Stoddard Arms and waited.

"Waterford here."

"Judge, you don't know me but I know all about *you* and the Colonel."

"I know you, Detective Groton. I know your voice very well."

Taken by surprise, Mike stammered, "How the hell could you?"

"There's an old child's saying, Detective, 'that's for me to know and you to find out.'"

"Well, I'll be..."

"What did you want, Detective?"

Mike collected his thoughts but stumbled over his words, "I...I knew that...phone call from...from the Captain was a phony. I also know about the garage and the passageway to the Plaza so I followed them to the Temple. I know they're here but they won't answer the damn door."

"The Temple. What Temple?"

"Your Honor, you're playing games with me."

"Exactly, son, exactly. We're playing games with each other and have been for years. We ought to cut it out. We're on the same side."

"I need to talk to Judge Hickman. I have a message for him."

"Stay where you are, Detective. I'll arrange it."

Judge Waterford hung up the phone and quickly re-dialed.

Joe Hirsch put his drink down as he was saying, "One more thing, Your Honor, I know you want to know how we are involved in the business of your court. Felix and Judge Waterford will tell you all about that. Right, Felix?"

"We started to tell him about our involvement but the details will have to wait for his decision after being offered a federal judgeship."

Before Hick could ask what he was thinking, the phone rang and Joe answered with, "What now?"

"What now? What a hell of a way to answer the phone, Joe. It's Sam."

"Sorry, Your Honor, I was waiting for a response from Judge Hickman, regarding the possible federal judgeship."

"Evidently you finished your presentation. How did that go?"

"Here, you ask him."

Joe stood, walked to Hick and handing him the phone said, "It's Judge Waterford. He wants to know if I made a believer out of you."

A big smile crossed Hick's face as he took the phone in his hand and spoke, "I believe, Sam, I believe. Joe is very convincing."

"Not only convincing, Hick, he's brilliant, but you would never guess it to look at him. I'm interested in whether there is one thing that caught your fancy?"

"Certainly, it came through loud and clear and it dovetails with the concerns that brought me to you, via Sam Hirsch. The creative force of the Universe is a supreme being. I, you and others prefer to say God. Also, this man that plays Rabbi, but isn't, has twin auras. One is obvious scientific brilliance; the other aura is the willingness to bear witness, through his thoughts and deeds, to his unrelenting belief in God.

Thank you for the opportunity to come to know this man and his work."

Hick's words caused Sam to pause before he could answer. He felt satisfaction giving way to emotion as he thought, *"Hell, this is the man, Sam Hirsch knew what he was doing,"* and then continued, "Well, ah, Judge, I mean Hick, you are special as well. I know Joe mentioned the federal judgeship. No immediate decision necessary. I would like to go into more detail about it with you at Sam Hirsch's wake. It would be appropriate to do so under his roof and all. After all, he sent you to us."

"Did he really, Your Honor, or was he a willing decoy *for you?"*

Judge Samuel Wenter Waterford's voice became judicial, "Sir! Are you inferring that I would consort with Sam Hirsch, or anyone for that matter, so as to bring about a desired result for the federal judiciary?"

"Yes."

"Well, ah, maybe and maybe not. We can discuss this further…later…Goodbye."

Hick never had a chance to say goodbye before the phone went dead. Joe and Felix were listening and Felix spoke, "I think *you* have His Honor's number, Your Honor."

Joe interjected, "He is very special, Your Honor, the man called Waterford. His life is the judiciary and he takes great satisfaction out of finding those to succeed him and his understanding."

"I sense that, gentlemen. He has a tenor about him."

The phone rang again and as Joe reached for it he exclaimed, "This time I'll be more careful about how I answer this damn thing. It might be the Judge. Hello there."

"It's me again, I forgot what I called for. *No,* I didn't, my mind is preoccupied with Judge Hickman. Anyhow, Detective Groton is at your door, ready to break it down. Says he has a message for the Judge."

"I'll go get him before he becomes history."

"Work on the Judge, Joe."

"I will, Your Honor. Goodbye."

Joe walked to the office door and suddenly turned and suggested, "Felix, Judge, why don't you come with me?"

The three men returned to the back door of the Temple and after several maneuvers by Joe the door slowly opened. Detective Mike Groton stood, hands on hips with a frown on his face and with a degree of disgust in his voice said, "The least you could do, Rabbi, is have a damned doorbell on this place."

"Sorry, Detective, we don't have visitors."

"Why?"

"We don't want any. What can we do for you?"

Mike Groton shook his head and looking past Joe Hirsch at Hick said, "Your Honor, your secretary left a message for you to call her as soon as possible. She has called twice and is a little upset at us."

"Why?"

"She's afraid something has happened to you. I tried to reassure her but the warning about the hit has her upset."

Mike knew he had said too much and his face reddened as Hick asked, "What hit? On who?"

"Just one minute, Your Honor," Joe interrupted. "Let me talk to the Detective. Detective, you've spilled the beans. What do you know?"

"About what?"

"Well, for starters, this place and how these two men got here?"

Mike Groton knew he had let the cat out of the bag just by showing up and he knew these men were somehow involved with this Judge who had the protection of the Kansas City Police. That meant his Captain wasn't squaring with him on the details. So he thought, *"Go ahead, tell 'em."*

"Well, I've told Judge Waterford so I'll tell you. I was cruising one night," and pointing at Felix, "spotted you in the limo with the Judge. We have been detailed in the past to observe you."

Felix interrupted with, "Observe us, a retired federal judge and Marine? What for?"

"I don't write the book, Colonel, I follow directions."

"Colonel, is it?"

"Yes, sir, we've been briefed on you both."

"You seem to know a lot, Detective, go on with your narrative."

"Yes, sir. When I spotted you I followed out of curiosity and saw you go in the Plaza garage and disappear on the lower level. I parked, went behind the wall of boxes and saw you disappearing down the passageway. I walked through it, what a climb, to the elevator. I took the elevator up and realized when the door opened it was a direct way to your apartment. I was afraid you heard me or the elevator but you didn't because I returned to the basement and passageway."

"We wouldn't have heard you. We care less about the elevator because there's a security light we turn on and off when it's not in use. Somebody wasn't doing their job."

"I figured as much that I lucked out. I've also followed you to the Temple several times when on stakeouts. So I figured today when I received the phony call from the Captain you were going to leave."

Joe Hirsch was listening attentively and asked, "Phony call?"

"Sure it was. Sounded like the Captain but it was pieced together."

"What was pieced together?"

"The words. They were pasted together."

Joe lowered his head as if embarrassed and muttered, "In a way you're right. We need to improve our technique. How are *you* involved?"

"Oh," Mike countered, "it's one of those 'it's for *you* to know and me to find out' deals. Right? Well, I've just recently been told that."

"Sounds like Judge Waterford," Felix prompted.

Joe's head popped back up and he barked, "Enough! Come on in, Detective, and follow us; but first; do *you* swear to Almighty God anything revealed to *you* will be kept only to *yourself?*"

"Come on, Rabbi, which *you* are not. You aren't going to tell me anything and I know it. Just let me use your phone."

Joe heard the antagonism in the Detective's voice and responded with, "You're right, Detective. Come on, there's a phone right around this corner."

"Here's the number your secretary gave, Your Honor. It's long distance, Rabbi."

"No problem, just dial nine and the number."

"Before I dial anybody, what about the hit you mentioned? I better know about it before Manning starts on me."

"We have an intercept since we are concentrating on…" Joe stopped abruptly, realizing what he had said and looking at Mike Groton snapped, "See, I have told you something. Do *you* so swear?"

"Okay, okay, I do, I do, Rabbi."

"Since we are concentrating on a particular group of men, about which, Your Honor, *you* have some knowledge. They have contracted for a hit on you while you are here in Kansas City. We so informed the Kansas City police and they in turn informed your office."

Hick looked at Mike Groton, "Do I have much to worry about?"

"Yes, sir, always. If it can happen to Sam Hirsch, it can happen to anybody. I don't think anything will happen to you while you're here, for we have you literally surrounded with protection, even as we speak there is backup waiting."

"Good." Hick dialed the number and waited.

"Office of Nicholas Hickman."

"Manning, it's me. New greeting?"

"No. It's your private line. I arranged it first thing this morning. Are you all right?"

"Don't I sound all right? Should I be worried?"

"You know, don't you?"

"Yes, I do, so what's new?"

"Besides someone trying to kill you? Oh well, we have received a special delivery letter marked urgent from the Department of Justice. The special delivery was followed up ten minutes later by a personal call from the Attorney General of the United States. He was inquiring if you had received the message. I told him no."

"Open the letter, Manning. Read it, then tell me what it says. I'll wait."

"Really? Okay, just a minute." There was a pause followed by, "Wow! They want you to be a federal court judge here in Omaha. Your appointment is for life on an as-needed basis to any district of the court system. You have been recommended by the president and Judge Waterford. Also, your appointment has been passed by the Senate and you are to replace Judge Samuel Wenter Waterford of Kansas City. I quote, 'if you agree to accept this appointment you will be sworn in by Judge Waterford'."

"I'll accept, Manning…wow! But it presents a problem. I've just joined a new firm. Only one day on the job."

"I don't think that's a problem, Hick. They'll be proud to have you accept. I'm certain. They are all here. Want me to run it by them and call back?"

"How long will it take?"

"Not long. Stop worrying. Give me your number."

"What's this number, Joe?"

"508-333-6363."

"Hear that, Manning?"

"Got it. I'll be right back to you."

Hick hung up the phone and turned to the men hanging on his every word and remarked, "It will be a few minutes. My firm is going to consider the offer of my becoming a federal judge."

The phone rang. Hick picked it up saying, "So soon, Manning?"

"It's a conference call, Hick. We're all here."

"You all right, Your Honor?" Henry Justin asked.

"I am, Henry. How do you feel about what has happened?"

"Your Honor, Mr. Harding wants to speak for us all."

"Good morning, Hick, Your Honor, it's Lance Harding. We all voted and have unanimously agreed you ought to take the judgeship. It is an honor afforded very few. The office of special federal judge will only come once in a lifetime. We want what is best for you. We are proud you did associate with us, even if only for two days, but it proves what the legal profession here in Omaha knows. Your judicial temperament, your personal values and conduct have led to this honor."

There was a chorus of, "Congratulations, Your Honor!" from all gathered on the conference call.

"Thank you, one and all, for your vote of confidence. I will need your support."

There were several clicks and then Manning broke in, "Hick, they've gone. It's just Henry and me. Please be careful. When will you be home?"

"This evening. Whatever flight it was you set me up on. In the meantime call the Attorney General and tell him where I am, what I am doing and that I will accept if you and Henry are included as clerk and bailiff. I will need one week to finish up what I am doing, and that I will call him tomorrow."

"Me, clerk?"

"It will be the same as you have always been, Manning."

"Oh, then good as done. Henry and I will be waiting. Here's Henry."

"Proud of *you*, Your Honor. A federal judge, my, my, my. Praise the good Lord and be careful."

"I will, Henry. The law school thing still goes. See you both later this evening. I'll call before the flight leaves."

"You listen to me, Nicholas Hickman. Be careful, Your Judgeship."

"I will, Manning. You two watch out. Those after me might strike out at the two people I love the most."

Hick hung up the phone before Manning could reply.

"From what I heard, I believe congrats are in order, Your Honor," Joe said, extending his hand.

"You're right, Joe, I'm going to accept."

Felix stepped forward, as did Mike, to shake Hick's hand and Mike said, "Judge, I need to have you go with me to see my Captain. I'll get you back to your hotel so you can freshen up and then to the wake before you have to leave for Omaha."

"Why?" Felix asked belligerently.

"My Captain makes the demands, Colonel, and I follow orders."

"Very well, but watch after him, and, Judge, I'll inform Sam of your decision and we'll see to it you're sworn in at the wake, before you leave."

Hick threw out his hand saying, "Thanks, Colonel, Joe, it has been an informative day to say the least."

Joe and Felix watched as Hick and Mike got into the unmarked police car. Joe spoke, "Think they'll be all right?"

"Why? What's bothering you?"

"That Detective looks wet behind the ears, Felix."

"Believe me when I tell you he's not. Thurmond, his Captain, is well informed. We clued him into this operation."

"You always have operations. What have you called this one."

"Operation Five."

"Operation Five? Just what does that mean?"

"Secrets, Joe, secrets."

"Nuts!"

*   *   *   *

Mike took note of the car that was following them after they left the Temple. He spoke through his teeth, "We have company, Judge, but what they don't know is they have company. We'll go down the Parkway and let their company get along side of them if they try to come along side of us, which they will. Never fear, the glass is bulletproof and so are the side panels. When the shooting starts, if it does, get down. There's an extra gun in the glove compartment, just in case."

Hick moved his hand to the glove compartment and opening it saw a .44 Magnum police special. A small Kansas City police badge was embedded in the black handle causing him to remark, "Now, that's classy."

"Nothing but the best, Judge. Watch yourself. I'm slowing down so they can make their move. Here they come…they've stuck a Tommy gun out the window. Looks like there's a silencer on the end of it."

Hick felt the impact of the bullets on the window but it held. The noise was extreme as Mike slammed on the brakes, allowing the trailing police car to cut in and pass them. This move confused the pursuers and as the police car moved ahead of Mike and Hick they came abreast of the shooters car. Immediately the car slammed into the side of the shooters; there were multiple shots. Mike yelled out, "Look, Judge! There go their tires. They've had it."

The shooters car slipped to the left and began to tilt and then rolled violently across the expressway, slamming into the median cement wall and then exploding. The fireball was enormous but Hick and Mike saw a body as it was thrown clear of the explosion. Rolling to a stop, Mike instructed, "Stay where you are. There's one left. I want to see who it is."

Mike ran to the body and turned it over with his foot. He waved at the other police car and climbed back into the car with Hick. Grabbing the radio microphone he called out, "Car 55 requesting backup and an ambulance on Central Parkway at Troost."

"Car 55, we acknowledge. Backup and ambulance are on their way. You are to proceed to the station without delay."

"Car 55, over and out."

"Here we go, Judge. Keep your eye out for more trouble. The dead guy was Wally Falter, second best when it comes to blowing up places and people. In this city a guy named Nitro is the best. I can't figure what Wally was doing out after *you*. One thing for sure, you're no $250 hit."

"What's that mean?"

"Wally and/or Nitro never touch anything for less than five thousand. They get his kicks more from standing around and watching the aftermath then setting the bomb or getting the money."

"How do you know?"

"I inhabit the bars where these creeps circulate. They'll talk if they think you're not wired and even that doesn't worry them too much. They like to brag, but I can't figure who Wally was running with. He was a loner. Maybe they'll figure it out when they put the pieces of the other two together. That is, if there are any pieces left."

"Other two?"

"Yeah, there were three of them in the car."

"That's something. With all that going on, you had enough presence of mind to count heads."

"Part of the job, Your Honor, just part of the job. Keep your eyes peeled. I don't think we're out of the woods yet."

"Why?"

"That was pretty heavy stuff for the middle of the day. They usually sneak around in the dark. I would bet they're making a statement and they won't give up. They missed and whoever is paying the bill wants results...so...they'll be back at us."

The car pulled up in front of the police station and before Mike could reach over to stop him, Hick had placed his hand on the door handle and pulling on it pushed the door open with his hand in place as he slid sideways to exit. Mike saw the blood erupt from the top of Hick's hand. Grabbing the shoulder portion of his coat he pulled violently, throwing Hick down on the front seat as he yelled, "Watch out, Judge!"

Hick instantaneously slapped his left hand over the back of his right hand, for he felt the searing pain and knew what had happened. Hick yelled back, "I'm O.K., Detective, get your head down!"

There were two more shots shattering the door glass. Two officers walking from the building saw the glass explode and heard Mike yell at the Judge. Dropping to their knees they jerked their pistols from their holsters and one officer fired in the air as he yelled, "Watch out! Across the street! Open window, second floor!"

Two minutes passed and the street was covered with policemen, guns drawn. Mike whispered to Hick, "Bleeding much?"

"Nope."

"Good. The three we took out must have had back up. Don't move. I think the shooter is gone."

Mike, opening his door, slid down on his knees and heard, "You both all right?"

"Yeah. For now."

"It's okay, Detective, we've zeroed in on the shooter. Come around to the front of the car."

Mike stood and walked to the front of the car and was immediately surrounded by patrolmen with guns drawn. He insisted, "Forget me. Help me get the Judge inside, he's been hit on the back of his hand."

Mike ran to the car door and eased Hick back up to a sitting position. He pulled his tie from around his neck and tied it around Hick's hand asking, "You still okay? Not light headed?"

"I'm fine, son. I think I'll need a band-aid for my hand."

"Yes, sir. Come with us. Officers, let's crowd around His Honor, and get him into the building to Captain Thurmond's office. One of you get Sergeant Hanscom and his medical kit, pronto."

Hick was rushed into the building and down a large hall to Captain Rick Thurmond's office. Hick noted the sign on the door as they rushed him in and it read, Homicide Division, Captain R. Thurmond, Chief.

The Captain was waiting and called out, "Sit here, Your Honor. You all right?"

"I'm fine."

"Good. Mike, how many hurt?"

"One, Captain, the back of the Judge's hand. Hanscom should be on his way."

"Good. You all right?"

"Yes, sir."

The Captain turned his attention to Hick and asked, "How's the ole' nerves holding up?"

"Captain, I've been through worse."

"Right, but two attempts on you within ten minutes could unnerve anybody."

"Naw. I had great protection all the while."

Sergeant Wilson Hanscom walked into the room, medical bag in hand, and asked, "Who's been hurt?"

"The Judge. The back of his right hand."

Wilson Hansom had been a corpsman in Viet Nam. Multiple decorations and knew his business. Sliding a chair over to Hick, he put Hick's hand on his knee and as he unwrapped the tie from the wound asked, "Your name, sir?"

"Nicholas T. Hickman, attorney."

"Having much discomfort, sir?"

"No. None."

"Looks clean. Not deep. Tetanus lately?"

"Two years ago."

"Good…allergies?"

"None."

"Makes it even better," and as he reached down into his bag he warned, "this is going to burn like hell. Ready?"

"Go to it."

Hanscom poured a small stream of reddish brown liquid across the wound. "Damn, you're right, it burns like hell!" Hick cried out.

Hanscom quickly blew across the wound several times and then asked, "And now?"

"Better, much better."

"Right. Just like mother used to do."

"Iodine?" Hick asked with a smile.

"The one and only; like aspirin, you can't beat it. A trick of the trade that others have forgotten. Let the air get at it and in three days you'll never know it happened."

"Thanks, Sergeant, much appreciated."

"My pleasure, Barrister."

Captain Thurmond ordered, "You're excused, gentlemen, I want to talk to the Judge."

As the door closed the Captain pulled two glasses and a bottle of scotch out of his bottom desk drawer and asked, "Want to see a real Doctor?"

"Didn't I?"

"You saw the best. Two or three fingers?"

"Two, thanks."

Captain Thurmond poured and handing Hick the scotch added, "Quite a day so far. Sit back, relax; enjoy the scotch."

Hick rolled the scotch in his glass, and offered, "I think I'll count my blessings, too."

CHAPTER 9

$\blacktriangledown$

Gertrude Boltinghouse, Harold Batemen's secretary, looked up and away from her typewriter and was startled to see an older man, with the traces of once being handsome, standing in front of her desk. She spoke hurriedly, "I am so sorry. I didn't hear you come in. May I help you?"

"Yes. My name is Walter Givens. Is the Judge in?"

"Why, yes, of course, Mr. Givens. I'm Gertrude Boltinghouse. I've called your office many times for the Judge and have heard him speak of you but we have never met. I'm so sorry I didn't recognize you but..."

Walter Givens interrupted with, "I'm in a rush, is he in or not?"

Gertrude, taken aback by the harsh tone of his voice, was offended. Gertrude was a lot of things, and would and could put up with a lot, but not rudeness. It was always a key for her to exercise the little authority she held as the Judge's secretary. She looked at Walter Givens with her practiced "*You've* crossed the line" look and curtly replied, "He is in. I will ask him if he cares to see you."

Walter Givens never hesitated. He moved to the side of the desk, walked to the Judge's door and threw it open. Gertrude was behind him as he stepped in the room yelling, "You can't do this!"

"The hell I can't. Tell her, Harold."

Harold Batemen was sitting behind his desk reviewing the latest issue of Playgirl. Taken by surprise, by the door suddenly opening and Gertrude's yelling, he quickly slid the magazine off his lap and into the wastebasket under the desk. Looking up he called out, "It's all right, Gertrude. Close the door behind you."

"But, Your Honor, he was…"

"Tut, tut Gertrude, it must be important for Mr. Givens to burst in like this. Please close the door."

Gertrude's face was bright red. She stomped her foot, slapped her hands together, turned and as she slammed the door behind her, muttered loud enough to be heard, "Damned rude, I'd say."

Walter Givens looked after her as she left and snarled, "That broad could use a good screwing."

"What can I do for you, Walter? Something wrong?"

"Damned right there's something wrong."

"Why didn't you call?"

"Because my K. C. contact tells me two things, they missed…can that bitch hear us?"

"No. Go on."

"They missed nailing Hickman, and they've got some kind of tap on you. Has this room been swept?"

"Once a month, and that was two days ago. The phones are monitored."

"Well, that may be but you're wired somehow."

Harold, looking frightened, sat down asking, "What should we do?"

"I've done it. I figured this might backfire, or whatever, and I have a back up. You'll love this, Harold, Hickman is going to be appointed a special federal judge here in Omaha."

"What? Why, why he just quit and went across the street."

"That may be but he's going to accept the judgeship. Piss you off?"

"Absolutely. They're—he's up to something. What is a special judge for? I'll tell you what for. The Feds are getting ready to hand down indictments. You just wait and see."

"What kind of indictments?"

"How in the hell would I know? They're kept secret. You know that. Why don't you find out?"

"You're jabbering. How much time before they do?"

"Do what?"

"Hand down indictments, you dumb bastard!"

"This is my office!" Harold shouted, bristling at the words 'dumb bastard', "I'm a judge, don't you call me a dumb bastard. In this room, Walter, I'm king!"

"Sure you are, Harold. Now answer, how much time?"

"I don't know, it could be tomorrow or two years from now. It's too early to speculate. Let Hickman get situated and then the rumor mill will start to work."

"Well, if that's the case, I'll see to it we hurt him soon. We'll give him something to think about."

"What are you talking about?"

"They missed him in Kansas City. He's thick with that secretary and bailiff of his. I'll have one of them taken out and let the other one twist in the wind. That should get his attention."

"I don't agree. Something is going on and I think we may be the objects of their attention."

"You're paranoid, Harold, go back to your Playgirl. Playgirl? Why Harold.... tut...tut."

Harold was surprised, for he had thought he slipped the magazine into the wastebasket before Walter had seen it. Evidently not.

Walter turned and walking to the door remarked, "Sit still, Harold. I'll let myself out, just like I got in. If you hear anything, let me know."

Walter walked out, slamming the door. Gertrude looked up, removing her stenographer's earphones and watched as Walter leaned over her desk whispering, "Listen, if you ever want a good screw, don't hesitate to give me a call."

Gertrude was not what one would call quick or on the in but she rose to this occasion with a coolness of knowing and looking up into his eyes countered, "If I ever did, it would be the last screw you'd ever have. So...buzz off, Buster." Walter was taken off guard and hesitated; this gave Gertrude the time she needed to demand, "Get your hands off my desk and get outta' here, you, you...has been Romeo!"

Walter jerked his hands from the desk; standing upright he began to turn a bright red. He was angry but sensed Gertrude would have to be reckoned with if he persisted. He backed to the door, turned, and let himself out and, as he did, heard Gertrude shoot him her last remark, "No class is low class...blow that out your ass, you pond scum."

When the door shut, Gertrude looked down at her trembling hands and tears flowed copiously onto her lap. She sobbed softly and began to wring her hands in despair. Then she spoke out loud to herself, "Gertrude, you should be ashamed for what you said. Mother would have washed out your mouth if she had heard it. I'll tell you what you should do, what you need. You need to quit. Get a *new* job. You don't like this man that calls himself a judge. You know there's something wrong with him and the company he keeps. Who can help you, Gertrude? Manning, she'll help you. Just get your stuff together."

Gertrude wiped her face, reached in a drawer for a Kleenex and blew her nose. She took a small shopping bag from her desk and gathered up her personal belongings. She put on her coat and without knocking walked in Harold Batemen's office. He was doing what Walter Givens had suggested, reading his magazine with feet propped up on his desk. There was surprise in his voice as he looked up to see Gertrude looking down on him and he quickly folded the magazine, to say, "Whatever happened to knocking around here?"

"I didn't start it. I came for the final time to give my notice, as of now...this very minute, I'm leaving."

"What! Why you can't do that. Why are you doing this? Because of Givens?"

"I can do it and I am doing it. Mister Givens is a symptom and you're the problem. Something's wrong around here and has been since I started five-and-one-half-years ago. I don't like it and won't tolerate it anymore."

"What are you saying, girl? If you leave I'll see to it you never get another job in this town."

"Threats? Don't bother. I could care less, this isn't the only town in the world. Goodbye."

Harold threw his feet to the floor and began yelling after Gertrude as she walked out the door, "What about your pay? You won't get one cent. You don't deserve it, leaving like this."

"You keep it, Your Honor, I have a feeling you'll need it and all of the money you can lay your hands on before long."

"What do you mean by that?" was the last remark by Harold. He returned to his office, slammed the door, walked to his desk and picking up the magazine threw it in the wastebasket, screaming after it, "Damn, why doesn't somebody put out some good stuff!"

Gertrude rode down in the elevator, alone with her thoughts, and was relieved she didn't have to face anyone. It was late in the afternoon and courthouse activity always slowed down by three o'clock. She asked herself, *What now? Where do you turn? Where will you start over?* Then it suddenly occurred to her and she cried out loud, "Manning, Manning will know what I should do!"

Gertrude's spirits rose dramatically as her steps quickened and she made her way out of the Courthouse and across the street to the Law Offices of Harding, Kimball, Roberts, and now Hickman. As her hand reached for the doorhandle she saw the sign had been changed and now read,

Harding, Kimball Roberts,& Hickman
Attorneys at Law.

Gertrude's enthusiasm returned and walking in the building she started for the offices and as she turned the corner she ran into Manning, who was going to the courthouse at a furious clip to look over the new quarters that had been assigned to Hick.

Manning called out as she grabbed Gertrude's arms, "Whoa, there. Oh, it's *you*, Gertrude. Forgive me. I'm rushing, there's so much to do. Where are you off to? You all right?"

"No."

"What hurts?"

"Oh, nothing, Manning. I just quit Judge Batemen."

"Good! No, I shouldn't have said that."

"Yes, you should. I should have done it sooner. I need help, your help. I don't have anyone I can trust."

Manning heard the desperation in Gertrude's voice and without hesitation reached out and put her arm around her shoulder and with a gentle hug said, "Come on with me to my office. We'll talk about it. They've all left for the day."

Manning walked into her office and, seating Gertrude at her desk, instructed, "You sit here. Answer the phone for me while I go over and say Okay to the Judge's new digs. I'm certain they're the best if my memory serves me right."

"Where are they? In the courthouse?"

"No, they're in the federal building. Top floor, if you please. He's going to be a federal judge this time around. Surprised?"

"Yes and no. I listened in when Walter Givens was talking to Judge Batemen earlier. He said it had happened."

"Who said?"

"Givens to the Judge, and then he was rude to me coming into the office and I let him have it going out. I was vulgar."

"We'll talk about that later, the vulgarity, but most important, Gertrude, did you hear how he found out?"

"Something about a K. C. contact and the Judge's chambers being tapped. Also, they missed nailing Hickman and something about indictments. I swore, Manning."

"Gertrude, you should have sworn and quit a long time ago."

"Tell me what Judge's chambers were tapped?"

"Batemen's."

Manning was excited by what she heard but calming herself instructed, "Gertrude, what you have is important. I know quitting was and is tough on you but I'll see to it you have a new job before the sun sets. I have to go to the federal building, as I said. Sit here at my desk and carefully remember and write down everything you heard today and in the past. I'll be right back. Twenty minutes at the most. Henry's due back any minute. Will you do this for me?"

"Certainly, I'll do it for you. You can really find me another job?"

"Good. Do it and I'll keep my promise. Paper and pencil are in the top drawer."

Manning left in a swirl and Gertrude opened the desk drawer and finding paper and pencils settled into the chair and began to think and make notes about what she had heard. Ten minutes went by and as she sat writing, the door to the office opened. Gertrude looked up and saw a man looking down at her and in his right hand was a gun. She sat straight up in the chair, outwardly unafraid and asked, "Yes?"

"Manning?"

"Why…"

The 'psst' from the silencer was the last thing Gertrude heard. Only one bullet was fired and it penetrated her skull mid-point of her forehead. She was dead instantly and the chair in which she sat moved rapidly back and smashed against the wall, ejecting Gertrude's body to the floor. Looking over the desk and down at her, the killer smiled as he twisted the silencer from the barrel of the gun. He placed the gun in one pocket of his rain coat and the silencer in another.

He turned, opened the door and proceeded down the hall to the outside door. Walking out the door his black raincoat melded into the shadows cast by the now setting sun. Henry had come in the back way, for he knew Manning was in her office when he left, which was next to his. He entered his office from the corridor, as Manning and Gertrude had done, so as to avoid the reception area. Throwing his hat on the rack he walked to the door between their offices and knocked. There was no answer so he opened the door and walked in saying, "Manning,

I've gone and…" He stopped in his tracks and looking down stared into the open lifeless eyes of Gertrude and instantly yelled, "Oh, my God! What's happened?"

Reaching down he touched Gertrude's hand and felt its warmth. Instinctively he ran out of the office, down the corridor to the outside door of the building and burst out to the street, quickly looking both ways. There was nothing, not a person, not a car, nothing. Henry went around the corner of the building and tried to enter the main entrance but the door was locked. He returned to Manning's office, picked up the phone and dialed 911.

"Emergency. Can I help you?"

"Law offices of Hickman, Lance and what have you. There's been a shooting. We're on the corner of 15th and Grand. I'm Henry Justin."

"The police are on their way. Stay calm, Mr. Justin. Stay where you are and touch nothing."

"Sure." Henry hung up the phone and looking down at Gertrude began saying The Lord's Prayer.

The three police cars pulled up to the front of the building with their sirens blaring. Hearing them, Henry remembered the front door was locked and ran to the side door and around the corner to yell at them, "This way, officers!"

One officer looked at Henry and remarked, "Damn, he's big enough."

"No worries," came the reply from his partner, "that's Henry Justin, the bailiff in Judge Hickman's court."

*   *   *   *

Manning had half run the four blocks to the federal building. A tall, handsome man was waiting at the locked door. Seeing her approaching he unlocked the door and held it open for her and she strode in as he said, "Miss Manning, I'm United States Marshal Jed Palmer. Judge Sam Waterford and I go back a long ways. He called me to inform me the preliminaries of Judge Hickman becoming a Federal Judge are under discussion and are to be finalized this evening. He was most anxious for the Judge to have a new home on his return to the city tonight. If you approve."

"Glad to meet you, Marshal. Let's take a look."

"Follow me, ma'am."

While in the elevator Manning offered, "Marshal, I have the feeling we'll be working with and seeing one another quite often. Call me Manning."

"I will in private, ma'am, but officially you are to be the Clerk of the Court and Judge Waterford prefers the title of Madam Clerk. Mr. Justin will no longer be referred to as the bailiff but as the Officer of the Court. Judge Waterford feels formality is the foundation of civility for the Judiciary. Can you concur?"

"That's not for me to decide, Marshal. That's up to Judge Hickman. It will be his court and if the past tells us anything, he'll run it. On that you could bet and win."

"Yes, Ma'am. You are correct."

The door opened and the Marshal instructed, "Straight ahead is the Judge's courtroom. Please follow me."

The Marshal opened two large oak doors revealing a strikingly well-lit and well-appointed courtroom. The walls were library paneled in dark oak and large beams crisscrossed the ceiling. Manning's breath was taken away by what she saw and she hurriedly remarked, "I had no idea this was here. Why, why it's majestic."

"Yes, Ma'am, it is and it holds two hundred people. The courtroom is for the exclusive use of Judge Hickman. The door behind the bench leads to three offices, all contiguous with one another. They are for the Judge, the Clerk, and the Officer of the Court. There is a private entrance, as you leave the elevator, that connects to a hallway leading back to the three offices. As you enter that hallway there is the law library for his Honor to use as a conference room as well. We will go through this entrance, behind the bench and work our way back to the elevator so you can see the entire layout."

The three offices were completely furnished in brand new mahogany desks, leather chairs and all of the equipment needed for efficiency. All offices, like the courtroom, were library paneled in dark oak. Manning was overwhelmed and had nothing to say until they walked into the library and she exclaimed, "Why, it's like home! The whole place is like your home. The home you would always want but couldn't afford."

"Yes, Ma'am. Funny you put it that way, for that's the way I have always thought about it. We started it one year ago."

"It's brand new?"

"Yes, Ma'am. It was constructed by Judge Waterford for Judge Hickman."

"He used his own money?"

"Yes. The federal government put up the space and Judge Waterford did the rest."

"Why?"

"He told me he felt the office of special federal judge, based on his experience, at this time needed this environment. He created it."

"How did he know Judge Hickman would accept?"

"Have you ever met Judge Waterford, Ma'am?"

"No."

"When you do, you'll understand."

Manning walked to the large window overlooking the downtown area. Her eyes were immediately drawn to flashing police lights. Straining to see she remarked, "I'd swear those cars are by my office!"

Marshal Palmer walked to the window and, looking down, agreed by saying, "You are right. They are. Follow me. We'll take the elevator to the basement. My car is there and it will save time."

In a matter of minutes they arrived at the office and, with his badge held high, they stooped under the yellow crime scene tape and rushed down the corridor to Manning's office.

Henry was waiting at the door to her office and moving toward him Manning called out, "Henry, what's going on?"

Henry moved to her and taking her arm in his hand asked, "It's Gertrude, from Judge Batemen's office. She's dead. She's been shot."

"I know she was here. I left her for a few minutes to look at the new offices in the federal building and, oh, Henry, sorry, this is Marshal Palmer."

Henry nodded at the Marshal while saying, "I know the Marshal, Manning. Marshal, good to see you. What was Gertrude doing here?"

"She quit her job. She had some things she was going to write down for me, and I promised her that before the sun set I was going to get her another job."

Manning, without any warning, suddenly threw her arms around Henry's neck and pretended to wail, "Why Gertrude, Henry?" Putting her lips close to his ear she whispered, "did you see anything on the desk? Did she write anything down?"

Henry was surprised by her outburst, but with her whisper understood. Reaching up he unwrapped her arms, moved her back and with a voice loud enough for the Marshal to hear, remarked sadly, "Nothing. There's nothing. I can't explain why."

"No clues at all as to who did this?"

"None, Manning. I arrived and she was still warm but I couldn't find anyone inside or out. You'd best talk to the Sergeant. He's in your office. I've told him everything I know."

Manning walked into her office. Gertrude's body had been covered with a blue sheet. A small round man with sergeant's stripes on his sleeve was looking at her and, seemingly puzzled, asked, "And you are?"

"I'm Marsha Manning, this is my office. Gertrude was my friend. Who did it?"

"Miss or Mrs.?"

"Miss."

"Well, Miss Manning, right now we don't know anything more than this young woman was murdered. I'm waiting for a homicide detective and a criminologist to show up. Please don't touch anything. I won't ask you anything. We'll wait for the detective to arrive."

"Can I ask a question?"

"Go ahead."

"Did she suffer?"

"No. Looks like one shot did it. She was dead in a matter of seconds. No sign of a struggle and no sign she tried to escape. She must have been sitting at the desk, looked up, and was shot between the eyes."

Manning gasped. "You all right, Ma'am?"

"Yes, go on."

"Probably only two people involved. The lady and the shooter."

"That quick? She was dead that quick?"

"Yes, Ma'am. I'd say it was quick."

"I'll wait."

Manning, visibly dejected, moved back into the hall with Henry and the Marshal. Henry walked up to her and gently put her hand in his.

CHAPTER 10

▼

"Looks like today is almost history. I've enjoyed the drink and just sitting here doing nothing," Captain Thurmond said as he looked up at Hick.

"I needed this time to do a little thinking. Wonder if we'll hear anymore about the fellas who were out after me."

"Detective Groton should be back shortly. Smoke? I have some great cigars."

"Never touch 'em, but help yourself, won't bother me."

Captain Thurmond opened a box on his desk and removed a large cigar, after smelling it, reached in his pocket and removed his lighter. After rolling the cigar around in his mouth once or twice, he lit it. Drawing deeply on it, he seemed to savor the taste. Exhaling the smoke he remarked, "Too bad the whole smoke doesn't taste like the first few puffs." The phone interrupted him and, picking it up, he said, "Captain Thurmond, Homicide. Yes. Go ahead, Mike. I've got it. You should get back here to take the Judge to the wake. He'll most likely want to go by his hotel first. Fine. We'll be here. Goodbye.

"That was Detective Groton. He'll be here in a few minutes to get you back to your hotel. They can't I.D. the other two in the wreck. They have parts of several hands and the fingerprints are good. They're running them through the F.B.I. for a possible I. D. It will take a while. Another splash of scotch?"

"Better not, Captain. I'll have one at the wake and then I have to catch my plane. I don't really need to go back to the hotel. Can I use your washroom to splash a little water around?"

"You bet, Your Honor. The cabinet's full of what you need and fresh towels are underneath. Help yourself."

As Hick walked to the bathroom the phone rang again. "Captain Thurmond. Yes, Miss Manning, right here. Your secretary, Judge."

"Hi, Manning."

"Hick, Gertrude Boltinghouse was murdered in my office."

"What happened, Manning?"

Manning gave the details of Gertrude's coming to the office, her own trip to the federal building and meeting the Marshal, and about Henry's finding the body. Hick remarked, "Have you figured it out, Manning?"

"What?"

"You were the one they were after, not Gertrude."

With a shocked look, Manning covered her mouth with her hand and cried out, "Oh my God!"

Hick heard, understood, and commanded, "Manning, let me talk to Henry."

Tears were running down her face as she handed the phone to Henry. "It's Henry, Your Honor."

"Do you have it figured out, Henry?"

"Yes, sir. They were after Manning and I think you told her that. She's as white as a sheet."

"Then you understand, Henry. You and Manning are targets. They've tried for me and missed. Now you could be next...understand, Henry?"

"Yes, Judge."

"You are to be with her every second. Do as the Marshal says. I will be home soon. Now put the Marshal on the phone."

Henry handed the phone to the Marshal and said, "The Judge wants to talk to you, Marshal."

"Marshal Jed Palmer, Your Honor."

"I am pleased to know you, Marshal. I will look forward to shaking your hand and working with you. From what I am being told the two most important people to me, Miss Manning and Mr. Justin, are targets. Prime targets. I want them protected."

"I will do that, sir."

"What do you have at your disposal?"

"Whatever needed."

"Good, put them up in the Marriott Continental Plaza, with guards, around the clock. I want Henry armed. I'll be back as soon as possible. Can you do this for me?"

"Without question, sir, it will be done as you said."

"Good!. Put Miss Manning back on."

The Marshal handed the phone to Manning and she quipped, "I'll get use to the idea, Hick. Sorry, I feel stupid, it just didn't occur to me. You could think Gertrude was me if you didn't see us very much. What are you up to?"

"The Marshal will tell you and Henry. Do as he says. I will be there as soon as I can get a flight. One more thing, call Batemen, tell him about Gertrude, put it this way, 'She's dead, whoever did it thought it was me.'"

"You out to scare him?"

"I hope to scare the hell out of him. One of these days, I'll have a piece of his hide. I love you, Manning. Goodbye."

There was a click before Manning could answer. Henry and the Marshal watched as tears again streamed down Manning's face. Henry walked quickly to her side and as he placed his arm around her shoulder said, "Don't worry, Manning. You'll be all right, the Marshal and I will see to that."

"I know, Henry. I'm crying because I love him, too."

*   *   *   *

Hick, sitting on the edge of Captain Thurmond's desk, hung up the phone and looked worried. The Captain asked, "Not going well in Omaha?"

"No, they're out after my secretary but they mistook another secretary for her and killed her. They missed, but Henry, my ex-bailiff, could be next. There's a U.S. Marshal going to give them cover. I should go back immediately."

"I know Jed Palmer, the Marshal. Don't worry, they're in good hands. He was sent there by Judge Waterford. You have to be sworn in before leaving."

"How do you know all this?"

"I think I should let you know we work closely with Felix and Judge Waterford on everything. It's an agreement we have. Let me get Felix on the phone."

The Captain picked up the phone, dialed and spoke, "Felix. Rick. We have a problem in Omaha."

"I know. Marshal Palmer is there. The Judge had me divert Southern Air to pick up Jed, the secretary, and the Bailiff, a surprise for the swearing in ceremony. Just tell the Judge everything is under control."

"I'll tell him, Felix, and then send him on his way to the wake."

"Right, Captain, and thanks for the help."

Captain Thurmond hung up and turned to Hick, "Felix knows what happened. He said not to worry about a plane. He'll have Southern Air waiting at the downtown airport for you. He wants you to be sworn in first and to spend some time with Mrs. Hirsch."

"Southern Air?"

"Southern Air is CIA transportation. They work with Intelligence. Naval intelligence is their hammer."

"Their hammer?"

"It's a long story. I'm certain Felix and the Judge will get around to indoctrinating you."

"Indoctrinate me?"

"There are strings, Your Honor, that come attached to every federal job. You best wash up. I'll alert Detective Groton that I'm coming with you to the wake."

Captain Thurmond, tapping his desk slowly, exclaimed, "Even if I do say so, going with you is a good idea," reaching into his pocket he removed a small black pad. Thumbing through it he found the number he wanted and dialed the phone and heard, "Limousines and Escort Service, Monty's style."

"Monty there?"

"He certainly is. Could I say who's calling?"

"Captain Rick Thurmond, Homicide."

"Yes, sir! One moment."

A husky, cheerful voice barked, "Rick. My greatest friend. Long time no hear. What's the occasion?"

"Trouble."

"So what's new, that's when I usually hear from you. That's the way it's been since we were kids. You'd get in trouble and I'd bail you out and it's still going on. Tell me."

"I have a distinguished federal judge-to-be, I need to get to a swearing in and then to downtown Private Air for a Southern Air trip to Omaha."

"A Waterford man, I presume?"

"Right on the money, but this afternoon, twice, somebody's tried to take him out. I need heavy cover."

"Know who?"

"One was Wally Falter."

"Was...Wally?"

"Yup. He was playing gunsel."

"Something's wrong with that. That's not Wally's style. His rep was based on using TNT, dynamite, and stuff like that for blowing people up, not bullets."

"We're working on it and you're right, it's a puzzle. Can you help me?"

"No prob...1em. What you need is a motorcade with a heavy police escort and a phony judge. Me! All of which I will have waiting for you in fifteen minutes. However, about your judge. In or out of the car?"

"In."

"Okay. the phony...me, will be in the second car. Put your Judge, plain clothes please, in the third car. Give him an M16 and one of your Dick Tracy hats, pulled down *low.*"

"The hat I can do but the M16 is military issue. You know I have it but can't issue it."

"So be it. Give him something that looks like he means business. A Thompson. I'll take care of the rest. Remember, fifteen minutes."

"A Tommy gun? Can do but how'd you know I needed you in fifteen minutes?"

"Shoot, Rick, it's easy, that's what you always want. I have to rush if I'm going to make my own deadline and you be sure to make yours. Timing is everything, and by that I mean no delays. Have him at the door, the escort in place and everybody else ready to move when we pull up."

"Fifteen minutes?"

"Fourteen...now."

*   *   *   *

Monty Gabriel, as he said, was a lifetime friend of Captain Thurmond. They had grown up together and served together after college in Viet Nam. Monty was a chopper pilot and Rick Thurmond a ditch lieutenant in a search and destroy rifle company.

Monty took Rick and his men in and then went back to bring them out. Monty had modified his Huey into a gun ship with tremendous firepower and named it, "The Archangel Gabriel".

Monty was not only renowned for his piloting skills but also for his logistic abilities of where and how many of the enemy were in a given area at a given time. He would change drop off and pickup zones while in action and no ground lieutenant would argue. He could smell danger and had an uncanny ability to avert it time after time. On one mission Rick had been shot and had instructed his men to leave him and make a run for the chopper. A Sergeant entering the chopper was asked by a gunner, "Where's your lieutenant? Lieutenant Thurmond!"

"He's down about two miles back."

"Back where? Right, left, where?"

The Sergeant pointed and the gunner called on his mike, "Captain! Lieutenant Thurmond is down. North about two miles. He's the only casualty. Everyone else is on board."

"We're outta' here, Johnny. Keep your eyes peeled," the Gabriel had replied.

The chopper roared into the sky and in minutes Monty was instructing, "Gunners, I've got him spotted, we're going in. Do you see him?"

"Affirmative," came the replies.

"Good! I'll make one pass. Sweep both sides of him so as to clean out the Cong trash. Here we go!"

The chopper dove and the gunners swept the area and looking back one yelled, "There were a few and the ones left are hightailing it."

Bringing the chopper in, Monty called out, "They'll be back, keep your eyes open."

Once on the ground Monty jumped out and ran to where Rick lay and commanded, "Don't talk or argue with me, Lieutenant, I'm gonna' pick you up an' you better start shooting that gun you're holding. It'll keep their damn heads down. We're clean but not for long."

Monty scooped Rick up and as he turned back to the chopper, gun-fire erupted. He flopped Rick in the chopper, ran back to his seat and put the chopper back in the air. With his mike on he called out, "We take any hits?"

"Nope," came a reply.

"Damned good. What about the lieutenant?"

"Through and through wounds of the right and left legs, his side and two across his scalp. Lost a lot of blood but I'm puttin' fluids in him. He's one damn lucky cowboy. Go for home."

"Roger."

The wounds ended Rick's tour and Monty's time ended two months later. Both men were discharged and both entered the police academy but Monty didn't like the restrictions placed on his aggressive nature so he resigned and started the escort and limousine service.

$$*\qquad*\qquad*\qquad*$$

The fourteen minutes went by and everyone was in their place when Monty's cars drove up. In a matter of twenty-two seconds the cars were leaving and in eight minutes Captain Thurmond, Detective Groton, and Hick had entered Sam Hirsch's restaurant to find it crowded with people. Monty left the entire motorcade and police escort right where they stopped in front of the restaurant with the following admonition to Rick, "We'll be right here…waiting. Don't take too long. Have your men ready. The Judge sits with me to the airport. Oh, Rick, tell His Honor he looked for real with that Tommy Gun."

Sam Waterford and Felix had arrived early and were waiting with Kate Hirsch in Sam's office. The series of doors to the office had been flung open so the office was contiguous with the rest of the restaurant. A large crowd was milling around the tables covered with every type of delicacy imaginable. Hick noted that the Judge was in a wheelchair and asked, "Are you all right, Your Honor?"

"Damned hip. Gives out on me from time to time and Felix makes me ride."

"Well, it's better than hobbling around," Felix countered.

Kate, wearing a black sheath dress with a large strand of pearls around her neck, and her black hair held back by a large diamond tiara, moved to where Hick stood, cutting short the exchange between the three men.

"So nice to see you again, Judge Waterford, Judge Hickman, Colonel. I understand, Judge Hickman, that congratulations are in order. Judge Waterford is to swear you in and I understand we must speed you on your way back to Omaha. I only wish Sam could have been here. He would be proud."

"Thank you, Kate. I wish Sam could be with us," Hick replied.

Kate took Hick's hand in hers as she said, "I would like a word with you when His Honor is through,"and then turned to Sam Waterford. "Judge Waterford, whenever you are ready."

Sam Waterford moved forward in his chair and Felix helped him rise to his feet as he remarked, "Right, Kate, we best get on with it. Felix, the Bible."

Felix, carrying a small Bible in his right hand, extended it and Hick placed his right hand on the Bible as Sam Waterford announced, "Ladies and Gentlemen, we are gathered today for two reasons. Kate, to support you in your loss of Sam. Also, because of a friendship Sam had with Judge Nicholas Hickman of Omaha, the Judge was brought to my attention. Which brings us to the swearing in of Judge Hickman as a federal judge. If you will, Judge, repeat after me."

Which he did, "I, Nicholas T. Hickman, swear to uphold the Constitution of the United States of America. I further swear to uphold and enforce the laws of the United States of America. So help me God."

Sam Waterford continued, "So swearing I now announce you as the new Special Federal Court Judge from the District of Kansas City.

Please accept my personal congratulations and best wishes for your tenure, which is for life if you so desire."

There was a round of applause. Sam raised his hand and continued, "Ladies and gentlemen. In all of our lives there are people who take on a special meaning to us. Regardless of what we call these people, friendship is the basis of the relationship and the guarantor of its success. Judge Hickman has two such dear friends," Sam halted and turning to face Hick said, "Judge Hickman, Kate Hirsch informed me, and I took the liberty of having your two dear friends flown down so they could be present this evening. We wanted them to share this auspicious occasion with you. If you would turn around, sir. Ladies and Gentlemen, I have the honor to present to you Miss Marsha Manning and Mr. Henry Justin, dear, dear friends of Judge Hickman."

Hick had been very composed until now. Judge Waterford's words caused his hands to tremble as he turned to see the smiling, proud faces of Manning and Henry. The three stepped to embrace one another, their tears caused a hush to fall over the room. Judge Waterford's words, the embrace, the tears caused more tears from those watching and then a burst of thundering sustained applause.

Hick noticed the tall man standing behind Manning and Henry. He strode over to him smiling; and extending his hand so as to shake the stranger's, asked, "Marshal Palmer?"

"Yes, sir, Your Honor. Judge Waterford felt all things considered, Miss Manning and Henry would be better off with you here in Kansas City."

"He was right. I am told you will be assigned to my court."

"Yes, sir. I served Judge Waterford and I look forward to serving you."

"We will be busy, Marshal. Very busy."

The evening's congratulations, introductions, and words of kindness were anti-climatic to the swearing in. Soon Monty was prodding Rick to take Hick, Manning, and Henry to the airport, "It's been great, Lieutenant, I mean Captain. The ceremony, the conviviality, the wine, hors d' oeuvres, and the pretty women; but with each minute we are giving whomever a window, an opportunity."

"You're right, Monty. Get everyone ready to roll. Where do you want the Judge and his friends?"

"Middle limo. We'll pull the switch just before we leave the river road tunnel."

"Switch?"

"Yeah. We arranged to have a tunnel in a tunnel. It's a long story, but if you want to say goodbye to the Judge you'd better ride in his limo."

"I do, I will and the rest is up to you. Give me five minutes."

Rick walked to Kate and whispered in her ear. Smiling she opened her purse and handed him a sealed letter. "Give it to the Judge. Tell him he will know when to open it."

Rick put the letter in his pocket, returning Kate's smile and grasping her hand said, "Thanks, Mrs. Hirsch, for letting us mix business into Sam's wake."

"Not at all, Detective. I know you have to hurry but let me ask you one question before you run off. Did you like Sam?"

Rick paused thoughtfully then answered, "I never met anyone who didn't like Sam, Mrs. Hirsch, and that includes me. However, I didn't respect him because of what he did."

"Gamble?"

"No, Ma'am, not the gambling, it was always the doubt… whether…did he ever step over the line, and we know he did."

"Murder?"

"Yes, Ma'am, murder. I must be going."

Rick dropped Kate's hand and turning thought to himself, *"Damn, I wish I didn't have to say that but I did."* He moved swiftly around the room finding Hick, Manning, Henry, and the Marshal and escorted them to the waiting motorcade.

In moments Monty had the motorcade on its way to the downtown airport. Rick marveled at Monty's ingenuity, for as they pulled into a tunnel another duplicate limo pulled alongside. Their limo pulled off into a parallel tunnel and the replacement limo moved into place.

Monty was driving and as he brought the car to a halt commanded, "Please move out and over into the school bus. Now!"

Everyone did as they were told. The bus was filled with people of every description. Smiling, Monty instructed as they boarded, "Please sit in the seats grouped together in the middle of the bus. We are now a bunch of Church members on our way to Kansas City International Airport to catch a vacation flight to Holland. That's what the sign says on the side of the bus. I will signal you a few minutes before we stop at the airport. When the bus stops, immediately follow me out of the bus, three steps to a gate, three more steps to the Southern Air Jet. The plane will have the markings of your favorite overnight shipper. It will have just taxied up and will be ready for immediate take off. Only you four will be boarding the flight. Others await you in Omaha." Looking at Hick, a big smile broke out on Monty's face as he quipped, "The look on your face, Your Honor, tells it all. You're right! It's just like a military operation…because it is! That's my specialty, and the pleasure has been mine, Your Honor, Ma'am, gentlemen, and best of luck to you all."

Smiling back, Hick put out his hand and as he shook Monty's he remarked, "I know about you, Captain. I consider you and the once Lieutenant my friends. I can't thank you enough. I salute you." Which Hick then did.

The transfer to the plane and its subsequent takeoff went so fast that once in the air it caused Manning to exclaim, "Did this plane ever stop?"

"No, it was rolling the whole time we were climbing on board," Henry answered laughingly.

"Any more word about Gertrude, Marshal?" Hick asked.

A voice interrupted the Marshal before he could answer, "Judge Hickman, Marshal Palmer, Mr. Justin, and Miss Manning, I am Col. Bruce Meyers, United States Marine Corps. I am your pilot and your co-pilot is Lt. Col. Charles Browning, United States Air Force. We welcome you aboard. Our aircraft is a Boeing 737 and our flying time to Omaha will be twenty-three minutes. We have no other personnel on board. A completely stocked galley is in the forward portion of the cabin. Lavatories to the rear. The speaker is voice activated if you find you need anything. We can listen to anything you say and all conversations are recorded as a matter of security for the missions of this aircraft. You are guests of Southern Air, which is a joint military Air Operation. We have many missions, special missions such as yours this evening. We cannot come to the cabin to meet you nor can you come to the flight deck. Again, regulations. We will notify you five minutes from touchdown and upon completion of our flight will personally say goodbye as you leave the aircraft. Until then."

There were looks of puzzlement on Manning's and Henry's face but they were quickly shrugged off with Hick's words, "What about Gertrude, Marshal?"

"Not a thing, Your Honor. We left before much was said or postulated other than she met an instant death at the hands of an unknown person."

"You made the necessary hotel arrangements?"

"I did."

"Can you and I be included?"

"We are. I took the liberty of doing so."

"Good thinking, Marshal. Manning, what about our setup?"

"Fantastic, Hick."

"What about Paul Ortman?"

"He was taken in by the firm and will handle the Doctor's case."

"We will need Gladis Pitman as court reporter. Full-time."

"Judge Batemen will have a fit."

"Why? He doesn't give two hoots about Gladis."

"I know, but if you want her and get her, that will upset him."

"Then upset him for me first thing in the morning. We'll have breakfast together, alone, at the hotel. Invite Gladis tonight. We won't go back to our offices. We'll all go to the new ones in the federal building. Marshal, where's your office?"

"I don't have one, Your Honor."

"Manning?"

"There's an empty one next to mine, no furniture or phone, but I'll take care of that."

"Good. What about a conference room?"

"There is a library that can be used or your office would be large enough, Hick. I can take out your desk and put in a desk-conference table if you would prefer."

"I prefer, use my money for both office changes. The five of us are going to spend a lot of time together. We have a big task ahead and there's safety in numbers. We need to stay close and keep an eye on one another. Someone tried for me in Kansas City and someone tried for you, Manning, in Omaha. We have someone, or more, concerned about us and I plan to see to it they become even more concerned as time goes on. Enough for now. Breakfast at six in the morning at the hotel. Henry, let's find us all a drink. How about you, Marshal?"

"Scotch on the rocks, Your Honor."

Hick led Henry to the front of the cabin and found the liquor cabinet and asked, "Scotch, Henry?"

"Shouldn't touch it, but maybe just a drop."

Hick was watching Manning and the Marshal. When he was convinced they were engaged in a conversation and weren't listening he asked Henry, "How worried is she, Henry?"

"I don't think she is."

"Someone was out to kill her."

"I know, but Manning is tough."

"Watch her for me, Henry."

"I will, Your Honor. I'll watch over us all and ask the good Lord to do the same. We'll be all right."

"I know we will. Here's to us."

Hick handed Henry a glass and as they clinked their glasses, Manning called out, "How about us, you two?"

As Hick handed Manning her drink she asked, "Hick, are there going to be federal indictments?"

"I don't know, Manning. Do you, Marshal?"

"I've been told a grand jury will be convening soon. You will be informed by the District Attorney in the morning. The particulars will be kept secret until the jury makes a decision."

"Tomorrow is Sunday, Marshal," Hick questioned.

"You will find this District Attorney doesn't care what day it is or who he is after. The law comes first."

"Do I know him?"

"No, sir! Like myself, he has been sent to work with you. There will be separation so as to exclude the perception or challenge of collusion, bias, or discrimination."

"We're federal officers, Marshal."

"I know, Your Honor, I can't say too much, but from the little I know all hell is going to break loose as these matters develop and big, big guns are going to be rolled out."

"What's going on, Marshal? Have I been set up?"

"No, Your Honor, never, not by Judge Waterford. Absolutely not, you will be briefed tomorrow much better than I could ever do. I can truthfully say you were selected because of two reasons; your judicial honesty and your judicial prowess."

"I'm flattered and…"

"Judge Hickman, this is Colonel Browning, speaking for Colonel Meyers. We are now on final approach and will be landing in five minutes. Will you please store any loose objects, fasten your seatbelts, and extinguish any smoking materials. We have been assigned a special off-ramp for deplaning. There will be a car to take you to your hotel, and, Marshal, there is a police escort. Also, a reporter from the newspaper would like a quick interview, Your Honor, regarding your recent appointment to the federal judiciary."

Marshal Palmer called out, "Absolutely not, Colonel. Have whoever it is call me about it in the morning."

"I didn't think so, Marshal. Colonel Meyers and I look forward to meeting you all."

In a matter of minutes the plane landed and rolled to a stop at an off-ramp. A stairway rolled into place and at the precise moment Lt. Col. Browning opened the cockpit door, turned, opened the plane door, followed by Col. Meyers. Both men stood at attention as their startled passengers deplaned. Manning summed up all of their thoughts when she whispered, loud enough to be heard, "Oh, my God, they're beautiful!"

Both men stood six foot two inches. They had put on their uniform coats. The decorations displayed were numerous. Their smiles and the warmth of their handshakes was disarming. Manning was first to say goodbye and Hick last. He best summed up the feelings of the group when he said, "Gentlemen, your presence, demeanor, and flying abilities cause us all to be proud. I know I speak for everyone when I say we are sorry we cannot come to know you better. I hope one day to meet you again. I thank you and salute you."

Hick saluted, turned, and while descending the stairway heard "Thank you, Your Honor."

*   *   *   *

Robert Conway, publisher of the Omaha Sentinel, tapped his fingers slowly as he waited. Four rings, five rings, then Harold Batemen answered, "Judge Batemen."

"What takes you so damn long to answer your phone, Harold?"

"I was busy."

"I can imagine. We have a problem and I want to know: How well informed are you, Harold?"

"You mean about Gertrude?"

"Yes."

"Hickman's secretary, Manning, the one who was supposed to have been gotten, called me."

"Do you realize what you just said and that your phone could be tapped?"

"I went over all this with Walter. I am checked out for phone taps and listening devices. My home and office are swept monthly."

"That means nothing, Harold, and you ought to know it. The other thing, have you been told about Hickman's new judgeship?"

"Yes, I know."

"Well?"

"Well, what?"

"Harold, I'm losing patience with you. Why was he appointed? Are there to be indictments handed down?"

"You sound like you've been talking to Givens and I'll tell you what I told him. I know nothing. Let a day or two go by and we'll know a hell of a lot. I'm worried."

"Why?"

"Hickman doesn't like me and I gave him reason the other day to like me less. He takes his court and its decorum very seriously."

"So what did you do?"

"I called him names."

"You called him names?"

"Yes! He's gutter trash and lucky gutter trash, at that."

"Harold, you have a problem."

"And, Robert Conway, so do you."

"I know, Harold, it's you and that could be taken care of."

"Are you threatening me?"

"Sorry, Harold, forget what I said, I'm concerned. I have a feeling we should stick together. One more thing, Hickman was just brought in by Southern Air. He refused an interview by my paper."

"So what? That's what you'd expect. Goodbye."

Robert Conway was seething and after slamming the phone back in its cradle, he picked it back up and furiously re-dialed his phone. After five rings he hung up and then re-dialed, after two rings a voice answered, "Yes?"

"Walter, it's Bob. We have a problem."

"You must have been talking to Harold."

"I was. What's his problem?"

"The same one he was born with."

"What should we do about him?"

"Nothing for right now. Our success rate is poor."

"I know what you mean. Should we have a meeting with the others or decide for ourselves?"

"Decide for ourselves. To hell with the others. How do you vote?"

"My thumb is down."

"I agree. He won't answer his phone so I'll try again in the morning."

CHAPTER 11

▼

"Omaha Carlton. Good evening. Can I help you?"

"Yes, do you have a David Field registered?"

"One moment, please."

"Good evening, this is hotel services. We do have a Mr. David Haddam Field registered. May I connect you?"

"Please."

The phone rang four times and a voice stammered, "Hello, hello there. Sorry to take so long. I was in the shower, you know."

"Sorry to bother you, Mr. Field. My name is Paul Wentzel."

"Oh, the Police Chief."

"Yes, that's right. How did you know?"

"I'm new, Chief, but I do my homework. I was given this assignment six months ago and I've been working on who's who in Omaha ever since."

"Six months ago?"

"Yes. Judge Waterford is a thorough man and diligently sought his replacement."

"You mean Judge Hickman?"

"Exactly. I am looking forward to meeting the Judge."

"You haven't met him yet?"

"No, I haven't."

"Mr. Field, I am an attorney. Are you related in any way to the codification David Dudley Field?"

"Only as far as the Haddam is concerned."

"The Haddam?"

"Yes, he was born in Haddam, Connecticut and my mother was an actress and wanted to make a connection that wasn't there."

"I don't understand, Mr. Field."

"No one but Mother understood. Mother was a consummate actress until the day she died. Never got off the stage."

"Her maiden name was Field?"

"Given and acquired. She took the stage name Mary Stuart."

"Mary Stuart! The actress?"

"Right, Chief. That's what I've been saying."

"My mother worshiped her."

"Most people did. She had a way about her, on and off the stage."

"Fascinating. I'm finishing up here at the station, could I interest you in a drink at the Hotel Bar?"

"Absolutely, Chief. Give me ten minutes to get dressed. If you get there before I do just order me up an Old Fashioned."

"Ten minutes, Mr. Field. I'll see you in ten minutes."

David Haddam Field took twelve minutes and when he walked into the Hotel Bar he recognized Chief Paul Wentzel sitting at a table. His Old Fashion was waiting for him on the table. He walked to the table slowly for effect and it worked, for he saw Paul Wentzel was studying him.

*   *   *   *

David Haddam Field was six feet tall, two hundred and fifteen pounds, black hair, blue eyes, and his most distinguishing features were his massive hands. He was born in Haddam, Connecticut, thirty six years before. The only child of Joshua and Mary Field. His father operated Joshua Field Haberdashery on main street. His mother, Mary, met his father in the theater alley one night after a performance. She always affectionately called Joshua her "Stage Door Johnny."

The stage, her husband, and her son's education were the main concerns of her everyday life. Andover, Yale, and then—to her husband's surprise—the University of Nebraska College of Law, when David rejected her call for him to follow her in the theater.

"Why Nebraska, Mary?" Joshua asked.

"Midwestern basic values, if mixed with east coast self righteousness and arrogance, will better prepare him to be a person of the people and for the people since he would not consider the stage."

"He's an actor, Mary. He's your son, haven't you noticed?"

"Yes, I have, but if not the stage then where better than the law…to act?"

"What do you have in mind for him, Mary?"

"Criminal law."

And so it was.

Paul Wentzel's background was in sharp contrast to David Haddam Field. He was five feet, ten inches tall, two hundred and ten pounds, brown eyes, and receding light brown hair. His most distinguishing characteristic was his sharp pointed nose and a habit of closing his right eye when he was under stress. He was born to John and Trisha Wentzel of Bolton, Iowa. He was the eldest of seven children. His father was the county sheriff and his mother's calling as she would tell anyone was, "To grow children, flowers, vegetables, and any farm animal we have room for around here."

Paul's education was catch as catch can because of the shortage of money. He attended the University of Iowa on several occasions but was called home whenever funds ran out. He became a deputy sheriff and worked with his father. After three years he left to return to college.

His law degree was earned at night from Columbia University in New York. When he told his father of his plans to go to New York he had remarked, "Good. You'll see the other side of the coin. The side marked hell. When you're finished, come back to the good life."

Paul never practiced law and like David Field, never married. His law degree and experience as a deputy sheriff over qualified him for many positions as chief of police he had held in eight different towns and cities. He always resigned by simply saying, "It's time for me to move on."

No one ever asked, "Why?"

Paul Wentzel didn't stand as David Field stood at the table looking down at him. He commented, "Have a seat, Mr. Field, your drink awaits."

David reached down and Paul Wentzel was amazed by the size of his hand, for it seemingly engulfed and then swallowed the glass from view. The hand raised to David's mouth and when the glass appeared again, as if by magic, David dropped it on the table and it was empty. Paul Wentzel's right eye closed as he asked, "Another?"

"No."

"Have a seat, ah, can I call you David?"

"No. To both."

Paul Wentzel's right eye, still closed, twitched as he stood to face David. "What's the problem?"

"You, Chief. You play poker? Don't you?"

"What?"

"Poker! You know, the card game. If you do, you shouldn't."

"What's that have to do with?"

"Chief, I came down here for one reason to see if your eye is the dead giveaway it's purported to be. I didn't come to Omaha to sit with you. I drank the drink for the inconvenience."

"What inconvenience?"

"Having to go after scum like you."

Paul Wentzel was taken aback and reaching for his eye he began rubbing it as he demanded, "Just who in the hell do you think you are talking to me like that?"

"Let me tell you who I am…Chief. I'm the prosecutor who is going to see to it your ass is either parked in a mental health facility or preferably in the state pen without protective custody. You and your buds are a study…Chief, and they'll also be in one of the two places I mentioned. I'm here and ready. I'm coming after you. All of you."

Paul Wentzel's hand dropped from his eye and as it started to move to the lapel of his coat David's massive hand rose and he called out, "Stop, Chief! I can out-draw you and my .357 will stop you easily."

Paul's hand dropped to his side and he snapped, "You have a permit to carry a concealed weapon?"

"Two! Federal *and* state."

Paul's eye twitched again. Obviously flustered, he asked, "Just what the hell are you up to?"

"Tuesday I go for a grand jury. It's the beginning of the end for you and your buds. Chief, before you get any big ideas, turn around."

Paul turned and saw Jed Palmer staring at him. Looking back in David's face he asked, "Who's he?"

"A U.S. Marshal."

"What's that mean?"

"Don't mess. A Marshal will be watching you and your buds and me and my team all the time."

Speechless, Paul Wentzel moved around David and made his way to the door of the bar. He turned and looked back at both men momentarily and then disappeared into the lobby.

Jed Palmer moved to David and asked, "Scare him?"

"I don't think you can scare the likes of him, but you can worry him and his kind to death. That's what's kept him on the move all these years."

"What's that mean?"

"Have time for a drink?"

"Sure do."

"Good. Have a seat and I'll tell you about our friendly Chief of Police."

David raised his hand for the waitress and as he looked up he saw Paul Wentzel walking back into the bar. Keeping his eyes on him he whispered through his teeth, "Don't look now, but our worried Police Chief is on his way back. Stay put, Jed, but be ready. Desperation is sometimes a detonator for these sickos."

Paul walked to the table and looking down asked, "Can I join you?"

"Why?" David asked.

"I have questions."

David had handled men like Paul before and understood they possessed a high degree of arrogance as a mask for what lay hidden behind the mask. He also knew that to find the truth the arrogance must first be undermined. He retorted, "I thought you knew all the answers, Chief."

"Some I know, others I don't. Like, what are you after?"

"I told you indictments would be handed down by a grand jury."

David saw Paul's right eye begin to twitch as it closed, and sneered as he commanded, "Have a seat, Chief, and let's all put our hands on the table. Drink?"

"No."

"Go ahead then, Chief!"

"What are you after?"

"I've made that clear. I want to put you and your pond scum buddies away where you belong."

"For what?"

David clenched his hands and made fists. His fingers instantaneously turned white. His eyelids narrowed as his lips parted and they narrowed into a sinister smile enhanced by the whiteness of his teeth. This was the posture he assumed before cross examining a hostile witness or a witness he found offensive, for he was his mother's son...a great actor.

However, in this case there was a personal distaste for Paul Wentzel. He lashed out, "I've got the goods on you, Chief. You pretend to your associates your interest is only pornography but it's more than that,

Chief. Right now, this moment, I'll tell you I have you cold. I've gone back, found, picked up on and have followed your trail of lust for little boys."

David let his words sink in. Paul Wentzel's right eye was completely closed. He began to rub it as he asked, "How could you have such information? Where could you have gotten it?"

"Thought you covered your tracks pretty well, didn't you, Chief?"

"You don't know a damn thing."

David leaned across the table and hissed, "I've got you on tape. I have witnesses. I have those who have procured for you ready to testify."

"Tapes?"

"Your voice, Chief."

"How can you prove it's my voice?"

"You know about voice prints, Chief, but what you don't know is even if they are discredited as not being absolute enough for conviction in the past, new science gives us a voice mark that is yours and yours alone. If you want to argue with that, let me add that I have you and your associates all on one tape. Loud and clear."

Jed Palmer whistled in surprise at what he had heard and quickly remarked, "You can really do that, David?"

"It's perfected."

Paul moved to his feet and snapped, "I won't go down easy, Mr Prosecutor."

"I'll tell you what, Chief. You be a witness for the prosecution and I'll see to it you go to a mental hospital."

"For how long?"

"It doesn't make any difference. You can't be cured. A pedophile is a pedophile."

"How long?"

"Five years."

"I'll see. Good night."

David and Jed watched again as the Chief walked out into the Hotel lobby. Jed was first to speak., "Is what you said to him true?"

"Absolutely."

"What do you think he'll do?"

"He'll bow out."

"Bow out?"

"Yeah. He knows I'm after him and have the goods on him. He'll do one of two things, run or kill himself."

"Kill himself? You're serious?"

"Sure. He'll kill himself. He knows running won't do any good. He doesn't want the humiliation associated with public disclosure. He was always smart enough in the past to know when it was time to move on, but now he'll realize the jig is up."

"Doesn't it bother you he might do that?"

"No. It's his decision. He's brought enough misery to others, little children. I don't think killing himself can come close to evening the score. Only God can forgive him, not society. I think we need that drink."

"Dave, you're tough."

"Not really, Jed. You know as well as I do we represent the people's interest in finding justice as best we can and any way we can."

"You're right but sometimes it gets complicated."

"Sure does and I'd like it better if I didn't have to take after others, but it's my job."

"And you like it."

"Right! I hope and pray what I do makes people happier and safer. They have the right to expect the law is watching out for them. Like I said, let's have that drink."

*   *   *   *

Paul Wentzel walked to the station house, talking to no one as he walked past the desk sergeant. He entered his office, removed his revolver, and placed it on the desk. He picked up the phone and dialed Walter Givens's private number. The phone rang several times before he heard, "Givens. How can I help you?"

"Walter, it's Paul. We have a problem. A big problem named David Haddam Field. The new federal district attorney."

"Hi, Paul, you just caught me. I've been talking to Bob about Harold. Harold's a problem, but I think we've solved that. How's this Field person? He a problem?"

"I've been talking to him and he seems to know plenty."

"Get specific, Paul. Just what does he know?"

"About me for certain and the rest of you for sure, too. He seems to have recordings of what we've said and done."

"Do you know that for certain?"

"No, but I can read between the lines. I'm worried."

"He may just be poking around to see what he can find out or stir up. Get you worried so you make a mistake."

"Why is he suspicious of me, the police chief, unless he has something on me…us?"

Walter Givens laughed loud enough that Paul had to pull the receiver away from his ear.

Then he asked, "What's so funny?"

"You think your cover's blown, don't you? You've gotten away with it for years, being police chief and all, but now he's got you worried the cover is blown."

"Cover? About what?"

"That you go for little boys. That's what."

"How did you know?"

"You thought no one checked on you? Forget it. We wanted someone like you as Chief. It's easier for us to protect ourselves if the Police Chief is one of us. We checked on you. Seems you were always one step ahead of the hounds. You always seemed to know when to move on before they got the goods on you."

Paul's eye twitched and as he rubbed it he firmly said, "He's offered me a deal, Walter. A deal if I rat on the rest of you." There was dead silence on the phone and Paul knew what it meant so he laughed and shouted, "How do you feel now?"

Walter Given's neck veins were distending and his face was turning red. He lowered his voice as he tried to regain his composure and, half snarling, said, "Paul, what kind of deal?"

"Five years in a mental institution."

"What are you going to do?"

"Nothing that concerns you."

The phone went dead and Walter Givens slammed the receiver back into its cradle and swore, "Damn stupid bastard! All he has to do is keep his big mouth shut."

Paul Wentzel put his phone back in its cradle, picked up his service revolver and, placing the barrel of the gun in his mouth, pulled the trigger. The sound of the shot shattered the evening silence of the police station. The desk sergeant jumped from his chair, pushed the general alarm button and ran down the hall to the door marked Police Chief, Paul Wentzel. Kicking the door open, he ran to the desk and found Paul Wentzel lying dead in a pool of his own blood.

*   *   *   *

Hick saw to it that everyone was situated on the same floor and the floor was off limits to anyone else. Jed Palmer deputized three Marine sergeants and positioned them on eight hour shifts at the elevator door. The stairwell door was locked but the manager insisted it be welded shut with a one side breakaway in case of a fire.

It was seven o'clock when Hick entered his room. He and Henry had escorted Manning to her room and checked it out. Henry was in the room on the other side of Hick. He said he was tired and decided to shower and get some sleep. The breakfast meeting was early and he wanted to be up ahead of everyone else for his daily walk and Hick insisted, "There will be no walking the streets, Henry, and you know why. Manning suspects, or at least she should, there's danger out there for us all. Understand?"

There was a meek but differing reply in his deep voice, "Yes, Your Honor. I'll walk the corridors on this floor only."

"Good. You understand, knew you would. See you in the morning."

As Hick closed the door to his room the phone rang and picking it up asked, "Who is it?"

"Captain Bob Tyson, Your Honor, Omaha Police Department. I am second in command and I'm calling to inform you Chief Wentzel has committed suicide."

"I've never met you, Captain, but I've heard of you. Why are you calling me?"

"I saw the Chief just before he left and he mentioned he was going to have a drink with David Field, the new federal district attorney you brought from Kansas City."

"Captain, I didn't bring Mr. Field with me. He was sent by the court."

"I apologize, Your Honor, I didn't mean to imply anything."

"I beg to differ, Captain. You did imply something and I'll set the record straight. Yes, we are back for a reason and the reason is for Mr. Field to impanel a grand jury and return with a true bill."

"Against who and for what?"

Captain Tyson's voice reeked with contempt and Hick snapped, "Captain, when the indictments are handed down you'll know who and why. In turn I'll ask you, who do you suspect and who's side are you on?"

"Why, ah, I have nothing to suspect. My job is to uphold the law."

Hick sensed the Captain was flustered and changing the tone of his voice to subtly ridicule, asked, "Excellent. Then tell me, Captain, if you suspect nothing, why do you suppose your Chief committed suicide?"

"I don't know."

"No note?"

"None."

"He never said anything to you?"

"Never gave me any hint of contemplating suicide."

Hick felt the honesty in his answer. He detected a sincere concern on the part of the Captain for his chief. Even so, Hick bore down on him, "Then tell me, Captain, what did he tell you?"

"As I said, nothing."

"Your voice tells me differently, Captain. You suspect something! Didn't you, or don't you?"

"Yes. He alluded to his sexual orientation on several occasions. He was apologetic. I feel he was looking for answers."

"Were there ever any complaints against him?"

"None."

"Come on, Captain. What was his orientation?"

"Pedophile."

The answer caught Hick by surprise but he demanded, "How do you know?"

"I don't really know. I suspect it because one day I was looking for a warrant on his desk and under some other papers there was a magazine. A magazine about young boys…sexually explicit."

"Did you ever confront him about it?"

There was no reply. Hick waited. Suddenly the Captain exploded. His voice was very angry, "We've come full circle, Your Honor! My Chief is dead and I want to know what your David Field said to him to cause him to come back here and blow his brains out!"

"Captain, I don't know what was said. I wasn't at the meeting. If he was what you suspected, who's side are you on?"

"Law and order, just like I said. There's ways of dealing with these people. They are sick. They can't be cured, but they can be put away. They don't have to kill themselves."

"Captain, call me back when you get over the shock of losing your friend. Call about six o'clock in the morning. Ask the operator where we are meeting, she'll know. This is a breakfast meeting of those who, like yourself, believe in law and order to discuss our goals and objectives. You are welcome to attend the meeting if you believe as you say you do. It is not our purpose or prerogative to exclude those in the community of law who believe as we do."

"How do you know you can trust me?"

The question reassured Hick, he thought, *"The man is corning back to his senses,"* and answered, "I haven't been a Judge all these years for nothing, Captain. Judges judge character. As I said, call me in the morning if I can't trust you or just show up at the meeting if I can, so one way or another, Captain, I believe in answering legitimate questions and doubts, such as yours. I'll have what you want and need in the morning...one way or another. Good night...Captain!"

Hick hung up the phone, waited to think, then dialed David Field's room. There was no answer. He dialed the desk. "Can I help you, Your Honor?"

"Yes. Mr Field, David Field, did he leave any messages as to where he would be?"

"No, Your Honor, he did not."

"Please have him call me whenever he returns, and I need a wake up call at five a.m."

"Yes sir, and good night, Your Honor."

Hick re-dialed, "January, here," came the reply.

"Jason, it's Hick."

"I've heard the news. Congratulations, you ole' turkey. What's up?"

"I'll get to the point. I haven't asked Manning yet, tonight that is, if she'll marry me, tonight that is, and if she says yes, would you do it for us?"

"Earth-born matter. License?"

"We took one out years ago but never used it."

"I'll except that. In fact, Hick, I'd marry you two even if you didn't have a licence. This is marvelous. When are you going to ask her and need me?"

"I'll call her now and if she'll have me, about twenty minutes. Heck, I'll call you back."

"I don't think you'll need any luck but good luck anyhow."

Hick, without thinking, hung up and re-dialed the hotel desk, "Yes, Your Honor, you forgot something?"

"I forgot this a long time ago, young man. Connect me with Miss Manning's room. No, forget it, what am I thinking, she's right next door. I best talk to her in person."

"Very well, Your Honor. Good night again."

Hick hung up the phone and walked immediately to Manning's connecting door and knocked. "Is that you, Hick?"

"Yes, Manning. Can we talk?"

The door opened and Manning stood before him in a white night-gown with a champagne glass in her hand. Smiling she remarked, "I'm celebrating. Join me?"

"Celebrating what?"

"It's a secret. Champagne?"

"Yes, I believe I will. In fact, it's quite timely."

"For what?"

"I don't have a secret, Manning, but I would like to ask you to marry me."

Manning smiled, and walking to Hick took both of his hands in hers saying, "Marry you? Yes, of course, I will. I love you. When?"

"Tonight. Right now."

"Ah, yes Hick, right now. Oh, a licence, our licence, do you still have it?"

"Yes, I checked with Jason and he'll come right over. He says the license is good and even if it isn't, he'll still marry us."

"Good. Now, Hick, let me see, oh yes, here, I forgot."

Manning walked to the table and poured two glasses full of champagne and turning to Hick remarked, "You won't believe this but I ordered the champagne for courage. I was going to knock on the door and ask you the same thing, drunk or sober."

"Why, Manning?"

"Because I love you and I've…I guess we've both decided we've waited long enough."

"I love you very much, Manning, and I believe we need each other now more than ever."

"Well, that settles that. We'll need a witness. How about D. T. Osbon? I've promised him if I ever did marry he'd be the first to know and could give me away."

"Can you get a hold of him?"

"I talked to him about twenty minutes ago. I told you I was going to propose to you and I wanted him to be ready in case you said yes."

"Good, you call him, I'll call Jason."

Hick walked to his room and snatching the phone from its cradle began to whistle, "Here Comes the Bride", as he dialed.

Jason answered with excitement, "Well, what did she say?"

"The answer is yes. Get on over here."

"Terrific, Hick, I'm on my way."

D. T. Osbon answered Manning's call with, "Well, you did it, right?"

"Right!"

"Well, come on, Manning, what did he say?"

"Yes!"

"Goodbye. I'm on my way."

Manning yelled over to Hick, "He's on his way."

"So's Jason."

"What about a honeymoon?" Manning chirped.

Hick walked into the room and taking Manning's hands in his own replied, "We marry, we do our duty, we honeymoon one month at the Mauna Kea on the big island of Hawaii."

"That's a deal. In fact, it's one helluva' deal, Judge Nicholas Hickman!"

Hick released Manning's hands and placed his hands on each side of her face and slowly drew her to him while gazing with love into her willing eyes. After kissing her several times he drew in a breath and whispered, "It was about time, wasn't it?"

"Your timing is perfect, Hick. Let's get you ready. Put on your pajamas, slippers, and robe. I'll wear what I have on, it's a delightful wedding nightgown I've had in my hope chest for years. I'll call down for more champagne and you bang on Henry's door and get him ready to stand up with you."

"Oh my God, I forgot to tell Henry!"

"He knows."

"How?"

"I told him what I was up to and he said you would say yes so he'd be ready. You'll see. We talk about it all the time, my loving you, that is."

Hick took Manning in his arms and kissed her several more times and then guided her into his room. Knocking on Henry's door they called out in unison, "Henry. The answer was yes! Are you ready?"

The door flew open and Henry's face was glowing with a smile breaking all records for the smile of happiness. He stood proudly, dressed to the nines, with arms outstretched. Stepping forward he swept his powerful arms around them with his voice booming out, "Praise God! Praise God Almighty, for this night He will make you one. Praise The Lord!"

One knock after another brought D. T. Osbon, Judge Jason January, the desk clerk, a waiter with more champagne and a bewildered David Field who asked somewhat confusedly, "Your Honor, what's happening? I thought you might be in trouble?"

"Not trouble, David, a blessing; but first we must talk. By the way, Manning and I will marry in a few minutes. Can you stay?"

"Your Honor, why I, I didn't know, I didn't realize you both were...you know...I'll stay. About your message to contact you."

"Yes. The Police Chief, Paul Wentzel, has committed suicide. His second in command, Captain Robert Tyson, is upset at you. What's the story?"

"I'm not surprised. Wentzel called me. Wanted to have a drink. Jed Palmer was with me. I put the scare in Wentzel. He left but came back. I offered him a deal if he would cooperate. I felt he would resort to suicide and I told Jed he would."

"I like Tyson. He thought Wentzel was a pedophile. He's coming to the breakfast in the morning. Talk to him."

"Yes, Your Honor. First things first, what about the honeymoon?"

"That comes later, after we complete what we are here for."

The room was filled with the flickering light from dozens of candles brought from the dining room by the night fry cook. A three-tiered cake was hastily put together. The room was overflowing with people when Jason January called for their attention. Henry moved to Hick's side and D. T. moved to Manning's. Jason's words brought tears to the eyes that moved back and forth from him to Manning and Hick.

"To the bride, Marsha Manning, to the groom, Nicholas Hickman, and to you, Ladies and Gentlemen, I extend my greetings on this most special day of all days. Like some of you," Jason stepped forward to touch Henry's arm and then D. T.'s, "I have, over the years, developed a special fondness for Hick and Manning. They belong together, they are and were made for one another, for they love each other. The magic between them has always been apparent to those of us who are willing to take note of their interaction in their daily endeavors. They are a team. They are and from this day forward will really be one, forever."

As Jason recited the marriage vows his words came slowly, haltingly, and were filled with emotion as he concluded with, "By the power of Almighty God and that which is placed in my hands by the people of the State of Nebraska, I, Jason January, pronounce you man and wife."

Jason stepped forward and taking both of their hands in his went on, "God bless you both, and Hick, now's the time to kiss your bride."

Hick turned and as he kissed Manning, Henry began singing the Lord's Prayer. All present slowly and quietly left the room as Manning and Hick looked deeply into each others eyes. Henry and D. T. were the last to leave, and closed the door to the room, leaving Hick and Manning to themselves.

CHAPTER 12

▼

The next morning as Manning, Hick, and Henry walked to the break-fast meeting, Manning remarked, "I didn't mention it, Hick, but I asked D. T. to be present this morning. I know he's not a lawyer or what have you, but he is a very responsible person in the community."

"No problem, Manning, any responsible person is welcome. We have nothing to hide or to fear."

Henry opened the door to the meeting room, and as they walked in, at exactly 5:59, a standing spontaneous applause by all present, including waiters and hotel staff, took them by surprise. Hick walked to the head of the table and with Manning and Henry on either side of him remarked, "Ladies and Gentlemen, please be seated. On behalf of Manning and myself, I say thank you all so very much. I personally want to express to you the happiness of our decision last night to marry. Manning and I have been a team for many years. Caring friends and confidants, we are both dedicated to the law and of service to its administration."

Turning to take Manning's hand Hick looking at her said, "On a personal note, and there is no way better to say how you feel than publicly, I must confess I put off the matter of my heart, Manning, for too long. I believe I know now that we are one, our dreams for each other and especially mine for you will be fulfilled."

Turning back to face those present Hick continued, "We have been given a mandate, here in Omaha, to unearth and prosecute a corruption that eats at and tears away at our societal structure. We will lock horns and defeat our adversaries wherever we find them. We will do this together knowing we are upholding the law. I look forward to working with you to this end. Manning, would you like to say something?"

Taking Hick's outstretched hand in hers Manning stood and said, "Thank you, Your Honor. I join in thanking you all for your kindness. You all know the respect I have for my husband knows no bounds, and that's the first time I've used the word husband. I welcome the opportunity to continue on the journey with him, and with you in the search for justice. Thank you again."

Manning sat down and as she did Hick leaned over and kissed her on the cheek. It was a thrill she would never forget, and before Hick could raise his head she whispered, "Thank you, Your Honor, my love."

Hick smiled as he gazed around the table; stopping at a face he did not recognize and then exclaimed, "Ladies and gentlemen, let me introduce to you Captain Robert Tyson of the Omaha Police Department. I would assume you are all aware Chief Paul Wentzel of the Omaha Police Department took his own life last night."

Hick paused as he reached down to grasp Manning's hand and continued, "This loss is an example of life. In Manning's and my life there is much happiness today, in other lives much sadness. Let us bow our heads and remember Paul Wentzel in prayer."

After a few moments Hick continued, "Captain, have you been designated Chief?"

"Your Honor, the Mayor has designated me acting Chief. My official appointment will be on Wednesday after the services for Chief Wentzel."

"Good."

"Mr. Field, my court will be in session Monday morning at nine o'clock. Are you ready?"

"Yes, Your Honor, I will be ready to present evidence to the court to show cause for a grand jury."

"Good. The rest of us will spend the day readying our offices. Please order breakfast and socialize. I believe we are in for a fight and must know and trust each other implicitly."

Manning leaned over to Hick and asked, "Do you think you have won Captain Tyson over?"

"I think his being here and saying what he did makes me believe he'll be a player on our side. Work on him."

"Hick, I need a favor."

"Anything, Manning, name it."

"I want D. T. Osbon to help me."

"Do what?"

"You'll need information on some of these people. The quiet type of information a person like D. T. has access to. I've talked to him about it and he is willing to do it for nothing. As you know his wealth precludes the necessity of a salary."

"Everyone should have compensation for their efforts."

"He insists, Hick, no money."

"How about a title? The title I refer to will cause him to be diligent in his information and fact-gathering activities, and others will look up to him. Not many carry the title."

"What title?"

"Amicus curiae. I am inviting him to advise the court on matters of law to which he is not a party."

"He's not an attorney."

"Not necessary. His unbiased insight is what the court values. This will intensify his research and presentation. He can assist you at the same time."

"Will you tell him?"

Hick stood and tapping his glass asked, "D. T., I wonder if you would be willing to research and advise the court on matters before it on any occasion you or myself deem worthwhile? This will in itself designate you as amicus curiae."

"I would welcome the opportunity, Your Honor."

"Good. Questions?"

"Yes, I'm not an attorney."

"Not necessary. The court can designate or recognize anyone as an amicus curiae."

David Field called out, as if to second the appointment, "My office is available to assist you at any time about any matter Mr. Osbon."

"Thank you, Mr. Field," D. T. offered as he walked over to shake Hick's hand.

"Can you start today, D. T.?" Manning asked.

"Certainly. I have nothing but time and I have some information for you on the matter you have had me researching."

Hick smiled at what he heard, and asked, "What's she have you up to, D. T.?"

"Well, our Wednesday lunches always lead to some question needing answers. That's about all I'm up to."

"D. T., you should have been an attorney with answers as obscure as that one," Hick replied, shaking his head.

Both men laughed while Manning shook her head in agreement.

Hick heard a phone ring and watched Captain Tyson as he answered his cellular phone.

Suddenly he stood and as he snapped the phone shut announced for all to hear, "Your Honor, I must leave. I've just been informed Judge Harold Batemen has been found dead in his office. He was shot in the back of the head."

"Keep me informed, Chief."

When the Chief had left the room David Field stood and remarked to the group, "It seems to me the rats are circling."

Hick countered sternly, "Make your point, counselor."

The rebuke from Hick surprised David and he hurriedly responded, "I apologize, Your Honor, I know you had your differences with the Judge yet were associated for many years. I was insensitive to the moment. My point was it's hard to shoot oneself in the back of the head. It's not usually done. I'd say after the Police Chief's suicide, and now this, the targets of my inquiry are getting nervous and are cleaning house so they can circle the wagons and stonewall."

"Your apology is accepted and your point is noted and well taken, Mr. Field, but save your impressions and theatrics for the proper time and place: my court."

That Hick was hurt, annoyed, and angry was plain for all to see. Realizing this was the time and place for the remarks Hick made, Manning hurriedly reached over to take his hand and as she squeezed it Hick realized what he had said and continued, "I am wrong, Mr. Field, this is the time and place for you to say what you did and in any way you would prefer. However, Judge Batemen had his faults. We all do, but for him to presumably die at the hands of someone else I find unjust and stands against the Commandment, 'Thou Shall Not Kill.' As a Judge I should know this, and I do. I am learned and seek the truth and justice. I am guided in my endeavor by the knowledge I have acquired over the years and I am primarily guided by the Ten Commandments. The Commandments are simple, direct, and to the point. We, as humans, attempt to confuse the issues the Commandments spell out. Any attempt on our part to compromise or equate these divine revelations to our understanding of what is right or wrong is without prior thought or understanding of life and is immature, brainless, and insipid behavior."

As D. T. listened intently to Hick he felt his frustration and sensed the rising tide of anger and he thought, *"I must speak up as I have never done before, publicly"*. D.T. rose to his feet and looking at Hick asked, "Your Honor, is it not best for all concerned to adjourn until the facts of this matter are known and digested?"

All eyes and ears saw and listened to this mild-mannered man as he spoke. There was a reverent quality to his voice that was comforting and reassuring to all who heard him. David Field was pointedly impressed yet had reservations and leaned over to Jed Palmer and whispered, "His Honor made a brilliant tactical maneuver when he picked this man as amicus curiae."

Hick didn't really know D. T. Osbon all that well and what he did know came from Manning. At this moment he shared the same feelings about the man as the others in the room and he thought, *"I picked the right Amicus Curiae. When he speaks he captures those who listen, or was it Manning who picked him?"*

Manning leaned over and offered, "Hick! Let it go...listen to D.T."

Hick nodded in agreement as he responded, "We stand adjourned. My court will be in session at ten o'clock in the morning. Mr. Field, please schedule your pleadings with the Clerk. Judge January, Your Honor, can I have a word with you before you leave?"

"Sure can, Your Honor," Jason January called out. The room emptied leaving Hick, Manning and Jason. Hick reached over and took Jason's hand while saying, "Can't thank you enough for what you did for Manning and I last night and for being here this morning."

Jason leaned over and kissed Manning and looking up at Hick with a smile remarked, "That kiss and the many to follow make it all worthwhile. Now, what else do you want?"

"Simple. I want the J. R. Rollins case rolled over into my court."

"It's not a federal matter."

"Make it one."

Jason January was as perceptive as he was intelligent and direct. He knew to resist was out of the question, for he knew Hick was up to something. He stared at Hick for a few moments and then said, "I won't resist, Your Honor. I will say this, however, what you want is a little, shall we say, shady and unprecedented, but I'll twist Villella's tail and point his nose in your direction. You'll owe me one."

"Agreed."

"And Manning," Jason added, "You owe me one and I'll collect now, thank you."

Manning leaned over, kissed him, and added, "On your way, con man."

Jason smiled, turned, and was gone.

Manning saw Hick watching but sensed his mind was working on something else.

She turned to him and said, "Spit it out."

"I will. I've been thinking, Manning."

"I could tell that, Hick, it's written allover your face. Come on…spit it out. What do you want?"

"A very tight-knit group. You, Henry, D. T., and Jed Palmer. That's all."

"What about David, the new Police Chief, Jason, and on and on?"

"Too many. Let's enter into a conspiracy, just like the one we're up against, fight fire with fire, that's the only way to keep our activities under cover."

"Is it legal?"

"Certainly is. I don't think all conspiracies are necessarily an unlawful act. Just like propaganda, it can be to further or damage a just cause."

"A conspiracy it is then. When do we have our first meeting?"

"Tomorrow morning in my court before David Field shows up at nine. Let's go to the new offices. Where are Henry and D. T.?"

"They left with Jed and are heading for the courthouse."

"Let's join them."

*   *   *   *

Bob Tyson was met at the door of the Hotel and immediately taken to the county courthouse. He was met by Lieutenant John Kinmonth who informed him, "Before you go in and see for yourself, sir, it's as slick a takeout as I've ever seen."

"Why do you say that?"

"Just like his secretary, one shot, not a sign of a struggle or even the slightest evidence he knew what was going to happen. The doors were open, no signs of forced entry. He was sitting at his desk, with his computer on and evidently reading."

"Watching and reading what, Lieutenant?"

"Why, ah, a pornographic magazine, and his computer was tuned into a porno site, Captain."

"You seem stunned, Lieutenant, are you?"

"Yes, I am. He was a Judge and just last night Chief Wentzel..."

"Excuse me, Lieutenant! What about Chief Wentzel?"

"The word's out, Captain. No sense in trying to hide it. He was a pedophile. What's going on?"

"Trouble, Lieutenant, trouble for a few people in this town who never thought they'd get caught. That includes the Chief and Judge Batemen. Let's see what's what."

Walking in the room Captain Tyson saw Harold Batemen sitting at his desk, face down. His left hand dangled at the side of the chair and his right hand lay next to an open magazine that depicted two young boys engaged in sex. The computer had been turned off. There were no signs of a struggle and he noted there was no pool of blood. Looking at Lieutenant Kinmonth he asked, "The lab people been here?"

"Come and gone. That's why I turned off the computer."

"That was quick. Who found the body and when were you notified?"

"Security found him one hour ago, the front door to his office was open. We were notified immediately. I did what had to be done before notifying you because I knew you were in a meeting with Judge Hickman."

"What can I touch?"

"Anything. The place has been swept for prints and what have you."

"Find anything?"

"Nothing."

"Really," Captain Tyson sighed as he moved to Harold Batemen's body. He grabbed Harold's hair and lifting his head noted out loud, "Yup, there's a hole where the bullet came out. Notice, Lieutenant, there's not much blood on the desk. In fact, I'd say just a few drops. Doesn't make sense. Anybody look for a bullet?"

"Where, sir?"

"Opposite from where he was sitting here at the desk. If someone slipped in here and shot him without him knowing it was about to happen, he would have had to be looking out the window. See a hole in the window?"

"No, sir."

"Well, if he was shot while facing the wall, any signs of a bullet within one hundred and eighty degrees?"

"No, sir, we didn't find anything."

"That tells me something, Lieutenant. What's it tell you?"

The Lieutenant knew he had missed something important and muttered, "I need a moment to think."

"Take your time."

The Lieutenant walked around the desk and viewed the wall. Seeing nothing, he walked back to the desk and looked down at the small amount of blood and then exclaimed, "He wasn't killed here, sir!"

"You're right, Lieutenant. Tell me why he wasn't."

"No sign of a struggle. If shot while facing the window, there should be a hole in the window. If shot facing the wall, there should be a hole in the wall and there isn't enough blood."

"What if he knew his assailant and let him get behind him somehow?"

"There's still no bullet."

"The hole in his forehead is small and something else. What does that tell you?"

"Steel jacketed bullet."

"Look at the wound edges carefully."

Lieutenant Kinmonth turned Harold's head to one side and peering at the wound recounted what he saw, "Wound diameter a little under a half-inch. Smooth margins but contused and inverted. There's no substantial clot in the upper part of the hole. Very little swelling around the wound."

"Well? What's it *tell you?* That hole in his head?"

"It tells me he was shot elsewhere."

"Why?"

"Not enough blood on the desk. Someone shoved something in the wound to stop the bleeding. The wound margins are inverted and the pressure applied reduced the swelling."

"Good deduction, Lieutenant."

"Could anyone have heard shots if they were fired in this office?"

"Not likely and none were reported."

"What about his car?"

"Not in the parking garage."

"That's peculiar. How' d he get here? Did he sign in on the off hours registry?"

"From what we know I'd say he was brought here and carried to his office. The Security Guard says he never signed in or out, he didn't think that, as a judge, he was required to. There's one guard in the building so for someone with keys, knowledge of the place and the security setup, coming and going without detection would be easy."

"Do you smell something?"

The Lieutenant took a deep breath and remarked, "Right! I smell it. I thought it was me but the Judge has the odor on him."

"What is it?"

"Jean Nate' after-bath splash. It's a cologne alcohol based liquid, not oily. My wife uses it. It's for women but a lot of men use it as an aftershave lotion. I do."

"It's not a perfume?"

"No. It's scented but just a lotion and the odor doesn't usually last long. I think."

"Then somebody took a bath in it and I'd bet has the habit. Take a good whiff of the Judge."

The Lieutenant bent down and smelled around the Judge's head and remarked, "I'd say the smell comes from his clothes. No doubt transferred from whoever carried him in here."

"You use it. Where do you usually put it?"

"On my face and neck."

"Never on your clothes?"

"Sometimes I do. It seems to last longer."

"See, we just learned something else, Lieutenant. This after bath splash stuff evaporates faster from skin than fabrics. The cloth acts as a wick…what about the Coroner?"

"He was here and left. His people should be on the way up to pick up the body."

"Any relatives?"

"None. He lived alone."

"Put him on ice. We'll figure out later what funeral home to use when we find his attorney. Let's get back to the station."

*   *   *   *

The phone rang as Roberta Conway sashayed around in her kitchen. She always tried to be as sexy as she could when her husband was home and that wasn't very often. Roberta Conway was quite a catch for Robert Conway since her father was the publisher of the *Omaha Sentinel.* Robert rose to editor in no time and when Roberta's father passed on they inherited the paper. Roberta had suspected from the beginning of their relationship Robert was straying. His good looks and manners that had attracted her also gave her reason to believe he would stray "now and then." She didn't know he had a lust for young boys.

"Conway's," she said sweetly as she answered the phone.

"It's Walter, Roberta. Bob in?" he asked curtly.

Roberta had no use for Walter Givens. *"He may have everyone else fooled that he's a pillar of the community but I know he'd screw anything he could lay his hands on,"* she thought and then answered sweetly, "Why, Walter, how nice to talk to you. Yeah…he's home, just one minute."

The blood drained from Walter Givens's face at her reply and he thought, *"What in the hell has happened to that bitch? She's not usually like poisoned maple syrup."*

Roberta called out to her husband, "Bob darling, it's the phone for you. Walter Givens is on the line."

"Thanks, Roberta. I'll take it here in the living room. You can hang up!"

Robert Conway picked up the receiver and waited for the click as Roberta hung up and then answered, "Walter, what's up?"

Walter sneezed and at that moment Roberta Conway, still holding the receiver to her ear, carefully eased up on the phone's switch and heard, "Harold's history."

"Who'd you get.?"

"I didn't get. I did it."

"What?"

"You heard."

"I didn't think you could do a thing like that."

"Well, before whatever is coming is over you may be able to and even to yourself. Like Wentzel did."

"Nonsense."

"You sure that bitch of your's hung up?"

Robert Conway covering the mouth piece of his phone called out, "Roberta! Did you hang up?"

Roberta hearing what she did was horror-struck and taking a moment called back, "Why, ah, louder, Bob, I have the water running. Now it's off. What is it you want?"

"Forget it, Roberta," lifting his hand from the receiver he continued, "She's in the kitchen. No problem. What do you think we should do?"

"Get out of town for now. Take a nice long vacation."

"Ridiculous, Walter. If all six of us left at once, that could draw attention."

"Four. Two are dead. Remember?"

"You're right. It could be seen as just coincidence if we all left."

"I don't give a damn what it looks like. We better hang together like we have in the past or we're all going to jail."

"That's silly. What for?"

Walter Givens turned red and the veins in his neck stuck out as he yelled in the phone, "You dumb, simple ass! What in the hell do you think Wentzel killed himself for and why I killed Harold? You're a damned pedophile, Bob, and that's against the law. You've been in a state of denial since you became a big shot publisher. Well, listen up, the law doesn't give you immunity any more than the rest of us."

Without answering, Robert Conway slowly and methodically hung up the phone and sat slowly in a sofa, looking without purpose straight ahead. Walter Givens, on his end, slammed down his phone and yelled, "How in the hell did I ever get mixed up with these perverted clods?"

Roberta Conway put the receiver back and as she did tears welled up in her eyes to stream profusely down her cheeks, and holding her breath to keep from screaming, she sat at the kitchen table. Wiping her face with her lace apron and shaking her head she whispered, "Oh, my God. All these years and I didn't know. What will people think if they ever find out? I must do something."

Roberta stood, walked to the kitchen sink and turning on the cold water, waited and began to splash her face. Reaching for a towel, she wiped her face and walked to the living room where Robert Conway sat as if in a trance. Roberta sitting down next to him took his hand, kissed his cheek and said, "I'm so sorry for you, Robert. I heard." There was no answer.

Dropping Robert's hand she stood, walked to a table on which her purse sat and while opening it remarked, "Robert, we have to get away.

Why, the shame and disgrace would kill us both. We must hide quickly. I know just what to do."

Roberta, taking the car keys from her purse, returned to take Robert's hand and lead him to the garage. She helped him into the passenger seat and ran around to the drivers side. As soon as she entered the car she started the engine. Robert muttered, "Don't forget to open the garage door."

"Oh, of course. How forgetful of me. Put your head back and rest Robert, we'll be out of trouble…soon."

*   *   *   *

Bob Tyson, on returning to the police station, found the booking sergeant and several others had temporarily moved him into the Chief's office and Lieutenant Kinmonth had been moved into Bob's old office. Sergeant Booker was proud of himself as he informed the new Chief and Bob Tyson remarked, "Things never change, Sergeant. The King is dead, long live the King, and in this case we haven't even buried the old King. But thanks, it's the way it should be. We have to go on."

Bob Tyson closed the door to the office and sat down alone. As he sat pondering what had happened in the last few hours the door suddenly burst open and Lieutenant Kinmonth, obviously excited, stepped into the room announcing, "You'll never believe it!"

"Calm down. What won't I believe?"

"Conway, the publisher, and his wife tried to commit suicide."

"Tried to?"

"Well, he made it but she's hanging on."

"Back to the beginning, Lieutenant. Slow down and tell me what happened from the beginning."

"Well, the FedEx man went to the house with a letter. No one answered the doorbell and as he was leaving he heard the car running in the garage. He broke in and found them both in the car. He opened the garage door, dragged them out and called 911. He said, the driver that is, Mrs. Conway coughed but Mr. Conway was pronounced dead by the medic when he arrived. He's in the morgue at County Hospital and the Missus is in intensive care, unconscious. They think they can save her. I told them to call if and when she comes around. Can you believe this?"

"Yes, I do believe it. I think our Mr. Field initially pushed the right button. Call him and tell him, Lieutenant, to please inform Judge Hickman. Suggest that if he knows any others that might be in jeopardy or are related to all this in some way, we better round them up or there'll be more dead bodies. Since it's Sunday, writs would do."

Lieutenant Kinmonth whirled around and as he started out the door stopped, turned back, and asked, "Shouldn't you call Field and make the suggestion?"

"Not if I asked you to do it, Lieutenant, and for your information, I don't think Field trusts me."

"Why?"

"He knows I've known for some time, what the hell has been going on in this town, by certain parties, and haven't done a damn thing to stop it."

Lieutenant Kinmonth didn't pursue the matter any further, noting the look of guilt and then shame on the Chief's face. He turned and left to call the District Attorney David Haddam Field.

*   *   *   *

Hick was sitting in his office contemplating moves for J. R. Rollins when the phone rang.

Picking up the receiver he heard Manning say, "Judge Nicholas Hickman's office. Marsha Manning Hickman, Clerk of the Court speaking. How may I help you?"

"David Field here. That's quite a handle and a mouthful. How would you have me address you?"

"Manning, David, if you please. I was just trying it out and you're right, it's too long a handle."

"Manning, is the Judge in?"

"Yes, he is. I'll ring him."

"Good, and please, stay on the phone."

Hick spoke up, "I picked up the phone along with you Manning, and I agree, the handle is too long. What can we do for you, David?"

David recounted the recent death of Robert Conway. Manning and Hick expressed their regrets that suicide was resorted to and Hick asked, "And what would you have me do, Mr. District Attorney?"

"Well, Your Honor, out of the seven targeted, only four remain."

"And?"

"Well, sir, from our information one's a skirt chaser with more material on him coming in. One is a pedophile and the other two purportedly are predators of young girls."

"Why aren't they classified as pedophiles?"

"They don't chase young boys."

Manning, fuming at the suggestion interjected, "Young girls are children. You are mixed up, Mr. District Attorney, it's pedophiliac."

"I know, Manning, but that's the way they're classified in my rap sheets."

"Rap sheets?" Hick asked.

"Yes, sir. FBI sheets and they're a mile long."

"What do you want me to do, David?"

"A written order commanding them to surrender themselves into protective custody. I'll have Jeff and his deputies serve them. I'll put them up in our hotel and guard them with Marshals."

"You want four writs?"

"Yes, sir. I think their attorneys will buy it for two reasons. One; They won't be in jail; two; It's obvious a trend is developing and anyone of them could be targeted for suicide or murder."

"Won't their attorneys object on the basis of grounds for this suspicion? Based on association?"

"I don't understand, Your Honor."

"And I don't like to conduct legal proceedings over the telephone. My court will be in session in thirty minutes to consider any request and to hear any pleadings you have, Mr. District Attorney."

"Thirty minutes could be valuable time, Your Honor."

"Manning. What say you as Clerk of the Court?"

"Go sit in your court, Your Honor, Henry's there waiting and Gladis is next door working on her office. It will take me three seconds. How about you, Mr. Field?"

"Three minutes. I'm at the hotel but I'll run. Goodbye."

Manning stood next to the bench waiting with watch in hand. The door to the courtroom flew open and David Field rapidly, but quietly, walked to the prosecutor's table, standing erect with perspiration running down his forehead and cheeks. He started to called out but Henry interjected, "Hear Ye, Hear Ye, the Special Federal District Court of Kansas City is now in session. The Honorable Nicholas Hickman presiding."

Hick rapped the gavel and David Field called out, "If it pleases the court. Could the clerk give me my official time?"

"So ordered," Hick said smiling.

"Two minutes and thirty three seconds. You have met your schedule and it will be so recorded," Manning said sternly.

"You have pleased the court with your promptness, Mr. Field, or would you prefer Mr. District Attorney?"

"Whatever pleases the court, Your Honor."

"Very well then, Mr. Fields, what can this court do for you?"

"I need four writs from the court for a Mr. Walter S. Givens, Mr. Clyde D. Tyler, Mr. Donald S. Remco, and Mr. Tad O. Beasley to surrender to Marshal Jed Palmer, United States Marshal, for protective custody."

"Based on what cause, Mr. Field?"

"The recent suicide of Police Chief Paul T. Wentzel, the apparent murder of Judge Harold J. Batemen, and the completed suicide and/or murder of Mr. Robert I. Conway and the attempted suicide of Mrs. Roberta M. Conway. Her death has not been confirmed. Also, I have in my possession information linking the above-named people to a conspiracy of common purpose that could predispose the remaining living members live's to be in jeopardy from a party or parties yet unknown."

"Interesting. A Conspiracy. Do you intend to seek a grand jury to obtain a true bill?"

"In good time, I do, Your Honor."

"So ordered, Mr. Field. The writs will be prepared immediately, then you can have the Marshal serve them. Also, as you know, the Marshal can arrest who he wants without a warrant but this will make it more demonstrative. The court will be in recess until such time the attorneys of those served appear to object. Which they will."

"On what basis, Your Honor?"

"Simply put, Mr. Field, to whatever the attorneys are, man or woman, they will put aside the safety of their clients because of the supposed taint of guilt by association," Hick looked over to Manning and further declared, "Manning, you go ahead and prepare the writs while Mr. Field and I discuss the inevitable," Then turning back to David, Hick went on by saying, "You said on the phone they would not be incarcerated but under the protective cover of Marshals, but I venture much will be read into the fact that this is Sunday and you are asking for extreme measures out of the blue. Also, their attorneys will want the court reporter, you have met Gladis Pitman, the court reporter, haven't you, Mr. Field?"

David looked over at Gladis, smiled, and offered to Hick, "Yes I have, Your Honor, a striking looking woman and I understand she is the best court reporter hereabouts."

All eyes turned to look at Gladis and as she blushed, Manning mumbled under her breath, "Striking my eye, she's a knockout."

David heard Manning and mumbled back, "I concur with the clerk of the court."

Hick, shaking his head at the interplay, suggested, "Back to the matter at hand, Mr. Field. The attorneys will want the court reporter's notes on what has been said."

"All we've said is we want to protect them, their clients."

"Miss Pitman, take Mr. Field into my office and read back to him what has been said. He'll find it interesting. This court stands in recess until such time it is petitioned to hear the pleadings of the attorneys of the aforementioned parties to the writs I have issued."

Henry called out, "Please rise."

Manning walked to Hick as soon as Gladis and David left the court room and suggested, "Come with me while I prepare the writs for your signature."

While going about her task, Manning asked, "Well, what do you think about the way Gladis looks?"

"She took my breath away. Jealous?"

"I'm serious, Hick. You mean you didn't notice any difference?"

"I did."

"Well, stop being coy."

"I stand by, 'she took my breath away.' You did a good job. She won't be single for long."

"Did you see the way David looked at her?"

"Yes, but do you think he could be interested?"

"Well, he's single, she's single, and I'd bet they get together."

"Good," Manning said gleefully, "here, the writs are done and need your signature. I'll go get David to call the Marshals so they can serve them."

As Manning walked away Hick quipped, "Manning, you're something else. Sit here, preparing writs, and also working on Gladis's case. Only woman I know that can do two things at once."

Exactly one hour went by and Manning's phone rang. She answered, "Clerk of the court speaking."

"What court?" came the reply.

"Federal court, David Skultetty, and you know it."

"Manning! Just kidding. I'm proud of you and I secretly love you and I am crushed to hear you married without consulting me first."

Manning liked David Skultetty. He was young, well mannered, knew the law, and—most of all—understood how the court worked. She snapped back at him, "What would your wife think if I had and what would she have said?"

"Good point, Manning, being married does complicate matters somewhat. But to the point. I need to object about the writ the court served my client twenty minutes ago."

"Who is?"

"Yes, that is important. Ah, my client, Mr. Walter S., not A. Givens. Manning, is the writ still good? You goofed."

"It's still good and you better honor it if you want to stay in my good graces. I goofed because I was trying to do two things at once. Plus working on Sundays. I'll white out the A. and put in an S."

David's voice turned serious as he said, "What gives, Manning?"

"The court wants to protect your client from a person or persons unknown as stipulated. The suicides and murders represent a possible clear and present danger to your client."

"Cause, Manning. How do the murders and suicide relate to my client?"

"I can't speak for the court, David, but if you want to object the court is prepared to hear you in an hour and a half. Want me to schedule you?"

"There'll be others."

"How does he know that if his client's situation isn't related to the others? I think you just gave something away, David," Manning thought to herself and then answered, "I know. Maybe you'll all like to do it together."

"I doubt it. Put me down as a single."

"See you at three, David."

"Three it is, Manning."

Within twenty minutes the four men and their attorneys met in Walter Givens's office. He demanded it, against David Skultetty's advise, "If you do this, Walter, you are establishing for the court today and the prosecution tomorrow that there is a relationship in fact between the four of you. Make them prove it, and Walter, as your attorney, I must ask, is there a relationship?"

"We're friends."

"Friends? There's no common denominator?"

"What the hell are you after, Skultetty? What do you want to know?"

"Simple, Walter! Did any of you commit a crime? Are you linked with the suicide and murder victims in any way?"

"They were friends."

"Walter, you're a very acute business man. You're smart. Your success is predicated on the fact you can anticipate. I'm telling you, something smells. This court is here in Omaha for a reason. I think you and your friends are the reason. There is a link and you better come clean with me or you had better find another attorney. Anticipate this, Walter, if you don't come clean with me and retain me, you'll do time. Big time and, Walter, it just occurred to me, you might even get the chair. That's what they use in Nebraska, you know."

"Just what the hell do *you* know?"

"Nothing! I'm waiting for you to tell me."

"What's it going to cost me?"

"How in the hell would I know? I don't know what I'm defending you against."

"The worst is murder."

"What?"

"Murder."

"The price tag is five million and don't try to intimidate me or yell anything at me. Cut to the quick, Walter, before the others get here. You don't have time to shop around."

Walter Givens didn't really like David Skultetty but he knew he was smart and had always performed for him in the past. He knew he was had by David and made his decision hurriedly in a panic he had never felt before. In five minutes he told David everything. David said nothing as he listened, and nothing when Walter finished. He sat with Walter in the company boardroom, thinking, as the other four men and their attorneys filed into the room and took a seat. Walter stood so as to speak, but taking Walter Givens by surprise, before he could speak, David stood and demanded, "Sit down, Walter, and the rest of you listen. Walter has told me everything about you and your 'Club'. Everything, gentlemen, your perversions, lusts, and failings. I'm certain he'll tell me more as time goes on. I'll remind you and your attorneys, in my opinion, you are the subject of an ongoing federal probe into your perversions, and now suicide and murder. You're being studied and *played with,* like rats in a box, if my past experience with the Feds tells me anything. Also, by meeting here, you've lost your individuality and had better present a unified front, with one voice, and I want to be that voice. I'll answer your question…how much? One million a piece, and one third of that goes to your attorney to join with me in wringing out of you what we need to save your asses. You should know, right up front, that I think your activities are accursed, but I'm an attorney and my obligation is to keep you out of jail and/or the electric chair. There's no time for dickering, yes or no?"

There was a resounding, "Yes!" Even by the other attorneys.

"Good. Get to the federal courthouse. We have a date with a tough judge and prosecutor. One last thing, all of you: I do the talking. You keep your mouths shut, and there are no exceptions, or I walk the big walk out of your lives and at best, you walk into prison."

As the other men and the attorneys left the room, Walter sneered at David and snapped, "You think you're pretty hot stuff, don't you?"

"Walter, I have my suspicions about you and you'd better hope I'm as good as I know I am. Let's join your friends."

At exactly three-thirty David Field and Jed Palmer sat in the court-room, watching as David Skultetty led the group down the aisle to the defendant's table. He positioned each man next to his attorney and walked to the prosecutor's table and extending his hand remarked, "Good to see you again, David."

"Good to see you again, David. Meet U.S. Marshal Jed Palmer."

"Glad to meet you, Marshal. I want to thank you for the courteous manner in which your deputies served my clients."

"They're all your clients, David?"

"They didn't think paying four attorneys made sense."

"The other three are here to learn?"

"Hardly, David. They're all personal friends."

David Field smiled and as he was about to speak Henry boomed out, "Hear ye, Hear ye, the Special Federal District Court of Kansas City has reconvened, Judge Nicholas Hickman presiding. Please rise."

David Skultetty returned to his table. Manning, sitting to the right of the bench, smiled at him, and moved her fingers as if to be waving. He smiled back. Hick strode into the courtroom, banged his gavel and said, "Please be seated."

David Skultetty remained standing and Hick taking note of this said, "The court presumes you wish to be recognized, Mr. Skultetty?"

"Yes, Your Honor, I do wish to be recognized in the matter concerning the four writs served by the court upon my four clients."

"As you say, I am aware of the writs, Mr. Skultetty. You are to represent all four of the clients in this matter?"

"I have been so retained, Your Honor."

"Highly unusual...proceed, Mr. Skultetty."

"My clients object to the writs and do not wish to comply with the Court's order unless cause is shown."

"Very well, Mr. Skultetty. Mr. Field, can you show cause as to why the court should overrule Mr. Skultetty's objection?"

"I have presented to the court cause for the action. The court issued the writs."

"I know that, Mr. Field. They want to know what you said to convince the court."

"The recent suicide of Paul Wentzel. The murder of Judge Harold Batemen and his secretary, Gertrude Boltinghouse, and the apparent murder-suicide of Robert and Roberta Conway, give us reason to believe these men's lives are in jeopardy from a party or parties unknown."

"That's fine, Mr. Field, but get to the point. Mr. Skultetty wants cause, commonality. Am I correct, Mr. Skultetty?"

"Yes, Your Honor."

"They meet on a regular basis and have a common cause and purpose for meeting."

"I object. How does the prosecutor know this, Your Honor?"

"Now, Mr. Skultetty, you are on the threshold of understanding. The prosecutor divulged to the court what the court needed to know to take the action it did. This is protective custody, Mr. Skultetty, not incarceration."

"They meet on a regular basis, or so it is alleged. What evil of purpose would cause them to be in danger so that they must give up the individuality of their person?"

"Now that's a mouthful, Counselor. Your reply, Mr. Field?"

"Is this an informal session, Your Honor?"

"Not on your life, Mr. Field. This court is in session, period. Reply, Mr. Field."

"I believe these men could be in danger. I have given the court cause and the court agreed with me. I do not intend to divulge more at this time."

"Can I appeal the Court's decision?" David Skultetty called out.

"You can appeal anything this court does, Mr. Skultetty, as you know full well, but until the appeal is heard, I will remand these men to the custody of a U. S. Marshal. It will not be voluntary. I will have them arrested and thereby their surroundings will change dramatically from a luxury hotel to a jail cell."

"You can do this for how long, Your Honor?" David Skultetty asked with a worried look.

"Until the prosecutor can assure me these men are not in any danger whatsoever or your appeal is heard and I am overruled."

"My clients will surrender voluntarily, Your Honor."

"That was a wise decision, counselor." Then Hick turned his attention to the Marshal and advised, "Marshal Palmer, escort these men to the Hotel and assist them in any way possible so their protective custody will not be more of a burden than necessary. Their immediate families must have access to them at any time. Be certain their business needs are met. I will personally converse with them each day and keep them up to date. Questions?"

Hick looked at each man sitting before the bench. He saw solemn faces but there were no questions. Hick stood saying, "Since there are no questions, this court is adjourned."

Henry called out, "Please rise for the Honorable Judge Nicholas Hickman."

CHAPTER 13

▼

Tuesday, a dreary rain persisted throughout the day in Kansas City. There was a slight chill in the air and Felix always rose earlier than the Judge and went about cleaning up from the night before. He made his way to the kitchen to begin a hearty breakfast, for this was the meal the Judge enjoyed most. Before going to the Judge's room to awaken him, Felix started a fire in the study. He waited to hear the Judge singing, but Sam Waterford came instead to the breakfast table with a vacant stare. Felix knew the look and didn't even bother to gain the Judge's attention, and after breakfast the Judge moved to the study and sat in his chair, before the fire, all day without saying a word. Late in the afternoon he seemed to still be studying the flames, when Felix finally asked, "Well?"

Sam turned his head away from the flames to face Felix and grunted, "Well, what?"

"Sam, you're a study. I know what you're up to. Do you want a port or scotch? It's five o'clock."

"Five o'clock! My God, time goes faster everyday. That's what getting old can do to you. Why didn't you let me know sooner and what the hell do you mean, you know what I'm *up* to? Before you answer, Colonel, make it port, my tired bones tell me there's a chill in the air."

"Port it is and what I mean is, I know you're scheming."

"Scheming, Felix?"

"Yes, Sam, you're crafting a plot of a systematic design. That's a scheme."

"That sounds better. How do you know this, Felix?"

"Sam, you've been sitting in that chair all day. Never once getting up for anything, food, phone, or bathroom."

"Well, I have to go now."

"Then go. I'll get your port for you and then clue me in on what you have decided."

"How do you know I have decided anything?"

"Sam, it's easy. The twinkle is back in your eyes. Go take your leak or whatever."

Sam Waterford had made a decision and when he returned to his chair he sat down, letting out a groan of comfort. Chuckling, he lifted his glass of port and blurted out, "You're right as usual, Colonel, so stir up the fire."

Felix knew the instant Sam called him Colonel, he had in fact made a significant decision and pleaded, "Come on, Judge. Let me in on what you, ah, we are going to be up to."

"What did Jed say about the day's events to date in Omaha?"

"Nothing more than I reported yesterday about the protective custody matter. Said Judge Hickman handled it well. David's comment was, 'A sterling performance.'"

"I expected that from Judge Hickman. Now, Colonel, I want as much supportive information sent to D. T. Osbon, the amicus curiae, as we can lay our hands on. He's to be our conduit of support to Judge Hickman. Do not, and I repeat, Colonel, do not hold anything back from him that could arouse suspicion, and Colonel, I want him sworn in on the Q.T."

"As what, Judge?"

"Any title, say, Special Officer of the Court as directed by me. Hickman is in charge but I'm going to exercise quietly my senior status, based on longevity, for my experience tells me to never forget before this is over, they'll be looking for anything to throw this whole matter into the appellate court."

"Couldn't his association with us be contested?"

"Anything can be contested but he'll be an officer of this court, my court, and he can still act as an amicus either in Judge Hickman's chambers or publicly in his court. Appellate Judges don't like to interfere with the way another Judge runs his court."

"Yes, sir!"

"And, Colonel, I picked Judge Hickman for this matter, or I should say matters, but they're both really one, because I believe he will bring to the bench an insight based on judicial wisdom yet human sensitivity and disgust for the trivial manner in which the laws of God that have influenced our society are being disregarded in many camps. Do I make myself clear?"

"That you're angry about something, most likely the same thing Judge Hickman is angry about, but what it all adds up to in Omaha I don't seem to have a clue."

"You will, my dear Colonel, you will. When is the J. R. Rollins case to be heard?"

"Tomorrow."

"Good. After tomorrow things will start to fall into place. Call Joe Hirsch. Get him over here for some port."

*   *   *   *

Wednesday, 9 AM, Judge Jason January's court

"Hear ye, hear ye, the District Court of Nebraska, Judge Jason J. January presiding, is now in session. Please rise."

Jason January swept into the room and as usual left no doubts in his trail that there would not be anything practiced in his court but the letter of the law. His reputation had preceded him for many years. He was sixty-three years of age. Upon graduating from law school at the age of twenty-seven, he joined the Navy rather than practice law.

Asked why, he replied, "I'm not ready. There's other things to do and to learn. First!"

He joined the Navy to fly and for fifteen years served as a naval pilot. Quickly rising in rank during and after the Korean war, he attained the rank of Captain. One day he resigned at the age of forty-two and returned to Omaha to practice law. After five years of distinguished engagement in the courts he was appointed, at the age of forty-seven, to fill a seat on the district court. Sixteen years passed swiftly but brought with it the complete respect of the legal community. Jason January was an all business, no nonsense Judge. No one dared to come to his court unprepared.

This day he called out, "Please be seated. Mr. Villella, I'm up to date on this case but tell me, what's Mr. Field have to do with the matter before this court?"

David Field shifted in his chair nervously with the early recognition of his presence. Joe Villella replied, "May I approach the bench?"

"Why? Secrets already?"

"To explain Mr. Field's presence."

"Shoot…it's an open Court, Mr. Villella. Explain so we'll all know."

"We have a true bill, Your Honor," Joe Villella said nervously, "ah, in the case of the State of Nebraska vs J. R. Rollins, M.D."

"A true bill for what?"

"Attempted murder."

"Allow me an aside, Mr. Villella. Is the grand jury still in session?"

"As we speak, Your Honor."

"Without you, Mr. Villella?"

"My deputies are present, Your Honor."

"Okay, back to Mr. Field."

"It is our opinion that the indictment should be a federal one."

"Interesting. Why?"

"Federal laws were broken."

"Really? Give me the big one, Mr. Villella, that was broken."

"Crossing state lines to contract for the murder of a person or persons."

"That's a good one, Mr. Villella. What say you, Mr. Field?"

"I concur, Your Honor."

"I had that figured, Mr. Field, or you wouldn't be sitting in my court. Go on…tell me…why you concur."

"We have the evidence. Prima facie evidence."

Paul Ortman had been listening and watching intently but had not shown any outward concern, but at this point he jumped to his feet and called out so as to stall and confuse, "I'll contest the fact that he feels uncontested would establish the fact or raise a presumption of guilt. Whatever it is."

"Nicely put so as to obfuscate. I wondered what happened to you, Mr. Ortman, since Doctor Rollins is your client," Jason January snapped back with obvious glee, "but Mr. Villella has an indictment, so the twelve true grand jurors feel there is an inference as to the truth of the evidence presented to them based on probable reasoning. The ball is in your court, Mr. Ortman, but this time spit out what you have to say so we understand it."

"And the definition goes on to say in the absence of, or prior to, actual proof or disproof. I didn't have access to what was presented, so I could accept the taking for granted guilt of my client. To leave no doubt I want an open court presentation of the so-called evidence. Twelve jurors or not. The presentation, whatever it was, was one-sided at best and this court knows it."

Jason January was surprised by Paul Ortman's initial outburst, so as to obfuscate and collect his whits but not offended by it. He drummed his fingers on the bench and leaning forward commented, "Bravo, Mr. Ortman…you got to it…and you are right but I think the real question is whether this case should be bumped into a federal court because it is asserted that interstate activities took place."

Paul Ortman's face flushed and his words were strident as he replied, "Maybe that's what the presumption of guilt or the true bill was really based upon."

David Field jumped to his feet while calling out, "The facts presented to the Grand Jury gave them cause to indict. Part of the facts do involve interstate use of the telephone for purposes of committing and or being a part of a felonious activity."

Jason January sat back in his chair, folded his hands in front of his face as if pondering what had been said. The attorneys' eyes were focused on him and he sensed their wanting him to make a decision. He countered, "I've seen the evidence, Mr. Ortman. I've enjoyed the scrimmaging but this case has greater implications as related to other felonious activity. I'll accede to the federal prosecutor, Mr. Field. This case, Mr. Field, is remanded to Judge Hickman's court for disposition. Mr. Ortman, do you want to object?"

"No, Your Honor. We do not."

"Now that is wonderful. Approach the bench."

Paul Ortman didn't object because he knew the cards were stacked against him and to appeal meant more delay. His gait and facial expression gave testimony to his displeasure. As he stood before Jason January he half-smiled and then saw him push a phone across the bench while saying, "Call Manning now. On my phone. Right here in this court. The number's on this paper. Ask to be given a trial date."

Paul did as he was told and heard Manning's voice say, "Paul, is it you?"

"Why, yes. How did you know it would be me?"

"No questions, Paul. Judge Hickman will hear your case Friday at nine. Are you prepared?"

"Yes, I'm prepared, but isn't it the prosecutor who sets the date?"

"I know that, Paul. You questioning my ability as Clerk of the Court?"

"No. It was just a reminder."

"Mr. Field chose the time."

"When?"

"One hour ago."

"Manning, am I being set up?"

"No questions, Paul, remember?"

"Yup!"

"That's a good answer to most questions. You'll be ready Friday, Paul?"

"Yup!"

"See ya' in court then."

Paul hung up the phone and pushed it back to Jason while saying, "Seems we're all set for Friday, Your Honor. May I ask a question?"

"Certainly, Counselor."

"Am I—are we being set up?"

"Why Counselor, how unprofessional, but I'll answer your question. Yup!"

The answer startled Paul but before he could reply Jason called out, "Court dismissed," and the Bailiff followed with, "Please rise for His Honor Jason January."

Paul returned to the defense table and J. R. Rollins asked hurriedly, "What's it all mean?"

"Sit down, J. R.. Let me think a minute."

J. R. studied Paul's face as he sat thinking. Suddenly a broad smile crossed Paul's face and, lifting his eyes to J. R., he whispered, "More times than not cases are decided in the judge's chambers. Usually both attorneys are present but in this case I have the feeling they know you aren't guilty of anything and are using your case to catch bigger fish. Judge Hickman's appointment, the presence of a federal prosecutor and his entourage, all from Kansas City, all connected to Judge Samuel Wenter Waterford. They're out after a big, big fish. Are you certain you aren't a part of all this?"

"What, who, why? What's it all about?"

"I don't know but if I had to guess, they're after your nemesis."

"Walter? Walter Givens?"

"Yup!"

"Why?"

"You are kidding, J. R., after what he's put you through and is trying to do to you and, for that matter, has already done to you. You are
kidding, aren't you?"

Paul's voice was no longer a whisper as he jumped to his feet and
going on, disregarded the fact David Field and Joe Villella were listening, "This guy is treachery incarnate. Where have you been? He's sto-
len your wife, alienated your sons to a point where they are willing
players in trying to have you convicted of a phony felony. You're an
ostrich of good with your head stuck in the sand. You better get your
head out of the sand and up looking around for who in the hell is trying to do you in!"

Paul's voice was now thundering as he gulped for air and continued,
"I believe your interests are being looked after by the likes of Judge
Samuel Wenter Waterford, Judge Nicholas Hickman, and Judge Jason
January. Something is rotten, really rotten here in Omaha. You're a
ploy between good and evil and you have some heavy hitters on your
side…our side."

Joe Villella and David Field smiled at what they heard, stood and
walking toward Paul extended their hands to shake his. Joe Villella
spoke first, "Paul, I'd say you've precipitated out."

David Field added, "And smart, too."

Paul, still agitated, was taken by surprise by their words but uttered
impulsively, "Well, am I right?"

Joe and David looked first at one another and then at Paul and in
unison answered, "Yup!" turned and walked away. David leaned his
head over as they walked and commented, "So far, so good."

$$* \quad * \quad * \quad *$$

On Thursday at nine A.M. Manning was sitting at her desk in deep
thought as she studied a report that had been sent to D. T. Osbon by

Joe Hirsch in Kansas City. She became aware someone was standing before her desk. Looking up, she slid the report under other papers stacked on the desk. Seeing it was the mayor, Manning immediately rose to her feet while remarking, "Why, good morning, Mayor Gunderson. Forgive me, I was engrossed in paperwork and didn't hear you knock."

"I didn't knock, the door was open, Manning, so I took the liberty of walking in. My congratulations to you and the Judge on your recent marriage. He is a lucky man. Is the Judge in this morning?"

Manning thought, *"Peculiar his secretary didn't call for an appointment."* Manning never liked Dwight Gunderson, he was just too sweet and slick. He seemed to ooze his way around the city and she found him particularly obnoxious when he was running for office, for he would say anything anybody wanted to hear to get their vote. He had been on the city council, then ran for the state legislature, then congress. When defeated soundly after his first term in Congress, he returned to run for mayor and had been elected twice; much to Manning's surprise.

Manning replied, "He is in, Mr. Mayor. Let me see if he is free."

"It will only take a few minutes, Manning."

"I'm certain he will see you. Give me just a minute."

Manning walked to Hick's door, rapped softly and heard, "Come."

Manning opened the door and turned to smile at the Mayor as she closed the door and whispered, "Our greaseball Mayor, is outside. He wants to see you and says it will only take a few minutes."

Hick smiled at her remarks. Rising from his chair he asked, "What do you think he's up to?"

"You got that right. He's always up to something. I don't have a clue as to what he wants. Let's check and see what he's doing."

Manning and Hick walked to the office door and slowly opened it a crack to see the Mayor thumbing through the papers on Manning's desk. She covered her mouth to stop from saying anything. The Mayor had taken note of Manning's action of slipping the report from Joe

Hirsch under her other papers. Retrieving it, he began studying it intently. Hick closed the door ever so carefully and signaled Manning to walk to the other side of the room and quietly remarked, "Looks like he found what he wanted. What is it?"

"It's a report to D. T. from Joe Hirsch. It's not even for your eyes."

"How'd you get it?"

"D. T. asked me to review it and to help him prepare to present it as Amicus Curiae."

"What?"

"You didn't know?"

"No! I'm beginning to get the feeling there's more, a lot more to all of this than I know or have even suspected. You sure you aren't in something up to your neck that I don't know about?"

"Really, Hick. We'll discuss this later. I better cut the Mayor's snooping off before he finds out too much."

Manning walked to the door and in a loud voice said, "I'll bring the Mayor right in."

The Mayor, hearing her, slipped the file back where he had found it and turned to face Manning as she opened the door and called out, "Come right in, Mr. Mayor. The Judge will see you."

With his right hand extended, and an expression on his face he couldn't or forgot to hide, the Mayor walked into Hick's office as Manning walked out, closing the door behind her.

Hick walked around his desk and shaking the Mayor's hand suggested, "Please, have a seat, Your Honor."

"Thank you, Judge Hickman, I'll only take a few minutes of your time."

"I have plenty of time, Mayor Gunderson. You look very concerned about something…actually you look worried."

Dwight Gunderson's face immediately lit up and waving off Hick's remark replied, "To the contrary. I came to let you know, personally, how pleased Mrs. Gunderson and I are for you and Manning."

"Why, thank you both, Mr. Mayor, and please carry my regards to Mrs. Gunderson."

"Certainly, Judge. I also came to have you understand that my administration is prepared to assist you in any way it can."

"About what, Mr. Mayor?"

"Why, sir, rumors are flying, but they seem to be coming from reliable sources, that two very large cases that could reflect on the city are about to begin in your court."

Hick stiffened in his chair and his hands slipped noticeably out onto his desk as he answered sternly, "You can't put much faith in rumors, Mr. Mayor. They usually are to serve the person or persons starting them and promulgating them. District Attorneys do it quite frequently to flush out suspects. Have you consulted with Mr. Villella?"

"No, I haven't. The rumors seemed to have started yesterday after Judge January remanded Mr., I mean, Doctor Rollins's case to your court."

"Yes, well, it seems that in Judge January's opinion federal laws have been broken."

"I find the institution of your court in the first place very interesting."

"In what respect?"

"A special federal court?"

"Found it interesting too, Mr. Mayor, but also found it intriguing and couldn't resist. How else can I help you?"

"Judge Hickman, I've taken too much of your time. I must leave, but again our congratulations to you and Manning."

Hick stood and, walking the Mayor to the door, saw him out. As soon as he closed the door he moved to his desk and buzzed Manning, "Yes, Your Honor?"

"Manning did you…"

Manning interrupted, "I've carefully slid the report out from under the other papers and have called Chief Tyson. I've informed him of the sensitive nature of the matter and he insisted on his coming over to dust the report for latent prints of His Honor, the Mayor. I might add there was glee in his voice when I told him what had happened."

"You're too good to be true. He doesn't like the Mayor?"

"That's why you married me and it should have been sooner. Yes, it would appear, and has been rumored there is some animosity between the Chief and the Mayor. The Chief says he'll discuss it with me when he gets here."

"I agree. I just never had the courage. You should have been a detective. Find out what you can."

"Detective my eye, it's just that I know a snoop when I see one. I have the strange feeling our web is enlarging. I'll find out everything I can."

"You know, Manning, you haven't told me what the report is about."

"I'm not supposed to. Your next question is, who says so?"

"Right. Who says so?"

"I know what you're up to, Hick. You'll work on me until I tell, or give you enough, and you'll figure it out yourself. Not this time, my love, not this time, but…I'll tell you this, the report is about DNA."

"DNA? I'll let that rest…for now, Manning. I have to prepare for tomorrow."

*   *   *   *

"The Honorable Nicholas T. Hickman presiding. Please rise," Henry intoned.

Walking slowly into the courtroom, Hick's eyes swept the room in its entirety. It appeared only the principal parties were present, which surprised him. Hick sat down and Henry instructed, "Please be seated."

Hick called out, "Mr. Justin, please approach the bench."

Henry quickly walked up to the bench and with a surprised look on his face asked, "What is it, Your Honor?"

"I note, Henry, only the principals are here. No spectators?"

"Yes, there are spectators, Your Honor, but Misters Villella and Field requested they be held in abeyance until you have ruled."

"On what?"

"I agreed with them, under the circumstances, Your Honor, but you'd best ask them."

"Henry, you're beating around the bush. I'll get to the bottom of this." Hick's eyes made contact with the attorneys. He thought, *"They're anticipating me, all right, I'll find out what's going on,"* "Mr. Villella, Mr. Field, approach the bench. Oh, and you too, Mr. Ortman."

Again, Hick was taken by surprise, for the three men stood before him before he even finished the sentence. Obviously frustrated, he commanded in a low voice, "What's going on? Henry says you said no spectators. It's my court."

David Field cleared his throat nervously and added, "Until…"

"Until? Until what, Mr. Field?"

"Until we clarify a witness."

"That doesn't make sense. How in the hell do you clarify a witness? Is it butter?"

Surprised by the remark, the three men laughed. Hick sensed the collusion between them and growled, "You think it's funny? You won't give me an answer? You can't give me an answer? You're up to something and the court, and that's me, gentlemen, is losing its patience. We have a lot to do. Spit it out or sit it out in the slammer."

Paul Ortman interjected, "Please, Your Honor, we meant no offense to the court. If you would indulge us and allow the matter before the court to proceed, it will become very clear, very soon that the dilemma we have regards a matter that will come before the court. We all agree on the matter but the court must make the final decision, so as not to jeopardize any rulings made relating to the matter that will come before the court."

Hick looked at the three men and shook his head from side-to-side. A minute went by as he drummed his fingers on the bench. He then purposely answered, "Mr. Ortman, I detected a tone of sensitivity as to my frustration and my dilemma as to the matter I don't know anything about. Throwing the three of you in jail, I fear, won't bring the dilemma to fruition. I'll proceed as you wish. Sit down."

Hick waited for them to return to their seats and then asked, "Mr. Field, is the prosecution ready to proceed?"

"It is, Your Honor."

"Very well. Mr. Ortman, is the defense prepared to proceed?"

"It is, Your Honor, but a point of clarification is needed."

"Here we go again, Mr. Ortman, make sure I understand this time. Clarification about what?"

"The prosecution has informed me there is to be an amicus curiae in the matter before the court."

"Correct, Mr. Ortman. And you know this is not usual. The courts have always been willing to recognize someone, anyone who comes before the court with information to assist the court in its deliberations. Understanding this precedent as a matter of acceptable law you wouldn't disagree with this decision…would you…Mr. Ortman?"

"I agree, Your Honor, and I welcome it, especially in this case but…"

"For heaven's sake, but what, Mr. Ortman?"

David Field, rising to his feet, asked, "With the Court's permission, may I suggest we introduce the amicus and satisfy the court about him?"

"I'm satisfied about him, but evidently there's some point about him that is causing you three trouble." Hick swung around in his chair to face Henry and ask, "Where is Mr. D. T. Osbon, Henry?"

"He's outside with the other spectators, Your Honor."

"Get him, Henry."

"And Mr. Joseph Hirsch, a.k.a Rabbi Joseph Krupinsky," Mr. Field added.

"Mr. Field!" Hick demanded, "It's my court, remember?"

"I meant with the court's permission, Your Honor."

"Sure you did, Mr. Field. Oh well. So ordered, Henry."

D. T. and Joe Hirsch were ushered by Henry to seats directly behind the railing separating the defense and prosecutors tables from the courtroom general seating. D. T. seemed nervous as Joe Hirsch's smile captured everyone present. When seated Hick offered, "Mr. Osbon, Mr. Hirsch, seemingly you are now officially recognized. There has been some confusion in my mind as to what the counsels for the defense and the prosecution have in mind. Therefore, Mr. Fields, how would you like to proceed?"

"I believe Mr. Ortman wishes to call Mr. Osbon to the stand."

"All right, all right then, Mr. Ortman; you proceed. Pa...lease!"

"Your honor, the defense in the matter of the United States of America vs. J. R. Rollins as a part of an alleged conspiracy to commit murder before this court wishes to call Mr. D. T. Osbon to the stand."

"So be it. Mr. Osbon, please take the stand. Henry, swear him in."

"Please state your name, city and state of residence, and, after placing your hand on the Bible, repeat after me."

"I am Derrold Terrance Osbon of Omaha, Nebraska."

"Now, sir, repeat after me."

"I, Derrold Terrance Osbon, swear to tell the truth, the whole truth, so help me God."

"Thank you, Mr. Osbon," Henry said removing his left hand that had rested over D. T.' s right hand as he was sworn in.

"I guess Mr. Osbon is your witness, Mr. Ortman, proceed," Hick muttered, now totally confused as to what the purpose for this calling of D. T. to the stand was all about. Smiling at D.T., Paul Ortman asked, "Mr. Osbon, are you planning to offer yourself to the Court as amicus curiae in the aforementioned matter before this court?"

"That is my intention."

"About what, Mr. Osbon?"

Hick saw no activity on the prosecutor's part and queried, "You don't intend to object at this point to this line of questioning, Misters Field or Villella?"

"We do not, Your Honor," Joe Villella offered.

"Very well. Please answer the question, Mr. Osbon."

"I have information pertaining to DNA specimens. DNA research and development has been a lifelong endeavor of mine from laboratory research to clinical application."

"Will you please tell the court of your training, Mr. Osbon?"

David Field interrupted, "We are willing to accept Mr. Osbon's credentials as stipulated in the field of DNA research, Your Honor."

"As stipulated when and how?" Hick said, somewhat agitated.

"In discovery."

"When was that?"

"Yesterday, Your Honor," Paul Ortman volunteered.

"Yesterday! Why wasn't I informed?"

"The discovery dialogue brought matters to the surface that made contesting Mr. Osbon as an amicus curiae no longer mutable but for one matter. We felt only the court could make the final decision."

A large smile crossed Hick's face as he slapped the bench and further startling everyone cried out, "Ah-ha, Misters Ortman, Field, and Villella, my judicial savvy and temperament now leads me to believe we are finally arriving at the point we should have arrived at twenty minutes ago. Am I correct, Mr. Ortman?"

"You are correct, Your Honor," Paul Ortman said meekly.

"Then in the name of everything Holy, why haven't you gotten to it sooner?"

"I am...we are...apprehensive, Your Honor, about...about your reaction in your court."

"The plot is thickening again, Mr. Ortman, and I don't like it one bit. You're acting like a child about to be scolded. If I scold you all, so be it, but as I said, I have decided not to throw you all in the slammer, so relax. So, in the name of expediency, get on with it. NOW!"

Paul Ortman walked up to D. T. Osbon and as he prepared to ask the question, there was utter silence in the room. Hick leaning forward in anticipation heard, "Mr. Osbon, are you related to anyone in this trial, and if you are, do you believe this should disqualify you as an amicus curiae?"

Hick, immediately interrupting before D. T. could answer, pleaded, "Mr. Ortman, believe me when I say I want to get to the answer but you're answering your own question with a question. We all now know Mr. Osbon is related to someone in this matter. Let's find out who that is and then determine if it disqualifies him, and I'll make that decision."

Paul Ortman grasped his now trembling hands and asked, "To whom are you related in this matter, Mr. Osbon?"

"I am related to Judge Hickman."

Hick flinched but before he could react Paul Ortman snapped, "How?"

"I am his father. He is my son."

The silence, mixed with Nicholas T. Hickman's seeming astonishment, made for a moment like few moments most experience in a lifetime. Hick's first rational thought was, *"No, couldn't be."*

Then he looked to Manning for an answer and saw the "yes" written across her glowing smile.

Next, looking at Henry he heard him whisper, "Praise God." Now fortified by those he loved he looked to D. T. Osbon who broke the silence by saying, "Yes, my son. I am your father."

Paul Ortman, David Field, Joseph Villella, Joseph Hirsch, Marsha Manning Hickman, Henry Justin, J. R. Rollins, and Gladis Pitman, court reporter, rose to their feet, and with understanding, in unison began to softly applaud. Tears streamed down cheeks as Hick, with a quietness to his voice instructed, "This Court will be in recess for fifteen minutes so that I might confer with my father. Will the clerk of the court and the bailiff please escort my father to my chambers."

Henry called out, "Please rise."

When Manning, D. T. and Henry joined Hick he was standing by his desk and his eyes were concentrated on D. T. as they moved toward one another. Without any reservation whatsoever, Hick moved to his father and wrapped his arms about him saying, "Praise God, indeed, that we have found one another."

"I never lost you, my son. I always knew where you were," D.T. answered softly.

"How could that have been?"

"Please be seated, everyone, so I can tell Nicholas what happened."

Once seated around the conference table D. T. continued, "First I must ask, Nicholas, can you accept that I am your father?"

"Absolutely."

"Why?"

"I can see by the look in Manning and Henry's eyes the research as to who you are has been validated."

"You are correct. Manning asked me to begin a search for your father, not knowing who I was. Then, as matters in the two cases pending evolved, the powers that be wanted me included and it was felt my identity should be made known to you. Judge Waterford has always postulated that timing is the key to success in many things."

"You know Judge Waterford?"

"I have been involved with Naval Intelligence most of my life."

"Naval Intelligence? Judge Waterford is part of Naval Intelligence?"

"It would seem I let a cat out of the bag. It is but something else for us to discuss. You are pressed for time and I would like to say something of how you came to be and what happened."

Hick leaned back in his chair and it was obvious to Manning he was comfortable and at ease with the turn of events. Grasping his hands in his lap Hick asked, "How would you have me address you, Father?"

"D. T. would be fine, and I would like to address you as Hick."

Both men smiled as they nodded their heads in approval. "Your mother," D. T. went on, "and I were young and from very wealthy families. Your mother was Catholic and I was Protestant. Both families opposed our love for one another."

D. T. stopped momentarily to sustain his composure. He went on, "This however did not deter our love for one another. We ran away and secretly married. When it was discovered, your mother was taken away and the marriage was annulled by the church. I was restrained from seeing your mother on many occasions by force. You were placed in an orphanage and it took me years of diligent effort to find you. I have followed your every step, all of your life."

"D. T., you were responsible for my coming to Nebraska's Law School."

"Correct, Hick. It was my greatest achievement only made possible by the fact you were an excellent student and the Dean and I happened to have served in Naval Intelligence. It gave me the opportunity to be closer to you than I had ever been. I sat in your classes and your courts many times. Your mother died six years after you were placed in the orphanage. I pleaded with your grandparents to allow me to take you into my life but was rebuffed on many, many such quests. My appeals to the courts met with denial but my many contacts allowed me to follow your growth and development. I am an old man and when Manning offered me the opportunity to become even closer to you, I never hesitated. I am so pleased you have married such a wonderful friend as Manning and that your other ally, Henry, stands by your one side and I would like to stand at your other side…if you can forgive me."

Tears came to D. T.'s eyes and seeing this, Manning rose and moved quickly to his side and took his hands in hers. Hick stood and as he searched for words momentarily, Henry joined Manning at D. T.'s side. Hick found the words he was looking for, "D. T., there is nothing for me to forgive, for I honor you. As your son it is not for me to judge or forgive you. I thank God; he has given me the opportunity to be able to come to know you and to be at your side as long as we both shall live."

"And through eternity," Henry cried out, and then added, "praise God."

Hick moved to the other three and as their arms locked about one another there was a silence of knowing and understanding that passes from father to son from generation to generation, withstanding the test of time. Manning was moving from one to the other, wiping tears from their cheeks as she informed, "Your Honor, I am sorry but we must return to court; it has been twenty minutes."

Hick, clearing his throat, replied, "Manning's correct, D. T., Henry. Back to work and the matters at hand."

Hick embraced Manning and whispered in her ear, "Thank you for what you have done for me."

Manning whispered back, "My pleasure, my dear husband."

D. T. shook Hick's hand as he patted his shoulder but seemingly could not speak. Henry was last to leave and as he did, whispered, "A few more minutes won't hurt to reflect. It's been a lifetime of loss to now regain. I will wait for your door to open."

Hick understood and returned to his desk and to his thoughts. Five minutes went by. He rose to his feet, walked to the window overlooking the streets of Omaha and cast his eyes skyward exclaiming, "Thank you, God, for Your understanding. Give me the strength I need to do what is demanded and to follow Your will. I ask for Your guidance in the name of the Father, the Son, and the Holy Ghost."

Henry's eyes were riveted on the door and when he saw the crack of light he jumped to his feet and called out, "Please rise for the Honorable Judge Nicholas Hickman. This court is now in session."

Hick walked to his chair and looking down at those gathered announced, "The matter before the court of a possible conflict between amicus curiae Osbon and myself because of our familial relationship has been considered. I see no, nor do I anticipate, any conflict; on the contrary, because of the circumstances, of which you all shared, I expect a special contribution to the court from the amicus. If there are any opinions to the contrary now, or as this matter before the court proceeds, the avenue of appeal is always open. We will proceed."

Hick rapped the bench with his gavel and looking at both counsels asked, "Mr. Field, Mr. Villella, Mr. Ortman, are you prepared to proceed?"

David Field stood and replied, "Your Honor, in the matter of the United States of America vs. J. R. Rollins as an accessory to murder, I would like the court to know that impaneling a jury was agreed upon by both sides. We are willing to accept the first twelve jurors from the jury list without interrogation and waive our rights to excuse any juror without cause."

"That, Mr. Field, is astounding and expeditious considering the nature of the indictment. However, I have a feeling you are up to something but I must ask; Mr. Ortman, has your client been informed of his rights in this matter?"

"He has, Your Honor, and concurs with our attempt."

"Your attempt to do what, Mr. Ortman?"

"As you said, Your Honor, expedite the matter before the court."

"It will do that, Mr. Ortman. Mr. Field, I have a hunch you are leading me somewhere. Where is it?"

"To a matter of fraud, Your Honor."

"Fraud, Mr. Field?"

"Fraud and deceit, Your Honor."

"They go together, Mr. Field, but let me get one thing straight. I don't like to go around in circles. I can take on anything you want to present to the court for its consideration, but I don't like pussyfooting around and why I am going to add this word I don't understand, but deception comes to my mind. Am I being deceived, Mr. Field, by your office? No wait, save that answer, just get to the point."

"The defense and the prosecution in this matter before the court would like to expunge from the record the evidence used against Doctor J. R. Rollins. To the court's satisfaction."

"I'm confused, Mr. Field, your joining with the defense means, in fact, you didn't have a true bill. What goes on? Are you dropping the charges?"

"We have a true bill, but to drop it we feel we must satisfy the court as to the fraud and deception in this matter because it has a bearing on another matter I am bringing before this court. We value the opinion of the court as to what extent those guilty of the fraud and deception should be pursued."

"I don't understand, Mr. Field, but there's that word, deception. Go on, I am willing to listen, proceed but carefully."

"I call Victor Donner to the stand."

"Where is he, Mr. Field?"

"In the hall, Your Honor."

"Who else is in the hall relevant to this case? No, I guess it's now a matter before the court."

"We have Patrick and Joshua Rollins and their mother, Mrs. Susan Givens."

"Henry, please escort all the witnesses in; we'll wait."

Hick had seen Victor Donner before, but the other three were a study. The ex-Mrs. Rollins was dressed in a black sheath dress someone had poured her into and her lipstick was as red as red could be. Her black hair was so black it was obvious it had been dyed. Her blue eyes were accentuated by colored contact lenses. She sashayed down the aisle so as to attract male attention. She was followed by her sons, both of which looked like Ichabod Crane. They were stooped over and shuffled their feet. They looked like they had been in their clothes forever and meekly followed their mother to sit directly behind their father.

Victor Donner was dressed in a navy blue business suit. He strode with his head held high to the Prosecutor's table where both David Field and Joe Villella shook his hand and directed him to a chair. The contrasts of appearance upon entering caused Hick to muse, *"I know who would influence a jury."*

When they were seated Hick recognized them by looking at each one while nodding his head. Hick spoke, "Good morning, madam and gentlemen. The trial matter before this court concerning Doctor J. R. Rollins has been delayed so the court can hear about a matter of fraud and deceit from the defense and the prosecution jointly. This is highly unusual, but the court seeks the truth and could not deny such a pleading be heard since it arose jointly from those sworn to defend and prosecute. We will start again, Mr. Field."

"I call Mr. Victor Donner to the stand."

Victor Donner strode to the witness stand and after Henry swore him in,. David Field asked, "Mr. Donner, you have appeared before this court regarding the matter regarding Doctor J. R. Rollins, have you not?"

"I have appeared before His Honor, but the court wasn't a federal court."

"I stand corrected, thank you. Did you lie to His Honor's previous court?"

Hick moved forward in his chair. "I did not."

"Have you told this court everything about yourself?"

"I have not. I wasn't asked."

"I am asking you, Mr. Donner, to inform this court about that which it needs to know."

"I am now retired from Naval Intelligence so I am now free to speak in open court with some restrictions."

"When did you retire?"

"Yesterday."

"That's convenient, isn't it?"

"No, my involvement was planned, as was my retirement, from the beginning of this governmental operation."

"Governmental operation, Mr. Donner?"

"Yes, sir! Intense surveillance of persons yet unnamed by the federal prosecutor's office of Kansas City has been going on for over six years."

"What was the surveillance about?"

"Interstate murder, pornography, prostitution, extortion, and pedophilia."

"How did the federal government become involved?"

"There was no willing cooperation from local or state officials when approached. Commission of the crimes mentioned on an interstate basis is a federal crime."

"Who are these people?"

"I cannot say, sir. Indictments have yet to be handed down."

"Will they be?"

"You ought to know."

David Field turned to Hick and remarked, "They will be handed down, Your Honor, when this matter is concluded."

"That could be today, Mr. Field," Hick interjected.

"Then they will be named today, for I have true bills against six people."

"Mr. Donner, I have only recently been assigned to this court and this matter. For that fact, why has it taken so long to seek indictments?"

"The people, as you know, have influence. A great deal of influence. Also, to acquire the preponderance of evidence needed for convictions is time consuming."

Hick interrupted, "Mr. Field, you're off on another matter. Let's get back to Doctor Rollins."

"Yes, Your Honor. Mr. Donner, specifically in the matter of the tape purportedly to be Doctor Rollins contracting for the murder of his partner, Doctor Watland, what can you tell the court?"

"It is a fake."

Paul Ortman was on his feet and cried out, "But you were to testify for the state as an expert witness regarding the tape!"

Hick didn't want to interfere so he instructed, "Go on, Mr. Donner. You can answer, this is about as informal as you can get."

"I never testified. I was stipulated as an expert witness. The trial never went anywhere and if it had I was to throw a monkey wrench in the proceedings so as to flush out the real criminals we are after. Doctor Rollins is innocent of any wrongdoing. He has been cooperating with us the entire time."

Hick, smiling and tapping his fingers on the bench, asked, "Mr. Donner, you're telling this court Doctor Rollins was in on this whole thing from the beginning?"

"I am. And a lot of other people for a long, long time."

"That's quite a ruse, Mr. Donner. Why such an elaborate ruse?"

"What we are trying to get to is extensive in nature. Corrupt beyond my comprehension or understanding. We have gathered the evidence necessary over a long time and have concocted many ruses and no one will escape what they have done."

"Okay, Mr. Field, I think I know what's coming next."

"Your Honor, I ask the court to dismiss the true bill and to dismiss all charges against Doctor Rollins."

"One question, Mr. Field, before I do. Was the grand jury in on this too?"

"They were, Your Honor, there was no deceit on our part."

"I still don't get it, Mr. Field. All of this turmoil and taking of the court's time to pull off a ruse?"

"I think and hope, Your Honor, as the guilty are tried and convicted on the evidence this ruse allowed us to gather, you will better understand the necessity for it. The element of surprise of this moment alone is about to ripple through the community and the attention on the part of the citizens and the guilty will have a lasting effect so that what has transpired in the past will never happen again."

"That's quite a speech, Mr. Field, and I hope you're right in what you say. Doctor Rollins, please rise."

Hick waited for J. R. Rollins to stand and as he did, Paul Ortman, Joe Villella, and David Field moved to stand by his side as Hick addressed him, "Doctor, evidently you are to be congratulated. Not only are you a good physician, as I can testify to, but you are a superb actor. I hereby dismiss all charges against you. I thank you for the cooperation you have given to the cause of justice. I am most anxious to observe how this plays out. Would you like to say something?"

"Yes, Your Honor. I want to thank everyone involved who came to help me defend myself from my enemies by including me in such a way that my enemies wanted to humiliate me, rather than kill me, as they originally intended to do. I have but one regret. I have lost the love and favor of my sons because I had to hide the truth from them. Thank you, Your Honor."

"No thanks due to me, Doctor. It's our wonderful, sometimes circuitous system of justice, that leaves itself open to the inventive minds of defense lawyers and prosecutors, in this case. I wonder just how much more has been kept from the court."

Hick had been watching the Doctor's ex-wife and two sons. He saw the ex-wife listening intently to everything said. She now had a worried look on her face. The two sons' faces, however, he never saw, for they never looked up and Hick thought as he observed them now, *"Floor watchers, no guts."*

As Hick started to raise his gavel to adjourn the court, the voice of D. T. Osbon called out, "If it pleases the court."

Hick never hesitated, "It does, Mr. Osbon, please approach the bench."

D. T. walked from the back of the room where he had purposely sat, for he knew when he walked down the aisle there would be an element of suspense. He walked slowly for additional effect. All eyes were on him. His newly established relationship with Hick had had its effect. It was Paul Ortman's idea to identify him as Hick's father first. Standing before the bench with a dignity befitting the moment he intoned, "I come before the court, Your Honor, as amicus curiae."

"The court has so recognized you and so ruled, Mr. Osbon. What would you offer to the court?"

"There is a matter the court should be aware of for final closure of the charges against Doctor J. R. Rollins. The relationship between a father and his son or sons is a special and unique relationship of life.

Considered so important that God, in his infinite wisdom, subscribed to it as all encompassing in the Fifth Commandment. This Commandment has been broken by Patrick and Joshua Rollins and this must be brought to the Court's attention today. If Doctor Rollins is to heal, he must know the truth."

As if his being had been suddenly captured by a supernatural force of inaccuracies, Hick recoiled from the words, 'He must know the truth'. Hick felt isolated in time and space and had to struggle to regain his sense of the present. Doing that, a greater strength catapulted him back to reality and he spoke with a determination, "Excuse my momentary lapse, for your words have seized within me a curiosity of just what is the truth. What is it, as amicus curiae, you would have the court know, Mr. Osbon?"

D. T. swallowed away the tears, wiped his face, and, instantly composing himself, went on, "I have spent my life quietly establishing an in-depth understanding of deoxyribonucleic acid, or DNA."

"Your Honor," David Field's voice implored.

"Yes, Mr. Field, what is it?"

"I have for the court's information the academic standing of Mr. Osbon. His work with DNA is original, for the record he is a father of this scientific endeavor. He has no equal."

"Thank you, Mr. Field, the court accepts Mr. Osbon's credentials and takes note of your remarks. Go on, Mr. Osbon."

"I stand before the court to add supplemental support. As it became known in the matter of Doctor Rollins that he was being used to cover up other criminal activity, facts began to become tangled and to separate the truth from lies it became necessary to attempt to understand the criminal actions on the part of conspirators yet to be named. I was asked to turn my attention to why the two sons of Doctor Rollins would so willingly turn against him and actually participate in trumping up charges against him. The letter he wrote to his sons concerning their mother was not that deleterious to her reputation or her standing as their mother. There was no personal attack against her on the part of the Doctor's words. Their actions were contrary to most human behavior toward parents. As a corollary to my investigation of Mrs. Susan Givens's activities, Doctor Rollins ex-wife, I determined through blood and tissue samples from each son that neither was the son of Dr. Rollins and they were not parented by the same father."

J. R. Rollins lowered his head and his cry of anguish was heard by all, "Oh, my God!"

Susan Givens jumped to her feet, and cried out, "It's a lie!"

The two sons looked up dumbfounded at one another as they jumped to their feet and tried to restrain their mother who broke free from their feeble attempt and was making her way toward D. T.

As Hick's gavel crashed down on the bench his voice erupted with, "Henry! Restrain Mrs. Givens."

Joe Hirsch, with a smile on his face leaned forward over the rail separating him from David Field and grabbing his arm half whispered, "The cat's out-of-the-bag. This is going to turn into a donnybrook."

Henry wrapped his arms around Susan Givens but she screamed out, "You old sanctimonious bastard! You can't call me a whore and my two sons bastards and get away with it!"

D. T. didn't move and his facial expression never changed. He waited, as did the court.

Susan Givens raged on, "This old bastard and you're his son, I hear, has inferred I'm a criminal as well as a slut! Where's the evidence, where's the charges! Don't I have any rights in this kangaroo court?"

Susan Givens was beet red as she struggled to free herself from Henry's grip. She failed and as she struggled, Hick called out to her, "You have rights in this court, Mrs. Givens. No one has charged you with anything. Mr. Osbon, as amicus curiae, has supplied to this court evidence to support his allegations. These facts have been given to Mr. Field, the federal prosecutor, and I believe he has sought an indictment against you and will you give us the results of the grand jury, Mr. Field?"

"I have a true bill against Mrs. Givens, Your Honor."

"Very well, Mr. Field, and the sons?"

"Not enough evidence, Your Honor."

"Very well. Mr. Justin, find out who Mrs. Given's attorney is and call him. Tell him I want him in my Court, now! Take Mrs. Givens to my office and…wait. Marshal Palmer, do you have a federal warrant for her arrest?"

"I do, Your Honor."

"Good, arrest her. Mr. Justin, call her lawyer but first turn her over to Marshal Palmer until her attorney gets here. Marshal, handcuff her right now, and read her, her rights."

Jed Palmer moved to Susan Givens. Henry held her and as the Marshal prepared to handcuff her, a notable silence fell over the courtroom and all eyes were fixed on a subdued Susan Givens. Marshal Palmer took delight in slapping on the handcuffs, for he knew the charges against her. There was an audible "click" as the cuffs locked into place. Susan Givens winced, but as the Marshal led her to the Judge's chambers, she cried out, "You'll pay for this! All of you will pay dearly! Just you wait and see!"

When the door to his chambers closed, Hick turned back to the courtroom and spoke directly to the two sons who stood in disbelief of what they had just witnessed. "I direct my remarks to you, Patrick, and you, Joshua Rollins, in open court. I am aware of what you have done and the dishonor you have heaped upon your father and the sorrow you have brought to his heart."

Joshua Rollins yelled out, "Didn't you hear? He's not our father!"

"Oh yes, he is!" Hick snarled, "He has the power to forgive you without demanding retribution. He has nurtured you, guided you, fed you, clothed you, and educated you to the best of his ability. Tell me, tell them, Doctor Rollins, no matter what, do you consider them your sons?"

J. R. Rollins stood. Everyone in the courtroom waited and rose as a body to hear, "These are my sons, Your Honor. My love for them can never be diminished and I will honor them always as my sons."

Everyone sat down. Hick let J. R.'s words sink in and then instructed, "Patrick Givens, Joshua Givens, go to your mother. Henry, escort them and then return to the court."

Hick waited and when they were gone he sat back in his chair and remarked to D. T., "The court thanks you, D. T., please be seated. Miss Pitman, did you get all that? I know you did, it's a silly question, but I'm looking forward to reading that transcript. I'll bet there's nothing in the annals of court procedure that can compare with what we have just been through."

"I have it all, Your Honor. "Thank you, Miss Pitman. Manning, I'll bet David Skultetty is Mrs. Givens's attorney. See if Henry needs help finding him. Mr. Field, Mr. Ortman, Mr. Villella, how far out on a limb are we?"

"What do you mean, Your Honor?" David Field asked.

"What I mean is, has what happened here this morning jeopardized in any way the main purpose? This was all part of a Judas goat tactic. Does the court's prior knowledge of this tactic set us up for appeals?"

"I think, Your Honor, there are some very worried people right this moment. They deserve to be worried. We will present to the court the evidence needed. No matter what we did or do, there'll be appeals. When Mr. Skultetty arrives we will present to the court the true bills and Joe Hirsch will give prima facie evidence to support our contention that the defendants should be removed from protective custody and placed in the county jail to await trial, and that includes Mrs. Givens and Mrs. Conway, when and if she recovers."

"Is that likely?"

"No, sir. The Doctors tell me that for all practical purposes she is brain-dead. She is not expected to live. She has a flat EEG. Her children are to arrive to determine if her organs can be harvested and the plug pulled. That's the medical recommendation."

"I'm sorry to hear that. Let's just sit back and take five minutes or until Mr. Skultetty barges through the door. He'll be upset, if I know David Skultetty."

"No defense like a good offense, Your Honor," Paul Ortman called out.

Hick smiled and thought to himself, *"That young man played his role of ineptitude so well I can't believe it."*

CHAPTER 14

▼

Before five minutes went by, the door to the courtroom swung open and David Skultetty and his three associate attorneys strode down the aisle. Seeing them, Paul Ortman and J. R. Rollins vacated the defense table and moved to seats behind the prosecutor's table. David Skultetty dropped his briefcase on the table with a loud bang. Hick shook his head and slid forward in his chair, obviously dissatisfied with the display of anger and said, "Well, well, Mr. Skultetty, I hear you're here. We've been waiting for you."

"I object, Your Honor."

"To what, Mr. Skultetty?"

"The high-handed manner in which this court has acted against my client."

"Pish, pish, Mr. Skultetty, watch what you're saying about this court, my Court. Answer me, and be civil with your answer, who is your client?"

"Why, Mrs. Susan Givens, you know that."

"That's what I suspected, Mr. Skultetty, now you've made it official. Have you conferred with your client?"

"I have, Your Honor, and Mrs. Givens related to me the high-handed proceedings of this court earlier this morning."

"High-handed, is it? I know and you know that everything done in this court is subject to review but unnatural proclivities and aberrant behavior can necessitate seemingly questionable tactics on the part of all involved. Even so I'll overlook your remark just this once. Anymore cavalier remarks like that and you'll do time for contempt. So, with some restraint on your part, let's go on. And what, Mr. Skultetty?"

"That this court accepted evidence, DNA evidence of a questionable nature from a questionable witness, that her sons are not J. R. Rollins's."

"Now that's a mouthful of innuendo and damn near slanderous words about this court again, my court, Mr. Skultetty. You are in effect challenging the integrity and judicial acumen of this court, my Court, to evaluate what is and what is not evidence."

David Skultetty knew he had overreached himself and had offended the court. This wouldn't do and he knew it. His demeanor and the tenor of his voice changed instantly. "I ask the court to forgive my brashness, Your Honor. I was completely taken by surprise by the sudden turn of events. Please accept my apology, Your Honor."

"Mr. Skultetty, I want you to understand you can differ with this court, my court, anytime you want. The avenue which you take to differ on a basic concept ends at the appeals court. But...in open court remember you can challenge my decisions but I can overrule your objection. Consider yourself overruled. What else can I do for you?"

"I would like you to set a reasonable bail for Mrs. Givens."

"I object to bail, Your Honor," David Field called out, "Mrs. Givens is an accessory to murder and fraud."

"Your Honor, Mr. Field is out of line, Mr. Givens is in protective custody, and this leaves Mrs. Givens the sole provider for her sons. She can't flee, she has no money. The sons are emotionally distressed at this time and need their mother."

"Mr. Skultetty, this court realizes Mrs. Givens has some explaining to do to her sons. Bail is set at one million dollars."

"But, Your Honor!"

"No buts about it, Mr. Skultetty. Mr. Givens can make bail for his wife without any difficulty and you know it. I should have made it steeper but I am going to hold you responsible if Mrs. Givens walks away. Have I made myself clear?'"

"Yes, Your Honor. I have one question."

"Which is?"

"When the grand jury was impaneled who instructed them?"

"I did, Mr. Skultetty. Why?"

"It all seems to have happened so fast and no one had any prior knowledge."

"You don't have to advertise about impaneling a grand jury, Mr. Skultetty. It was all done very legal-like and it was secretive to a degree and fast because we didn't want anyone fleeing."

"What about my clients in protective custody?"

"It is fortuitous, Mr. Skultetty, that you are here. We will get to that right now. I believe you have something to say about that, Mr. Field?"

"Your Honor," David Skultetty said leaping to his feet, "this all seems like a setup of some kind. You know what David Field has to say about that?"

Hick was once again visibly irritated at what he heard; his voice cracked with subdued anger. "One hundred dollars, Mr. Skultetty, and one more innuendo and it will be thirty days. Pay the bailiff, Mr. Justin, now!"

A very shaken David Skultetty wanted to leave but he pleaded, "I don't have that much money with me, Your Honor."

"Come, come, Mr. Skultetty, between the four of you there is one hundred dollars. I'll wait."

The four attorneys conferred and quickly produced one hundred dollars and handed it to Henry. Hick outwardly was stern but inside he was tickled to see the four of them scrambling to come up with the money. He continued, "Now that you have enriched the court's coffers, Mr. Skultetty, let's proceed."

"Yes, Your Honor. I shall proceed with caution but with the court's permission I would return to my question, but rephrase it for Mr. Villella."

Joe Villella stood, and leaning over to David Field whispered through his teeth, "Here it comes."

"Swear Mr. Villella in, Mr. Justin."

Duly sworn, Joe Villella sat looking up at David Skultetty with a big fixed smile and said, "Good Morning, Mr. Skultetty."

"Yes, yes, good morning. Ah, Mr. Villella, you were the prosecutor in the state versus Dr. J. R. Rollins, were you not?"

"I was."

"Why did you seek and obtain an indictment for murder against Doctor Rollins?"

"I was presented with evidence by Mr. and Mrs. Walter Givens and subsequently Mrs. Givens sons, by her former marriage to Doctor Rollins. They filed suit against the Doctor for slander and libel. Against their father! Can you believe that?"

"Hold it," Hick growled, sliding forward in his chair and peering down on Joe Villella and then instructed, "Mr. Villella, you know better. Stick to the question asked; don't volunteer anything, and no sarcastic side comments…even if you think they're warranted."

"Yes, Your Honor."

"Go on, Mr. Skultetty."

"What evidence?"

"Tape recordings."

"Who taped them?"

"I can't reveal that at this time."

"Your Honor."

"Yes, Mr. Skultetty?"

"Your Honor, I…"

"I'll ask for you, Mr. Skultetty. Mr. Villella, tell us why."

"The evidence is germane to the case for racketeering, fraud, and murder against the four men presently in protective custody, Mrs. Givens and Mrs. Roberta Conway and two unnamed co-conspirators."

David Skultetty was clearly taken by surprise at what he heard. He paused as he thought.

David Field leaned over to Paul Ortman and whispered, "Now we have him rattled."

"What was on the tape?"

"Purportedly Dr. Rollins's voice contracting for a hit."

"Was this evidence presented to the grand jury?"

"It was."

"Was it substantiated by your expert witness? Don't answer, wait one minute," David Skultetty walked back to the defense table and after conferring with his associates returned to Mr. Villella and continued, "Was it one, Victor Donner?"

"It was."

"He wasn't much of an expert, was he?"

"He never said it was Doctor Rollins's voice outright. He said it might be, could be, sounded like, and so on."

"Why? To deceive the grand jury?"

"Hold it, Mr. Skultetty," Hick interjected, "let me ask. Mr. Villella, was there any deception?"

"That depends on how you want to interpret our motives. Mr. Donner was never asked to state if this was a word by word forgery of the Doctor's voice. The indictment and subsequent hearing before you gave impetus to flushing out the big fish we are after."

Hick snapped, "Big fish, you are after, Mr. Villella?"

"We, Your Honor, my office, Doctor Rollins, Mr. Ortman, all were and are part of an ongoing federal investigation of the charges I named against the named parties."

"How come I wasn't told?"

"Not to offend, but the more who know, the less likely it stays a secret, Your Honor."

"I concur. I take no offense. But is this a conspiracy?"

"There is no precedent, Your Honor. The details should be explained by Mr. Field."

"Mr. Field, consider yourself sworn. Mr. Villella, return...excuse me...any more questions for Mr. Villella, Mr. Skultetty?"

"No."

"Change places with Mr. Field, Mr. Villella. Now, Mr. Field, what led up to all of this and why, in your opinion, shouldn't the court consider this conspiratorial in nature?"

"There has been an ongoing federal investigation of interstate racketeering, prostitution, gambling, drug distribution, and murder between the cities of Chicago, Omaha, and Kansas City for many many years. Recently very sophisticated and newer investigations were called for. There did not appear to be any connection with the mafia. This was a new organization, a big organization, not in the numbers of people but by the dollar amounts involved in the various criminal activities. The hub was determined to be here in Omaha by the Chicago office of the FBI who constantly monitors mafia activities in all major cities. As our plan developed we felt an innovation of some sort was needed to flush out the participants at various levels of involvement. Judge Waterford was placed in charge. Under his direction a special project office was instituted and we have been in operation for three years, and to answer your question, it is a conspiracy."

"You are refreshing, Mr. Field. I heard what you just said and you haven't told us much of anything. I'd say you're being obsequious. Why?"

"I am respectful to the court but not fawning, Your Honor. Indictments or no it is still an ongoing investigation and the element of surprise is essential to our cases. I want to cooperate and not agitate. To be honest, I'm stalling."

"And, I know you're not *even* going to permit me discovery. Go on, Mr. Skultetty."

The door to the courtroom opened and four people walked in and sat in the last row of seats. Hick saw them enter and remarked, "Hold on, Mr. Skultetty. Mr. Justin, please approach the bench."

Henry made his way to the bench and Hick asked quietly, "Who are they, Henry?"

"Your Honor, they're witnesses for the prosecution. Two are. The man and the woman. The other two are deputy Marshals."

"Ah, a surprise. Mr. Fields, stall," Hick whispered and then burst out with, "Okay, Mr. Skultetty, proceed."

"How many indictments are there, Mr. Field, in this pending matter?"

"Eight."

"Please name them."

"Mrs. Roberta Conway, Mr. Walter Givens, Mrs. Susan Givens, Mr. Clyde D. Tyler, Mr. Donald S. Remco, Mr. Tad O. Beasley, and Mr. Donald S. Hirsch."

"That's only seven," Hick exclaimed, "What is Donald Hirsch charged with?"

"Murder, attempted murder, extortion, prostitution, gambling, interstate and international drug running, racketeering. The eighth indictment is silent. For now."

"Okay, seven for now, but for the murder of his father?"

"No..."

"If Your Honor pleases," David Field asked.

"Yes, Mr. Field."

"I would like to call a witness to further substantiate for the court the charges we are bringing to bear in this matter."

"The stall, Mr. Field?"

"Yes, sir."

"Very well. Mr. Field, you are excused. Mr. Skultetty, any objections?"

"Not right now, Your Honor, but I'd welcome some clarification."

"All right, Mr. Field, call your witness."

"Your Honor, I call Mr. Samuel Hirsch to the stand."

Sam and Kate Hirsch rose together, and Kate supporting Sam's arm walked to the Prosecutor's table where they were joined by Joe Hirsch. Sam reached out to grasp the table, paused, then looked up as Hick rose to his feet exclaiming, "Sam, Sam Hirsch, is it *really you?*"

"Yes, Your Honor, forgive me for being so slow. I took a bullet to my side, bulletproof vest or not, and I can't walk too far without help."

"But, you're alive, Sam! Take your time, but I can hardly wait to hear what happened."

Kate smiled at Hick and reaching over to the table poured a glass of water for Sam and before handing it to him turned back to Hick and asked, "With the court's permission?"

"That it could be stronger. Permission granted. Good to see you again, Mrs. Hirsch. I am pleased for you."

As Kate waited for Sam to drink his water she remarked, "Thank you, Your Honor. I am pleased it worked out the way it did, and I thank my cousin, David Haddam Field, and Sam's brother, Joe."

Hick shook his head and exclaimed, "This is a day of surprises. Good surprises, Mr. Field. Your stalls have paid off handsomely…this day."

Kate and Joe assisted Sam to the witness stand and when he was seated Henry swore him in, and when Henry finished, Kate reached over the bench to take Hick's hand saying, "Congratulations on your marriage."

"Thank you. We will celebrate, the four of us, thank God, the four of us," Hick replied and then instructed, "continue, Mr. Field."

"Your name, sir, age, and occupation?"

"Samuel T. Hirsch, fifty-six, and I am retired."

"What did you do before your retirement?"

"I was a gambler."

"What prompted you to retire, Mr. Hirsch?"

"My *son* attempted to have me murdered."

A hush fell over the courtroom. The words, "My *son*,", reverberated over and over. There was dismay on every face. Hick was infuriated. The words and the looks on the faces had their effect on Sam. There were tears and then Sam's head dropped and his sobs caused further dismay.

Hick offered, "Take your time, Sam. There is no hurry. All of us understand."

Kate stood, walked to the stand and gently lifting Sam's chin, wiped away his tears with her handkerchief; kissed him and turning to Hick said, "Sam's ready to go on, Your Honor."

"Mr. Field, please go on."

David Field walked to where Sam sat and patting him on the shoulder asked, "You're sure you're ok, Sam?"

"Go ahead, David."

"Your Honor, before Mr. Hirsch continues I…"

David Skultetty leaped to his feet bleating out, "Your Honor, I object. May I ask the court, what purpose, at this juncture, will it serve to have Mr. Hirsch relate the details of the horror of what happened to him?"

"Your objection is overruled, Mr. Skultetty. Go on, Mr. Field."

"I wanted to suggest to the court that before Mr. Hirsch tells his story that the two sons of Doctor Rollins, Patrick and Joshua, be present to hear what Mr. Hirsch has to say."

The excitement on Hick's face was evident and caused David Skultetty dismay. Leaning across to one of his associates he whispered, "This is way out of line. He's letting us be set up."

"Very good idea, Mr. Field. A very good idea. Can you get them?"

"I have them waiting outside with the Marshal, Your Honor."

D. T. Osbon called out, "Your Honor, as amicus curiae, may I suggest the young men sit with me?"

"Good idea, Mr. Osbon. Sit halfway back. Young people have an aversion to the front row. Mr. Field, bring them in but first to the bench."

Patrick and Joshua Rollins walked with heads down as they were escorted to the bench by Marshal Palmer. Hick instructed, "Look up at me, Patrick, Joshua, and listen to what I say. The people in this court, well most of them, maybe even Mr. Skultetty, want you to hear about a sin. We want you to hear how the Fifth Commandment was not just broken but scurrilously disregarded and mocked by a son. You will sit with my father, who until today I did not know, and sits in this room as a friend of the court. Questions?"

Patrick Rollins, with a surly tone to his voice, asked, "Do we have to?"

Hick shook his head in disgust and replied, "Not really...but you will, for this is my COURT and I so order. Marshal, escort them to Mr. Osbon."

D. T. shook their unwilling hands, sat between them and in a low voice said, "If you have any questions, ask me."

"We're about ready, Mr. Field," Hick saw David Skultetty start to rise but then sit back. Hick inquired, "A question, Mr. Skultetty? Don't be hesitant."

"A comment, Your Honor. I believe all of us know where Mr. Field and now yourself are going with this and as a father, I must agree publicly with the court."

"You're aware of Mr. Hirsch's testimony?"

"No, sir, but I can imagine."

"Well, it will be a first for most of us, Mr. Skultetty, and I don't think any of us will like what we hear. Thank you for your indulgence. Mr. Field, if you please."

"Mr. Hirsch, Samuel Hirsch, tell the court what happened."

"I was, as I said, a gambler. No drugs, no prostitution no mur..., mafia-like activities, just gambling. I sent my son, Donald, at his request, at the age of twenty-five to learn from who I felt was the best in Chicago. Names I cannot reveal. He was to join with me but after two years he decided he wanted to expand his capabilities and expanded into what was not acceptable to me. He said he would work with me on the gambling for Omaha and Kansas City. I felt if he did, I might win him back to the path I walked. I was informed by Mr. Field of an ongoing investigation by the federal government into racketeering in Omaha. I was also approached by Judge Waterford and informed that a Chicago group, headed by my son, wanted to take over my Omaha and Kansas City operations. I was informed that my son had contracted for me to be murdered so as to further his lot in life. Me, Sam Hirsch, his father. I wouldn't believe it and couldn't until my brother, Joe, who is associated with Judge Waterford, came to me with the recordings of my son's voice making arrangements for my murder. A contract. I agreed to cooperate and stage my death. I informed Kate, Mrs. Hirsch, of what I had found out, and of what I decided to do. She agreed I had no other choice. She was not surprised Donny would do this to me. Kate just said, 'He is a bad seed'."

Louie Donato, one of my phone men, killed Charlie Umbigolata, who ran the Sapphire Diner on the North Kansas City river road. Louie was an angry man. He came to my office where he met my son, at my son's bidding. He opened my private office door and shot me. I rolled over and pretended I was dead but saw my son standing right outside the door. He shot at Louie, missed, and then disappeared, as did Louie. The bulletproof vest, sleeves, and pants supplied to me by Colonel Felix Brannigan worked, but one bullet went through my side somehow. First I heard a helicopter and imagined it was Donny. Then came the explosion, that was Louie being blown up. As planned, Colonel Brannigan and my brother were waiting to help me. They wanted to intervene but I thought I might have a chance to change Donny's mind; it didn't work, it went too fast. They took me to the funeral home and I was given medical attention. I was flown to Barbados and have been there since. I just can't explain it. My son, that is, but with God as my witness, I forgive him."

There was silence. Hick was visibly disturbed by what he had just heard. He cleared his throat and asked, "Mr. Field, what action have you, are you about to take regarding this whole unholy affair?"

"I have an indictment and a warrant for the arrest of one Donald Hirsch. A Marshal will serve him the minute he sets foot off the airplane this afternoon."

"What time?"

"Our sources say he took a ten-thirty flight from Chicago and should be landing momentarily."

"Can you be certain?"

"Your Honor, since the attempt on his father's life we have had a tail on him twenty-four hours a day and are in contact with the plane. We didn't arrest him because we wanted to keep a tight lid on this whole affair."

"Good. I'll recess for lunch. You have him in court at two o'clock. Marshal, I want to have lunch with Mrs. Hickman, Patrick and Joshua Rollins, Mr. Justin, and yourself. We will make the arrangements at the Omaha Country Club for a private dining room. If there are no further questions, this court is now in recess until 2 P.M."

Henry called out, "Please rise," waited for Hick to leave the courtroom, and finished by saying, "for the Honorable Nicholas Hickman."

Manning was waiting and as he sat down at his desk she looked at him quizzically and exclaimed, "Quite a morning."

"Full of surprises, Manning. How long have you known about D.T.?"

"About one month. It was hard to keep the secret."

"I would imagine," Hick answered speciously.

"What's that really mean, Hick?"

"You can read me. Right, Manning?"

"A question answered by a question. The plot thickens."

"Later, Manning, all things come in their time."

"Whatever that means, Nicholas Hickman. Lunch arrangements have been made. Your father is having lunch with David Field and Joe Villella. The Marshal is on his way with the young men and there is a car waiting for you, Henry, and me. Tonight we dine with your father at home, alone."

"Good. I don't mean to be secretive or deceptive but sometimes it is necessary."

"I understand, but tell me, do you think the Rollins boys were influenced in any way?"

"Not one damn bit. They're under their mother's influence and it is going to take time for them to wake up to the real world, but hearing what they did is a beginning."

"I hope you're right for their sake. Let's go, Henry is waiting."

"Manning, bring along the Bible."

The private room at the Country Club was tastefully decorated with flowers as Manning had instructed. The lunch was salad, a sirloin steak of considerable size, potatoes, and peas. Patrick and Joshua ate with relish, causing Henry to ask as he poured some iced tea for them, "When did you boys eat last?"

Patrick answered solemnly, "Last night. A Big Mac and fries."

Henry turned with the pitcher of iced tea, held it up and asked, "Anyone else need more tea?"

No one answered and Henry took his seat next to Patrick. Hick stood and directed his comments to the two young men, "I must tell you I am disappointed in your demeanor concerning your father. This outward manifestation of dislike and distrust had to be learned, for you certainly weren't born with it. In fact, the pretrial investigation of your family tells me you were at one time very close to your father." Hick paused for effect and time to observe their reaction to his words. Their heads hung down, as Hick continued, "I will not lecture you or interfere in any way with the feelings you now have for your father other than this: I'll finish my remarks by reading the Fifth Commandment from the Ten Commandments and please pay attention. All right, I read from Deuteronomy 5:16., 'Honor thy father and thy mother, as the Lord thy God has commanded thee; that thy days may be prolonged, and that it may go well with thee, in the land which the Lord thy God giveth thee.' I would add for all of our benefit a reading from Matthew 22:36., "'Master, which is the great commandment in the law?' Jesus said unto him, 'Thou shalt love the Lord thy God with all thy heart, and with all thy soul, and with all thy mind. This is the first and great commandment. And the second is like unto it, Thou shalt love thy neighbor as thyself. On these two commandments hang all the law and the prophets.'" I never had a father I knew until this day. I will tell you your father is your one true friend. Unfortunately this is not discovered by many until fathers die, for only then the magnitude of a father's love is realized. You can go on your way or return to *court* to see and hear from a man who wanted to kill his father. Questions?"

Patrick and Josuha whispered one to the other and then Joshua spoke haughtily, "We thought there was a separation of church and state."

Understanding the challenge and bringing himself to his full height, Hick replied, "Not in my court. This nation and its laws were conceived under God and are carried out by God-fearing men. I will say only this, for your sake, I hope you come to understand the power of Almighty God and in knowing His power, this knowledge will give meaning to your lives."

"A-men, Dear Lord, A-men!" Henry cried out.

Patrick screamed, "Yet your father says our father is not really our father!"

"Maybe not biologically, but in his heart, in his concern for you and the abiding love he carries about and for you, he is your true and only real father."

Manning, wiping the tears from her eyes, stood and went to Hick. Wrapping her arms around him she kissed his cheek and turned with defiance to face the young brothers. "Hear me, you two! The man that stands before you is reaching out to you. He was denied the love and the nearness of a father until this day. Judge Nicholas T. Hickman is your mentor and you would be wise to heed his words."

"A-men," Henry interjected and went on, "this man, this judge, turned my life around and gave back to me the dignity I might have lost were it not for his belief in the Almighty. I, too, say, heed his words."

That both young men were angry and confused was evident. Hick signaled for Manning and Henry to leave with him. While walking from the room Hick remarked, "It will take time for them to understand. They'll turn back to their father, for he is all that they really have. Let's be on our way. The Marshal will bring the young men along."

CHAPTER 15

▼

Casting his eyes around the courtroom, Hick noted David Skultetty and a sullen looking younger man in handcuffs and the Rollins brothers sat together toward the rear of the courtroom. This pleased Hick and he spoke, "Seems our numbers are somewhat reduced but we will proceed, Mr. Field."

"Your Honor, Mr. Donald S. Hirsch is, as you see, in custody. The warrants for arrest and the true bills handed down by the grand jury, against the various defendants, have been submitted to the court and are before you."

"They are, Mr. Field, and they have been reviewed. Mr. Skultetty, are you prepared to plead for Mr. Hirsch?"

"We are, Your Honor."

"Mr. Hirsch, please rise."

Donny Hirsch was helped to his feet by David Skultetty, for he was handcuffed and wore leg irons. Hick took note of the passive attitude he displayed, yet there was defiance. When he finally looked up, Hick continued, "Mr. Hirsch, you have been charged with racketeering, specifically gambling, prostitution, drugs, and as an accessory in the attempted murder of your father. How do you plead?"

David Field sat with Joe Hirsch and directly behind them were Kate and Sam Hirsch. Donny Hirsch turned and for the first time since the fateful day of the attempted murder his eyes met his father's. Sam sensed the contempt his son held for him when he saw the small smile dart across Donny's face. The cold stare lasted but a moment and Donny quickly turned back to face Hick and in a loud voice say, "Not guilty."

"Your Honor," David Skultetty interjected, "I request bail for my client."

"Denied."

"But, Your Honor…"

"But nothing, Mr. Skultetty, this man is charged with multiple felonies, but in my opinion the most heinous charge is that of attempted murder upon his father."

"Your Honor, these are charges. My client is innocent until proven guilty."

"You, Mr. Skultetty, are only confirming what this court knows only too well. That will be another one hundred dollars which you can pay on your way out. Be more careful, Mr. Skultetty, for you have exhausted my forbearance. The charges against your client are of such a serious nature, bail is denied. I remand Mr. Hirsch to the Marshal."

"Do I get to say something?" Donny Hirsch called out.

"Marshal, remove the defendant from the court and lock him up, now!"

"Hold on with this locking me up. Your ole man is no more pure than mine is."

Hick glared at Donny Hirsch and a flash of anger made him grab his gavel and slam it down on the bench. The bang reverberated throughout the court and caught the participants by complete surprise. Hick commanded, "Sit him down, Marshal. Mr. Field, Mr. Skultetty, approach the bench."

Hick's eyes moved to where his father sat with Patrick and Joshua Rollins. D. T. was on his feet. Hick turned to Henry and demanded, "Will the bailiff stand by Osbon."

The two attorneys stood at the bench and watched as Henry went to stand next to D. T. They turned to face Hick and he whispered, "Mr. Field, I've had my suspicions and I believe now is the time for you to reveal the silent indictment mentioned earlier."

"How does this effect my client? What's this about, Your Honor?" David Skultetty asserted.

"It will become evident in a minute, Mr. Skultetty. You won't like the scope of this discovery but I feel now is the time for you to know the magnitude of the involvement of your clients. All seven of them. What say you, Mr. Field?"

"You knew all along, didn't you, Your Honor?"

"I've known for a few days. Kate Hirsch confirmed what Joe Hirsch had to tell me when I was in Kansas City."

"How about Mrs. Hickman?"

"She knows and is devastated by it but she was innocently entangled."

David Skultetty, looking perplexed, whispered, "What is this about, Your Honor?"

"You know, Mr. Skultetty. If you don't know, you had better get your clients to start telling you what you need to know to defend them."

"I know, Your Honor," David Skultetty admitted sheepishly.

"Nicely done, counselor. Back to your seats, gentlemen, then we will proceed."

The two attorneys returned to their seats. David Skultetty leaned over to whisper to Donny Hirsch and when he was through Donny smiled and yelled out, "I think you'd better disqualify yourself, Judge!"

Hick, as was his habit when aroused, slid forward in his chair and calmly said, "Marshal, please remove Mr. Hirsch from the courtroom."

As Donny was led from the defense table he turned to his father and laughingly cried out, "I shoulda' never trusted Louie! I shoulda' done it myself from the start...earlier!"

Everyone in the courtroom rose to their feet, and Kate Hirsch reached out to help Sam and as she did cried out, "You swine! God waits to judge you!"

The last words heard from Donny as the Marshal pushed him through the door were, "Mother, I..."

Henry had been forewarned and as Donny was calling out, it diverted D. T.'s attention. As it did, Henry's hand slid under D. T.'s coat and with the deftness of the pickpockets trade he had learned on the streets, the nine millimeter pistol was removed from its holster, without detection. When those present turned back to face the bench Hick instructed, "I am sorry for the outburst, please be seated. Now, Mr. Field, if you please."

"Your Honor, I am prepared at this time to present the eighth true bill handed down by the grand jury."

David Skultetty was on his feet in an instant. Hick anticipated him and snapped, "Let him finish, Mr. Skultetty."

"The indictment names Mr. D. T. Osbon. Mr. Osbon is accused of racketeering, murder, interstate gambling, drugs, and prostitution. I am prepared to ask that no bail be extended and I have a warrant for D. T. Osbon's arrest."

"Now, Mr. Skultetty," Hick retorted.

"Your Honor, I represent Mr. Osbon."

"I had that figured, Mr. Skultetty."

All heads turned to face D. T. He stood stoic and motionless and the faces of Patrick and Joshua Rollins looked up at him, smiling. Manning's eyes were fixed on Hick for his reaction to the public pro-nouncement. There was none as he waited with everyone else in silence. D. T. leaned over and cupped his hand over Henry's ear and whispered, "I need to use the comfort room."

"Walk ahead of me, to the bench," Henry instructed.

When they stood before Hick, Henry, holding on to D. T.'s arm, leaned over and quietly said, "Your Honor, your father needs to use the restroom."

Hick was staring at his father but it was evident there was not the surprise one might have expected. Hick shook his head knowingly and said, "This court will stand in recess for five minutes. No one leave the courtroom unless it is absolutely necessary. Henry, escort Mr. Osbon to my facilities. Do you need assistance?"

"No, sir, I disarmed Mr. Osbon."

"Disarmed him?"

"Yes, sir, he carried a nine millimeter in a shoulder holster."

"In my Courtroom? Do you know what this means, D. T.?"

A hardness not seen before surfaced and D. T. said, "Just another felony."

"Go with him, Henry. Mr. Field, Mr. Skultetty, approach the side bar."

Henry led D. T. to the Judge's chambers as the two attorneys walked to the side of where Hick sat, and Hick asked, "Mr. Skultetty, tell me what I already know."

"I am Mr. Osbon's attorney, Your Honor. He's elderly and I'll ask for bail."

"Ridicu…"

David Field began to say but Hick interjected, "I'm not that far behind the curve, Mr. Skultetty. As you would say, I am up to speed in this whole damnable mess."

"You are?" David Skultetty said, obviously surprised, "I just found out this…", he stopped.

Hick found a smile and used it while saying, "Looks like I'm ahead of you, Mr. Skultetty, *way* ahead of you."

"Yes, Your Honor, I should have suspected."

"It's big, David, very big."

"Since he's your father, maybe you should step aside?"

"There's no doubt about that, but for now I must rule on the indictment and the warrant. Mr. Field."

"I have nothing to offer, Your Honor. Judge Waterford…"

Hick stopped him by raising his hand and quietly commented, "Later, Mr. Field."

"I'd like to hear what he has to say, Your Honor, one way or another," David Skultetty remarked, back in his defiant mode.

"At this moment, Mr. Skultetty, we have become adversaries. It will keep us honest and thinking, even though it's my court. Go on, Mr. Field."

"Judge Waterford is prepared to step in at any time, Judge Hickman."

"Thank you. Mr. Field, notify him. Mr. Skultetty, we just gave you a head start. Judge Waterford is tougher than tough. He instituted the deceptions used to entangle my father and the subsequent events leading up to this very day."

"Thank you, Judge Hickman, I have a feeling we'll need all the help we can get."

Henry walked through the door from Hick's chambers alone. He strode to Hick's side and leaning over so only the three men could hear, impassively announced, "You gentlemen had best come with me. Mr. Osbon hung himself."

The two attorneys were startled and Hick warned, "Easy, gentlemen, easy does it. What happened, Henry?"

"He went into your bathroom, Judge, and I waited. He seemed to be taking too long so I opened the door and he was hanging from the exposed pipe in the ceiling. There had been a small leak under repair. Your Honor, I never thought he would…"

"How could you, Henry? Get a Marshal, call the coroner. Gentlemen, come with me."

David Skultetty flushed as he said, "I'm sorry, I can't."

"Yes, you can and will, Mr. Skultetty. We need you as a witness."

The three men walked into the Judge's Chambers and Manning followed. The four walked to the bathroom and found D. T. with his pant belt around his neck, hanging from a pipe in the ceiling as Henry said. His facial appearance left no doubt he was dead. Holding tightly to Manning's hand, Hick instructed, "Mr. Field, you cut him down. I'll hold onto him."

Hick went to his father. Grabbing him around the waist, he pushed him up to reduce the tension on the belt. David Field stood on the toilet, with open pocketknife in hand, and cut the leather belt. Hick carried his father to his cleared desk and gently laid him down; reached for the book Manning was handing him and placed it under D. T.'s head. Manning had cleared the desk and now offered Hick an afghan to cover the body. Gesturing to wait, by holding his hand up, Hick said, "Wait, please wait, Manning."

Bending down, Hick kissed the now distorted and grotesque face of his father, stood and without any outward sign of grief said, "This I have known, I would be that much better a judge by being blessed with these three things; faith, Manning, and Henry, to see me through. Everyone, we must now return to court."

Henry walked into the courtroom and called out, "The court is now reconvened, please rise for the Honorable Nicholas T. Hickman."

Hick swept back into the courtroom and announced, "I must tell you, ladies and gentlemen, Mr. Osbon, my father, committed suicide. His arraignment this morning is now null and void. This court will reconvene on Monday at 9 A.M. I would leave you knowing I appreciate how difficult this day has been. The scope of this case must be evident. Evil has always been with us and takes many forms. It is for us all to do whatever we can to maintain law and order in our society. I have never done this before, and before I do, I would have you know I consider this room and the many like it throughout our nation hallowed. I will shake each of your hands as you leave, for it is because of people like yourselves this system of government has prevailed. May God Bless you all until we meet again."

Hick stepped down from the bench and walked solemnly to the back of the courtroom. Opening the large doors, Hick turned to greet Kate and Sam Hirsch. Kate, taking his hand in hers, reached over and gently kissed him on the cheek and he felt her tears. Kate turned her face away so only Manning could see the copious flow of tears.

Sam, extending his hand, warmly said, "Thank you, Your Honor, you are the very best."

"Thanks, Kate, Sam. In a way, Sam, we struggle with the same relationship of father and son. Manning will call for dinner tomorrow."

Patrick and Joshua Rollins looked confused, awkward and embarrassed. Hick sensed their dilemma and took their extended hands in his and remarked, "Young men, there are more difficult days ahead for us before we sort this all out and go on with our lives. I ask you to discuss this day with each other and the failed relationship you have with your father. I further ask you to keep asking yourselves why. I am available to you at any hour of the day or night. I may not have answers for you, or you for me, but maybe just talking about it could help us find some."

Hick dropped their hands and immediately threw his arms around their shoulders and, turning, instructed Henry, "See to it, Henry, the Marshal takes these young men to their mother."

J. R. Rollins extended his hand and as he did, Hick motioned toward his sons and instructed, "Go after them, Doctor. You take them to their mother."

J. R. smiled but said nothing. Turning, he started after his sons and called out, "Wait, boys, wait for me."

Manning squeezed Hick's hand and sighed, "You always know."

David Skultetty and his three associates were next and he took both Hick and Manning's hand to offer, "I am truly sorry, Your Honor, Manning; and thank you, Your Honor. I appreciate the way this court has extended its hand," and the three associates nodded in agreement. "I concur with my colleagues," David Field added, "and I will call in about one hour to help in any way I can, Your Honor."

"Thank you, gentlemen, thank you is all there is left for me to say."

Gladis Pitman was last and she sobbed, "Judge Hickman, I..."

Gladis Pitman was the personification of all that a genteel woman represented. Professionally, as a court reporter, she was second to none. Hick and Gladis admired one another for the other's dedication to purpose. Hick knew Gladis couldn't handle the emotion of the moment and nodding to Manning, who also understood, moved forward to enfold her in their arms. Moments later Henry returned to close the courtroom doors and seeing the embrace, held back. After a few moments Hick said, "Come on, I believe we all need a drink."

Paul Ortman had left the police station where Susan Givens was being processed. He wanted to try and talk to her about her sons but was rebuffed by, "Outta' here, scum," and was now on his way back to the courtroom. David Field and David Skultetty walked side by side in silence and when David Field saw Paul Ortman he called out, "Over here, Paul."

Paul walked over to them and remarked, "Court's over, I see."

"Yeah, until the Judge can bury his newfound father," David Field said dejectedly as David Skultetty solemnly shook his head.

Paul studied them carefully and from what he saw felt somehow he was out of the loop and suggested, "How about Theodore's and you can bring me up to speed."

"Theodore's?"

"Mr. Field, you haven't been to Theodore's? I know you're new to Omaha but like every city, town, and hamlet, we have our Theodore's too."

"A bar."

"Not just a bar, but the *in* place. It has more dark corners wherein light can be shed on any number of subjects, and most important it has Theodore. The number one grouch in Omaha."

"And for about fifty miles in every direction," David Skultetty added.

David Field, smiling at the remark asked, "Do you think it would be kosher for us to be seen together?"

Paul Ortman, reaching for his arm, replied, "That's what all the dark corners are for. Just ask Theodore."

The three men walked a block, then turned on Harney street. Looking up, David Field saw the sign, "The Only Place, Theodore's".

Paul went first and as he opened the door a gruff voice chided, "Well, as I live and breathe, two Barristers, and I would presume you're Mr. Field, the other great Barrister?"

David was surprised he knew his name but never missed a beat and snapped back, "There's only one, truly great Barrister…me!"

"And…I can see…he's humble, like all the rest of you lawyer louts," Theodore countered.

"Theodore, you know who he is, shake his hand and then hide us someplace and make it three glasses, bourbon, scotch, water, soda, and as little growling shit as possible," Paul ordered.

"Your usual order, I see. You wouldn't need the soda and water if you were any kind of men. Drink it straight…that's the only way, but what the hell, we'll serve anybody," Theodore snickered as he shook David Field's hand and then turning into the dimly lit room, raised his hand and condescendingly decreed, "Follow me."

The corner booth was dark and secluded and the walls around the booth went to the ceiling and everything was padded so sound was muffled and would not travel. They had no sooner sat down and were positioned than what had been ordered was deposited on the table and Paul spoke out, "Thanks, Helen. What took you so long?"

"Growing old, who's your new friend?"

"David Field, Helen Theodore."

David's face brightened as he answered, "Glad to meet you, Helen. If you're Helen Theodore, what's the main man's name?"

"He goes by Charlie, and we both go by Theodore."

She turned and Paul added, "I don't know how those two do it. They get these drinks here before they should. Somehow they seem to know when you're coming and are ready."

"They're married, Paul. Have been so, according to Charlie, forever."

Each man poured himself a drink and each man savored the smooth taste of it. David Field remarked, "Best bourbon I've ever had."

"Charlie's booze is the best. He'll never tell you what it is other than it's premium," David Skultetty added.

"What's going on in Judge Hickman's court?" Paul asked.

"What do you mean?" David Field answered, somewhat puzzled by the question.

"Well, it does seem orchestrated. The legal stumbling and fumbling and challenges just don't seem to dominate."

While he poured himself another drink David Field added, "And it isn't. He's a well organized Judge and we respect him. We don't try to play games with him because we know it won't work for very long. I'd say he's not legalistic, he's more humanistic in his approach to the law."

Paul gestured and was about to speak but David stopped him by saying, "Let me go on. Judge Waterford researched this man extensively. Education, demeanor, temperament, and if he was willing to listen and cooperate."

"Cooperate with whom," David Skultetty asked and added, "about what?"

"Our investigation of your clients."

"We haven't breeched the confidentiality of our findings. We wanted to see how he would react to our methods and we knew of the involvement of his father and he had to be informed."

Paul Ortman jumped in saying, "When did he know D. T. was his father?"

"Kate Hirsch told him at the staged wake for Sam."

"My God, how could he contain himself? Did Manning know?"

"Manning knew months before the Judge did. As far as the Judge containing himself, Kate Hirsch gave him the double whammy. Telling him D. T. Osbon was his father, and by the way, he's the long time head of the criminal activity being investigated in Omaha. Also, she threw in about her son trying to kill his father."

"How in the world could he handle all of that?" David Skultetty exclaimed.

"He is a man of substance. A very unique man and as Judge Waterford determined, a very necessary and special man needed for the investigation to succeed."

"It hasn't yet and won't if I have anything to say about it" David Skultetty said, seemingly somewhat irritated.

"Don't get your underwear in a bundle, Dave. I have a deal for you. I'll drop all charges against Mrs. Givens if you will agree, regardless of the trial matter and any circumstances, not to reveal Judge Hickman's mother was a child victim of the pedophile D. T. Osbon and bore him as a result of this man's lust for children."

"My God, is that true?"

"It is."

"Why would I do such a thing? He's hurting enough."

"The heat of battle causes us to sometimes forget. You might want to use that to disqualify the Judge."

"Then why did you tell me?"

"I would have anyway in disclosure."

"I will so agree and stipulate nothing. However, you must know I will use every other means at my disposal to get my clients off your hook."

"Noblesse oblige, sir!" David Field countered.

Paul took note of the two Davids' interaction and thought to himself as he watched and listened, *This trial is going to be a humdinger…or is it?"*

Another drink was consumed and then they agreed to leave. Walking to the door and the awaiting Charlie, Paul asked, "I always thought your name was Theodore."

"It is."

"I mean your first name."

"It is, but they call me Charlie…less questions and confusion."

The two David's laughed and Paul muttered, "Theodore, Theodore, you're a study. Next time I'll find out."

"Wanna bet," David Skultetty quipped.

CHAPTER 16

▼

The services for D. T. Osbon were nondenominational and grave side. Manning made all of the arrangements, for she could tell Hick's heart wasn't in it. The staff of D. T.'s house, the butler, cook, and upstairs maid was the way in which they introduced themselves but not one word was said after the introductions. At the conclusion of the services they abruptly turned and left in the limousine provided by the mortuary. Henry, David Field, David Skultetty, and Marshal Palmer were the only other people attending.

David Skultetty watched the staff leave and as the limousine pulled away, scoffed so all could hear, "They'll be back and be more civil when I notify them about what's in the will, and the conditions."

"Conditions?" Hick remarked.

"Yes. D. T. was a very insightful as well as wealthy man. He didn't earn the money, in fact he never worked a day in his life. He just plain, old inherited it and compounded it through criminal activity. Oh, he was an authority on DNA, but he never used it for monetary gain. I think he liked the quiet recognition it gave him, and it helped cover up his criminal and deviant behavior."

The word deviant made Hick flinch inwardly but he asked, "As I said, what conditions, David?"

"The conditions are, that you personally hand them the checks for their very generous inheritance."

"You're stringing this out, David!"

"Sorry, Your Honor, they each receive five hundred thousand dollars and you receive six million."

"I don't want a penny of it."

"I would have suspected as much, Your Honor, and I believe your father did, too. There is a stipulation you can give the money to whomever you please."

Hick never hesitated, "Five hundred thousand to Henry's church and the balance to the Children's Hospital, both anonymously. No names are to be attached to the gifts."

Henry was stunned and moved immediately to take Hick's hand, "That's very generous, Your Honor, are you certain this is what you want to do? Five hundred thousand dollars is a lot of money."

Hick smiled as he patted Henry's hand, "Yes, Henry, it is, but maybe it will help some children to make up for the children he hurt in his lifetime."

"And, he was a liar, too," David Field cried out with anger in his voice.

"What's that all about, David?" Hick asked.

"Shall we discuss it here?"

"If it's about him I can't think of a better place than right here at his grave. Maybe he's listening."

"Well, it's about your mother. He was never in love with her or any of his other victims. He just lusted. The love story is a phony he and his family concocted so he wouldn't be thrown in jail for statutory rape. He should have been because your mother was only thirteen when he impregnated her. Instead they made a love story out of it and got him off by marrying him off to your mother. He never honored it and had it annulled after one year. He never even lived with your mother. Her wealthy family wanted it covered up and so did his wealthy family. When I say the family wanted it, I mean the whole damn family, parents, uncles, aunts, cousins…they're more like a clan than a family. You were summarily disposed of by sending you to the orphanage and your mother belittled to a life of rejection and despair."

"How did she die?"

"She didn't, Your Honor, she's alive."

"Where?" Hick's voice pleaded.

"We don't know. Her family is tough to deal with. The only way we were able to get what we did about your mother was because D. T. cooperated when he knew we had the goods on him and the rest. Your mother's family is very prominent and has a great deal of influence and have been and are fighting us every step of the way."

"What are you trying to do?"

"Reunite you, Your Honor, with your mother."

"What?"

"Yes, sir. We didn't know she was alive, as I said, and when we found out we wanted to try and balance the emotional scale in some way for you. We never suspected D. T. would do what he did. When he told us about your mother we knew he was going to jail or wherever and we wanted to set the record straight."

"Is she in good health?"

"They won't tell us a thing, Your Honor. Judge Waterford is seething and is actively pursuing every avenue to reunite you and your mother."

"Is it possible?"

"Knowing Judge Waterford, sir, it's just a matter of time."

Manning reached for Hick's hand, and as she squeezed it he remarked to David, "Keep me informed."

"Every day, sir, every day. I would like to spend some time with you this morning, for we have a problem brewing since all of this is coming out. Plus!"

"Drive back to the hotel in the Marshal's car with us and we'll talk."

David said goodbye to David Skultetty and joined Hick, Manning, Henry, and Jed Palmer.

Hick had noticed that Jed hadn't let him out of his sight, but said nothing to him about his suspicions as to why. When in the car and on their way, Hick broke the silence and asked, "What's up, David?"

"I have word the *Omaha Sentinel* is coming out with an editorial about you, the court, and what we are doing here. It's a blistering attack filled with innuendo."

"About what?"

"Your father. The indictments of prominent citizens, and they have hired some fancy Kansas City lawyers to put you, Judge Waterford, and Joe Hirsch's facility under heavy attack."

"Where are they getting information about Joe Hirsch?"

"Your Honor, as you know, if there's enough money somebody will talk and you can get anything done you want."

"Well, that may be true, but I would have to believe someone on our list knows more than we think they do."

"I think Donny Hirsch is our man."

Hick was obviously irritated as he said, "He's no man. He's a weasel. Have him stuck in with or next to one of ours. He has a flunky or gunsel, find him and put the pressure on him."

"Her."

"Her?"

"Yup. He has a woman, if that's what one could call her. Her name is Beth Gutchow. She's thirty-two and has one hell of a reputation on the streets of Chicago. We've shaken her down twice on simple charges to size her up and to see what she carries."

"And?"

"You won't believe this but all she carries is a hand grenade or two or three."

"That's illegal, you've got to be kidding us."

"No, and we've been told she uses them and that's how she gets her counterparts to back off. She terrorizes them with the thought of her using a grenade. She creates the idea she doesn't care if she goes up protecting 'the boss' as she says, and he is all she cares about."

"Sick! What's happened to society?"

"Back to the newspaper. Who's the editor on attack?"

"His name is Peter Conway. Robert Conway's son. He's infuriated and blames all of us and the system for his father's and now his mother's death. He's a radical communist socialist pig, and if you don't believe it read what and how he writes."

"That's two strikes against us."

"How right you are."

Nothing more was said as Hick sat thinking. Manning could tell he was hatching something in his mind. Hick always thought matters through before he instigated anything. Manning broke in, "Hick, what are you cooking up?"

"Well, it's obvious we have several problems and it's time to force our hand and not have to go through a series of lengthy, expensive trials. I have a plan but I need all of you to help. First; Manning, rearrange the court dates to begin on Wednesday. Henry, I want you to form a coalition of Omaha ministers opposed to the exploitation of our children. David, you call David Skultetty and get him to agree to go to Kansas City with you. I want him to be informed about what we have in the way of evidence against his clients. Call it discovery. I'll call Judge Waterford and Joe Hirsch. Just one question: Is Skultetty clean?"

"Yes, he is. Squeaky clean. Show him the facts and he'll steer his..."

"Clients to plea bargain," Hick interjected.

"Brilliant idea, Your Honor, it will work."

"We need to neutralize this woman, Beth Gutchow. I'll talk to Colonel Brannigan and Joe about her. I don't understand, David, why you couldn't charge her with carrying a hand grenade."

"We've picked her up on several occasions and all she was carrying were dummies."

"Dummies! They're afraid of dummies?"

"It would seem one never knows when they will be live ones. I think Donny has connections, and when we bust her I'm certain she has been forewarned."

"I'll talk to the Colonel about her. He and Joe, along with everything else, are ordnance freaks. Now, about Mrs. Givens, the ex-Mrs. Rollins. Just what do you have on her, David?"

"Plenty, but it's passive."

"What's that mean?"

"She's present during some illegal planning, but never becomes an active part of the crime by suggesting or contributing in any way."

"Will you—can you drop all charges against her?"

"I could and can, but not legally. Why?"

"The element of surprise and dividing her from her husband of record could possibly, as the evidence unfolds, drive her attention back to her sons and even her ex-husband, my friend J. R. Rollins, not that he would necessarily want her. I think Givens turned her head using devious means."

"But most mothers, wives, women wouldn't allow that to happen. They don't stray."

"I know, David, but we all make mistakes. Remember, 'He that is without sin among you, let him cast a stone at her'."

"Touche', Your Honor, touche'."

"All right then, David, there's no time like the present to begin our attack to save time and end this battle. Manning, one hour and we're back in session so we can drop charges against Mrs. Givens, and, David, then you and Skultetty are off with Joe Hirsch to K. C. One other thing, Manning, notify Gladis and call the paper and tell them a reporter should be in court in one hour. The one, you know, what's her name?"

"Have you forgotten one thing?"

"What?"

"It's Sunday."

"So what, time waits for no man...or woman."

"Right, Judge. Shila Wadsworth. Sob sister…extra ordinaire'. That's who you want."

"Right, Shila should be in court for the first round of 'Operation Blight.'"

"Operation Blight, Hick? That's corny!"

"Maybe so, but it will get their attention and divert them away from how prepared and how serious this whole affair is, and if these people and their crimes aren't a blight upon this community, I don't know what could be."

Manning smiled and waving her hand cried out, "Touche', as our Prosecutor says, touche', Your Honor, brilliant husband of mine."

Henry looked away and snickered.

*   *   *   *

"Please rise for the Honorable Judge Nicholas Hickman."

Henry turned and as he did, Hick swept into the courtroom with his eyes fixed upon Susan Givens. Their eyes locked and every fiber in Susan Givens's body shuddered. The fierce determination of the man pierced her every defense, real or imagined. She knew at this moment his only purpose was to punish her. Henry called out, "Please be seated. This court is now in session."

Hick broke his stare and turning his head to face Henry, smiled as he thought, *"Now that was a nice touch for the sake of effect, Henry."* Hick turned back to face David Skultetty and began by saying, "Mr. Skultetty, thank you for responding to the short notice of the court on a Sunday. Our purpose in the people versus your numerous clients is to expedite justice. A speedy trial, as you are well aware, enhances justice. Have you conferred with your client about the matter that brings this court back in session?"

"I have not, Your Honor, there wasn't enough time."

"Very well, we will proceed. Mr. Field, if you please."

David Field stood, walked to the defense table, and looking down at Susan Givens, made eye contact, scowled in his best courtroom fashion and then spun around and announced, "Your Honor, in the matter of the people versus Susan Givens for aiding and abetting interstate murder, attempted murder, prostitution, racketeering, sodomy, statutory rape, and dealing in drugs..."

"Your Honor," David Skultetty cried out, "I object to the nature of the charges spouted by the Prosecutor. They don't match the charges on the indictment, they've been expanded."

Hick recognized what David Field had done and for more effect let David Skultetty rave on, "The prosecutor is leveling the full weight of guilt upon *one* person, my client, a mother, a housewife, an innocent bystander. Her role at best was passive. She, ah, she..."

"You seem to be at a loss for words, Mr. Skultetty, are you?"

"Yes, Your Honor."

"Very well. You know, Mr. Skultetty, I like you. You don't, as they say, 'mess around.' You get to the point of law as fast as anyone who has come before me. You nailed it, but your objection is overruled. Tell him why, Mr. Field."

"As I was saying, Your Honor, the charges before the court regarding Mrs. Givens are being dropped."

Hick's eyes first met David Skultetty's and the look of complete confusion had encompassed him. Hick moved his eyes slowly to Susan Givens. She had risen to her feet in disbelief at what she had heard. Hick saw and felt her changing. She reached for the table to steady herself and then moved to David Skultetty to embrace him and whispered in his ear, "Can this be true?"

David Skultetty regained his composure and answered, "Yes, it can and is. I must address the court. Your Honor, all we can say is thank you."

Susan Givens, with head down, sat at the defense table, crying and sobbing softly. Hick offered, "No thanks are necessary, Mr. Skultetty. It was a close call, or so Mr. Field tells me. We can all stray and become encumbered with other's failings and inadequacies if we fail our own standards of behavior. This court will pause for your client to regain her composure. I reserve the right to make the final discharge of the whole matter."

David Skultetty leaned over to Susan Givens and put his arm around her to comfort her. Hick waited. Henry caught his eye and nodded. Hick responded by saying, "Bring them in, Mr. Justin. Mrs. Givens, your sons are here to share this moment with you."

Henry escorted Patrick and Joshua to their mother. They embraced, Susan wiped the tears from her face and stood to face Hick, and said, "I am ready to face the Court, Your Honor."

Hick stood and answered, "I believe you are, Mrs. Givens, but not only this court. However, regarding this court, I've been a judge for many years, Mrs. Givens. I have seen many people, from all walks of life, pass through this valley of judgement only to return. Many more, thank God, never return. Rather, from their experience they climb back to the summit of life and soar. I don't expect you to do that, I know you will. I would ask you to do one thing. Find the love your sons once had for their father and return it to them. On a personal note, I had a father for one day, and Mrs. Givens, there are no words for me to express to you each day a man doesn't spend with his father that he could have, if reason prevailed, is a day lost and one day regretted. For 'The land shall mourn every family apart', a family being a father, a mother and their children. Mr. Skultetty, Mrs. Givens bail is revoked and she is free to go. This court stands adjourned."

"Your Honor."

"Yes, Mr. Skultetty?"

"Mrs. Givens would address the court with the court's permission."

"Granted, Mr. Skultetty. Mrs. Givens."

"Your Honor. I have understood what the court has said and done. I will, Your Honor, once again soar."

"I know you will, Mrs. Givens, I can now see it in your eyes."

"Your Honor," David Skultetty said, "I would like to thank the court. You, Your Honor, for justice has been and will be served."

Hick swallowed hard at what he heard and could only respond, "As I said, this court stands adjourned."

Hick rose and as he moved to the door to his chambers, Manning joined him, placed her arm in his and leaned over to kiss his cheek and say, "I love you, Judge Nicholas Hickman."

Henry was at a loss for words and knew even if he knew what to say, he couldn't. A voice rang out. It was Shila Wadsworth. Manning realized she had forgotten all about her. "Your Honor! Judge Hickman! A moment of your time, Your Honor, if you please."

"Her name, Manning," Hick whispered.

"Miss Wadsworth," Manning whispered back.

"Oh, yes, Miss Wadsworth, follow us."

Shila Wadsworth picked up on the "follow us" and was shortly sitting across from Hick. After Manning and Henry excused themselves she quickly said, "Your Honor, I know you're a busy man and it being Sunday and all, I'll cut to the chase. What's going on?"

"Miss Wadsworth, just what does that mean?"

"Your Honor, you have this whole town talking and wondering. You, a special court, special U. S. Marshals, a special Prosecutor. Protective custody of some of our city's leading and wealthiest citizens, suicides, murders. I repeat, what's going on?"

"Now that you put it that way, I can see where you might be interested, but how come it has taken this long to get your newspaper's attention?"

"You're modest, sir. We knew you were coming, we have ears in Kansas City. Give yourself and those who surround you credit. We haven't been able to get a word out of anybody and haven't been able to get near you until Manning called today. It's a good thing I don't go to church."

Hick smiled at her remark and was going to respond to it but thought better of it since this was the first time he had met this woman.

He had a feeling, being in her presence, that she was a straight shooter, or Manning would have never recommended her. That was his key. "For starters, Miss Wadsworth…"

"Call me, Shila, and I'll call you, Hick. Less formal; takes less time."

"Agreed, outside of my court. Is it with an E, an I, or both?"

"Some ask, some don't, which goes to show how many people really care. Thanks, it's with an I…S-h-i-l-a."

"Different."

"Goes back to my grandfather. You ready to let me in on something?"

"Off the record…Shila."

"Good way to start, Hick."

"Okay, it's Sunday, and as of today we begin Operation Blight."

"Blight?"

"Yes, the one that is on our city."

"Which consists of?"

"Preying on the town's children for sexual gratification primarily, and prostitution, racketeering, drugs, murder, and attempted murder; locally and interstate. How's that for starters?"

"To be honest, Hick, it's what I suspected. We've all known for quite some time about what goes on around this town and the coverups. We knew and suspected some of the upper crust. A few of them have crossed the river into Iowa and gotten caught. The top dogs in this town have been in bed with one another, in more ways than one, but I don't think the town, it's a big town you know, the town doesn't really know how deep and wide this corruption runs."

"It will now. Your point about not suspecting how deep this runs is the reason we have what we do. It's called neglect. This corruption has been going on without interference and now the big time operators from Chicago are moving in to once again tie this city to their organizations in Chicago and Kansas City."

"Once again?"

"Sure, it has happened before. Get out your history book or just go talk to Henry Justin, my Bailiff, he was a runner years ago."

"Wow, you're prepared, aren't you?"

"That's my job."

"Why did you want me here this morning?"

"Heard your Editor, Peter Conway, is coming out after me, we, us."

"You heard right! He's out to skin you alive, if he can, or at least he'll cause you a lot of embarrassment through innuendo, insinuation, and falsehoods. He and his have covered up for his father's proclivity toward children with money and heaping recognition. Plus, Peter is a communist socialist just like his mother and father were and makes no bones about it. He has on occasions advocated to me what I consider treasonous."

"You don't like him or them very much, do you?"

"You said it's off the record, but try me in your court."

Hick laughed but realized he shouldn't have and offered, "I apologize. I find your honesty refreshing."

"How about yours?"

"My honesty? Yes, I'm feeling you out and I'm satisfied. In a nutshell, what I'm up to is simple. I don't want to knock this city to its knees with these revelations. I want it to be as quietly resolved as possible but do it so a positive message of intolerance for future activities will be understood and not tolerated. I want it done with dignity. I want enough on these people so they realize they can't squeeze through any loopholes. I'm closing them down. I want them to come to my court and plead guilty in hopes of receiving clemency from those who stand in judgement of them. I am prepared to recommend a panel of three federal judges be appointed to hear the evidence and mete out the sentences. They will have to agree to this or jury trials will be mandatory."

"You're vulnerable, because of your father."

"How? I didn't know he existed until I went to Kansas City a week ago."

"You allowed him, as amicus curiae, to speak in your court and to offer up evidence against Mrs. Givens."

"You're better informed than you let on, Shila."

"It's my job, Hick."

"Well, knowing what I knew I had to trap her into a realization of what was happening to her and her sons."

"They were by somebody else."

"J. R. Rollins had no knowledge of that. He loved, nurtured, and raised them as his sons and even to this day he feels they are a part of him, regardless."

"Peter will come after you."

"I've anticipated that. Henry Justin, my Bailiff, is forming a coalition of area clergy to be a part of the revival."

"You're something else, Hick. Do you mean to revive the city or just have evangelistic meetings?"

"Both! I'm upset about sons turning away from their parents and I'm upset about daughters doing the same. It's simple, we must live as the Ten Commandments would have us live, if our cleanup is to prevail. I'll give you a tag line. In this investigation my anger was initially directed at those who would break the Fifth Commandment, now I can say all the Commandments have been broken not just one...by these people and many others not in our gunsight.".

"Can I print that?"

"Yes! Rework the tag line I just gave you when you feel and know the time is right."

"You're a devil, too, Judge Hickman."

"In what way?"

"You've woven your web, you've covered your bases, and now you know you have me in your court ready to fight what I have known about, yet looked the other way."

"We all make mistakes."

"When does this all start?"

"Wednesday, 9 A.M., my courtroom."

"I'll be there and ready. Don't laugh but I'm going to put Peter Conway on the ropes with counter columns if he comes after you, which he will."

"He's the Editor, he can shut you off."

"Maybe. Watch and see. I need a story line for starters, we're now back on the record."

"Right!"

"Judge Hickman, why were the charges against Mrs. Susan Givens dropped?"

"Insufficient evidence, which was determined by the prosecutor."

"Can you expand on the evidence?"

"No. Talk to Mr. Field."

"Can I have the court's permission to talk with Mrs. Givens?"

"Why would you ask me a question like that? This is a free country and Mrs. Givens is a free woman."

'Thank you, Your Honor."

Shila Wadsworth rose from her seat and extended her hand across the desk to Hick.

They both felt the warmth of a friendship start as their hands touched. Shila turned as if to leave, then stopped, turned, and said, "Off the record, I have one more thing to do and say…" Shila walked around the desk and wrapped her arms around Hick, and after kissing him on the cheek went on, "you are a fine man, Nicholas Hickman. You and Manning are cut from the same cloth and deserve one another. I'll work with you for the same cause."

Shila spun around and as Hick's eyes followed her, she left. Moments later Manning walked in and asked, "What did you say to her?"

"Why?"

"Tears, my husband, tears. Shila Wadsworth gave up tears years ago. She's as tough as an ole boot."

"Yeah, yeah, yeah, Manning, just like you. She's on our side."

"Shila…on our side? Tell me about it over dinner."

"You mean a late Sunday brunch."

CHAPTER 17

▼

Judge Waterford hung up the phone and called out, "Colonel, I need you."

Felix was in the kitchen cleaning up after breakfast and sticking his head around the door asked, "Who was it and what's up?"

"Mondays, my dear Felix, Mondays. I think you'll have your hands full with this one."

"Cut to the chase, Judge, who was it?"

"Judge Hickman. He's named his operation, Blight, and he is trying to close out the whole affair without any trials, just plea bargains."

"Blight? That's up for grabs."

"Grabs? Sometimes I don't understand your use of words, Colonel."

"I just mean you could go for it or pass it up. I'd pass it up; sounds corny. How does he expect to get everyone to plea bargain?"

"Have enough ironclad evidence. Seems the lawyer for the defense, a David Skultetty, is smart, reasonable, and knows when he's licked and when it's time to try and get a better deal with plea bargaining. He has been known to cooperate, for that end result."

"That's a lawyer that is too good to be true. No offense, Judge, but most of you guys like to fight until there's no more blood on either side."

"You don't have a very high opinion of us, do you?"

"I have the utmost regard for you and Judge Hickman, but the guys in the trenches bear watching."

"Felix, I won't argue with you, your mind is made up. I can always tell. I'll get on with it. Judge Hickman needs your help, your expertise."

"Sure, wonderful, lay it on me, Your Honor."

Felix was unpredictable and that was one of the many reasons Judge Waterford liked him. He kept life interesting. The Judge closed his eyes, shook his head slightly as if he were clearing out cobwebs, and went on, "Hick is after Donny Hirsch. Needs the goods, as you would say, on him, and his best bet is to get Donny's gunsel, bodyguard, to turn states evidence."

"Interesting. How do I fit into his plan and why?"

"His gunsel is a woman named Beth Gutchow. She has a quirk. She uses hand grenades to intimidate and to kill. She never packs a weapon, my mistake, a gun."

"Yeah, if a hand grenade isn't a weapon I don't know what is, but Judge, something doesn't add up. She can't be carrying live grenades around in her pockets."

"She does but one never knows. Some are duds."

"There's a screw loose in this head."

"I'd concur with that but she's effective. Hick says no one ever knows when she is pulling the pin on a live one or a dud and no one stays around to find out."

"How am I suppose to get her to come over to our side and spill the beans?"

"First, Colonel, are your contacts good in Chicago?"

"Our contacts, Judge, are good everywhere."

"Then you'll find a way if you're willing."

"Consider it done."

*   *   *   *

Colonel Felix Brannigan landed in Chicago at 2 P. M., and as he walked down the concourse a mild mannered looking young man fell into step with him and softly said, "Colonel, welcome to Chicago. I have a car waiting and the information you wanted has been collected and organized for an immediate takedown."

"Good. You lead the way."

The young man led him out of the airport and down a ramp to a waiting black, four door Lincoln. Once inside the young man said, "Colonel, I am a Naval Intelligence operator, as is the driver. We have no names or rank. We have been assigned to you by Naval Intelligence at your request thru Inter-military Intelligence."

"Son, the labels change faster than I can keep up with. Aren't you NICOPs?"

"Those were our fathers, sir. We're a new generation. The labels change frequently, sir, because of the attack we are under from within, but our purpose is the same."

"What's your I.D.?"

"We have none, sir. Our numbers are very small."

"Okay son, whatever you say. What do you have for me?"

"We understand you don't want to neutralize this individual, just to have her cooperate with law enforcement in Omaha. We have found her weak spot…arachnids."

"Arachnids…doesn't like spiders. I'll be darned. Sometimes it's all too simple. You know she's kept that a secret. How did you find out so soon?"

"She has enemies, Colonel. People she's intimidated with her hand grenades. Plus, she has a dirty mouth and a bad attitude toward men. We are surprised to find she is not in Omaha with Hirsch. They're interdependent."

"Symbiotic?"

"Yes, sir. Their strength comes when they are together. They rely on each other to bully and intimidate. They benefit from their relationship, for they need the reinforcement each brings to the other. It would appear the only thing they don't do together is sleep. She's that way; he's not. I'm quite certain with him gone she's carrying around live grenades and would pull the pin and suffer the consequences since he's gone."

"Seriously? It's that bad?"

"Or that close, sir. We'll have to watch out."

"Have a plan?"

"Yes, sir, we're going after her right now. This is the plan. We are going to Cicero, that's where she and Donny hang out. It's traditional for this kind of hood. She lives over a small Italian restaurant. Since he's in Omaha she only leaves her room at night to eat. She comes down wooden steps at the back of the building and must walk down a short alley to get to the front door of the restaurant. The time is always the same, seven o'clock. No one else is allowed in the restaurant one half hour before and while she eats. She takes forty five minutes and always consumes one bottle of Chianti. We have rented a small storefront one block away so we can change clothes and return with her for the indoctrination as to the cause and effect you desire. This is her complete dossier. You are scheduled out on Southern Air at nine o'clock with her and by then she will be more than willing to cooperate."

"I've heard it before; you don't miss a trick."

"Never, Colonel. It will be quick and effective."

Felix read the dossier and when finished exclaimed, "She is a study."

"Yes, sir, she has a modification of the Y chromosome. She's as much male as female in many ways. She's strong as an ox and it will take the three of us to take her down and to do it quickly is the key. We have an inhalant that will knock her out, right now."

The car pulled down an alley and parked. The three men walked to the back of the building and entered. The storefront windows had been blacked out and two racks of hanging clothes stood next to the door of a small room taking up one corner. The men changed into dark pants, shirts, and caps. They smeared their faces with black grease and one checked the small room and quickly closed the door saying. "They're ready. Let's go."

Returning to where the car was parked they walked past it down the alley, turned right, and found themselves behind a dumpster. Felix looked around the corner of the dumpster and saw the wooden steps leading down from the apartment. Turning to one of his companions he whispered, "How are we going to take her down?"

"My associate with the inhalant will be at the end of the alley and around the corner. We will stay here. When she comes down we will rush her; knock her down. My associate will hear our whistle through a special ear plug and will rush to cover her face with the cloth saturated with the inhalant. You strip her pockets. We understand you are an expert with hand grenades. She will be unconscious in less than fifteen seconds. We will carry her back to the store front. Let's get in position. Put in this ear plug. The plug will allow us to hear the whistle if our associate needs us or wants to warn us. I'll be right next to you."

Beth Gutchow never knew what hit her. She made a slight sound as the air was expelled from her lungs when she hit the ground, with Felix and the operator on top of her. The second operator covered her face as she gasped for air and as they had said, within seconds, she was unconscious. Felix found three hand grenades and announced quietly, "They're live rounds."

They carried her to the storefront and she was quickly revived with an intravenous injection. Propping her up against the wall, her eyes suddenly went from an emotionless, fixed stare to rapid movement, then a knowing fixed stare of anger. She growled, "Just what the hell is going on?" Feeling her pockets she added, "Who in the hell took my grenades?"

"Shut up and listen," the first operator said. "We want your cooperation and we don't have very long to hear you give us a yes answer."

"Cooperate how, and who the hell are you? Do you know who I am?"

"We want you to testify against Donny Hirsch, by telling everything."

"Go to hell. You've got to be stupid or something. Kill me if you want but not one word from me about him."

"Like spiders?"

Beth recoiled as the operator stuck his hand out, holding a large tarantula, then she snapped, "Heck, this one's non poisonous."

"Good," one operator chided as he threw the spider at Beth's face. She moved violently to one side and attempted to stand as she screamed, "Get that damn thing away from me!"

The second operator kicked her legs from beneath her and slammed the arch of his shoe across her wrist and bending down picked up the spider and put it into her free hand. Beth started to whimper as the spider moved up her arm. The second operator spoke, "She knows that one's nonpoisonous, let's stick her in with the blacks, northern greys, and the browns. They are!"

"Black widows!" Beth screamed out.

"Seems she knows about spiders. Open the door."

Felix watched as the two young men dragged Beth across the floor, opened the door to the small room and pushed her in, turning on the lights as they closed the door. Beth began screaming immediately, for the room was filled with spiders of every description and size. Felix, looking through the window, recoiled and then saw Beth flailing her arms around while she attempted to step on as many spiders as she could, and he asked dispassionately, "How long before they kill her?"

"They're all poisonous but they have little amounts of venom, but collectively it shouldn't take too long."

Beth was screaming as she writhed around on the floor, "Get me the hell out! Get me the hell out! Get me outta' here!"

"She certainly likes the word *hell*, doesn't she? " Felix called out. The one operator opened the door and grabbed Beth by her shirt collar and dragged her out of the room. He brushed away the spiders on her face and looking down at her asked, "Well?"

"Well what...*you*...you bastard?"

"Tsh, Tsh, such language. Are *you* going to cooperate?"

"Not with *you* or anyone associated with *you*. You prick!"

Smiling the operator replied, "Help me strip her."

"What?" Beth screeched.

The two young men began tearing the clothes off Beth's body. Felix held her shoulders down and soon she was naked, and writhing in anger. Still resisting as they dragged her back in the room with the spiders but to no avail. One operator looked at Felix and said, "The big box in the corner of the other room. Would you get it and bring it in and pour the contents over Miss Gutchow?"

Felix retrieved the box and as the spiders spilled out over Beth's body she began to tremble and scream for pity, "Please! Oh God, please! Don't! I hate them, they're biting me to death!"

"That's the idea," one operative snarled.

Felix yelled at her, "Cooperate or else! Will you cooperate?"

"Yes! Yes! Anything...get them off me!"

"Think she'll back down?"

"No. She's convinced we mean business."

The second operative opened a small canister and began to spray Beth as they dragged her out of the room. Soon the spiders were dead and she huddled in a ball, sobbing. Felix sat next to her and placing his hand on her chin, pulled her face around to look in her eyes and demanded, "You'll cooperate, keep your word, or I'll let the spiders eat you alive."

Beth clamped her eyes shut and through her teeth spat out the words, "You win."

"We'll dress her, Colonel, like we are and then head for the airport and your trip back to Omaha on Southern Air."

As the one operator shoved Beth in the back of the car, Felix asked the other operator, "Would you have let them kill her?"

"Why not?"

"Really?"

"No sir, Colonel, we wouldn't have let her die. You need her alive, but we had an alternative plan."

"What?"

"Snakes. Rattlers and cobras. She doesn't like them either."

*   *   *   *

The Southern Air plane was on a ramp of Executive Private Air Terminal. Felix and Beth were immediately taken aboard and the two Naval Intelligence Operators said goodbye. Beth was handcuffed to her seat and admonished by a male attendant to cause no trouble, "Or, I'll turn my pet rattler loose on you."

When Felix sat down another attendant asked, "Need a drink, Colonel?"

"How'd you know?"

"I know, experience. Name it."

"Scotch on the rocks. Make it a double."

"Yes sir, and Colonel, the pilot and crew welcome you aboard. The pilot, who must remain anonymous, extends the amenities of Southern Air to you and your prisoner. Also, Judge Waterford wants you to call him at this number. He is in Omaha and you are to meet him there. I'll get the scotch while you make the call, here's a phone. Oh, and my snake is secure in his cage."

Felix smiled knowingly, dialed the number, and waited. "Hello, Felix," Judge Waterford said, "How'd it go?"

"Where are you, Judge?"

"I'm in Omaha, Felix, get to the point. Did you get her?"

"You know we did."

"Will she testify against Donny Hirsch?"

"Before we left Chicago she said she would. I'll ask her again."

Felix looked over at Beth who was still recoiling from fear and thought to himself, "*For someone used to lobbing hand grenades at people she sure has mellowed,*" then asked curtly, "Beth, haven't changed your mind, have you?"

"No."

"She said she'll testify, Judge. She's scared spitless. She's whimpered out. Those operatives were good and they had her read. What should I do with her?"

"The Marshals will be at the airport to take her off your hands. They also will have transportation for you to the hotel. We are with Judge Hickman's group. They have the entire floor and you are to join me here. This whole affair appears to be shaping up as Judge Hickman planned and he will be ready for court on Wednesday."

"How about the main player? Has he capitulated yet?"

"No, but in about ten minutes there is a meeting with his lawyer, David Skultetty, to let him know what is happening and to appeal to him to have his client plea bargain."

"Good luck!"

"Oh, Felix, I mean Colonel, thanks, you did it again."

"Judge, it brought back fond memories of Doctor See. Let me tell you again the young operatives are just the same, tough, thorough, and efficient. They did their homework and should be commended to their superiors."

"Good to hear that, Colonel. I'll inform the source while I'm waiting for you…enjoy your scotch."

"How'd you know?"

"I'm the one who told them to be sure to have it. Goodbye."

$$*\qquad*\qquad*\qquad*$$

Monday Morning

"Good morning, Judge Hickman's office, Manning speaking. Yes, Mr. Mayor, the Judge is in. One moment please."

Manning pushed the intercom button and said, "Line one, Hick, the Mayor."

"Good morning, Mayor. How can I help you?"

"Good morning, Your Honor, I'm downstairs and wondered if we might talk for a few minutes?"

"Certainly, Mayor, I'll tell Manning to expect you."

Hick rang for Manning and she answered, "Yes, Hick."

"Come on in quick, Manning."

Manning slammed down the phone and half ran to Hick's office and opening his door heard, "Close it. The Mayor's on his way up. David Field is due in about ten minutes. When he arrives, cool his heels until I call for him."

"Going to set the Mayor up, Your Honor?"

"You got that right, now on your way."

Manning had no sooner sat down when the door opened and Dwight Gunderson oiled his way in. A big smile covered his face and he carried his hat under his arm. He was very thin and tall with sharp facial features that made his smile grotesque, for when smiling his upper lip became a thin line revealing gum tissue around his teeth. He looked like a Jack-o-Lantern because of the spaces between his teeth.

Manning squirmed in her chair and greeted him cordially, "Good morning, Mr. Mayor, go right in, the Judge is expecting you!"

"Why, thank you, Manning, thank you."

Hick watched the Mayor as he walked through the door and greeted him with, "Good morning, Mayor, please be seated. What can I do for you this morning?"

"I know your time is limited, Judge Hickman, and I know the matters confronting you are heavy ones and demanding of your time. But, as Mayor, I feel certain responsibilities to various organizations, groups and people who make up our city and contribute to it. I have been informed Mr. Dwight Givens is under arrest and facing some very serious charges. Are my sources correct?"

"They are, Mr. Mayor, but remember I am not the prosecutor, I'm the Judge. I can do nothing to alleviate your apparent distress about Mr. Givens. The charges against his wife have been dropped, however."

"So I am told."

"Yes, she has agreed to cooperate with Mr. Field, the prosecutor."

"But she can't testify against her husband."

"We know, but she can and has pointed her finger at parties and matters known and unknown to us. 'Us', Mr. Mayor, refers to the fact I don't sit in court and not pay attention…"

The phone buzzed. Hick stopped, picked up the phone, and said, "Yes, Manning."

"Mr. Field arrived, Your Honor."

"Good timing, send him in," and looking at the Mayor said, "Mr. Field is here, Mr. Mayor."

David Field walked into the office and nodding at the Mayor said matter-of-factly, "Good morning, Mr. Mayor. I would have suspected you would be with your lawyer."

The Mayor was taken aback and his broad smile faded as he stammered, "Just, ah, just, what does that, ah…that mean?"

"Mr. Givens mentioned you in some way and we are looking into your relationship with him."

"Into me?"

"You attended one of his group's meetings and you were being considered for membership. Are we right?"

"Why, I, I attended a meeting but it was informative about city matters. I'm not perverted like…", the Mayor stopped short and knew he had said too much.

David Field finished his sentence, "Like they are, Mr. Mayor?"

"Why, I, I didn't mean to imply that."

"You said it, Mr. Mayor, you said it, and I have you under investigation as we speak."

"Are you trying to intimidate me?"

"Why should I, you just incriminated yourself."

Hick turned his head to hide the smile on his face. The Mayor stood in a huff and said indignantly, "Your Honor, this young man is brash and disrespectful of my office. I object."

Before Hick could control himself he countered, "Overruled."

Dwight Gunderson's face flushed as he spun on his heel and was out the door before another word could be said, Manning bounded into the room shortly and asked, "What in the world happened to him?"

"I insulted and insinuated the Mayor," David Field said gleefully.

"You insinuated the Mayor? What's that mean?"

"Yes, I alluded to, hinted at, implied forcefully, suggested straight-forward, and meant entirely that he is sleazy and might be tied up with Walter Givens, for you know what."

"What?"

"Perversion."

"David, I'm beginning to think you see that in everybody."

"No, not really, Manning, but it helps to infer. That puts them on the defense and right now that's where we want them until they capitulate and the Judge sentences them on Wednesday."

"You're doing that well?"

"I confronted Donny Hirsch with what Beth Gutchow told us last night at eleven o'clock. He had me called at seven this morning and struck a deal with us through his attorney."

"Is David Skultetty his attorney?" Hick asked.

"No, believe it or not, it's Lance Harding."

"Interesting," Hick replied. "Who's next, Manning?"

"Appears there's only one left, Walter Givens. Mr. Skultetty is due any moment, as planned."

There was a knock on the door and Hick called out, "Come in, David."

David Skultetty opened the door and walked to Hick's desk, leaned across it and shook his hand. He turned and repeated the gesture with David Field and sat next to David when Hick gestured to the chair. He took a deep breath and said, "I don't know if it's a good morning or not but good morning to you all."

Manning sensed his despondency and walked to the back of his chair and squeezed his shoulder as she announced, "I'll be in the outer office, Your Honor, if you need me."

"Just the coffee, Manning."

"It's on the table next to you, Your Honor."

"I should have known. Gentlemen?"

Both attorneys responded with, "No thank you, Your Honor."

"No coffee means you're bent on business. All right, let's get underway. I want you to know, Mr. Skultetty, I set this meeting up with the prosecutor at your request. The court in no way is a part of any negotiations or agreements you might strike other than to consider them when court is in session."

"David, why did you want His Honor present?" David Field asked of David Skultetty.

"You know as well as I do that most cases are really settled in chambers. We want the Judge informed. Totally informed, if justice is to be served."

"Well, that's interesting and I'll tell you that in addition to the evidence I presented to you on discovery I now have additional evidence from Donny Hirsch against your client. Forget everything else we have on Givens, the most serious crime is the murder of Judge Batemen. I won't go for the chair if he'll plead guilty to murder one."

"Second degree."

"It was premeditated."

"Second degree, and I'll agree to life without parole."

"Done. Agreed."

David Skultetty breathed a sigh of relief and looking at Hick asked, "Your Honor, I believe if the exact nature of the perversion of these men were known to the public it would serve no purpose. I would like to see them convicted and sentenced on the basis of the murder counts."

"You don't want us to recite in court what they have done. How then can I confine three of them to the state mental facility, as agreed to by you, without stipulating to the court why I think they need this help and not prison?"

"It will tear this city apart. There are others who have a proclivity for the same aberrant behavior and are not suspect."

"They will be if they carry on their perversions."

David Field and David Skultetty were at opposite ends of a dilemma. David Field looked at Hick and remarked, "Have you read Peter Conway's editorial this morning?"

"No. I didn't take the time to even look at a paper."

"Well, sir, it's not flattering. It calls you and your court suspect. It asks a lot of why's. Why are prominent citizens in jail? Why are they being harassed and why are investigations of the Mayor and others being conducted? Is it a witch hunt? Are you seeking notoriety because *you* have political ambitions? Are you trying to cover up the story about your father? The editorial is why the Mayor was here. I thought you knew."

Hick shrugged off David Field's remarks with, "What about an article by Shila Wadsworth?"

"What article?"

"Most likely it will come this evening."

"Don't bet on it. Especially if it favors you in any way. He's the boss and he wants a piece of you because of his father and mother."

Reaching for his phone, Hick flushed and then dialed, "Mr. Robert Conway, please. This is Judge Nicholas Hickman speaking."

Hick's eyes darted between the two men as he waited, then he heard, "Robert Conway, Your Honor, it appears you read my editorial."

"On the contrary, Mr. Conway, The federal district attorney, Mr. David Field, recited it to me. I am personally ambivalent about the purported innuendos and would prefer a face to face confrontation now. I have Mr.'s Field and Skultetty in my office and would have you join us now…if possible."

"I'll be there in a matter of minutes."

Hick hung up his phone and remarked, "Relax, gentlemen, he's on his way. Mr. Field, forget about Mr. Skultetty being here, what do you have on Mr. Conway?"

"Plenty."

"Name something."

"Gambling, interstate and local. Big time amounts not reported. He consorts with very questionable Mafia types. The FBI has been watching and monitoring him for years."

"Do you want him to know you have him under surveillance?"

"Your Honor, this city has looked the other way for so long I just want two glaring examples, Givens and Hirsch. The others will trip themselves up once they realize the jig is up, and the public is finally alerted. My office will eventually be a revolving door of mea culpa and wanting to make a deal."

"Then go after him for me."

"Done."

Hick looked at David Skultetty and asked, "How do you feel about it?"

"I never liked him or his editorials. Thank God I'm not his lawyer, and if you don't mind I'll stay while you have at him."

It was only a matter of minutes before Peter Conway was escorted into Hick's office by Manning. Introductions were made and reconfirmed and when all were finally seated Hick started out by saying, "Mr. Conway, it is obvious you are aware of what the federal district attorney is doing and that you basically don't approve for one reason or another. I have been informed about your editorial and the concerns you have expressed therein about me and this whole process. I have talked to your reporter, Miss Wadsworth, and she led me to believe she would have articles to counter your attack."

The word 'attack' visibly irritated Peter Conway. He shifted in his chair as he blurted out, "I make all decisions on opinion articles regardless of the byline or source. The red line is my best stroke."

"I surmise that is your way of saying her articles won't see the light of day."

"Correct."

"Then you are not amenable to listening to our side of the story?"

"I'll listen to anything but I know my facts are correct and my suspicions of what you are up to are merely history repeating itself."

"Sounds like you have a closed mind, Mr. Conway. I don't think any evidence of complaint will meet with your understanding, but I believe Mr. Field has some hard evidence that will gain your attention…Mr. Field…if you please."

"Mr. Conway, are you aware of a person named Charles Goldsmith of Las Vegas?"

Peter Conway instantaneously became agitated and countered, "I am, he's my bookie."

"Last year, Mr. Conway, you made bets in excess of $700,000 with Mr. Goldsmith and received through unreported illegal transfers $136,000. You have personally established a book here in Omaha with the help of Mr. Goldsmith. Plus your male lover, Henry Gerard, and his activities are known to us."

"This is blackmail!"

"*No*…it is not. We can prove everything I've said about you. Plus there is a lot more. Let's call it tit-for-tat."

"What do you want from me?"

"Prove what you've editorialized or retract it."

"What else? I have a feeling that won't be enough."

"You're right. I want to maximize. I want Shila Wadsworth's ruminations to go forward."

"Ruminations. You want her to reflect on what?"

"No, no, Mr. Conway, not that definition, mine. I want Shila to chew the cud about you and your kind, and then spit you out in your paper, in black and white, so the people of Omaha will know what has been feeding on them and their children and getting away with it...until now. She'd make a good editor for your paper, in your absence, Mr. Conway."

Peter Conway was overwhelmed. He had never expected this. He thought when Hick called, he had Hick on the run. He didn't expect this counterattack quite so soon. His vulnerability was evident even to him and he felt he must fall back and develop countermeasures to neutralize this smear on his person. He countered calmly, "I must confer with my attorneys. I must take into consideration what you have said. I must leave."

"Do all those things, Mr. Conway, but when you get back to your paper, go to your ad layouts for tomorrow. Mine has been paid for and it's about you."

"That's libel."

"I'm ready to defend what it says. More than ready."

"What would you have me do?"

"You know what to do, Mr. Conway, and I suggest you do it before Wednesday or I'll have you indicted."

Peter Conway looked at Hick for some support but only received his scorn, as reflected in his words, "You are dismissed, Mr. Conway, and I would recommend you listen to what the district attorney has suggested. Good day."

Peter Conway stood and walked from the room in a huff. He was not used to being dismissed out-of-hand and with no response. He scurried out of the building and down the street to his paper. He saw nor heard no one, for his anger had totally engulfed him. Marching directly to Shila Wadsworth's office, he burst through the door. Shila looked up from her desk and dropping her pencil blurted out, "Peter, you...look...just awful!"

"I'm mad as hell! I've been with Judge Hickman!"

"Oh, my ally."

"Your ally? Hell, Shila, I would remind you…you work for this paper and this paper is me."

"Peter, our agreement is I write the truth."

Peter flushed, then sat down and as he did grabbed some papers from her desk and began to fan himself. Shila handed him some Kleenex and saw that the distended blood vessels in his neck were receding. His pique was over and he returned to his usual form.

"You all right now, Peter?"

"Well, I've calmed down, but I'm still damn mad at you for taking his side."

"You leave me no recourse, Peter. We both know where you're coming from and you've slowly but methodically burned your bridges and cut your own throat. What has happened was inevitable."

"Damn it, you're preaching to me! I won't have it! I've been preached to twice in one day and I won't have it, Shila. You're fired."

"Are you sure you want to do that, Peter?"

"No, I don't, but what choice do I have? Let me think."

Peter twisted in his chair several times, then stood. He looked down at Shila and as he did she observed his clenched fists. He spoke in enveloping tones, "Shila, a compromise is in order to preserve our relationship and trust, not only to one another, but to our purpose as journalists. My editorial this morning is causing a ruckus, let it steep for two days then write what you will."

"I'm going to try and cause you one hell of a lot of trouble, Peter. You and yours have gone too far."

"Maybe, maybe not. Is it a deal?"

Shila was wary of Peter, for he had double dealt her before. He was what he was and believed what he believed and that meant the end justified the means. She knew she had no choice and agreed, "I'll do it just this once, but be careful, hold true to what you say."

"Shake?"

That, Shila didn't like to do, for his hand was always moist and limp. Never was there a sign in his handshake of sincerity. Shila put her hand out and shook Peter's and as she did a smile slid across his face and touching him made her skin crawl. Peter turned and as he walked from the room Shila wiped her hand off on her dress...and shuddered.

CHAPTER 18

▼

Hick, David Field, and David Skultetty had agreed on the pleas and the sentencing was to be at nine o'clock on Wednesday morning. Lance Harding, Donny Hirsch's attorney, had also agreed to the terms of the sentence and was to be present with his client. Hick requested J. R. Rollins and his sons, Joshua and Patrick, be present. Susan Givens refused to be present. Sam and Kate Hirsch had in kind requested to be present. Shila Wadsworth would represent the press.

Judge Waterford, Colonel Felix Brannigan, and Joe Hirsch had returned to Kansas City, on Southern Air, when it was determined a panel of three Judges would not be necessary for trial. Beth Gutchow, on Tuesday, was returned to Chicago where she was to be indicted for racketeering and murder.

On Wednesday morning after Judge Nicholas T. Hickman had kissed Manning she followed him into his courtroom as Henry Justin called out, "Please rise for the Honorable Nicholas T. Hickman. The Special Federal Court of the Fifth District is now in session."

Hick sat down and those in the court followed. Hick caught Gladis Pitman's eye and gave her a quick thumbs up. Henry stood with Marshal Jed Palmer on either side of the door to the Judge's chambers and Manning sat a small desk to the right of Hick. David Skultetty sat with Lance Harding at the defense table and David Field sat alone at the prosecutor's table with Sam and Kate Hirsch. Kate looked radiant but dejected. Sam was somber. J. R. Rollins sat, reunited, between his sons. Paul Ortman and Joseph Villella had asked to be excused for other cases.

Manning had arranged the order of sentencing. Hick's voice rang out, "Will Misters Clyde D. Tyler, Donald S. Remco, and Tad O. Beasley please stand before the bar with your attorney, Mr. Skultetty." The three men walked dejectedly to stand before Hick and heard him say, "Misters Tyler, Remco and Beasley, I hereby sentence you to the State Mental Health Unit, in Lincoln, Nebraska, for a minimum of ten years or until such time it is felt you are no longer a threat to society. Do you wish to address the court?"

David Skultetty stepped forward saying, "Thank you, Your Honor, my clients wish to tell the court and the people of this city and state that they are sorry for and regret their actions. They hope to receive the help they need to prepare them to return to society."

"Thank you, Mr. Skultetty. Please return to your seats. The Marshal will escort all defendants out when the sentencing phase is completed. Will Mr. Donald S. Hirsch and Mr. Lance Harding please approach the bench for sentencing."

Kate Hirsch's one arm wound around Sam's shoulder and her other hand went to cover her mouth as Hick recited, "Donald S. Hirsch, I hereby sentence you to life in prison without parole. Do you wish to address the court?"

"I do!"

Kate gasped as Sam sat bolt upright in his seat.

"I have plenty I would like to say but counsel recommends I keep it brief, not that you could put me away for any more time than you already have. Business is business and I did what I had to, and needed to...do."

Hick was visibly angered and slid forward in his chair rapidly and sprang from his seat to reply angrily, "That's all you have to say to this court, to your parents, there is no contrition, no asking them for forgiveness? No remorse? You participated in an attempt to kill your father!"

"No! What are you talking about, Judge? Look what your old man did for *you*."

Hick was now seething and his fists slammed down against the bench as he sat back down, all the while glaring at Donny. Lance Harding stepped forward as if to come between them and pleaded, "Will the court please understand; will the court please forgive what my client says in this the darkest moment of his life?"

"Mr. Harding, please. The darkest moment of his life?"

"I don't think he understands, Your Honor."

Hick just sat looking at both of these men and not understanding. The anguish of his life without a father crushed down on his very being, all in the court could see the effect the words had on him. He waited and stared, then calmly asked, "Do you understand about the Ten Commandments, Mr. Hirsch?"

"Sure. I've heard about them. So what?"

"Are you aware of what the Fifth Commandment states?"

"No. I don't know them by the numbers."

"The Fifth Commandment says, 'Thou shall honor thy mother and father with all honor love and fidelity and submit myself to their instruction and correction with due obedience and to bear with their weaknesses and infirmities since God so planned to govern us by their hand.'"

"So?"

"So! You have no love or feeling for your parents who sit in this room?"

"Judge, I've lived by the Commandment do unto others as they most likely will do unto you…if they get the chance. Also, Judge, you're mixing up government and religion. Don't throw any religious rot in my face. I messed up, I got caught. So what, I'll appeal."

"This is a Christian Country and is composed of many other religions. As a Nation we have stated in God we trust. The Ten Commandments are part of our heritage, part of our governing, and in this court part of the court's insight. One more thing, the last Judge you will come before is God. You are yet to be judged. Sit!"

Hick took a deep breath and looking at Manning saw the agony she felt for him. She smiled, closed her eyes, shook her head from side to side, opened her eyes and whispered, "Next, Your Honor, go on."

Hick turned back to the court and clearing his throat asked, "Will Mr. Skultetty and his client, Mr. Walter S. Givens, approach the bench."

Walter Givens's face was drawn. His eyes were blank and he was slowly led by David Skultetty to the bench were Hick imposed his sentence, "Walter S. Givens, I hereby sentence you to life in prison with a minimum sentence of twenty five years for the murder of Judge Harold Batemen."

Tears began to flow down Water Givens's face, and a hush of finality fell over the courtroom. No one moved, nor was a sound heard.

EPILOGUE

▼

The plane, Continental Flight 202 to Kansas City, had taken off and was heading due North and after a few minutes banked slowly to the left, bringing the plane around to a due South point on the compass. The passenger in seat 5A had moved to the window seat 5B and opened his briefcase when the seatbelt and no smoking lights had been turned off. He gazed out over the city of Omaha and back and to the North he saw the federal building. He waited until the plane was passing over the stockyards and then extended a small antenna on a black handheld control box. His deformed index finger on his right hand, burned from a quick fuse, pressed down on the red button and he saw an instantaneous reaction on the northeast corner of the federal building. The building appeared to swell and then turned inward to collapse and a large ball of dust and smoke shot up into the atmosphere. Felix N. Harding, alias Nitro, smiled as he joyfully watched the cloud of destruction rise even higher. He couldn't take his eyes from what he saw and with a silent glee pushed the antenna back into the device and closed the briefcase.

"Ladies and gentlemen," the pilot interrupted, "it would seem a building has been demolished in downtown Omaha. If you look out the left side of the airplane you can see the cloud of smoke and ash from the explosion. It's strange they'd do it on a Wednesday, and not on a Sunday when there's not much activity downtown. Hope no one was hurt. If there's more to report, I'll get back to you. Our flying time will be twenty six minutes. Have a good flight and thank you for flying Continental."

Moments later the cockpit radio crackled with excitement as the control tower issued an alert to all planes having taken off from Eppley Airfield in Omaha. The pilots listened intently and then looking at one another muttered in unison, "Oh, my God!"

Nitro looked out the window until the cloud of destruction was gone. He then went to the sky phone and dialed, "Joe Umbigolata," a voice answered.

"Joe, it's Nitro."

"Yeah, what's up Nitro?"

"It's done. Revenge for Charlie. Call Peter."

"Sure. Anybody left?"

"I never leave anybody. I used eighty sticks"

"Good. Your reward is in the usual place."

The phone went dead. Passing the stewardess, Nitro asked, "Enough time for a beer?"

"Certainly. What kind?"

"The best you got, I'm celebrating."

ADDENDUM

All present in the court of Nicholas T. Hickman were killed. The explosion was expertly confined to the corner of the building where the special court had been established. Twenty-two other people beneath the court were killed. Felix Harding, alias 'Nitro', after landing in Kansas City retrieved a small case filled with money from a locker before he left the airport. He was watched and followed by Officer Mike Groton after Peter Conway had tipped him off. 'Nitro' was never seen or heard from again.

Peter Conway died two years after the explosion with AIDS.

Officer Mike Groton left the police force and joined Joe Hirsch's laboratory.

Joe Hirsch married Kate's assistant, Mary Beth. They never spoke of Sam or Kate again.

Judge Samuel Wenter Waterford returned to Omaha to attempt a reconstruction of what had happened so as to bring the guilty to trial. He failed and died in 1992.

Colonel Felix Branigan's last known words were, "I'm going fishing once and for all." He has never been seen again.

Dwight Gunderson was defeated as Mayor and was divorced by his wife. He lives in a downtown Omaha apartment and is often see aimlessly wandering the streets.

Joseph Villella immediately resigned as County Attorney and took Lance Harding's place in the law firm of Kimball, Roberts, and Ortman.

There were no identifiable remains of anyone in the courtroom that day. The community at large struggled with how those killed, the innocent and the guilty, would be remembered.

A common grave was established and three truckloads of intermingled remains were buried. The names of those killed were listed in alphabetical order on a large grey headstone. Captain R. Thurmond, Chief of Homicide, and Joe Hirsch talked about the similarity of the gut wrenching finality of the explosion with the deaths of Captain Thomas and Laura See, as recounted in the novel "Death Will Wait" by Stuart I. Haussler. They suggested the following inscription be added following the names of the victims. Their suggestion was accepted by the community.

Here Lie
The Remains Of Those Killed Together
OnThe Morning Of Wednesday June 21, 1986
Their Souls Are With Our Lord In His Heavenly Mansion
That Has Many Rooms
We The Living Testify
The Foolishness Of Man Is Only Exceeded
by
The Arrogance Of Such Foolishness

THE END

Printed in the United States
23384LVS00004B/82-114